Also by
Molly McAdams

THE REBEL SERIES
Lyric

THE REDEMPTION SERIES
Blackbird

Firefly

Nightshade

THE THATCH SERIES
Letting Go

To The Stars

Show Me How

THE SHARING YOU SERIES
Capturing Peace (novella)

Sharing You

THE FORGIVING LIES SERIES
Forgiving Lies

Deceiving Lies

Changing Everything (novella)

THE FROM ASHES SERIES
From Ashes

Needing Her (novella)

THE TAKING CHANCES SERIES

Taking Chances

Stealing Harper (novella)

Trusting Liam

STAND-ALONE NOVELS

I See You

REBEL NOVELS STILL TO COME

Limit

A Rebel Novel

LOCK

Molly McAdams

New York Times Bestselling Author

Copyright © 2018 Molly McAdams
Published by Jester Creations, LLC.
First Edition
All rights reserved. Except as permitted under the U.S. Copyright Act of 1976, no part of this publication may be reproduced, distributed, transmitted in any form or by any means, or stored in a database or retrieval system, without prior permission of the publisher.
Please protect this art form by not pirating.

Molly McAdams
www.mollysmcadams.com
Cover Design by RBA Designs
Photo by ©Regina Wamba
Editing by Ashley Williams, AW Editing
Custom Illustrations by DeepFriedFreckles

The characters and events in this book are fictitious. Names, characters, places, and plots are a product of the author's imagination. Any similarity to real persons, living or dead, is coincidental and not intended by the author.

Print ISBN: 9780998420097
eBook ISBN: 9780998420080

Mom and Dad . . .
I am unbelievably lucky to be your daughter.
Thank you for always being there. Thank you for your support.
Thank you for my wonderful life.
This is for you.

prologue

Maverick
ELEVEN YEARS AGO

"Fries."

"Jesus." I groaned and ran my hands over my face, the chains binding them sounding like windows shattering in the eerie quiet of our cell.

A cell I was fucking positive the government kept off the radar so they could hide people like us. People they wanted to contain and control and silence. Considering we'd been brought in blindfolded and were the only prisoners here, I doubted I was far from the mark on my assumption.

"Smothered in melted cheese. Oh God, I'm dying. I'm wasting away," my identical twin brother cried out from where he lay facedown on the floor. "I haven't had a good burger in so long that I can't remember what they taste like anymore."

"If you don't shut up, I'll kill you myself."

He scoffed. "You would get bored after a day without me."

I waited for him to continue with the food cravings rant he'd been on for the last . . . shit, I didn't know, felt like hours, but he was silent except for the little *scrape, scrape, scrape,* that endlessly came from his side of the room.

I was about to ask if he felt it, that *off* feeling, but stopped.

It was always quiet here in our cozy new home. Especially at night when our babysitters were preoccupied with themselves instead of their taunts and god-awful attempts at interrogations.

But this was a different kind of quiet.

It was as if the silence had come alive.

There was a charge in the air, making the hairs on my arms stand. Anxiety pulsed through me, as if I was waiting for something to happen. It was like the anticipation between the blinding flash of lightning and the thunderous crack that follows.

Scrape, scrape, scrape.

I forced myself to lay on my rock-hard bed and closed my eyes.

"Pancakes. Oh, *yes*, pancakes with powdered sugar. Fuck me."

I cracked an eye open. "Shut up, Evan."

My eyelids flew open when the power shut off.

"See? Even this place knows I'm dying. It's warning me that if I don't get real food, I'm gonna die."

I tilted my head slightly when I heard a rustle near my feet but didn't shift my position.

"We've been here for years, man."

Weeks.

We'd be there for weeks.

I opened my mouth to, once again, tell him to shut up just as the backup generator kicked on and the dim lights within our cell glowed, revealing three new people.

The solid metal door was wide open behind them.

I scrambled from the bed, stumbling over curses as I tried to get them all out at once. "Fucking shit—fuck, who the fuck are you?"

My brother didn't move. Wasn't even fazed. "Told you I was gonna die," he said matter-of-factly.

I stared at the people in front of me. Two guys and a girl. All three had black bandanas covering the lower halves of their faces.

The girl looked pointedly at the chains connecting my wrists and ankles. "Those look comfy."

"They don't really trust us anymore." My tone was hard and had an edge that let her know I would still take all three of them on, even bound. "I asked who you were."

She laughed softly and lifted the tablet she'd had hanging at her side. "You don't know us, but we know everything about the two of you. You have . . ." She glanced behind her.

"Two minutes." The burlier guy grunted the answer.

"Less than that to decide if you want to come with us or stay here. If you come and cross us, you'll wish you'd stayed."

A laugh punched from my chest.

"If you come over here, I'll make you want to stay," my brother said suggestively.

The burly guy took a threatening step toward Evan, but the second guy blocked him. "Johnny," he said in warning before releasing him.

"Your loss," Evan said, not caring that *Johnny* was looking at him like he wanted to murder him.

I shook my head. "Why the hell should we leave with you?"

I could already list three reasons.

Long reddish hair falling to her waist.

Wide eyes that had a wildness about them.

And a tiny body that had the perfect amount of curves.

Well . . . *four*. She'd also broken into a secret government prison.

But the three of them looked like they planned to kill us. I'd rather take my chances with the trial.

Instead of answering, the girl sighed, looked at her tablet, and then pointed to me. "Top Gun here—"

"The hell did you just call me?"

She glanced at me with those wild eyes before turning her tablet so I could see it. "This one is you," she said confidently.

I had only a couple of seconds to look at the screen. There was a lot of information—information I wasn't sure how she'd gotten her hands on—and multiple pictures. Military photos, my senior picture, and a couple of candid shots. The largest one was of me just weeks before our world turned to shit, and in it, I was wearing aviators.

I nodded.

How she knew which one of us was which, I had no idea. Our own parents were still mixing us up before we'd left for boot camp.

"Then keep up, *Maverick*."

Evan snorted.

I ground my jaw.

"As I was saying," she continued with another sigh.

"You're the sniper. You were the best marksmen in your battalion. Had a high number of kills on your first tour, but then you were both pulled for a black op that went extremely wrong and landed you here." She turned to Evan. "And Shawshank Redemption over here was his spotter—"

"It worked in the movie," Evan said defensively.

"You're using a plastic spork. And he did it to the wall, not the floor. Do you plan on digging to freedom or China?"

"Whatever gets me to food and a girl's bed, sweetheart."

"Well, by all means, keep digging." I couldn't see her mouth, but the smile was there in her voice. "Anyway, the spotter position was to keep the two of you together because *you* have a knack for getting in and out of places unseen and can apparently track *anything*. They called you a bloodhound. Am I missing anything?"

"The size of certain appendages," Evan murmured.

"Don't listen to him," I said quickly when Johnny lunged and was, once again, stopped by the second guy. "He's like this with all women, but he's harmless. It's worse when he's hungry."

I could hear Johnny's rough breaths as he jerked out of the other guy's hold. He looked at his phone and growled, "Forty-five seconds."

The girl dropped the hand holding the tablet to her side. "Well?"

"Well, what? All you did was prove that you can get in here and know who we are. You could lead us out into a trap. We don't know shit about you."

The fact that my brother hadn't jumped up the moment

she'd offered to get us out of here let me know he was thinking the same thing.

"That isn't how this works," she replied simply.

The guy who had stopped Johnny from charging stepped forward until he was only a foot away from me. With a glance over his shoulder to the girl, he murmured, "Free them."

I didn't have time to process what was happening before all four cuffs were off me and she was moving on to my brother.

It had taken her seconds.

"Look," the guy said once my brother was standing beside me, "I'm sure you think there's a trial coming, but there won't be one. This is your only chance of getting out. We're part of a family, and we take care of family. You two join us and prove you won't bolt at the first breath of fresh air, and we'll protect you."

"Why us?" I asked when he took a step back.

"If you come and stay, I'll tell you."

And then they turned to leave.

I looked from the door to Evan. "You alive?"

He nodded in quick jerks. "I'm alive."

"Keep it that way."

As soon as I finished saying the words, we bolted from the room to follow behind them.

There wasn't a soul in the hall when we set foot into it.

"Hurry," Johnny murmured. "We're five seconds behind."

"Behind what?"

But no one answered me, they just took off at a sprint.

The girl handed her tablet off to Johnny and accepted a small device from the other guy as we ran. And I watched in fascination as we came to bolted door after bolted door, and she used whatever that thing was in her hand to get us through within seconds.

It wasn't until we were outside and sprinting away that I wondered when it was going to come.

The shoe that was waiting to fall.

Because we hadn't passed a single person. It had all been too easy.

I looked over my shoulder at my brother, who was a step behind me. His face was pinched with the same apprehension that was sliding through my veins.

I slowed when we neared an SUV sitting in wait for us and grabbed Evan's arm to slow him with me.

The guy who'd had us released saw us hanging back when he rounded the front of the car and slanted his head. "If you're gonna bail, I'd suggest you wait until we get you farther away than this. Get in the car, and then you can decide."

I turned and looked at the building. It had felt like a fortress but appeared to be nothing more than a secluded, modern house. Cold. Straight lines. And a shit-ton of windows that gave it the illusion that normal people lived there. It seemed both inviting and intimidating at the same time.

Smart cover.

I growled out a curse, followed them into the car, and sat in silence as we sped away.

"Time," Johnny said from the passenger seat nearly a minute after we'd started driving.

"Good job, Einstein," the other guy murmured.

"You doubted me?" the girl said with a huff from beside Evan as she tapped rapidly on the screen of her tablet.

"Camera systems are back on. Three men just entered, which means Libby left."

"Good," the driver murmured.

"Walking, walking, walking," she whispered to herself. "Two are in the hall with the cells."

We all collectively held our breaths as we waited for her next words.

And waited.

Until she said, "And they walked right back out without checking."

I rested my head on the seat and released a strangled breath. My heart was racing from the adrenaline and disbelief and relief.

"Holy shit." Evan laughed and then added, "Figures. They don't usually check on us after taking our dinner trays away."

Despite the uncertainty still lingering, my lips stretched into a grin. "They don't really check on us at all anymore. Wonder why that is . . . *Evan*."

"Care to share?"

I looked over and found Einstein watching me. Excitement and curiosity practically poured from her as she waited for an answer.

"We told them not to separate us, and they did." I bumped my brother's shoulder. "So this one made our babysitters lives miserable by singing 'I'm a Little Teacup' all fucking day at the top of his lungs. Whenever an agent left, Evan slipped out of his cell and sat in front of mine."

Evan scoffed. "You're welcome for keeping you company."

"They kept thinking he was picking the lock somehow, so they stopped giving him utensils. But it was just a faulty door that didn't lock completely. Whenever they put him back in his cell, he said, 'I'll stop if you just put me with my brother.' After a few days, they did. Asshole got us put in the room you found us in. Solid walls and door. And we got fully chained."

"But we were together."

"Yeah, then I got to listen to you bitching about food."

He dropped his head back and whined, "I forgot I was dying. I need good food. Someone put me out of my misery and feed me."

The driver huffed and pulled off onto a shoulder. "Depending on your decision, we will."

A couple of seconds later, headlights appeared behind us.

I tensed and felt Evan do the same as we waited, but the others seemed unaffected.

"Truth or dare," the guy driving said.

When he turned to look at us, a breath of a laugh climbed up my throat. "Are you serious?" I lifted my shoulders in confusion when he only continued to stare. "I don't know. Truth," I said at the same time Evan said, "Dare."

"Your truth?" He looked from Evan to me then asked, "Did you do what they are pinning you for?"

My jaw clenched until it was painful. "No."

My brother just mumbled curses.

"I told you there wouldn't be a trial, and there wouldn't have been. The talking heads are saying you two went rogue and killed civilians. Einstein, who tends to research shit like that for kicks, dug into the black files and found out just how deep the cover up goes."

"It's bullshit," Evan bit out. "Every day they've been telling us that story. Telling us like they're waiting for us to agree with what they want the world to believe or some shit."

"Evan," I murmured.

"No, fuck this," he ground out. "We were sent in to find and take out a known terrorist. He wasn't there; it was someone who looked like him. We called it in and went to check in with our support guy before going to meet with the rest of the team in another town. Not three minutes after we cleared the outskirts of the city, a drone flew overhead and dropped a missile. A team came in and forced us to leave before the smoke could clear. Next thing we knew, we were Stateside and being transported here with bags over our heads. And we were *told* what we did. *Told* that we killed our support guy. He was found *shot*. He had been there—right fucking there—and alive when we were forced to leave."

Evan sat back with a huff. His teeth gnashed so hard it was audible.

No one said anything.

No one gave any indication of their thoughts on what really happened.

The guy in the driver's seat looked between us and said, "Your dare? Stay with us."

With that, he opened his door and stepped outside, the other two following just as a car pulled up behind us.

Evan sighed roughly. "We have nowhere else to go. Not if that shit's in the news."

"I know," I murmured and then pushed him toward the open door. "Come on."

We stepped out just as a tall blonde bounced her way out of the sporty car, her laugh filling the night air as she pulled off a wig and shook out her dark hair.

I looked at the three we'd come with as they all pulled their bandanas down to hang around their necks, and I froze when I got my first real look at Einstein.

There had been something about her wild eyes and hair and small stature before that intrigued me. Give any guy those small glimpses of her, and he'd want to spend a night with her just to get lost in a beautiful girl.

But actually seeing *her*?

Jesus Christ.

She was short and petite but stood like a giant surrounded by impenetrable walls.

She had a soft, angelic face, but those wild eyes gave her a seductive edge.

Her mouth was full and fixed into some mixture of a frown and a smirk. From the casual way she wore the expression, I wondered if that was her normal. If she was always amused and disappointed. And I had the strongest urge to know what was disappointing her and what made her laugh.

I wanted to know what she looked like when she fucking smiled.

Even if my brother and I had somewhere to go, I was sure I would've chosen to follow her anywhere.

"I just . . . I just don't know what happened to it," the new girl said, and I dragged my attention away from Einstein in time to see her gesture to the car. Her voice was high-pitched and whiny, and I was praying to any God listening that it wasn't natural. "It stopped driving the way it's supposed to. It started making this awful, loud noise and slowed down. It sounded like it was going to attack me." She winked saucily, giggled, and then slowly ran her fingers over her chest. "Not saying I don't want to be attacked. But my baby here is supposed to take me real fast, sir. Do you think you could make her go fast for me again?"

The guy who'd talked with us groaned and ran his hand over his head. "Jesus."

Another loud laugh and the new girl bowed. "You are welcome, little brother," she said in a throaty tone.

That voice fit.

Her dark stare found my brother and me. "Hello, fresh meat."

Einstein cleared her throat and gestured absently. "Diggs and Maverick."

"Not," I said quickly. "Evan and Andrew."

The new girl nodded. "Right. So, Diggs and Maverick," she said in confirmation.

"No—"

"You shouldn't have worn aviators," Einstein murmured from beside me as she pulled up her tablet and brought it to life. "Besides, I found you. I get to name you."

"Is that right?" I asked, the corner of my mouth slowly lifting when she made an amused sound in the back of her throat.

"I'm Libby," the new girl said before turning to Evan. "What's *your* story?"

"I was trying to dig our way to freedom," he said without shame.

"And how was that working out for you?"

"I would've gotten there in a couple hundred years."

I stepped closer to Einstein. "How'd you do it?"

She lifted her eyes in a brief glance and then looked up again quickly. This time her eyes searched mine for a few seconds before they shifted around us, her pupils widening in fear before her stare was back on her screen.

"Easy," she murmured. "Caused blackouts in different parts of the city and eventually on this grid. That way, it didn't raise suspicions and the electric company would be busy. That house had a number of different backup systems that we needed to beat, including different codes on each door, not that I had any trouble getting through them. Libby took care of keeping the CIA agents occupied, but that can only last so long without raising suspicions, which was why we were on a schedule."

"You asked 'why us.'"

I looked up and found the guy I still didn't have a name for standing directly beside me.

"We all have our talents." He nodded to Einstein. "Clearly. Your and your brother's would be useful to us. At the moment, we have a situation going on in Chicago we need your help with. After . . . well, there will always be a situation."

"Situation," I stated dully.

Who in the actual fuck was I talking to?

He shrugged unapologetically. "Unfortunately, this is where you decide."

I stared at him blankly for a few seconds, trying to figure out exactly who or what he was.

But whoever he was wouldn't make a difference. It was like Evan said, we had nowhere else to go. Come morning, they would know we were gone, and we would be bumped to the FBI's Ten Most Wanted list and then hunted.

When I said as much to the guy in front of me, he smirked and glanced at Einstein.

"Decision," she demanded.

"We're coming."

She lifted her eyes to mine. That disappointed smirk mesmerized me. "Then I've already altered your fingerprints in the system. If yours are ever run, they won't be linked to your old names. Same with facial recognition. I've also created everything you and your brother will ever need for new lives. Social security cards, driver's licenses, background stories and files to match."

I blinked slowly. "You can do that?"

Her mouth slowly stretched into that smile I'd wondered about. Bright. Captivating. Fucking beautiful.

"You doubt me?"

"Not after tonight," I said honestly.

Johnny stepped up behind Einstein and wrapped his arm around her neck, pulling her close and pressing his mouth to the top of her head.

Her eyes immediately dimmed and shuttered.

And I took a step back.

The guy in front of me held out his hand. "I'm Dare. Welcome to the family."

One

Einstein
TODAY

I COULDN'T REMEMBER EVER BEING more hungover.

Jesus, I couldn't even remember drinking last night in order to be hungover.

I tried to force open my heavy lids and gave up. A sound between a moan and a whimper slid up my throat but didn't make it to my lips.

I rubbed my eyelids as pieces from yesterday flashed through my mind.

Pain . . . but not physical.

My chest ached with echoes of the anguish.

My eyes burned with the memory of tears.

Maverick.

Maverick.

Maverick.

No, not Maverick. The guy. The guy from the—God, where had I met him?

We'd had dinner. No . . . *lunch*. And then nothing.

There was nothing. I couldn't remember finishing lunch. I still couldn't even remember drinking.

Only . . . *shit*.

An expectant, mischievous smile.

Losing the ability to speak or move.

Cruel, whispered words. *"You should've left it alone."*

Shit, shit, shit, *no*.

I sat up and cried out when my head threatened to shatter in protest. Out of reflex, I lifted my hands to cradle it but stopped when something tugged at my arm.

I was so panicked from the memory that I looked down without care. I stilled and then slowly followed the IV line to a full bag of saline. Attached to it was a bright yellow Post-it note with thick scrawl that read:

Hack your way out of this.

My stomach dropped, creating a hollow of fear and apprehension.

"Oh God."

Without moving, I let my gaze dart around the unfamiliar room.

I wasn't in a hospital. There was no one in the room with me. If there were cameras, they were well hidden.

After pulling the IV from my arm, I tried to stand, but my feet didn't move the way I needed them to, and my knees buckled.

I bit out a curse as I caught myself on the side of the bed and pushed myself up. The pounding in my head was unlike anything I'd ever felt before, and it threatened to roll my stomach. I blinked slowly and then squinted at the bottles sitting on the lone nightstand by the bed.

Water and aspirin.

There was no way in hell I was going to touch those.

"Nice try, asshole." My voice was nothing more than a pathetic rasp. The moment I opened my mouth, I realized just how badly I wanted that water.

Needed it to a point that was nearly unbearable.

It was so damn hot, and I felt dehydrated. The confusion and the pounding in my head only emphasized that.

My mouth was so dry I couldn't swallow. But that couldn't be right, I'd been—*wait*.

I put more pressure to my arm for a few seconds before releasing it, looking at the smeared blood where the IV had been, and then twisting to look at the bag of saline.

The full bag that wasn't dripping through the line.

What the hell?

I moved unsteadily to search the room, looking for windows or doors or anything that may aid in an escape. There was only a solid-wood door which had a cast-iron pull and keyhole . . . and it was securely locked.

A lock I was sure I would be able to get through had I been able to focus on anything without feeling like my brain was splitting in two.

And *why* was it so goddamn hot?

I pulled at my shirt with trembling fingers to air it out, but it came away too easily. I fell heavily against the wall and tried to look down at myself without falling over, pressing my hands to my body as I did.

My stomach. My chest and neck. My face.

They were all dry.

"No, no. Damn it."

I stumbled my way back to the bed, practically falling onto it as I reached for the bottles on the nightstand.

As soon as I had a water in my grasp, I twisted the cap off and tentatively took a sip.

The moment the liquid touched my tongue, my body sighed in relief.

In gratitude.

It took willpower I didn't know I had not to chug the contents of the bottle I was holding and all the others.

But I sat. And I waited.

There was no lingering aftertaste. There was nothing.

I slowly sipped more . . . and then more still, not caring about the uneasy way it fell straight to my stomach.

Once half the bottle was gone, I forced myself to put the cap back on. But when I reached forward to place the bottle on the nightstand, my hand missed.

My arm dropped heavily.

The bottle fell to the floor.

The sound of a lock sliding and a door opening.

I turned. Tried to look as the room spun and spun and faded.

Two

Maverick
TODAY

"Thought I got rid of you, but you keep showing up."

I blinked quickly and looked up from the bar. Zeke, the owner of The Jack, was glaring at me.

I didn't tell him he would be getting his wish soon enough. Just forced something that might've resembled a grin. "Now, what made you think you could do that?"

"I fired you and your brother."

"That was six months ago. And I thought we agreed we weren't quitting, and you weren't firing us—it was a mutual, loving breakup."

"You broke someone's jaw, Mav."

I shrugged and slid the empty tumbler from one hand to the other. "Shouldn't have tried to touch her."

Didn't matter what shit we were going through.

Didn't matter that she'd already been pushing me away at that point.

Einstein would always be mine, and I'd spent long enough watching someone else touch the girl who belonged to me.

Zeke grunted and smacked his hand down on the glass to stop it mid-slide. "Look at me, kid." When I did, he gave another grunt and poured me a drink. "Your eyes are still clear, and you're here without your carbon copy or posse."

I huffed out a laugh and stared down into the amber liquor. "Is this where you play shrink?"

"Could say I'm curious about recent events. Wanna talk about it?"

I cut him a cold, hard look. "No."

"Fair enough." He started walking away, but he hadn't gotten far when he said, "Ah. That was what I was waiting for."

Before I had a chance to see what he was talking about, a dark presence surrounded me, making my blood run cold and my body tense.

My fingers twitched, preparing to reach for my gun.

Right hip.

Two seconds to grab and aim.

All it took was a second to think it through. But even though I tried to block out the noises in the bar, I couldn't get a read on who was behind me until he was at my side.

"Fucking shit," I hissed under my breath.

Kieran Hayes.

Tall. Lean. Fucking terrifying. Pretty sure he was made of shadows. And the most notorious assassin alive.

Asshole.

Our mafia families had been sworn enemies until a

couple of years ago when our boss married their princess. But we'd only been in each other's faces for the last year.

It was hard to remember he wasn't my enemy sometimes.

This was one of those times.

"Where's Einstein?" he demanded.

I shook my head and grabbed my whiskey. "Hold on, trying to start my heart again."

A soft laugh sounded behind me, only betraying a hint of her wild personality. "Come on . . . still?"

I glanced to the side to see Kieran's wife sidle up next to him. "He materialized next to me, Jess. Yeah."

She grinned mischievously in response.

Hard steps sounded behind me, loud as a damn bull.

I gestured toward the man they belonged to. "He makes himself known. That's why we all like him." I brought the glass to my lips and mumbled, *"Liked."*

Conor shouldered between Kieran and Jess. The man was terrifying in his own right. Taller than the assassin and built like a brick house, but he had a dimpled grin that showed through his beard that always offset everything else.

For once, he wasn't smiling in the way that made him look like the happiest guy on the planet.

Not that I blamed him.

I wouldn't be happy to see the guy who hated me either.

That guy being me.

"Where's Einstein?"

I looked between the two when Conor echoed Kieran's question before turning to face the bar and rolling my neck. "Wouldn't know."

"Maverick—"

"You know what, Conor? The last thing I want right now is you—*of all people*—asking me where Einstein is."

He hissed a curse and leaned in, smacking his hand on the bar to hold himself up. "Nothing happened. You know that."

I did.

It didn't make me hate him less.

It didn't make me stop constantly wondering why she chose him.

"But right now, we need to know where she is," he continued, his words all whispers and bite.

"I don't know. Haven't talked to her in a couple of days."

Who knows if I'll talk to her again.

I dropped my head into my hands and grabbed fistfuls of my hair, remembering that last conversation I had with her.

That last fight.

All we did lately was fight.

But of everything she'd said and done in her attempts to push me away—to make me move on—nothing had slayed me like her last confession.

I didn't know how to process it. Handle it. Accept it.

I didn't know how to fucking talk to her.

I didn't even know how to look at her . . . the girl I'd waited for, protected, fought for, and loved for years.

"She hasn't shown up in two days," Kieran said, as though he were delivering hard news.

A sad laugh left me. "She never shows up to work lately."

Jess sighed and took the seat on my other side. "I know

things were hard between you and Einstein this weekend, but do you have any idea where she is?"

My head snapped in her direction, and my mouth fell open.

I wanted to know how she knew.

I wanted to know *what* she knew.

Before I could ask anything, she continued, her tone more subdued than I'd ever heard it. "And that isn't entirely true. About work . . . at least for ARCK."

"She's there for at least a few minutes each day around noon. That's why we think this is different," Conor said gently.

Jess tilted her head, her eyes drifting to the side like she couldn't hold my gaze when she admitted, "But it might not be. We might be paranoid."

I slowly looked from her to Conor to Kieran. "What . . . what am I missing?"

A strangled noise came from Jess. "Maverick, I'm sorry."

I stood from the barstool and took a couple of steps back so I could see all three of them at once. "Sorry for what? What the hell is going on?"

The three of them were usually unreadable, mostly because Conor couldn't stop smiling and Jess never stopped laughing.

But the way they were acting had a pit forming in my stomach.

It made it hard to breathe.

Conor's unease was rolling from him in waves.

Jess wasn't even trying to hide her nerves.

And Kieran . . . well, shit, Kieran always just looked intimidating.

After a heavy pause, Kieran said, "We were hoping you'd seen her. Because the last we did was Saturday afternoon, and she was going on a date."

My shoulders sagged.

A stunned breath pushed from my lungs.

Of course she was.

"No one's heard from her since she left the office. Her car is . . ."

I didn't hear anything else Kieran said, I just kept hearing all our fights in a jumble of words as the pit grew to an endless black hole in my stomach.

The day of her fucked-up confession.

The day she tore the ground from beneath my feet.

The day she took my world and shattered it.

For eight months, she'd been relentlessly trying to make me leave. And the instant she succeeded, she moved on with her life, forgetting about all the pain that had come with ours.

"I've told them . . ." I looked up in time to see Jess glance at the guys uneasily. "With the way she was acting before she left, I told them she just might not have come home yet."

"Two days," Kieran reminded her.

"How many times have we spent days in bed, escaping the world?" she whispered harshly, meaningfully.

My stomach rolled. I took a staggering step back.

Jess's face pinched with sympathy. "Maverick, I'm sorry. I didn't want to put you through this."

A pained laugh sounded deep in my chest.

I rubbed at the aching there.

"Why not? One more thing to break me before I go, right?"

"Fuck, man." Conor blew out a harsh breath. "You know that isn't what we want to do. And you know Einstein better than anyone, but this feels wrong. It felt wrong when she left."

"Very," Kieran agreed. "She'd been crying and wasn't herself. When she said where she was going, it looked like she wanted someone to stop her but wouldn't let anyone try. She's been missing a lot lately, but this is different."

"It had already been planned, but I think she only kept the date because of what happened with the two of you before." Jess tried to hold my stare but kept lowering hers to the floor. "She said she'd see me the next day, but she was trying to either numb herself or feel something. And that's why I can't be sure that we aren't making a mistake by coming to you."

I swallowed the bile that was quick to rise in my throat.

Anger mixed with the defeated feeling lingering in my veins. "Was it Lincoln?"

Jess shifted before lifting her chin and holding my gaze, as if she was preparing for my reaction. Whether or not it was him, Jess clearly knew about Einstein and the lead singer from Henley.

Fuck.

Kieran tilted his head just enough to be able to look at her when he said, "No. Einstein said he was a guy from the coffee shop. She mentioned him about a month ago, none of us remember his name."

"She thought he was lying to her about his name and where he lived," Jess added.

Icy fingers trailed up my spine as that morning at Brooks Street Café came rushing back.

"Alex," I said on a breath. "Has to be Alex. For the last

couple of months, if Einstein's somewhere, that guy shows up soon after. I finally said something when he showed up at Brooks Street one morning, but Einstein ended up fighting with me and defending him." I ran my hands over my face. "Tell me she ran a check on him."

Conor cut a hard look at Jess. "She was advised not to."

"It was a month ago," she snapped, as if she'd known the criticism was coming.

"You told her *not* to run a check on him?" I asked, my tone low and threatening.

I ignored the immediate reaction that got from Kieran. He could've had a knife to my throat, and I wouldn't have noticed in that moment.

Jess shot me an exasperated look mixed with regret. "He flirted." A frustrated huff burst from her chest as she lifted her fingers to her forehead and then flung them to the side. "Jesus, the guy was flirting so hard with her, and Einstein didn't have a clue because she's *Einstein*. She wanted to do a search on him because she'd been so sure he was lying and there was something off about him. But the conversation sounded like nothing more than a nice guy trying to pick up a girl, so I told her not to *Einstein* the guy and to give him a chance. That was all."

"You're standing there apologizing to me, saying you didn't want me to be put through this shit. But *you* told her not to *Einstein* some guy—whatever the hell that even means—so he could have a chance with her? Are you fucking kidding me? After everything she and I went through?"

"Choose your next words carefully," Kieran said in a lethal tone.

I bit my tongue and shook my head roughly.

"I *am* sorry, Maverick," Jess murmured. "And I'm sorry for what you've been going through. But the two of you haven't been . . . well, anything, for so long."

A broken laugh escaped my lungs. "And, yet, you're all here expecting me to know where she is. Funny how that works, isn't it?"

I stalked to the bar, grabbed my glass, and tossed back the last of the whiskey before turning to leave.

I ground my jaw and sent Jess a glare that said everything I couldn't without risking Kieran's wrath. "What I *do* know is that Einstein—" I swallowed back the words that nearly slipped free, words that weren't mine to tell. I cleared my throat and said simply, "She wouldn't do what you think she is."

Jess's shoulders sagged. "I know it hurts to think about, but we can't rule it out. We can't know—"

"Jessica," Kieran bit out, shaking his head for her to stop.

"*I* know," I said confidently. "Your guy Conor said it. I know Einstein better than anyone else does."

And what Jess thought might be happening were Einstein's greatest demons. She only trusted one person with them.

Me.

I looked at the phone Conor held in front of me when I tried to walk past him. "What—"

"Einstein's," he answered. "We tracked it before coming here when she didn't show for work. It was still at the restaurant. They found it under the table on Saturday."

Shit.

My legs felt weak.

I could no longer catch a breath.

I took the phone, checking to see her battery was nearly dead.

It didn't matter what they said, I refused to believe she hadn't run some kind of check on the guy. She checked everyone. Fucking *everyone*.

"Where, uh . . . where are her laptop and tablet?"

"Laptop's at the office," they answered in unison.

"Let's go."

I gripped her phone like a lifeline while reaching for my own. Within seconds, I had my brother on the phone.

"Get the others to ARCK. Now." I swallowed thickly and then added, "It's Einstein."

three

Einstein
TWO MONTHS AGO

Dare drummed his hands on the table at Brooks Street Café and sat back in the booth, a contented smile crossing his face. "No meeting tomorrow. Agreed?"

"Hell *yes* agreed," Diggs called out.

I snorted. "Obviously."

Maverick didn't answer at all.

"I don't plan to get home before the sun's up tomorrow," his brother continued, his words taking on a wistful tone.

Dare and his wife both rolled their eyes, but she shot Diggs an amused smile before turning it on Dare. "I'm just excited to go to a concert."

"Why was your life so sad before us?"

"Jesus," Dare murmured and tossed a sugar packet at Diggs. "We're not doing this again."

Lily held up the wriggling baby in her arms, her smile widening. "The last word I would use to describe my life is sad."

"*Before* us," Diggs argued.

I caught Dare's stare when I managed to wrench mine away from Lily.

His was hard and challenging. As if he were daring me to say something.

Something about their baby. About how he would only be seen as a target to old enemies. How he was a mistake.

Any number of the opinions I'd voiced before Beckham was born six months ago.

But I just dropped my head to stare at the table and mentally sang a simple code in the tune of "Twinkle, Twinkle Little Star" until my mind was on nothing but numbers and what I needed to do when I got home and—

That's my phone vibrating.

I snaked my hand across the top of the table to grab it from where it sat on the pile of other phones and let out a curse when Dare smacked my knuckles with the heavy end of a knife.

"Don't," he said sternly and then glanced at his sister before asking me, "About tonight . . . are you coming with us?"

"If Libby goes, I go."

If Libby hides, I get to hide.

I lifted my shoulders in a shrug, trying to appear indifferent about whether I went to the Henley concert.

Even before they became famous rock stars and expanded their world beyond Wake Forest, I'd never missed one of their shows. Mainly because Libby and the bassist, Maxon, had been on again, off again for most our lives.

He was her person. Plain and simple.

But the truth was, I didn't care if I went anywhere other than my bedroom tonight.

Alone.

Dare said Libby's name a few times before Diggs finally threw the sugar packet at her.

When she didn't respond, Dare snapped, "*Libby.*"

"I'm not hungry," she mumbled.

I chanced a look at everyone's varying degrees of shock and confusion but kept my mouth shut.

Dare's eyes dipped down to his empty plate. "Yeah. No. We got that when you didn't order. Are you working the Henley show?" When Libby just sighed and zoned out, Dare called out her name again.

Her reaction was instant and full of frustration. "*What?*"

Dare's expression shifted, softened. "Have you heard anything we've said?"

"Yeah, that's not likely," I murmured.

He ignored me, keeping his focus solely on his sister. "I asked if you're working the Henley show."

Libby sucked in a sharp breath and looked to me, the way her eyes filled with panic and pain answered Dare's question and screamed that she wanted nothing to do with this conversation.

I simply stared back for a few seconds.

Six months ago, gossip sites had gone crazy with news that Maxon was going to be a father.

The same day my world turned.

Flipped.

Righted. If only for a little while.

It came out a few days later that the pregnant girl was one of his closest friends—a girl who grew up here. And the baby in her belly? Put there by her husband and most definitely *not* Maxon.

If Libby had taken a few minutes to breathe, she would have known this. But after all of this time, she still didn't.

Maxon's name hadn't even been uttered in her presence since it all happened. Libby hadn't been able to handle hearing it.

He. Him. That was what Maxon had been reduced to.

More like He-Who-Shall-Not-Be-Spoken-Of.

It was bullshit if you asked me.

Not that anyone needed to. Libby already knew how I felt.

But as terrible as it sounded, there was a part of me that was thankful for her heartache and her detachment. If it weren't for them, I wouldn't have been able to hide my own pain from Libby—my best friend and roommate, who always saw too much.

But Maxon and the guys were coming back to Wake Forest to close out their tour, as they always did every couple of years.

I wanted to slap some sense into Libby as much as I wanted to continue hiding behind her pain.

To bury mine with it just a little longer.

"Does this mean we can skip giving E the numbers this week?" Diggs suddenly asked, his voice low.

I broke the connection with Libby and turned to shoot him a look. "I will gladly do whatever it takes to prevent you from getting laid for a month if I don't have those numbers before the show tonight."

Maverick gave a little huff from where he sat beside me, eyes on the table—as they had been for most of breakfast.

Diggs studied me for a moment. His playful tone turned passive when he said, "Torturing one brother isn't enough?"

I only caught a flash of Maverick's fist going into Diggs's side before I was able to tear my gaze away.

My chest wrenched open.

The place where my heart used to be felt so vast and hollow.

I was so absorbed in the echoes of pain that I flinched when Libby said, "No. No, I'm not."

What were we talking about?

Everyone stilled when Dare asked, "Are you *going*?"

Henley.

The concert.

Agony . . . no.

Lock it up. Bury the key.

Focus on Libby's hurt. Libby's pain.

"No," she finally said.

Not surprising.

Also not unwelcome.

I barely caught the end of Lily asking if Libby wanted to talk about what was happening when Libby simultaneously started trying to stand and shove me out of the booth.

Maverick needed to move for me to get out, and since I'd been tasked with getting Libby out of the apartment and to this booth, I sat back, refusing to budge.

"Do you . . ." Lily cleared her throat. "Do you want to talk about it?"

"Libby," Dare cut in. "He'll be back tonight."

"I know," she bit out while still trying to find a way to get free from the booth.

Dare grabbed Libby's wrist and waited for her to stop moving and look at him before saying, "I know you're hurting, Libby. Jesus Christ, I know. We've given you time, but it's gone on long enough. This isn't you."

I felt Maverick's stare on me, hot and accusatory, as if he was claiming those words as his own and shouting them at me.

Truth was, he'd said them to me over and over again these last six months.

And I'd brushed them off.

My chest shook from the power of my silent exhale.

My soul was screaming for me to look at him.

To tell him the words I'd been shutting down for months.

I love you, I love you, I will always love you.

To tell him *everything*.

About that day.

About what happened.

About how I'd failed him and myself.

My mind was warring with it, standing firm on what I knew and could no longer feel.

My heart.

Myself.

But still, despite it all, my neck twisted, my eyes drawn to his.

To the pain there.

To the questions.

The café and arguing at our table faded away.

It was only him. Only me.

Begging to know *why* and struggling to no longer feel.

You're better off without me.

As if he heard my words, he looked away, his head shaking subtly.

"I always love seeing these tables filled with my favorite kids."

I jolted at the unexpected voice, at remembering I was in public, and then tried to remember how to smile when I saw Dare and Libby's mom standing behind Diggs.

She sighed, her mouth pulling into a gentle smile. "Seeing all of you together like this gives me hope that, one day soon, you'll stop pretending to be something you aren't."

Always with both feet in the mafia. Forever with the heart and mind of a mafia boss's wife.

That was Sofia Borello.

She'd been firmly against Dare's decision to dissolve the family's ties to that world. But there was no talking him out of it. After his dad died and Dare took over as boss, his main objective had been to disband the organization.

But there was no leaving the mafia.

Not really.

Because enemies never forgot who you once were.

We all knew that—Dare included. But if he wanted to try his hand at a normal life, the rest of us had to follow until the day someone brought us and our black bandanas out of retirement.

Until then, I would keep doing what I'd always done . . . with a side job added here and there.

What could I say? It was hard leaving that lifestyle behind.

Then again, I never had to do any of the truly dirty work.

Locks and codes and puzzles.
Getting my family in and out of places.
Finding people—*helping* them.
Hacking into anything or anywhere . . . that was my forte.

"Who's pretending?" I asked Sofia, my lips twitching into a faint smirk. "I'm still doing me, thank you very much."

"You sure about that?" Maverick whispered before shoving out of the booth and storming out of Brooks Street Café.

The war within me raged and grew until it was so chaotic that it was hard for me to breathe. Until keeping up this pretense they all expected from me felt nearly impossible.

I need to get out of here.

"For a good reason," Dare reminded me. "Not for the old ones."

It took me a second too long to realize he was talking about the focus of my hacking and not was I was doing to Maverick.

I think I smirked. "Whatever you say, Boss."

A grim look stole across his face. "Call me that again. I dare you."

If I hadn't been so close to panicking—so close to losing my grip on who I needed to be—I might've laughed.

I'd handled cruel, sadistic Johnny for over a dozen years. His best days were more terrifying than the look Dare was giving me.

"Rain check?" I asked as I slid out of the booth, trying to remain calm even though I was trembling, desperate to be freed from their watchful stares.

Not thinking of how my betraying body would follow *his* to the ends of the earth, I stumbled into the parking lot just as Maverick turned in his pacing to face me.

He trapped me in his stare, which left me struggling to regain control of my emotions.

Lock it up.

Lock it up.

Lock it up.

I gritted my teeth when Maverick laughed, the sound low and full of frustrations and pain that only continued to grow whenever I saw him.

"You think you're still doing you?" he asked, throwing my words back at me. "Have you lost your mind?"

"My mind's still perfectly intact, thanks for asking."

"Einstein, have you seen yourself?" He shifted closer, and his voice twisted with torment. "Do you know what it's like to be the one looking at you?"

No, no, no.

Panic rose and swelled within me.

This was what I needed to avoid. This was what I couldn't allow to happen. This was why I had been keeping him at a distance for months.

"I look at you, and God, I see you." His jaw flexed and strained. "I fucking see you and this show you're putting on for everyone. But that's all it is—a show. Behind it, you've built these walls to keep me from getting too close."

"You ever consider that maybe you just never really knew me?"

"Bullshit," he snapped. "You're pushing me away because you're scared."

Of course I am.

Scared to feel. Scared to remember. Scared to let them *see*.

But I simply lifted a brow in amusement and tried not to sway toward him.

Tried not to remember what it felt like to be in his arms.

Tried to take hold of the pain and bury it deep once again.

"I wouldn't be so sure of that," I murmured and forced my lips to twist into a smirk.

Maverick ran his hands over his face before roughly gesturing to Brooks Street Café. "We're all here for Libby, trying to pull her out of whatever shit she's been going through the last six months. But I've actually *seen* Libby during that time. You're avoiding me. And when you can't —like at meetings—you pretend I'm not there."

I lifted a hand and motioned to him. "Clearly, you're here. I'm having a conversation with you."

"You know what I mean, Einstein." He released a pent-up breath, and I knew this was wearing on him. Knew what would happen soon.

The two times he'd managed to get me alone since *that* night, our conversations had gone the same as this one.

I had remained detached and had refused to give him answers until he left frustrated.

He started to turn, and I prepared myself for it. To watch him walk away from me again.

Exactly what I wanted. What I *needed*.

But at the last second, he rocked back and begged, "Jesus, what happened? Did I hurt you? Did I move too fast?" A wrecked-sounding laugh left him, and he rubbed at his chest. "I've gone over everything again and again, and every time, I end up at a loss. I had you for a second before I lost you . . . and I don't know what the fuck I did."

For a moment, my façade slipped.

I wanted to tell him that all he did was love me.

In a way I'd only dreamed was possible. In a way that was so pure and honest and beautiful that I'd hated myself for doing this to him.

Because I didn't deserve him. I never had, and I never would.

I opened my mouth to respond, but a choked noise was all I managed.

Betraying emotions.

I turned for my car, trying to force away the tears that were building.

"Einstein," Maverick called out, his footsteps sounding behind me. "Einstein. *Avery.*"

I stilled.

Goose bumps raced across my skin.

Only Maverick called me by my real name, and even then, he'd reserved it for special times.

His hands appeared beside me, hovering just over my arms before he let them fall with a defeated sigh. "Don't do whatever you're trying to do. Don't push me away. Not after everything we've been through."

I swallowed past the lump in my throat and turned to face him. "I want you to find someone. I want you to forget about anything you may have thought was happening between us."

"*May have thought?*" he asked, his voice thick with emotion.

"I want you to live your life apart from me."

His eyes widened, and he staggered back a step. "Avery—"

"And I want you to let me live mine."

He stared at me like he didn't recognize me. His broken expression threatened to shatter something in me . . . and I couldn't so much as crack.

Not again.

I needed to harden myself. Become immune to him and the emotions he incited inside me.

I turned before he could speak and didn't look back until I got in my car.

And regretted it the moment I did because it felt as if knives were being driven into my chest.

He was there, staring in my direction with his hands in his hair, walking slowly backward.

There was so much pain in love.

And my pain? It went so far beyond ripping myself away from the man I loved.

My heart had been destroyed, and there wasn't any recovering from it. There was only the struggle to survive. To breathe.

Maverick deserved a girl who could love him with every piece of her soul.

And I was no longer her.

I let the door to my and Libby's apartment swing open and didn't even bother trying to keep up any pretenses.

I didn't have the energy.

I folded my arms under my chest and leaned against the wall, watching Libby shuffle to her side of the apartment.

"It isn't too late to change your mind about the show. Love of your life will be at The Jack tonight. You could go . . . woo him. Fix everything and make your world right again." Every word was said with so little enthusiasm that it was a wonder she didn't charge at me in true Libby fashion and demand to know what was wrong.

Then again, she was *that* deep inside her own head and pain lately.

"The love of your life was just sitting next to you," she murmured as she turned the corner in her hallway. "I didn't see you trying to fix anything."

My chest pitched with a pained huff.

"Touché." I pushed from the wall and turned for my hallway, thankful for the escape of my room and my computer as the confrontation outside Brooks Street Café replayed in my head.

I wasn't surprised that Maverick and I had ended up there. In the same place we'd been for as long as I could remember.

Standing inches apart. Eyes trained on the other's. Voices low so the conversation wouldn't carry. Tones full of more passion than I would admit to.

And though all I'd been trying to do for the last six months was make him walk away, I wasn't surprised that *I* had followed him.

Because there had always been an undeniable, inexplicable pull between Maverick and I.

Always.

He and his twin brother had come into my life nearly eleven years ago, back when our family had needed to level the playing field with rivals. The mafia was as much about loyalty and family—blood or oath—as it was about the power you wielded over others, what you had to offer, and the tricks you kept hidden up your sleeves.

The brothers had been that trick. The two of them combined were very nearly the equivalent of Kieran, Holloway's silent-as-the-night assassin.

Finding them had been simple.

Breaking them out of a black site had been effortless.

I'd thought that them fitting in with our family would be the hard part, but only days later, it was as if they'd been with us for years.

They ended up being exactly what the Borellos needed.

And Maverick ended up being what I needed . . . and couldn't have.

For years, he stayed just as he had this morning.

Inches away.

Eyes trained on me.

Voice low and tone full of passion.

Everything I reciprocated because I couldn't stop myself. My heart begged for his. Craved his.

But to have closed that distance between us would've ensured his death.

Because until a year and a half ago, I'd belonged to Johnny.

I had been with him for over twelve years, and I loved him until the day he was killed.

Part of me still did.

But I'd fallen *out* of love with him almost as soon as we began.

To put it mildly, our relationship was toxic. He relied on me to keep him sane. He attacked strangers if they came too close to me. And over the years, I felt like his near-constant, unhinged state had turned into my responsibility. My burden to bear.

I was trapped. Suffocated.

Yet, I never left. Never attempted to.

Enough people had died at Johnny's hands, countless more would have if I'd ever walked away. If he would have known that my heart screamed someone else's name . . .

Bodies would have piled up until I could convince him that I only wanted him.

Maverick had never been a threat, though. The twins were family to Johnny. If Johnny had ever stopped to really look, he would've noticed something there . . . but he never stopped, and we never gave him a reason to look.

So, throughout it all, the man I *was* in love with was always by my side. Never touching me. Constantly breaking my heart with those wrecked, gray eyes.

The same eyes I'd been avoiding for the last six months.

I blinked quickly when my phone vibrated, and realized I was just standing in the middle of my room and reliving painful things the way Libby liked to do.

Awesome.

Glancing at the screen for a second to see a new email from Diggs, I sank into my desk chair and brought my computer to life—all five screens of it.

My eyes rolled when I opened up the latest email.

Here are the stupid numbers, fun-sucker.
    Threaten my sex life again, I'll hate you forever.
    Or at least until you come groveling with food.

I could have easily slipped into Diggs's system to get the numbers if he actually kept them all in one place. But he was consistent in his inconsistencies. At the end of each week, some numbers were in his laptop, some were in his phone, and the rest were written down.

I'd just opened the first attachment when an email came in from Maverick.

The subject was blank. The body was blank. But the attachments I needed were there, similar to the ones from Diggs.

Not that I expected much else after what had just happened.

I was actually surprised he'd sent the numbers in at all. Then again, what Dare needed, he received.

Not that it mattered. I'd hacked into Maverick's system before breakfast to get what I needed from him anyway.

While trying to legitimize the Borello family, Dare spent well over a decade buying business after drowning business in Wake Forest and loaning even more money until he owned or had a hand in most of the town.

With Dare wanting to devote his time to his new family, Maverick and Diggs had taken over managing the properties. That meant they sent their reports to me each week— including profits, losses, blah, blah, blah.

Seeing as it was the only reason we contacted each other anymore, it really drove home how much things had changed between Maverick and me.

I loosed a pained sigh and quickly scanned the reports, looking for the numbers I knew Dare needed and skipping over the ones that didn't matter.

After nearly seventeen years, it was second nature. Like breathing.

I'd been best friends with Libby since kindergarten when she asked if she could have my freckles. And since I'm not an idiot, I knew from a young age exactly who her family was and what they were involved in. But it wasn't until Dare was forced into the role of boss at thirteen that I was recruited into the family.

Ever since, I'd been his brain.

Every business he bought or helped out, I kept books for. Every move Borellos or their enemies made, I recorded. Cash and weapons that moved in and out were all logged through me.

It was all easy . . . *too* easy.

There was no challenge anymore. I had too much time on my hands, which was why I had started working for Kieran and Conor at ARCK Investigations, their private investigating firm.

Suffice to say, that decision caused a family fight that nearly reinstated our feud with the former members of the Holloway gang—our longtime enemies and the reason behind so many deaths in our family.

Then again, we'd been the reason behind a lot of deaths in Holloway as well.

But I stopped the fight before it could gain momentum when I reminded everyone that Dare had married the Holloway Princess almost a year before.

My fingers stilled over the keyboard when another email came in. My brows pinched tightly when I saw the familiar name pop up in the preview box of my bottom screen.

Sutton.

I thought over the name for only a second before recognition hit. I pushed out a frustrated breath and ignored it until I was done with the twins' reports.

Once I finished, I pulled up my email and tried to have an open mind even though I was wondering why I was entertaining this woman at all.

"All right, Sutton. Let's see what you've got this time."

I was ARCK's coder and hacker—most of which was still done illegally, but we didn't talk about that. Because there was a part of the company that wasn't publicized, and that was where I was needed most.

While Conor was the face of ARCK since he was so damn likeable, Kieran and his wife did the dirty work, including helping women and children escape life-threatening situations they felt trapped in. Then I helped them disappear.

They reached out to whichever account they found first —and sometimes that was mine.

Like with Sutton.

Only I'd never had a potential client so unwilling to cooperate. And I hated that with each new email, I became more irritated with her and the little information she offered me.

She claimed her name was Sutton Larson, that she was twenty-seven, and that she lived in Brentwood, Tennessee. Sometime before she first reached out to me, she witnessed a crime and the perpetrators wanted her silenced. There was also a child involved.

But it had taken three messages to get all that information.

Usually, by the time our clients sought us out, they were ready for help and ready to do whatever it took, so they would give the information I just read willingly. Sutton's first email came through to my account almost a month ago with nothing more than: "Is this real? Can you help?"

I hadn't even gotten her last name until today.

And after a quick scan, I realized why.

There was no Sutton Larson. Not in Brentwood, not anywhere.

I searched again, looking for different variations of the first and last name, but came up empty each time.

Frustration pushed slowly through my veins.

Someone had found out what we did for those who needed help, for those who desperately needed to get away from the situations they were living in, and was mocking us.

I started a reply to the email, my normally quick, rapid fingers sounded slow and clunky on the keyboard due to my aggravation.

We help those who genuinely need it.

Upon investigation, we've found there is no Sutton Larson in existence.

I'm not sure how you found out about us, whoever you are, but please do not contact us again unless you truly have need for us.

I pushed away from my desk as soon as the email sent and

finally let myself be consumed by everything I'd been avoiding today. Dismissing. Hiding from.

My heart was just a heart.

And it was shattering slowly. So slowly that it was piecing itself together in time to shatter all over again.

Four

Maverick
TWO MONTHS AGO

Everyone was arguing as they tried to figure out if anyone had known that Maxon hadn't actually gotten that girl in California pregnant.

Anyone other than Einstein, that was. She'd been the one to drop the bomb on us like we all should've known too. I wasn't surprised that she knew, because there wasn't a thing the girl didn't know.

Einstein and I were the only ones silent.

She was drumming her fingers on the tabletop, anxious to get her hands on her phone again. In all the years I'd known her, she hadn't been able to sit still for more than a few minutes at a time without finding something to hack into. A code to break or write. A mindfuck of a puzzle to defeat.

Not unless it was just the two of us.

Funny that *just the two of us* had happened a hell of a lot more before Johnny died.

Funny. Confusing. Frustrating. Agonizing. They were one in the same.

I'd been in a constant state of some mixture of them for the last six or so months.

And somehow, we'd ended up here.

Sitting next to each other. A world apart.

It'd been that way this morning and all tonight. It was how it had been since she shut me out of her life.

For anyone who didn't really know her, she seemed normal. She looked like she enjoyed the Henley show tonight, and her smartass quips and responses sounded like typical Einstein.

But there was no light in her green eyes. Even in relaxed positions, she looked rigid, like she was worried she'd break if she let herself loosen. And every once in a while, there was a sad lilt to her tone.

Before Johnny died—hell, even for nearly a year after—I knew that if something was wrong with her, I only had to wait. Eventually, she'd slip away from Johnny, or he would go on a work-related errand with Dare, and Einstein would find her way to me.

She had trusted me with things she hadn't trusted anyone else with. Had given me some of her grief so she wasn't the only one holding its weight.

This wasn't like any of those times. Something big had happened, cutting off the communication I'd once had with her and putting a wall between us. Something I could only assume I had done.

Assume, because she wouldn't tell me. Would hardly talk to me. Hardly look at me. Making it so that every time

I saw her, life slammed back into my lungs only for the agony of our situation to cripple them again.

When I'd walked into The Jack tonight and found Libby working and Einstein sitting at the bar, waiting for the Henley show to start, I almost walked back out. I didn't think I'd be able to handle another beatdown after the one outside Brooks Street this morning.

Turning around probably would've been the smart thing to do.

I'd never claimed to be smart.

Besides, I shouldn't have been surprised. Einstein rarely left Libby's side lately, and despite Libby's withdrawal these past months, she was as stubborn as they come. We all should have known she'd work the Henley show just to prove to Maxon that she was fine without him.

If the conversation we just had with Maxon was any indication, her plan backfired.

I glanced at Diggs, Dare, and Lily, and waited to make sure they weren't paying attention to Einstein or me before I reached forward and grabbed our phones from the pile on the table.

She didn't thank me when I slid hers over. I hadn't expected her to.

I leaned closer to her so I could drop my voice low, more out of habit from talking to her in secret for over a decade than my need for privacy. "Since you just gave your keys to Maxon to go fix things with Libby, I'm guessing you aren't going home."

"Looks like I'm not the only genius around here."

I let the comment go. "Where do you plan on staying tonight?"

"Not sure why that's your business."

"Einstein—"

"Stop," she whispered. Her eyes were shut, as if she were afraid to open them, and her thumbs were hovering over the screen of her phone.

I couldn't.

I couldn't, because none of this made sense.

If I honestly thought Einstein didn't want a future with me, I might be able to accept it, no matter how much the thought made my stomach churn and chest ache. But you couldn't love someone one day and then decide to cut them out of your life the next.

You couldn't have what Einstein and I had and have it suddenly disappear.

Attraction, lust, love . . . all those things could fade.

What Einstein and I had was all consuming. It was unending.

"You know what I don't understand?" I asked, my tone gruff. "You got on Maxon tonight for letting six months go by without coming to make Libby see reason. For not coming to fix things. Six months *while he was on tour.*"

Einstein stiffened, and her eyes shot open. She knew where I was going with this, but she didn't try to stop me when my next words came.

"It's been about that amount of time for us, and I've been begging for something from you. *Anything.* I've been here, and I've tried to fix whatever the hell went wrong. But that only seems to push us further apart."

Her head started moving, a slow rocking back and forth.

Whether she was silently asking me to stop or denying the truth, I wasn't sure.

"And why wouldn't it be my business where you stay tonight? From the moment you stepped into my life and started trying to boss me around like you had the right to, *everything* about you has been my business." I dipped my head even closer and said, "I want to know you're safe. I want to know you're okay. I want to know that you aren't letting that mind of yours destroy something so damn good."

Her eyes shot to mine, pain and hesitation swirling in their depths before she locked the emotion up tight and shut me out.

That . . . *that* was why I hadn't stopped fighting.

Because I could still see it in brief flashes—everything she was trying to hide from me.

"I'm fine. I'll *be* fine," she said harshly, her lip curling when she continued. "Wherever I end up, whoever's bed I end up in. I'll be fine."

I jerked back when the weight of her words hit me.

Drunken words I'd said to her such a long time ago.

I couldn't take a deep enough breath. It felt like I couldn't breathe at all.

Because when I'd uttered those words, I would've done anything—anyone—to be *fine*.

And I *had*.

She was looking at me the exact same way I knew I had been looking at her that night.

"Einstein." Her name was a rasp scraping up my throat, but she didn't react. She just held my gaze without wavering. "Why are you doing this?"

"Because this is the way it needs to be." She sank back into her chair, her eyes widening in horror when she looked straight ahead.

It took me a few seconds to tear my gaze from her, only to be met with three pairs of shocked stares.

My brother, Dare, and Lily were looking between us, expressions shifting from shock and worry for me to confusion and anger with Einstein.

I rubbed at the back of my neck, a strangled breath working from my mouth. "I, uh . . . fuck." I stood and tried to motion to them before letting my arm fall limply to my side. "I'll see you. I'm gonna walk."

The three of them called my name, but I didn't stop or look back. I let my feet carry me in the direction of my place as my chest cracked wide open.

As that night from six years ago haunted and tormented me.

I stumbled a few steps in the crowded bar before righting myself and turning to see Einstein standing there.

Eyes darting all around me, pain filling them so wholly it threatened to wreck me. But I was already so far gone that I wasn't sure I could feel my fucking tongue, much less my heart.

"Well, well, well . . . look who showed." A low laugh built in my chest. "Did you come to celebrate or gloat?"

"Maverick—" She jerked, her brows pinching tight when hands snaked around me, fingers searching under my shirt and raking over my lower stomach. "What . . ."

"Told you I'd be fine."

"Maverick, what are you doing?" Her strained voice somehow reached me above the music and the large crowd in The Jack.

I leaned back, spreading my arms wide and tipping my face to the ceiling to call out, "Having a damn good time!" I looked down at her and smirked. "You should try it sometime."

I felt more hands on my arm, pulling me closer to another body, and then lips were on my neck.

Einstein ripped her stare from the women before piercing me with all the hatred her little body could possess. She didn't need to say anything, her eyes said it all.

How could you?

I laughed loudly.

I dipped down until our faces were a breath apart.

Closer than we'd ever intentionally been.

I didn't even know if Johnny was there. And I was too wasted to care.

Too wasted to care that everything that was Einstein and me was kept secret. Hidden. Even from each other.

Don't get close enough to touch.

Don't voice our feelings for each other.

Don't let the world catch even a hint that I love you and you love me.

Tonight was throwing that last one out the fucking window.

"You're gonna look at me like that?" I asked, my mouth twisted into a sneer. "You're gonna look at me like I betrayed you? I just had to listen to him tell the whole family he's gonna marry you."

"What am I supposed to do?" she yelled. "What was I supposed to say? That I didn't want to? He didn't even ask me." She flung her hand out as if Johnny was standing behind her.

I looked.

He wasn't.

"I found out when you did."

I breathed out a laugh. "Like you said, what are you supposed to do? Not like you can leave the guy. Right? Because we can't hurt poor Johnny's feelings."

The words were out even though I knew they were wrong.

I knew why she couldn't leave him.

He was certifiably insane. He was cruel. He was a goddamn monster.

Considering I lived in a world full of the worst kind of people, that was saying something.

Her face pinched with grief. "Don't do this."

"I'm not doing anything. Oh, wait." *I lifted a finger and booped her on the nose.* "I am. I'm accepting the shit hand that life dealt me. I'm accepting that you're gonna be taken from me in a way that's irreversible."

"Maverick—"

"No, no. I'm fine. I'm gonna be *fine.* Clearly." *I lifted my hands to indicate the women clinging to me.* "Wherever I end up, whoever's bed I end up in. I'm gonna be just fine."

She looked at me as if I was devastating her. As if I were taking what we had—what we'd been pretending we didn't *have—and shattering it.*

I wasn't the one who was about to be engaged.

I leaned to the side and grabbed another shot glass off my table, and absently wondered how many shots I'd already had.

Not that it mattered.

I could still see Einstein. Could still register her pain. Could nearly feel my own.

I held the shot up between us and felt my mouth twist into a pained smile. Before I tossed it back, I said, "To losing what you never really had."

I'd woken the next afternoon to two girls in my bed. After forcing them out of my apartment, I'd run straight to Einstein, begging her to forgive me.

Because even during a time when she still belonged to Johnny, a time when we never crossed that line, I felt like I'd cheated on her and had nearly given up the greatest love I would ever know.

She didn't say a word to me for two days.

Two.

Even after what I'd done and said, she'd only lasted two days before falling apart to me about what she was going to do—about what *we* were going to do if she was forced to go through with a wedding.

A month after that, our world had been rocked when Dare's fiancée, Gia, had been ripped from their bed and murdered by the boss of the Holloway gang.

With Johnny's one-track, blood-seeking mind, his focus turned to keeping Dare's thoughts on nothing but revenge. He never mentioned marriage to Einstein again.

And not once in the last six years, had she or I brought up that night in The Jack, not until tonight.

Five

Einstein
SEVEN WEEKS AGO

You can do this.

I gulped down another shot—or two—of vodka straight from the skull bottle and roughly set it on the counter. I let my gaze drift to my and Libby's living room where the boys from Henley were lounging around after an impromptu practice.

They'd had a lot of impromptu practices this past week.

Someone said something that turned into Maxon singing the same words and adding a few of his own. Before I knew it, Ledger was drumming on anything close to him and one of the boys was grabbing a guitar as they tried to perfect whatever Maxon was envisioning.

It really was something to watch . . . it was also loud in our apartment. All the time.

After Maxon had gotten Libby to see the truth of the whole not-my-baby situation, they picked right back up where they always left off. Except this time, Maxon decided he wasn't going back to California and was moving in with us.

That somehow led to the rest of the Henley members crashing with us most nights instead of at their hotel. And I had a feeling the boys' nights were going to become more frequent, because Lincoln, Jared, and Ledger decided that, if Maxon was moving back to Wake Forest, they were all moving back too and had bought the old Holloway estate on a whim.

Rock stars.

Granted, mobsters weren't much better, but our family was subtle when it came to money.

Low profiles and all.

Lincoln's stare locked on to mine, as it had so often this week, and my gut twisted with guilt and remorse for something I hadn't even done.

Maxon and Lincoln had grown up in the same foster home, and since Libby and Maxon were together for most their lives, that meant Lincoln and I were often thrown together.

Either as the unwilling third and fourth wheels, or as covers so Libby and Maxon could sneak away together.

We couldn't have been more different. I was more interested in finding another code to break, and he was more interested in playing his guitar and the girls that followed him around.

I didn't know if I would've even considered us *friends* back then.

By the time I was made a Borello member, I was falling into my disastrous relationship with Johnny. So, unless we were all at a Henley show, Lincoln and I never said more than a few words to each other, and we sat as far away as possible when forced to tag along for Libby and Maxon.

After all, he knew Johnny.

Everyone in Wake Forest knew Johnny.

Just as everyone knew when he died. It was hard not to notice the absence of his darkness.

Lincoln noticed.

And he'd been acting differently from how he'd ever acted before.

A subtle touch. A tug on my hair. A wink and a smirk.

It all made something inside me want to die.

And at the same time, I couldn't help but consider wrecking another part of my soul and going through with what Lincoln clearly wanted. If only for the chance that my doing so would get Maverick to stop fighting for what was lost and find someone who deserved him.

Because that couldn't be me . . . not ever again.

I let my gaze drift to the counter and gripped the crystal skull in my shaking hands as I tried to think of any way to just get this over with while thinking of every reason not to go through with it.

I flinched when a hand palmed my waist.

Lincoln let out a soft laugh and took the vodka from my hands. "Drinking alone, little genius?"

"Seemed like a good idea."

"Usually better to have a partner." His lips met my ear and his voice lowered. "Or two."

I couldn't stop the shiver that ripped down my spine.

The thought made my stomach churn with acid and my head get light.

I swayed toward the counter and hurried to grip it when it felt like I would faint.

"Shit," Lincoln hissed as he slowly twisted me around so I was facing him, his eyes widened with worry as they scanned me. "How much did you drink?"

"Not—no, I didn't. I just, uh . . ."

Oh God, I sound like Libby.

I cleared my throat and reached for my forehead. It was covered in a thin sheen of cool sweat. "I'm hot, and I think I've been standing here too long. I must have locked my knees."

His brow furrowed as if he wasn't sure if he believed me. "All right. Well, let's go sit you down."

I let him lead me into the living room and then I sank to the floor in front of him when he sat.

My breaths were shallow and my hands were trembling, and I hoped like hell none of the guys noticed.

"Good God," Ledger said on a groan when Lincoln picked up his guitar and began playing. "What are you gonna do? Serenade her?"

"How is what I'm doing any different from Maxon?"

Jared snorted.

From where he was lying on one of the couches, Ledger lifted his beer in the air, saying, "Maxon's off in the corner being a fucking loner. You just brought the genius in here and started playing for her. *Serenading.*"

"I was playing before I brought her in here."

"Go. Play. Croon. Whatever the hell you do. Assholes." Ledger sighed loudly. "Can't serenade on drums."

Lincoln rolled his eyes but sent me a smirk.

"He isn't serenading me," I said matter-of-factly. "He's teaching me how to play."

Lincoln's fingers stilled on the guitar, and the room

went quiet, save for Maxon, who was too busy working on a song to notice us.

"Have you ever touched a guitar?" Jared asked from where he was slouching low in the chair behind me. When I only looked at him in response, he huffed. "Right, okay. It's usually easier to learn if you're holding one. Or, you know, have a general idea about what he's doing."

"I know what he's doing. His fingers are making patterns. Easy."

All three burst out laughing.

I glared at Jared before turning it on Lincoln. Dropping my stare to the neck of his guitar, I said, "Play that again."

He cleared his throat and slowly started again, muttering letters as he did.

"Whatever you're saying, stop."

"I'm telling you the chords," he murmured softly.

I looked into his gentle eyes and tried to ignore the way my body began subtly shaking.

Too close.

We were too close, and I didn't know how I thought I could make it through this when I could barely hold his stare.

"Maybe another time," I whispered, my voice strained. "Just play it how you did before so I can shut Jared up."

He tilted his head back and laughed loudly, his fingers already playing before his chest finished moving from his amusement.

I watched every shift. Noted the way his hand curled around the neck of the guitar tenderly. Absorbed the obvious and subtle changes in the way he positioned his fingers. It was almost beautiful.

And it was most definitely a pattern that could be memorized and replicated.

I made him play it once more, and then Jared was calling out, "Put your money where your mouth is, Einstein."

Lincoln didn't say anything as he passed his guitar to me; he just watched.

But the acoustic felt big and awkward as I set it on my lap. They always looked like they fit in the guys' arms so perfectly, as if they were meant to be there.

It most definitely was not meant to be in mine.

Maybe because I wasn't meant to be here doing this.

I had a life. I had work that filled my soul and gave me purpose.

I had a man my heart called for . . .

I was meant to be there. With him. By his side.

Always.

Not pretending I was fine living without him.

"No?" Jared asked, taunting me.

My apartment and the guys came rushing back. The awkwardly sized guitar in my lap was a glaring reminder of what I was supposed to be doing, and I gently ran my hand up the neck, feeling the strings and grooves beneath my fingers.

I forced a smirk and barely offered Jared a look over my shoulder. "You doubt me?"

Before any of them could answer, I envisioned Lincoln's pattern in my mind and mimicked it.

Slowly but flawlessly.

Honestly, they shouldn't have expected anything less.

I studied and memorized codes for fun.

But not long after I began, my mouth slipped into a

frown, and halfway through, I was shoving the guitar at Lincoln.

"That is extremely uncomfortable," I murmured before he even had a chance to grab it. "Why would anyone do that for fun?"

"Jesus," Lincoln whispered, his eyes wide with awe.

"Shit, girl," Ledger said on a laugh. "No way you've never played before."

I slanted a glare in his direction. "A warning that it was painful would've been nice." Looking at Lincoln again, I added, "I don't appreciate you making that look easy, by the way."

A smile broke out over his face. "Is there anything you can't do, genius?"

"I don't know. I've never tried the drums, but they can't be harder than that was."

He and Ledger shared a look before Ledger nearly fell off the couch laughing, but Jared scoffed. "She's hustling us. There's no way."

"Get over it," Lincoln said on a groan as he set his guitar behind him. "Admit she just owned that song."

"Hustler," Jared mumbled, but when I looked back at him, he was smiling.

I tensed and sucked in a shuddering breath when Lincoln curled his arm around my waist, pulling me closer.

"And there he goes." Ledger scoffed. "Lead singer always gets the girls."

Lincoln shook his head absentmindedly, his eyes never leaving mine. "Don't listen to him."

"I rarely do." My voice was soft as a breath, and I mentally cursed myself.

For sounding like such a girl.

For not being able to control my heartrate.

For my fear and uncertainty sounding like excitement.

"Something about you, Einstein."

Oh God. No. No, I can't do this.

"It's probably just how I talk to people because I know I'm smarter than them."

His chest moved with a silent laugh. He searched my face as his expression morphed into wonder and confusion. "I feel like I missed a lot of years really knowing you. But growing up? There was no talking to you, even before Johnny. You were too intimidating." The corner of his mouth tilted up. "Probably because you were smarter than everyone else." His stare fell to my mouth. "Now . . ."

I wished I'd taken a few more shots of vodka.

I needed them.

I was sure any other woman would die for a chance to have the man in front of me paying them any attention. Talking to them. Holding them.

But I wasn't just *any* woman.

He was undoubtedly attractive and had that rock-star charisma that seemed to radiate from all of them. But where Ledger and Jared were wild through and through, Lincoln was gentle and understanding.

I was positive it was a result of growing up in an abusive foster home since Maxon was similar in so many ways.

I was also positive it was why he and Maxon were always the ones in the headlines—because they were rare.

Bad boy attitudes with good guy souls.

But he wasn't Maverick. He wasn't the man I trusted implicitly. He wasn't the man I loved and belonged to.

"There is something I can't do," I whispered.

Amusement filled his words and expression. "I doubt that."

I swallowed thickly and mimicked what he had just done and glanced at his lips. "I can't do *this*," I admitted on a breath. "I don't know how."

The amusement faded, and his grip tightened, somehow feeling more protective than possessive. "What do you mean?"

"How to be with you when . . ." I didn't know what to say, how to continue. "I just don't know how."

"Is it the reputation?"

I'd been so absorbed in my own pain and suffering that I hadn't ever thought about that before he brought it up, and I didn't want to continue to. I was already struggling with trying to go through with this. Thinking about his reputation on top of it didn't help.

"No, it's . . ." I cleared my throat and looked him in the eyes. "I'm trying to move on, but I don't know how to."

Lincoln sat up straighter. "You're struggling to move on from Johnny?"

My body bowed as shame slammed into me. "What? No. He isn't—I don't need—I moved on," I stammered. "Long ago."

"*Not* Johnny." Surprise coated his words when he said, "A lot must have happened since our last tour."

"That was two years ago," I reminded him and then swallowed past the emotion tightening my throat. "This guy . . . I will never love anyone the way I love him, but we can't be together. If he thinks I'm moving on, maybe he actually will. And he deserves to."

A crease had formed between his brows before his eyes lit with understanding. His voice dropped so low I could barely hear him over the television Jared had turned on. "Is that why you were drinking? So you would be able to, what, go through with this?"

I pressed my lips tightly together.

A stunned laugh fled his lungs. "Don't think a girl has ever had to drink to hook up with me." The wounded expression on his face only made me feel worse.

"Lincoln—"

"You know," Ledger said, "there *are* other people still here."

"Shut up, Ledger." Lincoln's words held more pain and confusion than bite, and I wanted to apologize for being a terrible person.

I opened my mouth to say something—anything—when Ledger's voice boomed, making me jerk in Lincoln's hold.

"Hey, look who decided to grace us with her presence."

I didn't need to look to know Libby had come home.

I didn't need to look to see her disappointment in me. I could feel it slowly rolling from her and filling the apartment like a poisonous gas.

I stilled, torn between what I needed to continue attempting and wanting to repair my shredded heart.

"Shouldn't you be at work, Einstein?" she called out, her frustration clear in her tone. "Could've sworn you said there was a case being closed out tonight."

There was.

But Maverick wasn't the only person in my life I needed to pull away from.

The stronger the relationship, the more the person saw, and I didn't want anyone close enough to see the emotions I struggled to hide.

Certain people at ARCK knew more than most—there

was no getting past that. Even though they'd been sworn to silence, there were times the silence turned into too many questions and prolonged, probing stares.

The last few days, for example.

There was only so long I could handle that before I broke.

And with Libby back from her zombified state, I couldn't risk breaking.

So, there I was, trying to wreck a piece of my soul instead.

I dropped my gaze to the side but didn't let myself look at her as I shrugged in response.

I released a pent-up breath and leaned close to Lincoln to whisper, "It wasn't because it was *you*, it was because *I* honestly don't know how to do something that will be the final, crushing blow to my heart."

"I think that means you shouldn't."

A whimper of pain caught in my throat, and Lincoln gripped my waist in response.

"Does this guy even know what you're about to do to him?"

"He knows I would do anything for him. Even this."

"Fuck. Einstein," he whispered my name on a tortured groan and dropped his forehead to my shoulder. Moments passed in silence before he took a shuddering breath in and lifted his mouth to my ear.

"*Einstein*," Libby snapped from where she was stomping toward her room.

Shit.

I slowly loosed a sigh and carefully moved from Lincoln's grasp. "I have to take a call."

He smiled sadly. "Sounded like it."

I kept my head down as I followed Libby. Shame and regret and mortification swirled through me as I did.

As soon as I was in the room and the door was shut, she whirled on me. "What the hell, Einstein?" She lifted her arms out to her sides and hissed, "I'm going to skip past the work thing and go straight to you practically sitting in Lincoln's lap and *whispering in his ear.*"

I didn't want to talk about it. I didn't want to do this. Not with her.

Libby pressed her fingers to her forehead. "I've never seen you whisper in someone's ear for the sake of flirting. God, I don't think I've ever seen you *flirt*. What are you doing? What about Maverick?"

Hearing his name sent pain tearing through me, swirling and knifing like a path of destruction straight to my heart.

No, no, no. Lock it up.

I leaned back against the door to help steady myself and struggled to push the emotions raging inside away.

"What about him?"

She huffed, her shoulders slumping. "Einstein—"

"Am I a horrible person for not missing him?" I asked before she could go down that path.

She blinked quickly and stared at me for a few seconds, her wide eyes clearly showing she was trying to keep up with my rapid change in conversation. "Johnny?"

I nodded roughly, which only made her look even more lost.

Lost in the conversation. Lost in how to answer. Lost in what to do with me.

I felt the same, and I hated it.

When Lincoln had assumed I was trying to move on

from Johnny, I felt like the worst kind of human. I'd gone through my grief and moved on from him. How I'd felt then was nothing compared to the devastation of trying to move on from Maverick.

"I don't think so," Libby finally whispered. "I didn't know that you *didn't* miss him."

I dropped my head to stare at the floor. "There are days I do."

Like when I thought about the Johnny I'd first fallen in love with.

The *caring* Johnny.

The Johnny who used to make me laugh. Make my heart skip erratically. The one who would do anything for me.

But I so rarely saw that side of him throughout the years, and it was hard to miss the man who trapped me in a relationship for over a decade.

It was hard to miss the man who tried to murder innocent people because he just couldn't help himself.

It was hard to miss the man who made it nearly impossible to allow another man near me without fearing he would spiral into a rage.

"I know letting yourself love Maverick doesn't make you a horrible person."

My head snapped up and my stare went to Libby's.

Grief and want and pain swirled through me. But I couldn't let it consume me.

I grabbed the doorknob and opened the door. "He's better off without me."

Before she could say a word, I stalked out, intent on either going back to Lincoln or finding the vodka again.

I ended up in my room, standing beside my bed. My

arms were wrapped tightly around my waist like the action would keep me from falling apart.

It felt as if I were trapped under water, and every time I was able to break the surface and take a choking breath, another wave would come crashing down, pulling me under again.

I turned when I heard my door open and stilled when I saw Lincoln standing in my room, quietly closing the door behind him.

"Question," he said in a low, gruff tone as he folded his arms across his chest. "If you hadn't been drinking, would you have told me any of that?"

"Definitely not. There's a ninety-two percent chance I'm going to hate myself tomorrow for ever opening my mouth."

He nodded slowly for a moment, accepting the answer. "Why me?" When I stared at him in hesitation for a few moments, he asked, "Why did you choose me to try to move on with? Was it because of the image, reputation, what?"

The worst kind of human. That was what I was.

The hurt in his eyes that he couldn't hide went straight to my already excruciating chest.

I was never drinking again. I couldn't handle all of these amplified emotions and words that continued to slip out that shouldn't.

"Of course not. I just . . ." I shrugged helplessly, not knowing how to explain myself other than to give him the truth. But the truth was so close to giving him a part of me only Maverick was allowed to have. "It's hard for me to let anyone get close to me . . . physically," I whispered, choosing my words carefully. "With our history, I thought that when it came time, you would see that, and you would know to take care of me."

Lincoln's eyes slowly shut, and he released a hissed curse. "I want to be him." He finally opened his eyes and pierced me with a look that felt too personal. That made the space of my bedroom feel too small.

"What?"

"On a night when you haven't been drinking, if you decide you *want* to do this . . . I still want to be the guy you choose." His lips twisted into a sad smile. "But if you talked about me the way you talk about him, I wouldn't let you go for anything. I have a feeling he won't either. Just something about you, Einstein."

I didn't say anything as Lincoln turned and reached for the door. I stood with my heart shredded and walls shakily in place, waiting for him to leave so I could mourn in peace.

For the person I used to be.

For the person Johnny tried to destroy, but Maverick tried to hold together.

For the person who learned what it meant to love wholly and purely without a touch.

For the person who lost everything.

Six

Maverick
SEVEN WEEKS AGO

I RUBBED MY HAND OVER my jaw and snapped at Dare, "The fuck is he calling you for anyway?"

Diggs laid a hand on my shoulder but snatched it away when I jolted from the touch. "You just need to chill a little. Breathe. We're gonna get to the apartment. You're gonna walk in all white-knight status, and shit's gonna be cool."

I slowly turned to look at him, my jaw aching from the pressure it took to keep it closed.

He leaned back in his seat and raised his hands in mock-surrender. "Or brooding knight. Angry knight. Super pissed knight. Whatever. This isn't the power rangers, you can be whoever you want to be."

"Jesus," Dare whispered. "Do you ever hear yourself?"

"Often. You're welcome for gracing you with my angelic voice."

"Sounds like a dying cow," Dare mumbled.

"*Kieran,*" I snapped, my voice booming in the small car. "I want to know why Kieran is calling you and not me."

Dare spared me a quick look, worry creased the corners of his eyes. "Because of who I am."

"Were?" I corrected with a frustrated laugh. "You didn't want the mafia life anymore, so you don't have that title. And she's my—" I stared just past him, unable to finish the sentence.

Unable to even figure out how.

Because Einstein had never been anything other than *mine*.

And she was trying to make it clear these last months that she no longer wanted that.

Dare dragged a hand through his hair, shrugging as he let his hand fall back to the steering wheel. "Maybe Kieran knows or has an idea of what's going on between you two. Or maybe he called me because he expects me to keep tabs on all of you even if I gave up my title."

I knew he was probably right on both counts.

I was so filled with worry and confusion and anger that I couldn't think straight.

Einstein took care of the financials for all things Borello related and owned, so we had to be in constant communication whether she liked it or not. But not once this week had she answered any of my texts—even about the businesses I managed.

The only time I had run into her since the Henley concert was when she was leaving the coffee shop yesterday, weighed down with drinks.

When I'd tried to help, she cut me a hard look and said she didn't have time for *this*.

Whatever *this* was supposed to be.

Us?

My helping her juggle the drinks in her arms?

Her explaining why she'd been a ghost since the rock stars rolled into town?

When I mentioned the latter, she laid into me about having a life and being busy with ARCK. Then mentioned she hadn't seen the members of Henley since the concert as she sank into her car.

Every word was cold and unfamiliar. In a way that was different even from the past six months.

I'd texted her a few hours later, asking her to meet me at our tree.

Two hours after that, she finally responded, saying she was going to be at ARCK all night.

This morning, she hadn't shown for our weekly business meeting. I'd spent nearly the entire time staring at the empty spot directly across from me, unable to concentrate.

Just as we were finishing, Kieran Hayes called Dare, asking if any of us knew where Einstein was. Apparently, she hadn't shown to close out a case last night, and no one had been able to get in touch with her.

And that was it for me.

I'd shoved out of the booth and hurried out of Brooks Street Café with Diggs and Dare on my heels.

I'd barely made it to my truck before Dare grabbed my arm and shoved me in the direction of his car. "Get in," he demanded, leaving no room for discussion.

And the four-minute drive to the girls' apartment complex felt like it was taking an hour.

With everything going on between us lately—whatever the hell *everything* was—Einstein had still been there.

Work. Family shit. She was always there, pretending I *wasn't*.

At some point, I'd wondered if she was doing that to torture me. To rub it in my face that she seemed fine pulling away from me . . . fine pretending nothing had ever happened.

It wasn't until this last week, until this morning when we got the call, that I knew her distance was worse.

I would take her there, right there in my damn face every day for the rest of my life, just so long as it meant she was *there*. Meant Dare wouldn't get another call, asking where Einstein was.

As soon as we pulled into the lot, I was out of the car and stalking up to their door.

My keys were in hand, and I had theirs in the lock before Dare and Diggs were able to come jogging up behind me.

As soon as the lock gave, I pushed open the door and stormed inside. My eyes went everywhere, searching for the girl I knew I could find in a crowd, and landed on three members of Henley asleep on the living room floor.

Diggs shouldered past me and headed toward the kitchen, where Libby and Maxon stood, and shouted, "Oh, *oh*."

My chest pitched with ragged breaths.

My hands curled into fists.

"Can't you afford hotel rooms?" Dare asked as he passed by me.

"We were hanging out. It got late. They crashed here," Libby replied, her tone all bite.

I didn't hear anything else.

Everything had gotten too loud and too quiet at the

same time as soon as she'd started explaining the guys on the floor.

I wanted to demand to know where Einstein was.

I wanted to ask why she was lying to me. To know what else she was hiding from me.

Most of all, I wanted to hate the guys in front of me. Because their presence had changed everything.

"Oh my God."

My head snapped up at that voice to find Einstein walking to the end of the hall.

She was rubbing her hands over her eyes, her voice rough from sleep as she stumbled to a halt. "Can you be any . . ." Panic filled her eyes and covered her face when she dropped her hands and saw me there. "Louder . . ."

I wanted to laugh.

I wanted to yell.

I wanted to study this expression, because it was honest and bare and everything she'd been trying to keep from me lately.

But my pain and confusion and anger felt so big that I thought I was going to choke on them. I was afraid of what I would say if I let myself speak. I was afraid of what I would do if I let myself look at the guys sitting up on the floor, watching every part of my heartbreak.

And then she did it.

Straightened her back. Tilted her chin up. Forced that look of indifference back onto her face.

Could've shot me. Would've felt the same.

An anguished huff forced from my chest when I turned to leave.

It didn't hit me until I stepped out into the humid

morning air . . . what I'd so obviously missed yesterday outside the coffee shop.

I drove my hands into my hair. A laugh made of my pain and disbelief and frustration sounded in my chest as I replayed that moment when I saw her.

Juggling a carrier filled with four drinks. Another two carefully tucked into her arm.

Only four people worked at ARCK Investigations. She'd had enough drinks for the members of Henley, Libby, and her.

I didn't notice what she hadn't even tried to hide.

Didn't notice the lie because I'd been too caught up in the changes in her. In the way it felt to come alive every time I saw her, only to repeat a slow, painful death every time she walked away.

Seven

Einstein
TODAY

My eyelids felt as if they were being held down by weights.

But the pounding in my head had dulled.

I tried to sit up from where I was, once again, lying on the bed, but I paused when my stomach lurched.

Gritting my teeth, I tried to focus on nothing but breathing.

Because the last thing I wanted to do was throw up in this fucking hot room.

Once the worst of it passed, I pushed myself to sitting and fell forward onto my face.

A laugh burst from my chest, raspy and so odd that it made me laugh harder.

And then I realized I was still on my face.

"Oh God. Who put m'here?"

It took entirely too long to find my hands again.

To figure out how to put them on the bed.

To push myself back up.

"Shit."

I stilled, and my arms wobbled, making me feel as if I were on a bed made of Jell-O.

"Shit," I said again, listening to the way my voice dragged and slurred.

I need to lie down.

I flopped. Or fell. And twisted so I was mostly . . . sort of on my back instead of my face.

My eyelids alternated between slipping shut and popping open.

And I wasn't sure why.

Sleep sounded nice.

But the ceiling also looked nice. Comforting. The way my oak looked in the fall.

"Hey, Maverick? When I die, don't let Johnny bury me with the Borellos."

"Why would—why is this something you're worried about right now?"

"I don't know." I blinked slowly, heavily. My slurring deepened. "But I want to be buried under the oak."

I frowned and dropped my hands to my stomach, but pain lanced up my left arm.

A breath hissed from between my teeth. "Mav, you're hurting me."

When I looked to my side, he wasn't there.

My uneasy stomach turned.

Warning bells sounded.

"Maverick?"

I blinked, trying to focus on what was in front of me.

And who *wasn't*.

I followed the clear line down to where the IV was wrapped around my arm and secured into the crook of my elbow. Then lazily followed the line to the nearly empty bag of rapidly dripping saline.

Saline.

Something, somewhere, in the back of my mind told me it was more than that. Told me something was wrong with it.

Tainted.

Laced.

I hurriedly grabbed for the IV but missed. Over and over again I missed before finally catching the line and yanking as hard as I could.

My vision blurred and darkened for a few seconds as I tried to figure out what to do. Because there was blood everywhere, and I didn't know how I was supposed to survive.

The night.

The heartache.

This soul-searing pain that would surely destroy me.

Tears slipped down my cheeks and a quiet sob tumbled from my lips. "Maverick . . . I'm sorry. I'm sorry, I'm so sorry."

I cracked open my eyelids to the room. To the smeared blood leaking out from beneath where I was already putting pressure on my arm. To that night eight months ago, the one that changed everything.

My head rolled heavily to the bed.

My eyelids tried to shut.

But I didn't know what would happen if I slept.

I didn't know what I would wake to next.

I had to stay awake.

"Hey, Maverick? When I die, I want to be buried under the oak."

I had to . . . stay . . .

"Then that's what will happen."

"You promised," I slurred toward the ceiling.

Eight

Einstein
FIVE YEARS AGO

I SLANTED MY HEAD TO the side when Johnny crawled onto the bed behind me and pressed his mouth to my neck, but I didn't take my eyes from the medical files I'd been scanning.

Files from a mentally unstable patient who'd undergone surgery to remove a benign brain tumor. His outbursts and rage had completely disappeared in the weeks and months following.

I sighed and scrolled to another page of the doctor's notes from before the surgery as Johnny's hands tightened possessively and suggestively on my waist.

"What are you looking at?"

If I hadn't seen the detached look in his eyes when he'd walked into the room, his voice would've told me all I needed to know.

He was completely unhinged. He'd been that way for so long it had somehow become his normal.

Ever since Gia was murdered, he'd been on edge. Every little thing set him off.

Like the sun rising each morning.

We all grieved her death, but Johnny wasn't grieving. He was looking for revenge in every move the Holloway's made. Still. A year later.

The only positive in the whole situation was he never brought up the sickening idea of us getting married again, not once since the night he announced to everyone that we *were*.

Out of the blue.

Without ever mentioning the idea before or asking me.

All while Maverick stood just feet away.

"Looking for the right line to grasp and follow to help you," I finally answered.

A puff of disbelieving laughter sounded in my ear. "You saying I need help, babe?"

I twisted my neck to look into his crazed eyes. "Are you pretending you don't?"

He worked his jaw, his body tensing and vibrating with his anger. "Wanna know what'll help?" He gripped my shoulders and moved out from behind me while pushing me onto my back.

"No," I said firmly. "No. Not when you're like this."

The corner of his mouth twitched. "You weren't saying that a couple of nights ago."

"You weren't seeing red a couple of nights ago."

He ripped the tablet from my hands and tossed it aside, laying his body on top of mine and leaning close so his lips brushed mine when he said, "Baby, I'm always seeing red."

I struggled to stop him when he crawled onto his knees and grabbed for the top of my shorts, but his movements never faltered. "Johnny, stop."

"Red hair," he said through gritted teeth. "Red lips. Red blood. Red haze over everything. All I see is fucking red." He jerked my shorts off me so roughly it felt like the material left burns on my legs.

"Johnny—"

"Johnny, stop," he mocked in a terrifying tone. "Johnny, do this. Johnny, don't do that." One side of my underwear tore as he ripped them down my thighs. "Johnny, don't drink anymore. Johnny, do kickboxing with me. Johnny, do fucking yoga. Johnny, *just breathe*. Johnny, Johnny, Johnny."

Tears fell down my cheeks as I choked out, "You're being crazy right now."

He stilled above me, staring at me as weighted seconds passed, the tension pressing against us. "I know what everyone else calls me. Don't you ever fucking call me crazy again."

A sob burst from my chest. "Just *stop*. Stop. Don't do this—God, *please* don't do this. Let me help you. I'll find a way to make it go away."

"There's nothing to find, Einstein. Guys really aren't all that complicated. You don't need all your research to figure out how to *help* me."

He stood and reached for the top button on his jeans, the crazed look in his eyes making him look like an animal.

I pushed to my elbows and started scooting away. Another cry broke free when he grabbed my thighs and yanked me back. "I swear to God, Johnny, if you touch me when you're like this, I'll—"

"What?" The word ripped from his throat in a snarl.

"You gonna leave? Think you're gonna find someone better than me?" He jolted, his eyes narrowing with suspicion and rage. "Who the hell are you leaving me for, Einstein?"

"*What?* No one!"

"They're about to find themselves six feet under," he said through clenched teeth.

"There isn't anyone else," I cried out and tried like hell not to think of or imagine Maverick in any way. "I'm not leaving you."

He stared at me, eyes wild and nostrils flaring with his ragged breaths. "You see what you do to me? You see the kind of man you make me?"

"No. No, don't you put this on me."

"You get me riled up and so goddamn livid I can't see straight. Is this how you want me to be?"

"Don't put this on me." A strangled sob fell from my lips. "I know it's dark in your head. I *know*. I'm trying to find a way to get rid of it. But don't you ever blame me for it."

I quickly pulled my legs up to my chest and tried to roll away from him but was stopped with firm, shaking hands on my knees.

"What the fuck do you think you're doing?"

I looked at him pleadingly. "I'm leaving." When his face morphed into a terrifying mask of rage, I hurried to clarify, "This room. I'm leaving this room. You are not allowed to follow me, and I do not want to talk to you until the morning."

The rage shifted.

My stomach dropped.

I immediately wished for the raging Johnny to come

back. For him to snap out of it. For Libby to come home. For numerous things.

"Thought you wanted to help me," he said with a vicious grin.

"Not like this—*not like this*," I seethed when he slammed my legs down and spread them wide. "Johnny, if you touch me I will scream."

He searched my face and ground his jaw. "All right." After a few seconds, he cleared his throat and started pushing away from me. "All right, babe."

I warily pushed onto my elbows again and then onto my hands. When I had just started pulling my legs up under me, Johnny cocked his arm back and swung.

I didn't have time to flinch.

I groggily opened my eyes, aware of the light coming into the room from the sun rising and the aches in my body.

It took far too long to narrow down that the intense pulsing was coming from my temple.

And that there was a familiar, yet somehow foreign and nearly painful, ache between my legs.

Tears were already slowly leaking from my eyes. My breath hitched.

He didn't.

Johnny, Johnny, Johnny, no . . .

I tensed when I heard the agonized groan from somewhere near me.

I looked to the side and found Johnny crouched in the corner of my room.

His hands gripping and pulling at his hair.

His face twisted in torment and pain.

"What did you do?" My voice was soft but filled with hurt, the accusation no less powerful.

"I didn't—I don't—I—god damn it," he muttered and dropped his head.

His body lurched forward as he heaved, but he didn't move from his position and nothing ever came up.

"I'm sorry. I'm sorry. I'm so fucking sorry."

I blinked when the tears filling my eyes made it too difficult to see him, and then I looked at the ceiling again.

"I don't know—I mean, I do. I didn't—shit, how do I stop this?" he roared.

I didn't offer a response.

"I remember, but I don't. I know I came to see you, but that's it. I left to get a drink with Dare. When I came back and saw you unconscious on the bed, it all came rushing back. I wanted to die. I wanted to kill myself. I *want* to. Einstein, I—*fuck*."

I grit my teeth and tried to hide the tremble in my voice. "If you ever come near me again when you're out of control . . ."

A choked sob sounded from where he was in the corner.

"You can't leave me. Don't leave me. I can't live without you. There's no light without you. Without you . . . it's only dark. I can't live like that."

My eyelids slowly slid shut, and I swallowed the anguished cry that wanted to break free.

"I'll do anything. Name it, and I'll do it. Just don't leave me."

"I'm not leaving you," I whispered.

How could I?

I'd promised him long ago that I would fix him . . . and I hadn't.

And, after all, he meant what he said last night.

He would kill everyone I loved if I walked away.

Nine

Einstein
FOUR YEARS AGO

I TORE MY GAZE FROM the screens when Johnny curled his hand around my cheek. Shifting my face toward him, my fingers continued to fly across the keyboard for a few more seconds before I reluctantly let my hands fall to my lap.

His eyes shifted slightly back and forth as he searched mine. I tried not to notice the darkness swirling deep within them and bit my tongue so I wouldn't mention it.

If I said something, it would only go one of two ways: he would try to prove how wrong I was or it would set him off. Either way, he would stay. And I felt so damn suffocated with him this close all the time.

When there was an active threat against the Borellos, Dare brought us all to one place—his family home. That way when the threat decided to come after us, we would be together. We would be ready to fight back.

It was smart, really, especially considering what happened two years ago to Gia. But it also meant I shared a room with Johnny, and *we* shared a house with Maverick.

It was long, heartrending agony.

For nearly two years, Dare had been working with Kieran Hayes, Holloway's assassin, in hopes to one day overthrow the bastard who sat on Holloway's throne—the man responsible for Gia's death.

It was a risk and tensions often ran high as trust was called into question. But Kieran had come through this time with the location of a massive underground bunker just outside of town that held most of Holloway's cocaine and weapons.

Suffice to say, Holloway's boss had his suspicions that we were behind his precious bunker being cleared out.

If anything, he should be thanking us. I left him clues leading him to all the dirty politicians and government officials he worked with.

About an eighth of the bunker's contents were hidden on their properties.

But until things died down, we were all together, and I was in absolute misery.

"You good?" Johnny finally asked, his voice terse.

I nodded. "Just trying to find more information for Dare."

"You know that wasn't what I meant."

"Well, I don't know why you would ask." My tone was sharp and cold, but the words were soft as a whisper.

The muscles in his jaw flexed, and he blew out a harsh breath through his nose before dropping his head. "Einstein." My name was a tortured plea, but I wasn't going to spare him for what he'd done.

Again.

I knew I was the idiot who stayed. I was the idiot who had turned into everything I swore I would never be. But I'd found out far too late that men like Johnny weren't meant to fall in love. On the occasion they did, that was it.

Unconditional. Unwavering. Destructive. You-and-me forever.

Until death.

In no uncertain terms, that was the game I'd blindly entered into.

Johnny was dark and had a destructive mind. But despite his shattered soul and his cruel and deranged tendencies . . . despite it all, I'd fallen in love with him.

I had been young, and Johnny had been different when he had looked at me. When it was just the two of us, there had been rays of light that peeked through that darkness. I had been so sure that if I helped him, there would have been more of the light I saw glimpses of.

More of the light I knew he so badly wanted to grasp but couldn't figure out how.

But that love had nearly vanished over the years, had been destroyed by the monster he became when he lost control of himself.

I still loved him; only it was in a way that came from years of caring for someone.

I still wanted to help him, more than ever. Because it broke something inside of me when I saw the way it affected him on good days—the darkness he never seemed to escape. When I saw him get physically sick over things he'd done when he snapped. On the rare days he let me in and told me how it was destroying him.

But, mostly, I resented him.

I hated him for what he did to me during the times he truly became unhinged. I hated him for keeping me from what I truly wanted. And I hated myself for not seeing any other way.

"Einstein, I'm sorry," he murmured. "I'm so damn sorry. I love you. You know that. Right?"

"I know." The acknowledgment was said on a sigh, and it made Johnny cringe.

He pressed his mouth to mine and then stepped away. "Heading out with Dare. Have meetings. Don't leave."

His last words were said as a plea, nearly screaming their double-meaning.

If they were leaving the house, the rest of the family needed to be here—together.

And not to ever, ever leave him.

"Where would I go?"

The corner of his mouth turned up in a knowing smirk. "Nowhere."

Exactly.

I turned my attention to my screens before he could leave, my fingers barely moving across the keyboard as I listened for the moment they left the house.

I'd been waiting for this moment for days.

I held my breath as minutes passed and nearly jumped from my chair when I heard the front door close. I rapidly shut down everything on my screens and forced myself to slowly stand, my body vibrated as I waited for the sound of a car leaving the drive.

When it came, I walked from the room. Unaffected. Composed.

Anxious as hell.

I tapped rapidly on my phone so I wouldn't raise suspicions if anyone saw me, but there was nothing on the screen.

With each new hall and each new room, I allowed myself a quick scan to see if anyone was there. If *he* was there.

The closer I got to the theater room, the faster my steps came until I was running. My breathing was ragged by the time I reached the doors, and it had nothing to do with my pace.

I flung the doors open, my heart nearly pounding out of my chest, and loosed a sigh of relief when I found him already there.

Maverick.

His arms were folded over his chest, his furrowed brow smoothed the second I entered the room, and he seemed to release his own pent-up breath when I shut the doors behind me.

I dropped my phone as we hurried toward each other, stopping with a foot's distance still separating us. As we always did.

His gray eyes searched my face, as though he was trying to assure himself I was really there . . . that I was okay.

If he only knew.

"How are you?" he asked, breaking the silence between us. His voice was strained, and I knew it was because he was struggling not to say the words that were so clear on his face, he may as well have been shouting them.

I missed you.

I need you.

I love you.

Everything I reciprocated. Words we had never uttered.

"Struggling through being stuck in this house with everyone."

The pain that flared in his eyes told me he agreed. "Funny, the first time Dare said what we were doing, I thought nothing sounded better."

And then he realized he wasn't just in a house with me, but with me *and* Johnny.

"Nothing is better than our oak tree."

His mouth slowly curled into one of those smiles that got me through the difficult days.

Hesitant.

Secretive.

It was my favorite thing in the world besides the man himself.

"Nothing," he agreed and then nodded to indicate the room we were standing in. "But this is a good alternative."

The oak tree had always been special to me. It was where I went growing up to have time alone.

I could think there.

I could *breathe* there.

One night after one of Johnny's worse episodes, I asked Maverick to meet me there. He hadn't asked why we were there or why I asked him to meet me, he just sat silently.

Content to be near me.

Content to be my silent strength.

Since then, he had met me there a few times a week so we could talk about random nothings. Or just sit in silence.

"What would you do if you weren't here?" he asked when we were sitting on one of the couches.

On opposite sides.

Not touching.

As always.

I felt my brow pinch. "I'd be at the tree."

He laughed, but the sound was different. Full of longing. "No. If you weren't *here*. In this life. If you hadn't grown up in Wake Forest. If you hadn't been best friends with Libby and recruited into the mafia."

"The same thing." My response was immediate and sure. "Small town. Something with codes. It's all I know. It's all I've ever wanted to do."

"Do you think . . ." He paused and let his attention drift to the space of couch between us. Unspoken emotions swirled in the air as he thought for a moment. "Do you think you'd be happy?"

Once again, my response was immediate. "No."

Maverick's stare darted to mine, questions whirling deep within his eyes.

"I don't know how I could be." I didn't know how *Maverick* could expect me to be. "We desperately needed someone to match Holloway's assassin, and Dare put me on the task of finding one. So I did."

I found you.

Maverick sank against the couch, his expression shifting to one of understanding.

"If I weren't in *this* life . . ." I swallowed thickly but didn't continue on. I couldn't let myself.

The words begged to be voiced. My heart was screaming at me to breathe even a whisper of my feelings.

There wouldn't be you.

It would be so easy to release those words into the air. So damn easy.

I knew what would follow, though. We were already playing such a dangerous game being near each other, but I didn't know how to be apart from him.

It felt like I needed him to breathe. To get through the days. To survive Johnny.

But it took true strength to keep the required distance between us. It was physically exhausting when all either of us wanted was to close it. There was an energy binding us, making me feel alive whenever he was near. Teasing me with the idea of how it would feel if I were to just touch him. Taste him.

If either of us gave life to our true feelings, that energy would snap and there would be no going back.

"What about you?" I asked, quieting the words that had been on the tip of my tongue.

He blinked quickly and looked away, the edgy breath of a laugh tumbling from his mouth let me know he didn't like whatever he was thinking about. "Growing up, I only ever wanted to go to Notre Dame. I wanted to play football."

My mouth curled into a smile when I realized he was finally letting me in on pieces of his life I'd been dying to understand.

Sometimes, files just didn't give the full story.

"I got a full ride. But Diggs . . ." He shrugged and smiled sadly. "He didn't get in at all. We'd been banking on him getting in, and he only applied there because that was where I was going. So, after we graduated, he enlisted. I went with him."

"You guys really don't like being separated," I whispered, remembering the story they told me from the black site we'd found them at.

"No. Our parents were livid, but I never regretted it. You know, until we found ourselves in a cell."

A soft laugh fell from my lips, and his eyes shot to me

like he was drawn.

The tension between us started to thicken, and this time, I could practically taste it.

After a few seconds, he cleared his throat. "I think I would've played football. Probably wouldn't have gone pro, because that just isn't realistic. Would've met a girl and got married. My parents would've been happy with me . . . they wouldn't think Diggs and I had devastated a town."

"Starting to think it's a requirement with being in the mafia. Having disappointed parents."

An amused huff left him.

"Would you be happy?"

He was silent for so long that I wasn't sure he was going to answer. When he did, his voice was thick with emotion. "I would've been happy because I wouldn't have known what I was missing. But I feel like Diggs and I were born for this, so I think at some point, we would've stumbled into this life." His eyes flashed to mine and then away. "I would've found a girl under an oak tree, and I would know my life had meant nothing before that moment."

Guilt and pain sliced through me, hot and pure. My eyes burned with tears, and I hurried to stand from the couch.

"Einstein." Maverick's voice was panicked as he followed me across the room. "*Einstein.*"

He slammed his hand on one of the doors when I reached them, his body so close I knew that, if I turned, we would be only a breath away.

I gripped the handle of the door, trying to draw myself closer when my body betrayed me by slightly swaying back.

"I—shit, I know I shouldn't have said that. I just—"

"I'm sorry." My voice was barely a breath, but it stopped him as if I'd shouted.

"What?" Disbelief flooded his tone. "Why would you have anything to be sorry for?"

"For not knowing." I opened my eyes and looked straight ahead at the blurred door as I voiced things I knew I shouldn't. "For not realizing the most amazing part of my life was still coming. For destroying any hope of the life we both deserve long before I met you. For not waiting."

He released a shuddering breath. "*Avery.*"

"Don't," I pleaded when I felt him shift closer. "Please don't."

"Avery, I . . . *shit.*" His hand slowly formed into a fist against the door and gently hit the solid wood. "I'd wait lifetimes. I—"

"We need to leave this room," I said quickly, torment twisting my words. "This is dangerous. We're letting it go too far this time."

His silence spoke volumes.

He knew.

He agreed.

He didn't care.

I watched his hand fall away and dropped my head in time to see him slowly crouch down behind me. When I turned to see what he was doing, I wished I hadn't.

Because there I was, nearly pressed against a door, and Maverick was slowly rising in front of me. His body so close to mine I trembled. His heated stare locked on mine as he straightened, his mouth passing just inches from my own.

A needy whimper caught in my throat.

I jolted when he placed my phone in my hand.

"Oh." I swallowed thickly and blinked away the daze I'd fallen into. "Right. Thanks."

Agitation poured from him as he ran a hand over his jaw and stepped away, putting an awkward amount of distance between us.

It wasn't enough.

"You're right," he ground out. "We have to get out of here."

I twisted the knob but stopped just before I propped open the door. "Hey, Maverick?"

His head tilted slightly, letting me know he was listening.

"When I die, don't let Johnny bury me with the Borellos."

His expression instantly shifted to one of suspicion and jealousy and fear. "Why would—" He cleared his throat, his head shaking subtly. "Why is this something you're worried about right now?"

I gave him a comforting smile so he wouldn't look too deeply into my request. "We're in the mafia. None of us are guaranteed long lives. But I want to be buried under the oak."

His shoulders dropped and something like anguish sounded in his chest. He watched me for another few seconds before slanting his head in a nod. "Then that's what will happen. But when you die, know that I'm coming with you."

Ten

Einstein
THREE YEARS AGO

My head lowered and eyes unfocused as I listened for any indication of who had entered the apartment. My fingers were still above the keyboard. The only sound in the room was the near-silent whirring from my computers, which at the moment seemed as loud as a tornado.

"Babe?"

"Shit."

My heart thundered painfully in my chest as I scrambled for my phone and hastily entered the code. My thumbs moved too quickly for the phone that seemed to be working on a delay.

I shot off a message to Maverick. The message contained nothing more than a period but said everything I didn't have time to and couldn't risk.

Johnny was here.

Don't call.

Don't text.

Don't come over.

He wouldn't respond to it. He knew not to.

By the time Johnny opened the door to my room, my phone was on my desk, my noise-cancelling headphones were on with music blaring through them, and my fingers were tapping rapidly across the keys.

I forced myself to react slowly when Johnny touched my shoulder. Forced myself to take my time looking away from my screens when my body's automatic reaction was to feign surprise that he was there at all.

Johnny would know better. Even if I was caught off guard, I never showed it.

His eyes searched mine when I finally stopped tapping away and sat back in my chair, the carnal need lying deep within them made my stomach churn.

I swallowed thickly and forced something that felt like my version of a smile. Only one person earned my smiles, and it wasn't the man in front of me. "I didn't know you were coming over, did something happen?"

The way his brows pulled together in wonder made him look like he was ready to explode.

But this was Johnny, and no one knew him like I did.

To anyone else, every expression of his was menacing, terrifying, sinister . . . probably because they were.

You had to be brave enough to look into his eyes. They told you all you needed to know.

They told you when to run. Not that I'd ever been able to.

"Since when does something need to be happening for me to come over?"

Since Libby's at work, and I don't trust you when we're alone.

I rolled my eyes and looked back to the screens, to the cameras watching Holloway offices and storage containers, and to the accounts I needed to get into. "I was just ask—"

He grabbed my jaw and jerked my head to the side so I was facing him again. "I hate the way you roll your eyes."

I narrowed my eyes and clenched my teeth, the muscles in my jaw straining from the pressure and his tight hold.

As if I burned him, he released me and staggered back until he was pressed to the wall. "Shit. Shit, shit . . . *fuck.*" He raked his hands down his face, exhaling roughly as he did. "Babe, I'm sorry. I'm sorry."

The way he curled in on himself. The remorse that screamed in his eyes. The agony that bled from him. It left little room for denial.

Pain and guilt could be feigned. Not like this, not from Johnny.

I knew he was sorry.

Didn't change the fact that every day with him was a constant, exhausting battle with the darkness he was at war with. I was scrambling for any option to fix whatever was broken in his mind, but I felt like I was running out of time.

For him or for me, I wasn't sure.

I'd researched everything I could think of countless times.

I'd changed his lifestyle—even going so far as making every meal and forcing him into yoga and meditation.

I'd medicated him.

It had taken years of coaxing and begging before I'd finally, *finally* forced him to a doctor and to appointment after appointment, only to be told there was nothing physical causing Johnny's rage.

He'd reluctantly gone to a therapist a month ago, and I ended up having to pay the doctor off for his silence when Johnny attacked him. All because he thought the doctor was trying to hypnotize him. Trying to put him to sleep. Trying to leave him vulnerable and unable to defend himself so we could kill him.

The doctor had simply told him to relax and take calming breaths.

When I was settling things with the therapist, he told me people like Johnny belonged in a psych ward, heavily sedated and bound.

I hated that my first thought was: *Probably*.

I hated even more that my second was: *There'd be no saving your life if Johnny had heard you*.

Johnny was still willing to try anything simply because Johnny would *do* anything for me. But he would only try it once, which was long enough for him to claim that it wasn't working before he vetoed it for good. I was no longer allowed to mention doctors, and he refused to take anything, even homeopathic remedies.

I was back at square one, and he was worse than ever.

But I didn't know how to give up on him. So, I stood from the chair and walked to Johnny, falling into his arms and wrapping mine around his waist.

"I can't live like this."

I buried my head into his chest and squeezed my eyes shut. "Yes, you can. We're going to figure it out."

"And until then, what? I keep hurting you?" He laughed, but it sounded pained. "Keep waking up when I was never asleep, only to realize what I've done to you?"

"Here's a thought," I mumbled drily. "How about you don't hurt me, and we won't have to keep doing this?"

Another pained laugh.

He pulled me closer and pressed his lips to my ear. "I love you. Don't ever forget that."

I opened my eyes and stared at his shirt. "I know."

He passed his lips along my neck, his fingers digging into my side as he did.

I swallowed thickly, trying to think of a way to get out of this when he pressed his mouth to mine. Flashes from times before assaulted me, making my legs weak and turning my stomach sour.

And then he was leaning away.

Expression carefully blank.

Eyes so, so dark.

When he spoke, his tone warned of what would happen if I answered wrong. "Are you flinching?"

My head shook, and my lips moved with a soundless response before I was able to whisper, "No."

Screaming.

Begging.

Ripped clothes.

Rough hands and paralyzing fear.

Flash after flash slammed into me.

"Is that what you do now? You flinch? You fucking cower from me?" The words were all harsh growls, somehow making the crazed darkness in his eyes worse.

My head shook wildly, panic rising within me when I couldn't figure out how to speak.

Everything abruptly stopped when his fingers curled around my neck one at a time and then tightened.

Seconds passed like an eternity and the blink of an eye.

Then, all at once, we erupted into chaos. He turned us so our positions were switched, using the hand around my neck to slam me against the wall like I was a doll as I thrashed against his hold and screamed for him to let go.

"Prove you love me," he yelled, pushing me harder against the wall. "Fucking prove it. Or don't you anymore? Is that why you flinched? Is that it? Is there someone else?"

"Jesus, Johnny, *stop*," I cried out. "Stop being paranoid."

As fast as we'd exploded, we stilled.

The only sounds for long moments were our harsh breaths as he stared at me like a man possessed, and I clawed uselessly at his arm.

"Call me paranoid again. I don't think you'll like the outcome."

"You can't keep doing this. You can't," I said as tears rolled down my cheeks. I sucked in quick gasps when he finally released me and pressed harder to the wall when he crowded me. "You can't keep thinking there's someone else or that I don't love you. God, Johnny—can't you see what you're doing?"

The corners of his mouth slowly curled up in an ominous grin. "I see just fine."

Fear unfurled in my stomach and spread through me until I was trembling. "If I flinch, *this* is why. Because you force yourself on me and hurt me when you're seeing red. Now you need to leave, and don't you dare fucking touch me on your way out."

Instead of moving, he lowered his head until he was nearly eye level with me.

These were the eyes people saw before Johnny killed them.

I instinctively inhaled a sharp breath, my lungs trapping the oxygen inside and refusing to release it.

"Did you just say *Dare*? You're fucking my best fucking friend?"

Everything fell.

My expression.

My heart.

My stomach.

Before I could even think of how to respond to something so asinine, Johnny slammed his fists against the wall just above my head and let out an inhumane roar.

I didn't think. I just reacted.

I pressed my hands to his chest and shoved, squeezing out through the small space I'd managed to put between us.

I'd felt true fear with Johnny before, and it was nothing compared to that moment.

He kicked my feet out from underneath me, and I hit the floor with a pained *thud*. The air my lungs had been holding hostage rushed from me on a scream for help as Johnny turned me over and dragged me deeper into the room.

When he dropped on top of me and gripped the bottom of my shirt in his hands, I twisted away, knowing he would slam me back down.

Knowing he would get in my face.

When he did, I took all my fear and my anger and threw it into the only hit I would be able to get in.

His head snapped to the side. When he slowly shifted to look back at me, I would've sworn his eyes were black they were filled with so much twisted rage.

"Johnny, stop. Stop, stop, stop," I yelled, pleading and

crying. "Breathe and see what you're doing. Fucking *see* what you're doing."

But he didn't breathe.

He didn't *see* me.

He didn't snap out of it.

He left a half hour later, twitching and agitated and looking like he was ready to destroy the world.

Eleven

Maverick
THREE YEARS AGO

I was waiting under the tree when Einstein showed.

Even after the text she'd sent this afternoon to let me know Johnny had shown up at her apartment, I hadn't worried that she wouldn't be here tonight. Johnny never stayed long. He couldn't stay *anywhere* long.

He got too anxious. Felt too caged.

But the longer I went without word from her, the more I started to worry.

I'd already been here for nearly an hour, but I would've waited the entire night.

I shoved my hands into my pockets and shifted my weight from foot to foot as I waited for her to reach me. It was the only thing I could think to do in order to keep myself from rushing to her and pulling her into my arms.

My smile faded when I noticed her broken expression.

My hands were out of my pockets and in fists across my chest instantly. "What happened?"

Her brows lifted. "What do you mean?"

"I can see it."

If it hadn't been so dark outside, I would've sworn she held her breath until I spoke again.

"Your expression. What happened?"

"Nothing. Just, you know, another day with him frustrated with the world. It gets exhausting."

Bullshit.

I stepped closer but made sure to keep enough distance between us. "Don't lie to me."

"The last thing I want to do is talk about Johnny with you." Her voice was a tortured whisper. Her eyes were pleading.

All I wanted was to give her everything. I would give her the goddamn world if she asked for it. But something was twisting my gut, telling me not to drop this.

"Avery," I murmured, bending to look into her eyes.

"He said he can't live like this, with how dark his mind is and the way it takes over." She watched the ground as she spoke. "Is it horrible that some days I feel the same way?"

"Avery—" I grit my teeth and rocked back to keep from going to her. "Most days I don't know why Dare puts up with his shit. But you? I get why you're staying, I do. But no one would judge you if you felt like that *every* day. No one would judge you if you just disappeared one day because you couldn't find another way out of it."

The corners of her mouth tipped up in a sad smile. "Yeah. If only it could be that simple."

I didn't agree with it, but I respected her need to find a

reason for Johnny's psychotic behavior. I had to. That was the only option I had unless I wanted to constantly go head to head with her, which I didn't. It would only push her away, create a chasm between us.

The necessary distance we kept between us was already more than I could stand.

But of anything, I understood why she was still *with* Johnny. You didn't end relationships with men like him. Not without grave consequences.

Key word being *grave*. Any and all definitions.

To leave a man like him, you needed to disappear. Completely.

Einstein could create a new identity and life for someone in no time. She could erase someone just as easily. I knew if she really wanted to, she would do it.

"No one would judge you," I repeated.

"What would you do if I left?" she whispered so low that it was as if she was afraid of the words being picked up on the breeze.

"I would follow you when the time was right."

"You wouldn't get that chance." A short, frustrated laugh left her. "Johnny would do anything to bring me back, which means he would use you and your brother to find me. If you refused, he'd kill you." Her discouraged stare met mine. "You think I haven't already thought every possibility through?"

I ground my jaw, because I knew she was right.

"Then we'll stay here, doing what we're doing." I exhaled roughly and stepped beside her, so close our arms were nearly touching. My body trembled with the need to reach out and take her hand. "Or say the word, and we disappear together."

"Don't say things like that."

Don't mention you and me.
Don't mention thoughts of us together.
Don't mention our need for each other.
Don't mention that I love you.
I love you, I love you, I fucking love you.

That was the way it had always been. Ever since we both realized what we meant to each other. How much we needed the other.

All without ever saying a word.

I knew it was for our safety.

I knew it was because Einstein and unfaithful didn't mix.

I knew it was because once we gave voice to our feelings, actions would follow. There would be no containing them anymore.

But the girl beside me was mine—and she knew it. Just as I was hers.

I rubbed my jaw, warring with myself over what I knew I needed to do and what I wanted to do.

Finally, I dipped my head close to her ear and nearly groaned when she immediately reacted, as if it was instinctive. Leaning toward me and eyelids fluttering shut, her body sagging as if a weight fell from her.

"I know the roles we have to play. I know why. But I have a feeling a day's gonna come when I'll regret not telling you every day what you mean to me."

I started for the tree, to lean against it how I always did, so she could sit near my feet the way she liked to, but turned and stalked off toward where I'd left my car instead.

Hands fisted in my hair.

Heart racing and shattering.

She didn't try to stop me. I hadn't expected her to. I knew she understood.

This . . . *this* was why we never voiced our feelings.

Because neither of us could handle the impact of not being able to have the other when the words finally fell free. And I hadn't even told her I loved her.

Twelve

Maverick
TWO YEARS AGO

WHEN WE HEARD FOOTSTEPS HEADING toward the kitchen, Einstein slowly shifted away from me and picked up her tablet.

We hadn't been that close. But we could never be too careful, more so than ever before.

Johnny had torn up the Holloway guesthouse in search of the alleged dead princess and had been seething ever since.

Because the house had come up empty.

Because he'd fucked up by destroying the place and it wouldn't take more than a second for Holloway to know who had been behind it.

Kieran Hayes and Dare had been covertly working together for years . . . through Kieran's girlfriend supposedly dying and Gia being murdered in retaliation. For us to find out the princess's death had been faked, and Kieran had been lying the entire time?

A storm was building.

Death was imminent on one or both sides, which was why we were all under the Borello roof, waiting for their move.

And I had life-changing information that sat heavy on my shoulders. But I would bear the weight gladly as long as it eased it a bit for the girl sitting beside me.

I smacked Diggs's hand away when he hit my head and messed up Einstein's hair.

"Jesus Christ, I'm so damn hungry. Why isn't there any food in this house?"

A pleased sound rumbled in Einstein's chest.

I bit back a smile. "Dare and Johnny went to get food." I nodded toward the pantry. "That's stocked if you can't wait."

"Is that a purple rib—that's a white box," Diggs yelled as he raced toward the counter. "This is an empty white box." He turned, pointing at us with the purple ribbon that usually secured the coffee shop's white boxes. "I can smell them. Where are they?"

"Safe and sound in my stomach," Einstein murmured, the smile in her tone betraying her blank expression.

Diggs gasped. "You scone whore."

"I'll take that title."

"You couldn't have left one?"

Einstein glanced at him, giving him a look that clearly said she thought he'd lost his mind. "No, this is the price you have to pay for eating my entire box last time I got them. You know how important they are to me."

"That was one—" He stared blankly ahead for a moment and then said, "That was only three times."

A sharp gasp ripped from Einstein. "I knew it. I knew the other times were you."

"Insignificant detail right now!" he yelled. "I need them to survive. You can't handle their delicate deliciousness."

"I will eat you under the table in baked goods, and I won't care about the consequences."

His mouth slowly twisted into a wry grin. "You sure know how to turn a man on."

"Oh Jesus," she mumbled, her stare falling back to her tablet.

Diggs fell into the chair next to Einstein and made a pathetic excuse for puppy eyes. "Feed me."

"Is that supposed to work on me?" she murmured, never looking away from the screen.

"Yeah. You ate scones without me. You owe me."

She tsked. "It's funny that you believe that."

He looked from her to me. His eyes lit with an idea, and one of his hands reached out to me.

Something like a laugh escaped her mouth. Before he could speak, she said, "I won't do it if Maverick asks either."

Diggs scoffed. "Dude. What's up with this no love for us or breakfast?"

"You're grown. Feed yourself or wait."

I gave him a look that said I didn't plan to help him and laughed when he pushed from the table with a sigh. "Haters. All of you."

"There's only two of us," Einstein said.

"Don't bring genius logic minds into this discussion. I was robbed of scones."

The corners of Einstein's mouth turned up, but she didn't respond. Just continued tapping and swiping on her screen, as she always did whenever it wasn't just us.

When I got a glimpse of her screen, I leaned close so my voice wouldn't carry to where Diggs was raiding the fridge. "What are you doing? You already know who Elle really is." My brow furrowed and voice lowered to a hiss. "The fuck . . . are you creating a fake file for her?"

Einstein cut me a look, telling me to shut up.

She sat back in her chair and put her feet on the seat so she could rest the tablet on her legs, keeping Diggs from seeing what was on the screen.

After grabbing her phone, she pulled up her notes and started typing.

You think I can tell Dare who she is? What do you think Johnny will do when he finds out? He flipped over a couch this morning when he found out she stayed the night.

I made sure Diggs was still busy before grabbing her phone.

Forget Johnny. E . . . Dare's in love with her. One day he will figure out that she's Lily fucking O'Sullivan. What do you think he'll do when he realizes she didn't actually die four years ago?

She took the phone back, her fingers flying faster than mine ever could.

She's the Holloway Princess running from Holloway,

Mav. She's scared and hiding. Doesn't matter what may or may not happen, I'm gonna make sure her cover sticks as long as it needs to. Besides, she found out who we were and decided she loved Dare too much to leave. By the time Dare finds out, maybe it won't matter to him who she is.

A disbelieving laugh fell from my lips. Einstein couldn't be that naïve. She *wasn't*.

And we can say this file was made on her side. They faked her death, why wouldn't they create a new life?

Because people can't create new lives the way you can, and Dare knows that.

That weight on my shoulders grew heavier and heavier.

In the middle of all of this bullshit, Dare had fallen for someone for the first time since Gia. With the exception of Johnny, we all liked her—shit, what wasn't to like about a girl who could stand up to Johnny?

Then again, knowing what Einstein and I knew, it wasn't hard to see why she seemed to have a spine of steel.

Lily O'Sullivan—the Holloway Princess—had been with Holloway's assassin most of her life. They were born to be together and rule together.

And Johnny's rage had *nothing* on Kieran's silence.

But Holloway had kept Lily hidden for so many years before faking her death, that the last picture we had of her looked nothing like the girl we knew as *Elle*. That didn't mean the others wouldn't eventually find out who she was.

After another look to see Diggs chugging orange juice from the carton while standing in the pantry and grabbing at cereal boxes, I took the phone back.

It won't matter? Are you serious? Her dad killed Dare's old man. He ripped Gia from Dare's fucking bed and murdered her. Dare will kill her when he realizes who she is.

Within a second, Einstein had the phone and was typing.

If I were a Holloway, would you kill me?

She tried to hand me the phone. When I wouldn't take it, she grabbed my hand and shoved the phone into it.

I only typed one word, but it seemed to take forever. The weight and meaning behind it embedded into each letter.

Never.

I looked at her, but she refused to look away from the screen. "And Johnny?" I whispered so softly that it was nearly inaudible to my own ears.

She tilted her head toward me, her lips parted as if she was going to respond before she thought better of it.

Slowly taking the phone, she tapped out her reply and tilted the screen toward me so I could see.

He can never find out. You saw the way he attacked her just because he didn't know her. He's . . . he just can't find out. No one can know. Not right now. Understand?

"Of course," I mumbled as Diggs slammed into a chair and dropped three boxes of cereal, a jug of milk, a carton of orange juice, and the remainder of donuts from yesterday onto the table.

I watched as Einstein erased the content of the note before deleting it and putting her phone onto the table, ensuring there was no trace of our conversation.

"You're grown. Feed yourself," Diggs mocked as he grabbed a donut.

"So proud of you," Einstein said sarcastically and then quickly started closing out everything on the tablet. "And just in time."

I looked around in confusion seconds before I heard a key in the lock of the front door. "There's no way you heard them coming."

"You doubt me?" Her tone was all challenge wrapped in the slightest tease.

My mouth slowly lifted in a smile. My eyes held hers for the few seconds we had left. "Never."

"It's gonna be okay, man."

I shot my brother a glare, then resumed my anxious movements. Movements I couldn't stop no matter how hard I tried.

Rapidly bouncing knee. Trembling arms. Near constant movement of my hands . . . through my hair, over my face, across my jaw, or down my legs.

Anything so long as I was moving.

This must be how Einstein felt when she was so damn close to breaking a code. Or when there was something familiar about a stranger's face that triggered something in that genius mind of hers and she became wholly engrossed and determined to figure out what that familiarity was.

I felt like an addict about to go insane if I didn't get my next fix.

Only my fix was a girl hiding away in a room.

And I didn't know how to help her when she was so fucking shattered that she couldn't comprehend it, let alone deal with it.

An agonized groan built in my chest, crawling and scraping up my throat as flash after flash ripped through my mind.

Dare asking Diggs and me to meet him outside.

Johnny shot dead in the backseat of his car.

Carrying him in.

Einstein falling to her knees.

The grief and horror and denial streaked across her face.

Dare explaining it was his gun. His bullet. He pulled the trigger. If he hadn't, Johnny would've killed Elle—*Lily*.

Einstein's mouth opened, the pained silence that poured from her louder than anything I'd ever heard.

Diggs, Libby, and I all looked up when Dare came walking into the girls' apartment.

Libby sighed in relief and hurried over to him, begging him to talk to Einstein.

Falling. Grief. Excruciating silence.

Einstein, Einstein, Einstein.

Over and over, the flashes continued to assault me.

"She hasn't eaten in . . ." Libby twisted to look at us, the question and desperation clear on her face.

Too long. She hadn't eaten in way too long.

"I don't know when she last ate," Libby continued. "She won't sleep. She's obsessing over work to distract herself, but it's going to kill her. Didn't you see her today?"

I dropped my head into my hands and rocked slowly, my breaths shaky.

We'd tried to get Einstein to eat . . . to *sleep*.

I'd sat on the floor of her room day after day, trying to silently be there for her.

But she just worked without ceasing.

Never crying. Never saying a word to any of us until after the funeral.

I'd stood close by, watching her carefully for when she broke. Because I knew it was coming. It *had* to come.

She'd been staring at the ground, not giving any indication she'd known where we were, who was near her, or that we'd just buried Johnny. And then she tilted her head, just slightly, and murmured to me, "I failed."

Before I could react to the pain, before I could tell her how wrong she was, she'd turned and walked back to the car.

I rocked back when the yelling in the apartment grew louder and looked up in time to see Libby try to shove Dare.

"What do you want me to do?" he asked. "You're all grieving someone I killed. *Einstein* is mourning the loss of her boyfriend, who I fucking killed, Libby."

"I want you to fix it. I want you to keep this family together the way you always have. Johnny was sick. He was insane. No one blames you, Dare, but you can't just leave us when we need you."

"I would never leave any one of you, but that's . . . fuck, Libby." He released her as he stepped back, looking as though the weight of the world was on his shoulders. "I'm tired. I'm so goddamn tired. I've been trying to keep the entire family together since I was thirteen because it's always been, 'Dare will know what to do.' I *never* knew what to fucking do. That role shouldn't have been put on me then, and I don't want it now. People are still dying, and we're still neck deep in things I don't want us in, and at some point, I want all that to end. I don't want to be boss. I'll never be Dad, and it's exhausting trying to be."

Libby's response was low. Too low for us to hear.

After a few more hushed exchanges, Dare said, "All right. Let me go check on the genius."

I was standing before he finished talking. "I'll come."

"No, I've got it. I don't want her to feel like we're ganging up on her. Besides," he said on a sigh, "I've been avoiding this talk."

I'd been staying away since the funeral because Libby told me I needed to give Einstein space.

But there was no way in hell I could continue to if Dare was going to her.

I followed without giving him a chance to argue again, and I wasn't surprised that Libby and my brother were on my heels.

We were all worried about Einstein.

I shifted anxiously from foot to foot when Dare stopped in front of her door and stared at it for a few moments before turning, his eyes narrowing when he saw us.

"She's awake," Libby said. "Trust me, just go in."

With a hesitant look, Dare opened the door.

And my chest lurched.

Einstein looked the way she did any other day.

She was sitting at her desk with her headphones on. All of her monitors were on and littered with open tabs. She was studying one intently before she shoved the headphones off her head and rushed to the bed to grab her tablet.

In that one quick second when she twisted around to head back to the desk, she gave us the perfect view of her without ever realizing we were there.

I tried to step into the room, but Dare held up his hand to stop me. That single gesture had me biting back a yell of frustration.

Because Einstein was right there. Shaking. Wild eyes bordering on possessed. Looking as if she were being tortured from the inside out. Practically screaming that she was about to break.

And I had to stand there and *watch*.

I let out a ragged breath when Dare reached out and touched her shoulder and Libby mimicked his actions to me.

Libby let out a soft gasp when she felt the way my entire body was shaking. "She'll be okay, Maverick."

I nearly fell to my knees when Einstein spoke.

"Dare, look at this." She sounded like she'd run a marathon. She sounded out of it.

"Einstein—"

"See what he's doing?" she asked excitedly, her eyes on one of her screens, barely noticing that Dare was trying to get her attention. "He's got a tail following Kier—"

"*Einstein.*"

"—and he's gonna pin him for taking that girl—"

Dare grabbed her shoulders and turned her in her chair, forcing her to look at him. *"Einstein!"*

Both Libby and Diggs grabbed me before I could take a single step.

My breaths were rough, my body was tense, and I had so much pain that felt like rage rushing through my veins that, for a second, it fucking terrified me.

Because I felt like Johnny.

"You've gotta stop," Dare whispered to her. "You need to eat something and sleep."

I watched as she stammered. "But can't you see what's—"

"I don't care. I care that you're going to kill yourself if you don't *stop*."

Einstein's head began shaking, rapid little jerks that made her look unhinged as her stare darted wildly around the room.

She stood, her voice soft and distraught as she bent to tear through the mound of crumpled papers on the floor. "There's something else. Look at this," she said as she slammed back into her chair. "Mickey's changing his pattern—"

Dare hauled her out of the chair as quickly as she'd sat and wrapped her in his arms.

That should be me.

That should be me holding her.

That should be me comforting her.

That should be me taking her grief and her pain.

Dare gripped her tightly, murmuring apology after apology as she stood there, eyes vacant and body limp in his arms.

"I'm sorry, I'm sorry, I'm so fucking sorry." Repeated, tortured words until she broke.

I felt her heart shatter.

I felt her grief.

I felt every ounce of her pain rip through the room as she buried her face in Dare's neck and sobbed, her eyes finding mine over his shoulder.

"I tried—I tried to figure him out," she said through her body-heaving sobs. "I tried to fix him, and I couldn't fix him. I tried . . . I did. There was something missing, and I couldn't find it, but I tried. I tried so hard."

Fuck.

I shrugged Diggs and Libby off and ignored the years-old warning that sounded in my mind to keep my distance from the girl in front of me.

Because I knew if I only had one purpose in life, it was to be there for Avery when she broke.

"I tried too," Dare murmured. "But you can't fix someone like that. You can't change them."

"I could've," she whispered.

Dare looked at me from over his shoulder, a crease between his brows when I finally spared him a glance.

I tried to open my mouth, but there was a knot in my throat that was threatening to choke me.

So I just looked at him, silently begging him to give me the girl he was holding.

When he twisted so he could transfer Einstein to me, I didn't hesitate. I wrapped her in my arms and pulled her close.

As though I'd done it thousands of times.

As though this wasn't the first time I'd allowed myself to touch her.

I felt her pain leak from her as I stepped back to the bed and sat with her in my arms, my back against her headboard. Each sob felt like a knife to my chest. Each tear that stained my shirt felt like shrapnel tearing through my soul.

"I failed." I wasn't sure if she'd actually uttered the words again or if I was still hearing them in my mind.

"No—"

"I could've been what he needed to help him out of the dark," she said, her voice slow and thick.

"What'd you just say?" Dare asked, the look on his face was nearly a perfect reflection of Einstein's just a minute ago.

Slightly crazed and desperate.

I shot him a look, silently telling him to drop it. Silently begging them to leave.

"Johnny," Einstein said as she lifted her head from my chest. "He said it was dark in his head and sometimes he didn't know how to find a way out."

"You didn't fail," I whispered. "You did more than anyone could've."

A whimper of pain crawled up her throat as her head rolled back against my chest. Within seconds, her eyes were shut and her breaths had deepened.

"You good?"

I looked up at Dare's question and gave him a faint nod. "I'm not going anywhere."

I'd hold her forever if she needed me to.

I'd thought of this moment no less than a dozen times a day. I'd dreamed of the way she would feel in my arms.

What I'd never considered was that it would be under these circumstances.

I hadn't wanted *this*.

When a gentle cry escaped her parted lips, I knew I would do it all over again.

Watch the woman I love with another man.

Keep her close enough to touch, knowing the distance between us would never disappear.

I would do it for a hundred years if it took her pain away.

thirteen

Maverick
TODAY

Diggs had just returned to ARCK from searching Einstein's apartment.

Libby and Maxon were checking the places she'd been known to hide.

Dare was hitting up the places Alex had been seen and making sure the people still loyal to us would keep an eye out for him.

And I was losing my goddamn mind.

"There has to be something," I bit out and turned on Jess. "If you hadn't pushed her to go out without checking him, we wouldn't be in this situation."

Kieran stood guard behind her, his eyes like fire. "Maybe the entire last year would've been different if Einstein felt like she could talk to you."

I jolted back. "The fuck is that supposed to mean?"

Jess shoved a hand against Kieran's chest. *"Don't."*

Extending one toward me, she said, "Most people in the world date without doing complete background and facial recognition checks on the person they're about to go on a date with."

"Not in our world. And what the hell—" I looked up when the door opened to Libby and Maxon walking in.

Kieran's comment was instantly forgotten.

My heart painfully skipped a couple of beats while I waited for their news and then kicked back into a thunderous pace when they both solemnly shook their heads.

"The guys haven't seen or heard from her," Maxon said quietly.

"She isn't at Mom's," Libby added. "Finding people is what *she* does. How are we supposed to find her?"

"We do what she would do," I said, my voice rough. "We've all watched her enough times. If we can't do that, then we go out there and we just fucking *look*. She would do it for any of us."

Her face set in anger and her teeth gnashed so hard I heard it from across the room. "I didn't mean we wouldn't. You know I didn't mean that."

"When you were gone, she never wondered *how* she was supposed to find you. She just did it."

"I know that, Maverick!" She pulled in a deep breath, letting it out slowly. "And I know you're scared, but don't twist your fear into anger and take it out on me."

But I *was* angry.

I was so damn livid for so many reasons, not just with the current situation.

Dare walked into the office, his steps slow, his face drawn. Lily and Beckham followed closely behind . . . and my heart stopped.

I had a dozen things I needed to do.

I had my girl I needed to find.

But I couldn't look away from the baby in Lily's arms.

Mistake.

Target.

Was that why everything was being taken from me?

Was I being punished for everything I'd ever thought or said about a baby?

I couldn't get a handle on the mess of emotions rising in me and crashing over me like a tidal wave.

My legs felt weak.

I swayed.

I ground my jaw to stop the cry of pain and anger and fear that threatened deep in my chest.

"Maverick, uh . . ."

I forced my blurred gaze to Dare.

After a second, he cleared his throat. "Maverick, I think she's gone."

I had to brace a hand on the wall before I fell.

"No, no, no." I shook my head roughly, not believing Dare's words for a second. "No, fuck you."

He stepped forward and held out a hand as if to reach for me. "I meant from here. Physically. By her own choosing."

Libby spun on him and yelled, "She wouldn't!"

His jaw clenched. The hand he'd been holding toward me shifted to her. "Think about the last year for her, Lib. Something changed. She's different in so many ways. She doesn't show up to work most days. She . . . well, the whole thing with Maverick."

My knees finally gave, and I roughly fell to the floor.

"The whole thing with Maverick."

They didn't know half of it.

I'd just found out what had been happening this entire time.

I buried my head in my hands and grit my teeth against the fresh wave of pain.

"And fuck, come on, none of this makes sense for Einstein," he continued. "Doesn't matter if Jess told her not to search the guy. How many times have we told her not to do her weird shit on people? She doesn't listen to us. Not to mention, she never goes anywhere with at least two devices on her that can be tracked. And one of those is always, *always* in her hand."

"No. No, you're wrong." Libby's voice shook. "She wouldn't do this to us. She wouldn't do this to *me*."

I didn't add anything to what she was saying.

Eight months ago, I would've agreed with her.

After this week, I wasn't sure I could speak for Einstein at all. I felt like I didn't know her anymore.

Someone cleared their throat, and I let my head fall roughly back to the wall.

Conor looked from Dare to Libby and then finally to me. His expression was twisted in disbelief. "I think . . . I think Dare might be right."

My eyes slowly shut when he held out a paper.

I didn't want to know what was on it.

I could hear Libby's sobs and the others' whispering. It was as if this nightmare path Einstein and I had been on was rapidly approaching its end, and if I looked at whatever was in Conor's hand, I would barrel right off the cliff.

I wasn't ready for that.

Not when I'd spent over a decade *knowing* Einstein and I were supposed to be forever.

"Mav."

I cracked my eyes open and slanted my head to look at my brother, who was crouched next to me, holding the paper.

"Mav, you say she didn't go, and I'll stand behind you. I'll be outside tracking gasoline or the smell of exhaust or tire tracks. Whatever you want, I'll do it."

"What does it say?"

His eyes darted up to mine, concern filling them.

"Tell me."

Regret pulsed from him when he flipped the page around, showing me a printout with Einstein's indecipherable code scribbled across it.

But circled numerous times on the top of the page was the word that made my stomach fall to the floor:

Phoenix.

Phoenix.

Phoenix.

This wasn't making sense.

Einstein leaving . . . the way Dare phrased it, I could see it.

Especially after all the shit that went down on Saturday. I could see her disappearing without a way for us to find her before I could have a chance to leave.

But why leave a paper on her desk with the place circled?

Einstein didn't slip up. Not like this.

"What the hell is in Phoenix?" The question was nothing more than a growl as I tried to think this through.

"Apparently, a ton of people," Jess mumbled from where she sat staring at her phone. "Also one of the largest cities in the country."

My frown deepened.

"No. She wouldn't . . . no." I stood and went to stand behind Jess, my eyes darting over the screen and taking in everything she'd just been looking at.

"There's no way. Einstein likes *this*. Small towns. Places that don't attract a lot of attention. Why would she go to one of the largest and most populated cities if she was disappearing?"

"Maybe because she knows you wouldn't expect her there," Dare said, his tone defeated as he pulled Lily into his arms.

"I'm telling you, she wouldn't go there. I know that what you're suggesting is possible, but it doesn't sit right with me."

"And what? The thought of her being taken does?"

I grit my teeth and forced myself to breathe so I wouldn't lash out at him. "Of course not. But when they first told me everything, my gut screamed something was wrong—that she was in trouble. I *know* I need to save her."

Dare's eyes shifted to study his wife for a few moments before he met my pleading stare. With a subtle nod, he said, "Then let's find her."

I released a pent-up breath and nearly thanked him before Libby said, "But we still have nothing to go on. We don't know this Alex guy. She didn't leave us any clues about who he might be. We know nothing but his name at this point."

"That isn't true," I said. "We know where he's been

spending his days. We have people in town waiting to see if he shows up somewhere."

"And if he doesn't?" Dare asked bluntly. "Einstein was the one to break into traffic cameras and police databases. She was the one who found people trying to hide. The rest of us are extremely limited in what we know how to do because we relied on her to do it for us."

I gripped the back of my neck and rocked back on my heels, my gaze catching on the paper Einstein had written all over.

My head snapped up, and I turned to face Kieran and Conor. "Phoenix. It was on her desk, right? Are any of your cases from Phoenix?"

Kieran looked to Conor, who shrugged. "Not that have come through me," he answered, his tone nowhere near hopeful. "Some go through Einstein, though."

"We need to try to get into her computer."

Jess and Conor released sharp, disbelieving laughs.

"Everything in her computer is locked," Jess said, stating something that everyone in the room already knew. "*Everything*. Even if we do get in, we can't access anything."

"Well, none of you know her the way I do." I headed for Einstein's desk, my steps slowing when a thought crossed my mind. Turning to look at Jess, I asked, "Do you know for sure that she didn't do a search on Alex?"

"No, but—"

"Thank God." I dragged my hands over my face as hope swirled in my chest for the first time all day, and then I hurried to Einstein's desk. "That day at Brooks Street, Einstein said she'd thought Alex had given her a fake name. But that he hadn't."

Dare was instantly at my side. "That's right."

"That means she did a search." I opened Einstein's laptop and tapped on the keypad. "Whoever he is, he's in here."

I just needed to find out how to get in.

I stared at the screen, which was prompting me for a password.

Come on, Avery.

Help me find you.

Fourteen

Einstein
TODAY

I WAS DRENCHED IN SWEAT.
Positive.

One of the only ones I could find in that moment, considering I was also practically naked.

My jeans were down around my feet and my shirt was bunched up in one of my hands and pressed to the crook of my elbow.

Second positive. It looked like I'd undressed myself in my sleep and continued to try to stop the bleeding.

I looked around the room for a moment before trying to move and blew out a relieved sigh when I didn't have the urge to fall over or puke.

I grabbed for my jeans but hesitated.

The room was only getting hotter, and I couldn't imagine trying to pull on skinny jeans when my body was covered with a sheen of sweat.

And knowing the price of drinking the water, I wanted to stay hydrated for as long as possible.

I kicked them the rest of the way off.

I twisted to get off the bed, my entire body stilling when I caught sight of the Post-it on the floor below where the empty bag of saline hung.

I didn't reach for it.

There wasn't a need to.

The note was upright, just waiting for me to read it.

I'm waiting.

For a split second, I had one of those horror-movie visions where the murderer was waiting under the bed as the girl walked carelessly around her room half naked.

Yet, the first note had been on the saline bag. I had a feeling this one had been put in the same place before falling to the floor when the bag drained.

Just in case, I dropped to the floor, landing harder than I meant to due to the near-constant state of being drugged, prepared to look my killer in the face.

But there was nothing.

I rocked back to my knees and looked around the room with fresh eyes.

Well, as fresh as I thought they were going to get anytime soon. I still felt off-balanced whenever I moved, and my head felt heavier than usual, but I would take it.

I would take it a thousand times if the alternative was waking up like I had the last few times.

Other than the pole holding the empty bag of knock-Einstein-on-her-ass, there was still only the bed, nightstand, and bottles.

The only light source in the room came from the two long fluorescent light bulbs in the center of the ceiling. Not that the room needed more than that.

Without moving anything but my eyes, I looked at the door.

I remembered the feel of it beneath my palms. Too sturdy to attempt to break down, but there was a lock. And I'd always been good with locks.

Hack your way out of this.

My brow pinched as panic rose in my throat, making it difficult to breathe. Because that first note said so much in only a few words.

If I hadn't been so drugged and panicked, I would've noticed before. I would've grasped the underlying message.

It said he knew who I was . . . what I did.

It could've been a careless taunt, but there was something about it that felt like a challenge. That felt like a demand.

But what was I supposed to hack in a nearly empty room?

I slowly shifted my stare to the bed in front of me as I considered that.

Then I was moving. Ripping the sheets off and searching them for anything that shouldn't be there.

Another Post-it.

Writing on the bedding or mattress.

Just anything to lead me in a direction.

Once the mattress was on the floor and the frame had been tipped over and inspected, I moved on to the nightstand. After knocking the bottles to the floor, I roughly pushed the piece of furniture onto its side before slamming it repeatedly against the ground until it broke. Then I inspected every piece thoroughly.

When there was nothing, I moved on to the bottles. Emptying the contents of each one into my cupped palm slowly and then studying the caps and plastic wrapping.

Nothing. Still.

I tossed the last bottle to the floor and looked around, scrambling to my feet and around the mess when my gaze caught on the metal pole holding up the IV drip.

The bag.

The pole.

Nothing, nothing, nothing.

I swung it against the wall like a bat and yelled, "What do you want?"

I flinched when one of the hooks snapped off and flew back at me, narrowly missing my head. After glancing at the small piece of metal lying on the floor, I brought the top of the IV pole to my face to inspect the one still attached and noticed the push pin.

After easily removing the second hook, I righted the pole and grabbed the first hook before stuffing them both into my bra in case anyone came back.

With another glance around the room, there were only two options left.

I hurried to the door and pulled on the handle again—like an idiot—and then dropped to inspect the old-fashioned keyhole.

Blinking quickly, I leaned away and studied the door, my hands moving over the wood before I leaned in to get another look.

"No."

He wouldn't.

I grabbed one of the hooks from my bra as I told myself that I was wrong.

The hook wouldn't pick a lock, but I had a feeling I wouldn't be doing that today anyway. Because that would've been too simple.

I placed my ear flat against the door's surface, watching closely as I positioned the metal hook into the keyhole.

The low knock sounded in my ear and vibrated against my cheek and palm.

My eyelids slipped shut as I tried the hook again and again and again, only to be met with the solid wood of the door beneath the dummy cover.

I slammed the hook against the ornate cover. *"You fucking asshole."*

Hack your way out of this.

I'm waiting.

"What are you waiting for?" I mumbled to myself. I spread my arms out before letting them fall to the floor beside me. "There's literally nothing to do." Well, other than figure out how the hell I was going to get out of this room, but that wasn't hacking, that was breaking out.

It didn't make any sense.

I glanced up, narrowing my eyes in an attempt to see things that weren't there. Like a camera in the solid wood door or the frame or the damn walls.

"Is this fun for you?" I yelled minutes later.

Nothing.

What a surprise.

"Great." I nodded and choked out a laugh. "I'm talking to myself. *Yelling* at myself. That's awesome."

I walked to the center of the room and stared at the bright lights.

It was the only place in the room I hadn't checked.

With a sigh, I righted the bed frame, hefted the mattress onto it, and then grabbed the IV pole, all the while yelling for whoever might be listening as I dragged them below the lights. "If you're waiting for me to break down, you're wasting your time. I lost everything a long time ago. Myself included."

Climbing onto the bed, I gripped the pole in one hand and my shirt in the other and tried to see around the blinding glow.

After a few steeling breaths, I whispered, "Please don't break on me." Then I lifted my shirt to just below my eyes in case the lights did exactly that and guided the shaking pole to search the area directly surrounding the bulbs.

There had to be something.

Had to.

There couldn't be an entire room of nothing. There couldn't be *no* way of getting out.

Being stuck in here indefinitely wasn't something I was willing to entertain.

I dropped my head and brought the shirt over my face when the pole snagged on something. My breath caught in my throat. My heart faltered as I waited.

But there was no shattering of glass.

The room didn't darken.

I hesitantly continued the path the pole had been on, scrunching my face in preparation for whatever might happen and loosing a shuddering breath that sounded like a cry when the pole pushed a switch over.

I dropped both the shirt and the pole and looked up, blinking rapidly when I looked directly into the lights. When I didn't see anything right away, I turned on the bed and craned my neck to try to see more, but I had only looked for a second when I heard it.

The sound of a large system kicking on.

I froze and waited, not knowing what exactly I was hearing until I felt cool air blowing across my skin.

Air conditioning.

Oh my God.

The giddy feeling only lasted a second before I realized that if there was air conditioning that meant there was a vent in the room somewhere.

But where?

I whirled around on the bed, looking for where it could be coming from. Slowly, I lifted my hands and moved them in different directions until I caught the stream of invisible air hitting me.

Hopping off the bed, I followed where I'd felt it coming from, my eyes open wide so I didn't miss anything.

But there was nothing.

"No, that isn't right!"

Running back for the bed, I dragged it half a dozen feet away, climbed back on top of it, and raised my hands in front of me until I caught the current again. Then I repeated the process until the bed was pushed against the far wall of the room.

It looked like every other wall, but from where I stood on the bed, I could hear the air blowing.

Leaning forward, I curled my hand into a fist and then turned my hand to look at it.

A smile formed on my face.

I think I laughed. Maybe. But . . . no, this wasn't funny.

Why do I want to knock on walls?

I blinked quickly, studying the space in front of me.

Air. I needed to go where the air was. Because it was so sweet.

Has air always tasted sweet?

Before I could wonder about air and what it tasted like any longer, I hurried to bang on the wall. My fist went straight through, taking a large, rectangular section of the wall with it. I watched in disbelief as it fell backward and landed with a clang and small cloud of dust.

I stared at the dark hole in front of me, unblinking, and then burst out laughing.

"You look so real." I laughed harder, bracing a hand just to the side of the hole so I wouldn't fall over. When the wall didn't give, I slapped it. "Oh. You . . . you're a wall." Swinging my head back to the front, I scrunched my nose. "Imposter."

I let my head fall back and just stood there, enjoying the coolness on my skin and enjoying . . . *everything*.

When was the last time I felt so good?

Felt so free?

I wasn't even sure what I needed to feel free from in that moment. My body just felt light and perfect. I didn't have a care in the world.

I kind of wanted to lay back and just enjoy it.

A giggle slipped from my lips when I realized I was already on my back on the bed.

My head lolled to the side, and my eyes caught on a yellow note on the floor. I lifted my hand lazily to point at it.

"You mean something, don't you?" I clicked my tongue when I remembered and then lowered my voice to impersonate a man's. *"I'm waiting.* Ugh." I sat up and looked at the massive hole in the wall, pouring out sweet, cooling air. "All right, asshole. I'm coming."

I managed to put my pants on.

And my shirt.

But I was sitting on the bed, cross-legged, holding the shirt away from my body and wondering why there was blood streaked across it. It looked like I'd gotten in a fight with a bloody, declawed squirrel.

And might've lost.

Can squirrels be declawed?

My body vibrated with silent laughter until I fell onto my back. A contented sigh blew past my lips and ended on a groan when I saw the air duct in the wall.

I'd forgotten about that sometime between determining that I was going in there and imagining a squirrel without claws.

Rolling onto my knees, I mumbled about dark holes and all the evils that waited on the other side and began listing the pros to staying in the room.

There was a bed—beds were my favorite.

If there had ever been a squirrel, I was fairly certain it was gone.

And I wouldn't have to go down a rabbit hole like Alice and end up in some trippy land.

But there was a voice that kept telling me the room I was in was the last place I wanted to be.

Distant, subdued, kind of hazy . . . but persistent.

Get out. Get out. Get out.

You need to get out of here.

The corners of my mouth tilted up. "*You* do."

I placed my hands on the edge of the opening and lifted myself up, a laugh ripping from my throat when my arms gave and I faceplanted into the air duct, my body half-sticking out.

Get out. Get out. Get—

"Heard you," I grumbled, pressing my open palms to the metal beneath me and hoisting my body up. "Heard you the first hundred times."

Once I was fully inside, I crawled through the enclosed space that was big enough to fit two of me, trying to make as little noise as possible. Every time the metal gave beneath my weight and made a loud popping noise, I lost my battle with stealth and broke into a fit of giggles.

"If you didn't know I was coming before, you do now."

I drew in breath after breath, inhaling the sweet air blowing hard against my face.

I stopped crawling and struggled to swallow. To taste.

Not sweet, but there was a hint of something familiar that I couldn't place.

The next thing I knew, I had my head in my arms as tears fell from my eyes to the metal beneath me.

I wanted to laugh and sob and kick myself because I had no clue why I was crying at all.

But I couldn't stop.

And, oh God, it felt so good to close my eyes.

My body relaxed until it felt like I was a puddle.

You need to get out of here.

"Fuck off."

I didn't notice it.

Not at first.

The way my lungs screamed.

The way my muscles tensed. As if they were all being pulled . . . strained . . . set on fire.
Fire.
That was my lungs. On fire.
My mouth was open in a soundless scream.
Why wasn't I screaming?
Why was I trying?
My chest and shoulders jerked as I searched for air.
Air.
There was no oxygen.
My mind was screaming.
My brain felt fuzzy.
Wrong.
I was clawing. Clawing at the surface beneath me. Clawing at my face, my throat, my body.
I was drowning in a sea of nothing.
And my heart . . .
My heart was so loud. So painful. So slow.

Fifteen

Einstein
ONE YEAR AGO

"Ta-da," Diggs called out proudly, lifting his arms out wide to show off the transformed theater room in the Borello house.

I quickly counted the mattresses on the floor and then almost did it again, sure I had counted wrong.

But I was me, I never counted wrong.

I let my head fall into my hands and held back a groan. When I peeked back at the twins and Libby, I cleared my throat and asked, "Who's idea was this?"

Maverick and Libby pointed at Diggs.

Diggs huffed in offense. "Whoa, whoa, no. We all agreed long before, and the two of you helped me set up. Don't go throwing me under the bus now."

"We agreed on the sleepover—"

"See?" he asked, pointing at Libby. "There you go. We all agreed."

I looked to Maverick, but he was shaking his head, so I turned back to his brother and tried to let him down as gently as possible. "Diggs, we agreed *we* were going to have a sleepover. We never said Dare and Lily were staying in here with us."

Diggs looked as if I'd wounded him. "Why wouldn't they? It's a family sleepover."

"Because they just got married. They want to be alone. Also, Lily's pregnant, she probably doesn't want to sleep on the floor."

"It's a mattress," he argued defensively.

"*On the floor,*" I repeated.

His mouth opened and shut a few times before he waved his arms around, indicating the room. "But it's a masterpiece. Best one yet. It took *days*. They can't bail."

In all the years since this tradition started, which was the night Diggs thought it would be funny to lock us all in here since the theater room doubled as a safe room and we'd be stuck for five hours, the room had never looked so magical.

As always, the whole space was like one giant fort, complete with sheets hanging from the ceiling, pillows, blankets, food, and all of the mattresses from our rooms. Only this time, twinkle lights stretched across the ceiling.

But how could he think that Lily and Dare would sleep in here on their wedding night?

I looked to Maverick for help, but he just held up his hands. "I told him not to grab their mattress."

"Look at what I did before you say no again," Diggs said on a rush as he ran toward the far corner of the room.

Grabbing the sheets waiting to become makeshift walls

around the farthest mattress, Diggs quickly closed them and gave me a pleading look.

Silver glitter fell from the top of the hanging sheets like spilled paint—I assumed around that mattress only.

It was really hard not to smile at all Diggs had gone through to make it a little more special for Dare and Lily.

"Don't try to take credit for that," Libby yelled. "That was all my idea."

I sent Diggs an annoyed look.

"Whatever. Team effort. Get off the hate-train already," Diggs mumbled as he walked back to us. "So, what do you say?"

"It isn't up to me," I said with a frustrated laugh. "But I'm telling you, Lily won't be able to sleep on just a mattress. If you wanted a chance at keeping them in here, you should've brought their entire bed."

A sly grin crossed his face.

"Shit," Maverick murmured just as Diggs said, "Challenge accepted."

Not two hours later, Diggs had taken apart and put back together Dare and Lily's bed and managed to trap them in the theater room along with the rest of us.

Dare had looked like he wanted to punch Diggs.

Lily had laughed and then towed Dare to the front to curl up on a couch.

Before the movie could even start, the atmosphere was like any other sleepover. Food being thrown, everyone razzing each other and fighting over what movie to watch. Only this time, Maverick was by my side with my hand in his.

"You want to get out of here?" he asked a little while in to the first movie, his lips brushing along my ear.

A shiver moved through me when I looked at him, my mouth pulling into a smile for no reason other than he was right there with me. "Hate to break it to you, but we still have four hours and eight minutes before we can leave."

His lips tipped up at the corners. "Have that timer going in your head?"

"Always."

He looked around at the few couches pushed up to the front of the room. "I meant *here*."

I lowered my voice, the words all wrapped in tease and accusation. "You want to bail before the newlyweds?"

Maverick just stared at me as if I should have already known the answer. "I'll get the food," he whispered before slipping away.

My head tipped back in a silent laugh. After looking around to make sure no one was paying attention to us, I hurried over to Maverick's mattress, which was thankfully clear across the room from Lily and Dare's but also nowhere near mine.

Not that it mattered.

We'd never had ours near the other's before.

That didn't need to change.

I eyed his pillows and blankets for a few seconds, indecision wavering within me before I finally stepped around the side and opened the hanging sheet that separated his mattress from the line of leftover couches hugging the wall.

I dropped onto the couch seconds before Maverick set a white box beside me and took a seat on the mattress so he was facing me.

I sucked in a sharp breath and hurried to untie the purple ribbon keeping the box closed. "Are these mini blueberry scones from the coffee shop? These are my favorite,"

I continued before he had a chance to answer, before I even had the box opened.

But he knew that.

Of course he knew that.

Just as I'd known he would come back with M&M's and popcorn.

He shrugged nonchalantly, as if he hadn't just presented me with the best gift in the world. "Thought you'd want them."

I struggled to suppress my excitement as I flipped the lid open and snatched one of the scones from the box. "*Favorite*," I said on a moan when I finally bit into it. When I looked at Maverick, he was fighting a smile.

"There are more stashed away in your room."

I narrowed my eyes playfully at him. "Are you trying to sweeten me up for something?"

"Would it work?" he challenged teasingly.

I took another bite and pointed the last bit of scone at him. "Possibly." I already had a second baked gift from the gods between my fingers when a thought hit me. "How did you keep these from Diggs?"

"Hid them in an empty cooler under the table when he was disassembling Dare and Lily's bed frame."

I nodded in admiration. "Smart."

He huffed a laugh. "Civil war over scones."

I sent him a dry look. "First, they aren't just *scones*. Second, not my fault your brother doesn't understand that these belong to—*bastard*," I cried out when the box was snatched from my lap.

Maverick shot forward, grabbing Diggs's leg and sending him crashing down. He landed only partly on the mattress, and my box went sliding across the floor.

"I knew it," Diggs called out and tried to lurch forward as I scrambled over him to get to the box, kicking away his reaching hands as I did. "I *knew* I smelled them. I'm a fucking bloodhound, baby, nothing gets past me."

I picked up the box, inspected the contents, and then glared at Diggs. "You bastard, you could've ruined them."

"Then they would've been mine."

"The hell they would've been. They're mine whether they touch the floor or not." I held the box close to my chest when I stepped over him and went back to the couch. "You've eaten double your weight in food today. You'll live."

He made a wounded sound before turning to his brother. "Your girlfriend is so hateful."

My head snapped up and eyes widened. My pulse quickened and my breaths turned shallow.

Maverick slowly lifted his head to meet my stare.

I couldn't make out his expression through the darkened room, but I could feel his want and his need mixing with my own.

Maverick and I weren't anything, but we were *everything*.

I was his. He was mine.

That was all that mattered.

Things had changed—of course, they'd changed.

Sometimes he pulled me into his arms and held me.

Other times, he stopped me from walking by with a hand against my cheek and just stared into my eyes for a few moments before letting me go.

Our first kiss had shattered all the walls around my heart.

That first spoken *I love you* freed my soul.

But it had all begun slowly and continued the same.

"You know, speaking of, I've been wondering something . . ." Maverick was so focused on me that Diggs was able to push onto his elbows and face me again before he continued. "Now that the two of you are hot and heavy, what are the chances you'll mistake me for my brother?"

Maverick shoved Diggs away. "Fuck off."

Diggs scrambled to his feet and held his hands out in front of him. "Honest question. It isn't my fault I'm the better-looking one and all the ladies want this. I don't want to be taken advantage of by our favorite genius because she can't tell us apart."

I shoved the box at him. "Jesus, there's so much wrong with what you just said. Take this and stop talking."

He shoved an entire scone in his mouth and asked, "So, that's a *no*?"

"I just gave you my scones so you would leave. That's a *hell no*."

He shrugged as he stepped away. "Your loss. I could've rocked your world." Diggs jumped back when Maverick lunged for him. "I'm kidding, I'm kidding. Shit."

When Maverick sat on his mattress again, he didn't apologize for his brother, the girlfriend comment, or the loss of my scones.

There wasn't a need.

It was all just so *Diggs*.

He just looked at me and asked, "How do you tell us apart?"

A laugh crawled up my throat. "Taken you ten years and a comment from Diggs to ask?"

"I never cared." He loosed a slow sigh, his head shaking as he did. "Even our parents mixed us up. When we left for boot camp, my mom was crying and saying she was going to miss me. Called me Evan. I didn't even correct her."

I wondered what that felt like. To feel unnoticed but not for lack of being loved.

I'd been nothing but an irritation to my parents . . . so had my sister. There were so many days I'd wished they hadn't noticed me.

I cleared my throat and pushed thoughts of them away. "It was the way you looked at me when we found you." I glanced at Maverick and bit back a smile. "All the pictures I found of you had this intensity. Diggs . . . well, it's as if he was always in on a joke or playing one."

"Always," he agreed.

"You jumped up, and even though you were surprised, you still had this hard, challenging look, and I immediately knew you were Andrew. Helped that Diggs stayed on the floor without a care in the world. Ever since, it's been easy."

He breathed a laugh. "Yeah, well, things are when you're a genius."

"No," I said quickly, my voice soft but firm. "He doesn't look at me the way you do."

I could feel the shift in the air.

Feel the tension pressing down around us.

"And how's that?"

"Like you know me," I whispered. "Like you hear me without my ever having to say a word. Like you love—"

Maverick sat up and pressed his mouth to mine, swallowing my words and my surprised whimper.

And everything faded away.

The movie.

The room.

Time.

It was only us and this kiss as he parted my lips, his tongue teasing mine in a way that slowly drove me crazy.

"I feel like I've been waiting to kiss you my entire life," I whispered when he pulled away. "You told me once that you thought you and Diggs were born for this life. I think I was born to be with you."

His hands were in my hair and his mouth was on mine again before I knew he was moving.

"Avery, I love you," he breathed against my lips.

Chills raced across my skin. "I love you. I love you."

Then he was kissing me again, slowly, passionately.

Stealing another piece of my heart.

Leaving me feeling off-balanced in a way I was beginning to crave.

I never wanted it to end.

Sixteen

Maverick
TWELVE MONTHS AGO

I WAS BUZZING.
And it had nothing to do with alcohol or the lingering music ringing in my ears from the show.

It was her.

It was us.

It was finally having a night where we could be out and not keep each other at arm's length so we didn't raise any suspicions.

Touching her and pulling her close.

The way she moved toward me instinctively if she'd shifted too far away, as though her soul couldn't stand being away from me any more than mine could hers.

The way she looked at me and just fucking smiled.

That was what had me buzzing.

I closed the front door to her apartment behind me, watching her back away with her eyes on me in the dimly lit space. Pure heat and need and passion played out on her face, making me fucking ache to bury myself deep inside her. To make her mine.

The sound of the lock sliding home was like a gunshot prompting us to go.

I pushed from the door.

Her chest hitched as anticipation burned in those eyes.

And then we moved.

Reaching for each other and coming together so fast and fluid it was as if we'd done it hundreds of times.

I'd done this, I'd kissed her, I'd loved her *thousands* of times in my dreams.

But this . . . this was a decade in the making.

I captured her face in my hands and slanted my mouth over hers, swallowing her contented sigh when she opened for me.

Bliss.

I tilted her head back farther, kissing her deeper and taking everything that she willingly gave until she was breaking away, struggling to catch her breath.

I moved my mouth across her jaw and down her neck, leaving a trail of open-mouthed kisses and teasing bites. Savoring the way she whimpered and gripped my shirt, pulling me closer as if it would never be close enough.

My head spun, trying to remember every tease and touch that seemed to happen in flashes.

Fucking spinning.

Buzzing.

Her head arched back. Sweetest damn sound I've ever heard, low in her throat.

Then her mouth on mine.

Hands gripping. Pulling. Searching. Teasing my lower

stomach with the tips of her fingers.

This girl, this girl, this goddamn girl.

Her ass in my hands and her legs wrapped around my waist. Fingers sliding through my hair.

A laugh tumbling from her lips when I dropped her onto the bed.

My hand racing up the dip of her waist and over her breast, kneading and pinching. Reaching for the hem of her shirt and pulling it up, my lips moving down, down, down.

Popping open the button on her shorts.

And then trembling.

Choking.

Tears streaming down her face.

"Einstein . . . *Avery!*" I shouted frantically and gripped her shoulders. "Avery, what? What's wrong?"

But she just laid there, choking on nothing as fat tears fell down her cheeks. Staring straight at me but not seeming to see me. Shaking so hard that the bed was moving like a damn earthquake.

And I panicked because this was *Avery*.

I just stared at her for seconds or minutes or hours because I had no damn clue what to do when it was the girl I loved.

Finally, I blinked out of the daze and got off her, pulling her into a sitting position as I did.

"Talk to me, I need you to talk to me." I looked into her blank stare and clenched my teeth, pleading, "Fucking talk to me. Are you sick? Are you hurt?"

Just when I was about to ask if she was actually choking on something, she dropped her head and a pained sob wrenched from her body.

Literally. *Wrenched.*

Her entire body jerked and curled in on itself. But when I reached out to keep her from falling forward, she shot her arms out to stop me from touching her.

"*Don't.*"

I lurched back, sliding off the bed and barely planting my feet on the floor fast enough to keep from falling.

I held my hands in front of me, partly in surrender and partly in fear, and just studied her.

"Did—" I swallowed thickly, the motion seeming to take too much strength. "Did I hurt you?"

I thought back over everything before the trembling, wondering if I had pushed her.

Went back to when I locked the damn door.

Then the concert.

Every time, I got all the way up to that sexy, carefree laugh when I dropped her onto the bed, and then nothing. That was the last thing I remembered . . . from *her*.

I kept trying to think if she'd asked me to stop. Told me to. *Anything.*

But there was nothing.

She'd been still.

Too still, actually, and I'd been too caught up to notice.

"Avery . . ." I scrubbed my hands over my face. My shoulders sagged. I released a sigh as I sat next to her, but it abruptly cut off when she flinched away.

From *me*.

"Fuck, I'm sorry." I stood and went to lean against the wall, trying to give her the space she clearly needed. "This is moving too fast, I get it. I do. I'm sorry. I'm so damn sorry. I should've known it would be too soon after Johnny."

I thought she flinched from me, but she looked like

she'd been shocked when I said Johnny's name.

My brow furrowed.

I didn't move or say anything.

My girl was sitting there sobbing, and I couldn't touch her to comfort her. Couldn't pull her into my arms or even sit next to her.

She quickly wiped at the tears still falling and then lifted her head enough to look like my strong, confident Einstein but not enough to face me. "I need you to leave."

My chest heaved. My heart dropped. Pain sliced through me. "I'm sorry. God, what did I do? Just tell me so I won't do it again. Because one second we were both *right there*, and then we weren't, but I missed when it flipped for you."

"Leave." It was a broken, hopeless plea.

I slid my hands into the pockets of my jeans and shrugged. "No."

We stayed like that, wrapped in silence as minutes passed.

She never looked away from the point she was staring at on the wall.

I never stopped watching her.

For the first time in all the years I'd known her, I couldn't figure out whatever she was thinking.

But I tried.

I went through the entire night on a loop, looking for something I'd missed and coming up with nothing.

"I'm so sorry," she finally said when at least ten minutes had passed.

My eyebrows shot up. "*You?* You're sorry? Einstein, I'm going out of my goddamn mind trying to figure out what the hell I did. You don't need to be sorry, just put me out of my misery and tell me what I did."

"I don't know how to tell you." Her voice broke halfway through the sentence, making me push from the wall.

"You just tell me so I'll know what not to do, and that'll be the end of it. Simple."

She laughed.

Short, sad, with no humor behind it.

"If only it were." She finally met my stare, her lips trembling and eyes watering all over again. "I don't think I can have sex with you. I don't think I can do anything with you at all."

"That's fine," I assured as I walked toward her. "I've waited for you this long. I can wait longer."

Before I made it to the bed, she said, *"Ever."*

I recovered from the stumble.

I swallowed back the pained exhale.

"Oh." I somehow made it to the bed, making sure to give her room so I wouldn't have to see her recoil from me again.

I cleared my throat and nodded. I *think* I nodded.

"All right. Yeah. If it's because you aren't attracted to me, well then . . . I'm fucking screwed." I tried to laugh, but it fell flat. I felt fucking sick. "But I've loved you for ten years without ever being able to touch you. I don't need any of that to continue loving you. So, if it's because you don't think you can move on that way after Johnny, then I'll still be here. You know, if you want me to be."

Her body lurched and a cry sounded deep in her chest.

When she was finally able to speak, her voice was twisted in anguish. "Maverick, I want you forever. With me, by my side, *mine*. But I can't . . . I can't do this."

My chest felt empty.

I wasn't sure I was breathing.

Or if I knew how to anymore.

I dipped my head in something that resembled a nod and opened my mouth to tell her it was okay. To tell her I understood. But nothing came out.

I tried to tell my legs to stand. To carry me out of her room and the apartment.

Before I could move, she spoke.

Her words were barely above a breath and full of shame. "I thought it would be different with you. I've wanted this for so long. I was so sure things would be different."

Did she have any idea what she was doing to me?

How she was taking the remains of my heart and grinding them to dust?

"I'm sorry it wasn't." The words were thick with emotion and sat heavy in my throat. But I still managed to get them out before I forced myself to stand and walk away.

"It didn't start until after Gia died. A while after."

I stopped moving.

Confusion twisted through the agony already searing my veins.

"He was always just so angry and then he started getting paranoid. That was when it began. And it happened nearly every time after because I couldn't stop cringing when he came near me. Even if he was okay at the time, I still set him off. Somehow. And there was no stopping him."

I swallowed. Tried to. My throat was suddenly so damn dry.

My head moved. A faint shake. A denial.

The visuals her words created raced through my mind, burying themselves deep and burning their images in my brain so I would never be able to forget them. Slowly tearing me apart and making me want to die.

Unsteady. My legs were so damn unsteady when I turned to look at Einstein.

This had to be a mistake. I *had* to be taking her words the wrong way.

If I wasn't?

I'd bring Johnny back to life so I could kill him myself.

One bullet to the head.

Then I'd do it again so I could go fist for fist with him. Because there was no beating Johnny in a fist fight . . . and I had no intention of winning—of living. I didn't deserve to if I'd missed *this*.

When I finally faced her, she was sitting there with her legs pulled up to her chest, her eyes locked on the floor, and an emotionless mask on her face.

Typical Einstein.

Heart of stone, just like Johnny.

That was what she wanted our world to see. Someone who wasn't affected by what happened around her. Who didn't *feel*.

I'd always seen past it.

From the beginning, she'd bared her soul to me. Her happiness and pains and worries. Showed me her every emotion that made the cold, indifferent, mafia genius *real*.

But this?

"What are you saying?" I begged, needing to hear the words and silently begging her to tell me I was wrong.

Her eyes flickered to me.

Cold.

Detached.

Shit.

"Avery." Her name was wrapped in torment and denial. It felt like the air had been knocked from my lungs. I couldn't fucking breathe.

I was beside the bed in an instant, kneeling in front of her, my hands hovering over her legs before I dropped my head into them instead. "Ave—*God*. Tell me he didn't . . . tell me *I* didn't let this happen. Tell me—" The rest of the words caught in my throat, choking me.

Tell me I'm wrong. Please tell me I'm fucking wrong.

"No one *let* Johnny do anything." It was matter-of-fact. It was that arrogant way she spoke to everyone else, and it made me feel as if she'd put the remains of my heart back into my chest and lit them on fire.

I wanted to wrap her in my arms and tell her I was sorry for failing her. For not seeing what was happening.

I wanted to hit something. Some*one*.

My body and mind and heart felt pulled in so many different directions that I was only able to sit there. Head in my hands, body shaking as adrenaline and rage and shame and sorrow threatened to pull me under. Threatened to drown me.

Rage was the first to win out.

I'm gonna kill him.

I shoved from the bed and stalked toward the door.

When I got there, I gripped the frame and used it to push myself back into the room. "I asked you. I fucking asked you point-blank if you were scared of him. If there was something going on. If he'd ever *hurt* you."

She didn't respond. Only sat there watching me with a forced, bored look on her face.

My chest pitched roughly with my ragged breaths. "You lied to me."

"It happens in life."

I hit my chest. "*Me*. You lied to me, Einstein. I—*fuck*—I would've done anything if you'd told me. He would've been in the ground the *first time* it happened."

I walked back until I hit the wall and drove my hands into my hair when she became too blurry to see.

"I've been here." A choking sound caught in my throat, and my chest heaved. I dropped one of my hands to grip it, trying to relieve the pain. "I was *there* while this happened to you for, what? Years? And I did nothing."

I'd always prided myself on knowing Einstein in a way no one did, but I'd missed something huge. Damaging.

There'd never been a hint that she had been keeping something from me . . . that she had been lying . . . that she had been *hurting*.

The times I'd asked her were simply because I didn't know how Johnny could be such a monster to every person he came in contact with but still treat Einstein well.

What else had I missed?

At some point, I'd slid to the floor. My legs no longer able to keep me standing.

I scrubbed a hand over my face, wiping the wetness from my eyes and cheeks, and blinked slowly, trying to push away the pictures rapidly flipping through my mind. When I was finally able to focus on Einstein, she was watching me with a mixture of pain and horror on her face.

"How did I not know?"

"Because I couldn't let you," she said honestly.

A wheezing laugh sounded in my throat. "Einstein—"

"I knew one day it might go too far. He might not stop until it was too late. But I couldn't see a way out because one part of me was terrified of the consequences, and the other part of me still needed to help him."

I wanted to shake her.

I wanted to yell at her.

I wanted to demand to know why fixing someone who couldn't be fixed was so much more important to her than her own life.

The words all got caught up inside me, twisted and chaotic and unable pass my lips. I was hearing Einstein's voice in my head on repeat from the night of Johnny's funeral.

"I couldn't fix him. There was something missing, and I couldn't find it, but I tried. I tried so hard."

"I failed."

In that moment, I understood Einstein's feelings for Johnny in a way I never had before.

Her love for me? I'd never questioned it. Not once.

It had always been there. Yelled loud and clear whenever she looked at me but never spoken aloud while Johnny was alive.

I thought her only reason for staying with Johnny was because there hadn't been any other option unless she wanted to leave both Einstein and Avery behind. Become someone else completely.

I'd known she loved Johnny. Of course I had. But I'd thought her love for him had long been dulled, faded from his psychopathic tendencies. Until all that was left was a girl trapped with a man she cared for in the way you thought of your first love.

If she were truly wrecked after having endured years of whatever the hell he'd done to her, because she thought *she* failed *him?* Then maybe I'd had it wrong.

Maybe she loved him more than I realized.

And I didn't know what to do with that.

"I need you to leave."

My head snapped up to find her looking at me, her expression completely, utterly broken. "Why?"

Her face crumpled with pain. "Because I can't do this, Maverick."

"Do *what*? Love me? Be with me? I don't know what *this* means."

"Have you staring at me with that look on your face like you don't know what to do with me anymore." Her voice cracked and wavered and more tears slipped down her cheeks. "I don't know if I'll be able to give you what you want, and I can't do that to you. Not after everything we went through. Not after how long you waited for this."

I dropped my head back against the wall, a growl of frustration ripping from my throat. "You and I both know you're not vague, Einstein. So don't start now."

I spread my arms out wide and gave her a questioning look, my throat felt thick with emotion when she just sat there watching me with that devastated expression.

"How long I waited for this what? *You*? Yeah, I've waited for you for a damn long time. I would've waited my entire goddamn life just to tell you I love you, even if it took my dying breath to do it. And when they lowered me into the ground, they would be burying the happiest man who ever lived because I would have spent my life near you . . . *by* you. As for you not knowing if you'll be able to give me what I want? What exactly do you think I want?"

She looked away and locked her jaw, but it still shook fiercely.

"An actual relationship? I'll get over it. Your body? Like

I said—ten years. Never once touched you. I think I'll be okay. Showers and I have become best friends. But if you mean your *heart*? Then, yeah," I mumbled, barely able to make the words come out, "that changes things. That's something I always thought I had. If I don't . . . then what the hell am I doing?"

"Of course it's yours," she said, her voice strained.

"Then I don't give a shit about the rest."

"You can't know that," she said adamantly. "You can't know that you won't end up resenting me for not being able to sleep with you."

I nodded. A huff pushed from my lungs. "If we were normal, you would be right, I wouldn't be able to know that. But we aren't. We've spent a decade with a foot separating us, not saying how we felt. If we can get through that, we can get through anything."

"I hated what you went through for me before. I hated that you were waiting for something that might never be able to happen. I can't ask you to do this."

"Jesus, Avery. Don't you get it? I love you. I would go to hell and back for you. This is nothing in comparison."

I breathed a sigh and pushed from the floor. When I got to the bed, I sat with a foot between us. It felt like how it used to be, and I hated it.

Twisting to face her, I said, "But none of that matters if *you* don't want to do this with me."

"It feels like I've been waiting my entire life to spend the rest of it with you." Her eyes met mine. "I would let you go to give you a life you deserve, but it would kill me."

I searched her pained expression for a moment. "I'm not going anywhere."

Seventeen

Einstein
TEN MONTHS AGO

My lips tipped up in a hint of a smile when my headphones were pulled away from my head. I scanned my screens quickly, my fingers tapping faster as I hurried to finish.

An attempt that went to hell the second Maverick's hand smoothly slid around my waist and his lips ghosted along my neck.

In the last two months, these kisses had become one of my favorite things.

Light.

Playful.

Perfect.

Gentle enough to put me at ease.

Sweet enough to make me feel adored.

Enticing enough to leave me wanting more.

Every minute with him over the years—silent or otherwise—had always done the same. I should've known his feather-light touches and playful kisses wouldn't have been any different.

My eyelids fluttered shut, and my head rolled to the side, giving him easier access. "I thought you were working tonight. What are you doing here so early?" The question fell from my lips on a moan when his teeth grazed my skin.

"Early?" A rumble of a laugh sounded in his chest, and he pressed one last quick kiss to my neck before his fingers were at my chin, lifting my head so I was looking into his eyes. "Einstein, it's one in the morning."

I blinked quickly and then moved my head from his hand to check both my phone and the time on my computer.

"What time did you sit down?" His words were all a tease when I looked back at him.

Nearly ten hours ago.

I would've put money on it only having been two hours.

The look on my face must have answered for me because a knowing smile pulled on Maverick's lips. "That long, huh?"

I'd come home early from the ARCK office to continue working on an issue. It was something I could've done there—could've done anywhere—but my computer was the best for all situations, including this one. I'd built it that way.

It did everything I needed in a way that kept up with my mind.

A lot of computers and laptops had lost their lives because they weren't up to the challenge that was me.

So, I'd taken what I needed and built the perfect ones.

Frankensteins, sure. But they were the best.

"It was important," I said, an automatic response I used to use to explain or defend something Johnny had always been so frustrated with.

"I thought Dare needed you to pull something. Why aren't you working?"

"Why the fuck are you still working? You've been in here all day."

It had been endless and constantly changing, depending on his mood and whether Dare was keeping him busy.

Maverick folded his arms over his chest and gave an easy shrug before checking the screens. "Never doubted it was. What is it this time?"

I pulled my bottom lip between my teeth as I studied him.

I should've known Maverick wouldn't have said anything about my day. He never had before. Then again, I'd never done much work around him because I'd always wanted to give him whatever time I had.

His eyes found mine again when he realized I was still watching him. His face pinched in question.

"Is everything always okay with you?"

The crease between his brows deepened. "What do you mean?"

"Everything is always fine with you. You're never bothered by it. I stay with Johnny? You're fine. I work all day? You're fine. I don't show up somewhere because I'm locked in here? You're fine."

His jaw set. "You and I both know I was never *fine* with you and Johnny. There was nothing I could do about it, so there wasn't a point in making us more miserable than we were. And what are you expecting? Me to be pissed that you're working?"

I didn't say anything. Just continued to watch him.

Because I didn't expect that. Not from him.

But I was used to it.

And maybe there was a part of me that was waiting for it.

Things had been so easy between us since Johnny died—with the exception of that night two months ago—and I wasn't used to *easy*.

Watching Maverick and having him shamelessly watch me back.

Falling into his embrace.

Sitting on one of our beds or couches with my feet in his lap while I worked until long after he'd fallen asleep.

Everything between us was as natural as breathing . . .

It was all too perfect.

It left me happy and carefree in a way I didn't recognize.

And down deep, something was taunting me, telling me it couldn't last.

Maverick unwrapped one of his hands to gesture to the computer screens. "From day one, I knew exactly who you were and what you were passionate about. I'm not gonna get in the way of that. Not to mention, whenever you are locked in on whatever it is that day or hour or minute, it is usually for a reason. But the times when it is us, it's *just* us. There's no reason for me to be mad."

"And if this starts cutting in on our time more?"

Another easy shrug. Another look that told me he couldn't understand why I didn't already know his answer. "Before, I was lucky if I got you to myself for minutes or an hour a week. There isn't anything stopping us from being together now. Work will cut in on that sometimes. It's fine."

"Fine," I murmured with a soft laugh. "Like I said, always fine."

Confusion swam in his eyes. "Do you not want me to be okay with what you do? Do you want me to have a problem?"

"No. I don't. I just—shit," I said on a breath and turned to face the screens.

He huffed, sharp and bemused. "You know me better than to think I would. Or that I would stand in the way of what you do. Or that I wouldn't understand if you lost an entire day to your work—even if it did cut in on time with you."

"I know." I dropped my head into my hand and released a sigh.

An apology was on the tip of my tongue, teasing my lips when I felt him step up beside me.

Chills flashed across my body, and my breath caught when he slowly fisted his hand in my hair and tilted my head back so I was looking at him.

His words were gruff and strained when he said, "I'm not him."

"I know." I kissed the tips of his fingers when his other hand came up to cradle my face and then pressed my hand on top of his, keeping it there. "I've never thought you were, and I don't expect you to be. I don't . . . I think I'm just frustrated and I'm projecting it."

Warm lips passed across my forehead before he released me. "Tell me what's happening."

I released a sigh and went back to what I'd been working on.

"I noticed something wrong with the ARCK system earlier in the week. Really, when it comes down to it, it was minor, but still wrong." My fingers paused on my keyboard, and I chewed on my lip for a second before tipping my head back to look at him again. "It's like the equivalent of walking into the main Borello house and finding a paperclip had been slightly moved in the office."

He sent me a grateful smile before his eyes moved back to the screens. "So, this paperclip . . ."

A few more passes across the keyboard finished everything. "If I weren't me, I could've done it when doing any number of things. Changing the site. Securing the firewall. Anything."

"But you are you," he said when I didn't continue.

"Exactly. But there wasn't a trace of anyone slipping in to the system. There wasn't a trace of the paperclip being moved at all. It just *was*." I turned the chair so I could face him and folded my arms under my chest. "And I've been so distracted lately that I blamed it on that."

"On me."

I pulled my bottom lip into my mouth, but that somehow only fueled my smile when his heated stare followed the action. "On your lips."

On the way you've shown me what it truly means to be cherished.

On the way you've been so careful and gentle with me.

On the way I've fallen more in love with you every day.

"If you expect me to apologize, you're going to be disappointed."

"I'd be offended if you did." After a moment, my face fell. "But that paperclip has been bugging me. So every day since, I've been watching and watching and watching. Today, someone slipped right in while I was working. By the time I realized they were there, everything was already patched up behind them, completely covering their tracks, but they were still in there moving more than paperclips."

Maverick's body was tense, his face set in a mixture of frustration and anticipation. For the rest of what I would say. For orders to take care of the threat. To protect me and our family.

I tilted my head and scrunched my face. "Again, basically the equivalent of going through a house silently, picking things up and placing them back in their original spot. I just happened to see them being picked up."

"What were they looking at?"

"Trying to look at documents. They hadn't even made it into one of our folders before they must have realized that I was on to them and trying to track them. And then they were *gone.*" I waved my hand through the air. "No trace. No fingerprints. No DNA. No nothing." I tried to smile, tried to force a laugh at my attempt to tell Maverick in a way he would understand, but I couldn't find it in me to. My stare fell to the floor as frustration and unease crawled up my spine. "No one has ever made it past my security. And they've done it twice . . . that I know of."

Whoever was behind this was good. Not that I would admit that aloud.

"ARCK only?"

I glanced up, the question in my eyes.

"Did this only happen with ARCK, or did it happen with Borello businesses too?"

"ARCK. But I've spent the day reinforcing security on both, as well as my personal system, and moving important information elsewhere. Which might be pointless depending on how long they've spent in the system before."

He nodded, his eyes drifting to the screens. "What do you need me to do?"

"Kiss me."

Those eyes darted back to me, heat and amusement and mischief swirling within them.

I reached for him, fisting my hand in his shirt and pulling him closer and sighing against his lips when they pressed to mine.

"Forgive me for my moment of crazy," I whispered against the kiss.

"Moment?"

A breath of a laugh escaped my throat.

I pushed against his chest, causing him to stumble back a step, and feigned hurt.

His answering laugh was soft and throaty and had me already reaching for him again when he hauled me from the chair.

Take me to bed.

I didn't have to give voice to the words; Maverick was already stepping back and sinking onto the bed with me still in his arms.

It was as if we'd done this thousands of times.

I curled my legs around his hips, digging my knees into the mattress and giving him the opportunity to sit up against the pillows.

Our kiss didn't falter. It never did.

His lips moved against mine in a teasing combination of soft brushes and firm, passionate kisses. His tongue tortured mine in a slow dance of promises and hints of what he could give me—what he *wanted* to give me.

Every brush, every stroke, threatened to drive me mad.

As they always did. Chaste kisses that slowly built, each

time getting more frenzied until all I wanted was him on me. Against me. In me.

But he never pushed.

He always stopped us before we could reach a point where memories of Johnny could overrun my mind.

I had been thankful. I *was* thankful.

But I wanted us.

I wanted Maverick and me. I wanted to move past what had happened, but I wouldn't know if I could unless we tried.

And, *God*, I wanted to try.

I pressed my forehead to Maverick's and rocked my hips against his, a shuddering breath ripping from me when the friction from his jeans nearly set me off.

I could feel the kiss slow.

Could feel him start to pull away.

And I knew if I didn't do something, I would lose this chance.

Touch me, touch me, touch me . . .

But the words wouldn't come.

A knot formed in my throat, stopping me from speaking at all.

Not because I didn't want this, but because I didn't know how to do this.

I gripped his hands, and he shifted, moving just enough to taste my lips again.

My movements were shaky, but I'd never been more sure.

"Einstein." My name was a wary whisper from his lips as I guided his hands back to my body.

I opened my eyes to find him staring at me.

Eyes burning with need and want and passion and worry.

Begging.

Pleading.

I placed one of his hands just below my breast and released a shuddering breath when he pushed up, cupping and kneading and pinching.

His eyes never once moved from my own.

His breaths deepened and his grip on me tightened when I moved his other hand down.

"Einstein . . ." He curled his fingers around mine and stopped the movement just before we reached where I was aching for him. "Are you sure?"

I needed this. I needed his touch. I needed the feel of his skin on mine.

I nodded, the movement slight, but it was all I was able to manage.

A deep crease formed between his brows. Uncertainty wavered in his eyes. And I felt it, the second his muscles tensed as he began pulling away.

"Please." The word came out strained. "I want . . ." My chest heaved and my eyes shut as frustration and embarrassment nearly overwhelmed me.

I want you to touch me.

I want the feel of you on me.

I want to feel you inside me, making me yours.

So many thoughts swirled through my head, none of which I was able to voice. I wasn't that girl.

Never had been, probably never would be.

Maybe I could have been before . . .

But I would never know.

There was one truth, filling my mouth and *demanding* to be heard. "I need you."

It was a broken whisper.

A strained breath.

A gun shot that shook the room with its strength.

Maverick crushed his mouth to mine. His hands were in my hair and cradling my neck, deepening the kiss and demanding more.

More of the kiss.

More of my heart.

More of my soul.

More of me.

How could he not know that I was already his?

He could have it all.

My back was hitting the bed and Maverick was curling over me, hands searching and cherishing and worshipping.

Everything felt rushed and in slow motion.

Each grip was rough and sent the message that he couldn't get enough.

Each stroke of his fingers was slow, as if he had years to watch the bumps rise along my skin in his wake.

Our kisses were the same intoxicating mixture. Hard and breath-stealing that seamlessly transformed into the softest teases that had my heart and chest swelling.

Piece after piece of my clothing fell to the floor, leaving me nearly naked beneath him.

And it wasn't enough.

Because he was still dressed, and I needed to feel him against me.

When he dipped to press his mouth over the lace of my bra, I arched off the bed, trying to get closer to him and silently asking for more.

My hands stilled where I had his shirt halfway up his back when his teeth grazed my nipple. And then my nails were digging into his skin when he bit, rolling the hardened bud with his teeth.

I hurried to pull the shirt over his head when he released my breast, and then I reached for him, pulling him back to me and pressing my mouth to his in a fevered kiss I wanted to last forever.

"Need you," he said against the kiss.

"Yes."

I felt the corners of his mouth twitch into a grin. His chest moved harshly against mine. "Need you to tell me." He nipped my bottom lip before pulling away, his wild eyes searching my own. "Tell me to stop or tell me what you want. I won't do anything you aren't ready for."

Everything. Everything.

Please touch me. Love me.

My mouth was still slightly parted from our kiss, but all that left it was my ragged breaths.

"Avery," he whispered, his voice pleading.

"I can't," I finally managed to say. "I can't—I don't know how." A frustrated laugh crawled up my throat. "I know the words and what I want, but I don't know how to make myself say them. Not with you—especially with you."

"Why with me?"

My brows furrowed as I tried to figure out how to explain something I wasn't sure I fully understood. "I can talk about it, but not when it comes to me because I've always hated the thought of it—for obvious reasons—and I was scared of the thought of it with you."

His face fell, but I hurried to explain before he could question it or let his mind wander.

"I've wanted this with you for so long, but I think a part of me was always afraid this would come and it would change everything between us. That, once it happened, it would be the end of everything I've waited for."

Maverick's relief and confusion clashed, making him hunch in on himself at the same time as he dipped to brush his lips across mine.

"Death won't be the end of us."

A claim.

A vow.

On my heart and body and soul.

And then his mouth was slanting over mine, and he was begging entrance with his tongue. One hand was in my hair and the other was trailing over my breast and down the dip in my waist.

Down, down, down until he was spreading my thighs with his hips.

My body bowed against the bed when his fingers finally, *finally* touched where I was aching.

For him. For relief. For everything.

I broke from the kiss, struggling to catch my breath when it felt like the air had thinned and my head was spinning.

He teased me with strong, sure fingers. Moving against me in a way I'd only ever dreamed of. And then he was pushing inside me.

One finger.

Then two.

My mouth opened with a silent moan, and my body trembled.

Forever. I would've waited forever for this touch.

Every touch was a brand on my body.

Every touch was enough to make me fall into a place I never wanted to come back from.

Every touch was filled with so much control that, if I were to say stop, he would be gone from me and the bed before the word could finish leaving my lips.

Tentative, yet there was no doubting that each movement he made was another part of his claim on me.

And I got it . . . I finally understood why people cried.

Because I'd never experienced anything so gentle or filled with passion and love.

I'd known I deserved more than the emotionless sex that later turned forceful and abusive . . .

But I hadn't known it could *feel* like this.

And Maverick was only touching me.

Placing one hand on Maverick's chest so I could feel his erratically racing heart, which somehow perfectly matched mine, I threaded the fingers of my other hand through his hair and pulled until our foreheads were pressed together.

Soft, soft lips brushed across mine.

The words I'd only heard in my head for so many years blowing against my mouth as he breathed life to them. "I love you."

My heart lurched.

My spirit soared.

I pressed my hand harder to his chest. My lips moved with my muted words. *I love you. I love you. I love you.*

I shuddered when he pressed his thumb to my clit and pumped his fingers into me harder, faster, the passion fueling his movements in no way lessening.

My body tightened, and my stomach knotted and warmed, the feeling growing more pronounced as he built me up higher and higher.

Until I felt like I was flying and falling all at once.

Countless seconds suspended in the unknown until I came crashing down, my whole world trembling as pleasure rushed through me again and again. The feeling so pure and intense and just *everything* that I felt dizzy.

I never wanted it to end.

I never wanted this moment to end.

I wanted to take every feeling and every touch and find a way to make them last. To make this night last.

"So damn beautiful."

I opened my eyes to find Maverick staring down at me, the look in his excited eyes saying so much more.

A soft cry fell from my lips when he removed his fingers, and I wanted to beg him not to leave. Beg him to continue. Beg him to let *me* do something for him.

But every time I tried to work my throat to make the words come out, it continued to betray me.

His face softened with understanding. "This was enough. More than."

My head shook against the bed. "It will never be enough. Not with you."

I moved my hands down his bare chest and stomach, landing on the button of his jeans.

He opened his mouth, and I knew before he spoke that his words would be an echo of what he'd already said, that what we'd already done was enough. That he didn't want to push me.

"Please," I choked out before he could utter the words. "I want this." I swallowed thickly, searching his hesitant stare. "I want this if you do."

He huffed, something between amusement and uncertainty. "That has never been in question."

After another few seconds of studying my eyes, he pressed his hands to the bed and pushed himself up. A silent assent to continue what I'd started. The muscles in his arms rippled beneath his skin as he waited, his eyes on mine as I pushed the denim and his boxer briefs past his narrow hips and down his legs.

My chest heaved with ragged breaths.

I finally looked down. My heart thundered when I took in his thick length, standing proud and begging to be touched.

Gently, I ran my hand over the large symbol tattooed into his side, moving down, down to trail the tips of my fingers along his length. My mouth curved into a small smile when a tremor ran through his body and a breath rushed from him. It was as if just that simple touch alone had threatened to undo him.

I knew the feeling.

Glancing up, I fisted my hand around him, savoring the way his eyes closed, back bowed, and arms shook as I slowly stroked him.

The fierce look in his eyes when he opened them again had my breath catching.

Need.

Lust.

Love.

Promises of what was to come and what he wanted to give me.

And I wanted it all.

I curled my legs up around his hips, positioning him at my entrance as I continued to work him slightly faster, my grip tighter. The tip of him teasing my sensitive flesh and driving me wild.

His mouth crashed onto mine in a hard, quick kiss. His breaths fanned across my face and his chest moved roughly against mine.

"You're sure?" It was a tense plea that came tumbling out on a ragged breath.

I could hear it in his words and feel it in the trembling of his body. He was holding himself back, ready to do whatever I needed, but he was about to snap.

I lifted my head just enough so my lips teased his when I whispered, "I'm yours."

Within a beat of my thunderous heart, Maverick had my hands in his.

In another, one joined hand was locked in my hair, the other was pinned to the bed.

And then he was pushing into me.

Rough.

Hard.

As though he'd been held back for so long, and his restraints had broken. As though he couldn't get close to me fast enough.

It was everything I'd never wanted again, and everything I wanted with Maverick forever.

Because this wasn't an uncaring, forced act.

This was unrestrained passion.

This was love, finally set free.

Driving into me again and again until my whimpers and moans were nothing more than breathy, incoherent pleas.

Until I was gripping his hands tighter, knowing I needed to be locked to him so I wouldn't fly away.

Until that warm tingling began in my belly again, making my body buzz with anticipation of what was coming.

He moved our hands from my hair down between our bodies, his rhythm never faltering as he loved me in a way I never knew possible. When he brushed our intertwined fingers against my clit, my mouth opened on a cry that was muted by his lips.

My body was already so on fire, I wasn't sure I could handle more.

He didn't relent, though, as he coaxed the pleasure out of me.

His mouth moved down my jaw, and when he urged, "Come on," his voice was strained and gravelly and dripped with lust.

Another brush.

Another tremor rolling down my spine as his hips moved roughly. Thoroughly.

"*Avery.*" He pressed our fingers harder against my clit and grazed his teeth along the soft skin of my neck.

And I fell.

Into the abyss. Apart beneath him. More in love.

I succumbed to it all . . . to the pleasure racing through my veins.

To the sensation of him trembling above me as his movements became erratic for the first time before he found his release inside me.

To the profound love pouring from Maverick when he pressed his mouth to mine over and over again.

And I was left torn, wondering how I'd ever lived without this while knowing I would've waited forever.

His hips moved slowly, prolonging my orgasm and the moment before he finally rested on top of me, our bodies still connected.

He pulled his head back just enough so his lips brushed

mine when he spoke, and I felt the hint of my favorite smile on his lips before he said, "That . . . that was supposed to go differently."

I pushed against him until he leaned back enough for me to search his eyes. "What do you mean?"

Hesitantly, he answered, "I was going to take my time with you. Go slow." His smile widened, and he let his head fall. "God, I planned to go so fucking slow."

I shifted slightly beneath him, enough that a moan slid past my lips and sounded in his chest, and curled my legs around his hips again. "Then go slow."

His head snapped up. The change in his expression was instant.

Pure excitement and satisfaction immediately transformed to need and heat.

Chills flashed across my skin when Maverick swept the tips of his fingers up my spine before tracing the Borello symbol that decorated the base of my neck.

The same one that covered his entire left side.

Five lines.

Four horizontal—each shorter than the one above it.

One vertical—slashing through the middle.

All surrounded by a circle.

I mumbled something incoherent and shifted my head to look at him.

It was early. Or late.

Still.

The sun had risen, and for the most part, we'd spent the hours since he'd come over wrapped up in each other's arms. Kissing. Touching. Exploring. Loving.

Each time we'd had sex after the first had been slow, but never any less powerful.

Slow . . . that was what Maverick said he'd planned to do, and that was what he had done.

He'd taken his time with me, cherishing and worshipping me.

I was exhausted in the best way possible.

I ached in a way that made me crave more.

How could I have ever known it was like this?

How *didn't* I know?

I arched against his hand and lifted my bottom, seeking his touch as his fingers trailed down.

"Insatiable," he murmured.

The corners of my mouth tilted up. Before the smile could fully form, he slid a finger into me, stealing the breath from my lungs.

"More?"

My lips pressed into a thin line, and I buried my face into the pillow to hide the heat I could feel spreading across my cheeks. Part embarrassment. Part unease.

Maverick's lips went to my ear. "Even that? You really don't like talking about it at all?"

I could hear his confusion, but horrible memories that stemmed from darkness wasn't something I wanted to explain.

Not when Maverick was touching me.

Definitely not when I was still riding the high from this entire morning.

A slow chill crept up my spine as old memories invaded my mind before I could push them away.

"Tell me you want this."
"Tell me you like it when I fuck you. Tell me."
"Come on, Einstein. Beg. Beg for more. Scream."

Maverick's finger had stilled, but after a few seconds, he resumed. Tentative at first but then more confidently as my muscles relaxed.

I hadn't realized I'd tensed.

I arched my back more, silently begging for things I couldn't give voice to, and whimpered into the pillow when another finger was added.

I trembled, my legs nearly giving out when Maverick situated himself behind me and teased me with his tongue.

Slow, torturous licks and firm flicks against my clit.

Again and again until I couldn't take it any longer.

I twisted onto my back, grabbing and pulling him closer. My movements frantic and pleading.

His mouth twitched into a smirk. "You're gonna kill me, Avery."

A moan tumbled from my mouth when he slid inside me. When I spoke, my voice was barely more than a breath. "I won't apologize."

He was still smiling when he slanted his mouth over mine.

All Maverick with a hint of me.

Intoxicating.

Heady.

I wanted this forever.

Forever, forever, forever.

Hands searched and teased and drove me to the brink of madness as he pushed us over the edge. All the while his hips moved in slow, forceful movements. Long, rhythmic strokes.

"I love you," I whispered when he dragged lazy kisses down my chest before falling to the bed and wrapping me in his arms.

"Always loved you." His eyes slowly shut. "Always."

I let my eyelids follow. A nagging itch at the back of my mind finally formed into a thought and bubbled up. "You need to get condoms when we wake up."

I felt his chest move with his silent laugh. "Fuck that."

I cracked an eye open. "I'm serious. I'm not getting pregnant, Maverick."

Maverick tensed before his eyes slowly opened. "What about your birth control?"

"I stopped taking it when Johnny died."

It took all of five seconds for my words to finally click and his face to pale. He jerked to sitting and ran a hand through his hair, gripping at it. "Jesus, Einstein, what? That's something I should've known. You knew we were getting to this point. Or that we were going to," he said, his tone getting more agitated and frustrated as he continued. "After everything—the way you reacted to Lily and Dare's pregnancy—you would let us go an entire night without some kind of protection. Do you want to be in their situation?"

My gut twisted uneasily at the thought, but I didn't let it show.

I pushed myself to sitting and moved back to the headboard.

When he turned to look at me, I steeled my jaw and lifted my chin.

"Are you done? Because I have a few things to say about that."

He didn't respond, just locked his jaw to match me.

"You're rambling like Libby does when she can't find the right outfit, and it's kind of annoying. It's morning, not night. Also, fuck you if you want to blame this all on me. You could've asked me rather than expected me to be on birth control. But I'll take responsibility for my part and apologize. I'm sorry," I sneered with all the sarcasm I could muster.

Maverick's eyes narrowed.

"I'm sorry I was so caught up in you and what was happening and that it was *actually, finally* happening that I never stopped to say, 'Hey, Maverick. Why don't you leave and go get a fucking condom instead?' And, correct me if I'm wrong, but if for some reason—and please, for the love of God, someone kill me before this happens—I ever find myself in Lily and Dare's situation, I would think it wouldn't just be *my* situation. It would be *ours*. If that didn't clear it up for you, no, I don't want to be in their situation. You of all people should know that."

By the time I was finished, Maverick was staring at me with a mixture of helplessness and remorse.

"I'm sorry," he whispered, honesty ringing through his words. "For flipping out. For assuming. All of it." He dragged a hand over his face and lifted a shoulder in a brief shrug. "I panicked."

"That was obvious."

His chest jerked with a silent laugh. "I *assumed* because I knew you were on it before."

He opened his mouth to continue, but I quickly said, "I hated being on that."

A mumbled, dirty, confession.

That was exactly what that admission was.

When Maverick's brow pinched with confusion, I

explained, "Johnny was different from the rest of us, he wanted kids. Lots of them. He thought if there were more people like him—with his views—the Borello gang would eventually go back to the old mafia ways. He would've been livid if he'd known I was on birth control, I had to hide it in Libby's bathroom." I lifted my hands slightly before letting them fall to the bed. "After a while, even before it got really bad, I started associating the pills with him."

He nodded, just a hint of movement. "Understood." A few seconds passed before he said, "We'll figure something out. Because after this, there's no way in hell I'm going to want to use condoms."

I caught his stare for only a second before I dropped mine to the bed.

"Avery."

My eyes bounced back to his at my name.

My heart reacted wildly just from the gentle tone of his voice.

He swallowed, his throat bobbing with the action. His mouth opened and then snapped shut. Another swallow. Then he leaned forward and reached for my hand. "If *we* ever find ourselves in that situation, I swear to you it will be just as much my situation as it is yours."

Oh dear God, no. Please no.

Please don't do this to me.

I wouldn't be able to handle it if Maverick wanted kids someday.

That was the one thing I refused to give myself, him, anyone.

"Do you . . ." I licked my lips, which suddenly felt dry. "Do you want kids someday?"

He looked as if he were in pain.

I knew it was over how I would respond to his answer. But I couldn't figure out which way he was leaning, and it terrified me.

Maverick's eyes met and held mine. "I don't know if you didn't want kids before because it was with *Johnny*, but I can't—Avery, I can't. If we lived different lives, if we weren't involved in everything we have been and are, then yes. I would. But no, not like this. Never like this. I'm sorry."

My relief was so intense it made my chest ache from the force. "Don't be sorry." My head shook. "I meant what I said to Dare and Lily, they're putting a target on that kid's back. They should've known better. Bringing a child into our lives is the stupidest, most selfish thing any of us could ever do. I refuse to."

When he reached for me, I went willingly into Maverick's arms and settled against his chest when he laid us down. "I'm sorry for making that worse than it needed to be," he mumbled against the top of my head. "Sleep. I'll run to the store when I wake up so I can make it up to you."

My mouth twitched into a playful grin.

I could think of so many ways he could make it up to me where the store wouldn't be required.

Before I could begin to initiate any of them, sleep dragged me under.

Eighteen

Einstein
NINE MONTHS AGO

"You're cheating."

My chest pitched with a silent laugh as I covered his fist with my hand again. "Am not."

"There you go again. There's no way you can play this long without losing."

I looked up at him from beneath my lashes. "You doubt me?"

Maverick smiled that smile that always threatened to undo me. "Never."

I felt my mouth tip up in response just before I pounded my fist on top of his hand.

"Okay, but you're fucking cheating," he said confidently. "Pretty sure you're supposed to let me win on my birthday."

"*Pretty sure* that isn't how this works. And it isn't my fault I'm so much smarter than you."

Before I could start another round, he snatched my hands and used them to pull me against his chest. A giggle climbed up my throat when he passed both my hands into one of his so he could dig his fingers into my side. "What was that?"

"I'm smarter than yo—" My words cut off with a sharp laugh, and I jerked against him and the couch when he attacked harder than before. "Okay, okay, okay."

He narrowed his eyes playfully before leaning closer. "What was that?"

"You tell me what you're about to do."

Before our lips could touch, he jerked back, his brows pinching together. "What?"

My shoulders sagged in disappointment, but I sat up and returned to my position on the couch, facing him, legs crossed, hand in a fist in front of me. "Let's go again . . . go slow."

I kept my hand trained on his as we bounced our hands three times.

On the third rise, I called out, "Rock," and laid my hand out flat for paper.

Maverick just stared at me with wide, disbelieving eyes for a few moments. "How the hell did you do that?"

"When you're doing *rock*, you lift your hand all the way before doing it. *Paper*, you don't lift it at all. *Scissors*, you only lift it about halfway."

His mouth slowly twitched into my favorite smile again —all hesitation and secrets.

Ones I was dying to know.

"Tell me one of your secrets," I begged.

He blinked quickly, thrown by the sudden change. "Secrets? I don't have any from you."

"That can't be true. Everyone has secrets, and you smile at me like you have so many that are just waiting to be uncovered."

Surprise and embarrassment covered his face before he could drop his head to hide them both. "I, uh . . . I don't know how I smile at you, but the only words I've ever kept from you were words we couldn't say before. Now? There's nothing." He glanced at me. "Tell me one of yours."

A lifetime of nightmares flashed through my mind, making my stomach clench and my heart pound painfully.

Some, Maverick already knew.

Others, there was no reason to ever give voice to because they were better kept silent.

I shook my head and lifted my shoulder in a slight shrug. "I can't think of anything."

He gave me a look that told me he didn't buy it but wasn't going to push. "What did you expect me to say?"

"I don't know," I said honestly. "You're secretly smarter than I am and just didn't want to hurt my feelings?"

He dropped his head back and laughed.

"You prefer brunettes or blondes instead."

When he looked at me, the heat in his eyes told me that wasn't true.

"You want to get married someday."

Maverick's head jerked back, expression serious. "Wait, you don't?"

The question was out so quickly it stunned me into silence for a few moments. "No," I said slowly, drawing out the word. "I didn't realize you did. You know, in this life."

He'd told me about how he thought his life would've turned out if he'd never joined the mafia.

But he had.

This wasn't the suburbs—okay, technically it was. But the white picket fence life wasn't ours. It never would be.

"I didn't—I mean, before—that changed," he stammered and then shifted back against the couch to stare at me for a second. "Why don't you?"

"It comes with so many expectations, like having kids. I don't want that forced on me," I whispered. "I just want this . . . *us*—days and nights of you and me—for the rest of my life."

"We can have that. We *will*," he assured me, but his tone was different from just a minute before.

Quiet.

Reserved.

"You really planned to get married."

A breath of a laugh left him, but he didn't respond. He just gave me a look that said it no longer mattered.

In that second, something broke inside me. It made me ache and want to give him the world.

Because I knew he would do it for me.

"When you look at what we've gone through just to get here, it isn't important," he said quickly, trying to brush it off. "Being able to actually have a life with you is."

Those were my words he was saying. My thoughts.

How did all of this switch?

Why was I so against it in the first place?

The thought hadn't finished forming in my head before I knew. Because nearly a year ago, marriage meant a life sentence to an animal. It meant answers to questions I'd been evading—like *why* hadn't I gotten pregnant yet? *When* was I going to?

But that wasn't Maverick. That wasn't *us*.

A defeated sort of laugh sounded in his throat. "Let's just forget we talked about this."

I shifted to my knees and pressed against his side. Securing my fingers into his hair, I lifted his head so we were eye to eye.

"I would marry you a hundred times if that was what you truly wanted." The words were hushed, but the honesty in my voice rang loudly.

Want swirled on his expression before he shut it down. "You don't want that."

"I told you, I want you and me for the rest of my life. That means I want what *you* want for our life. Besides, now you've got me thinking about it, and you and I both know I won't stop. So, try to brush this conversation off all you want, but I can see it now, Maverick. I can see it all. One day, you're gonna give me a ring, and I'm gonna have your last—"

He crushed his mouth to mine, swallowing my words and my moan and shifting me so I was straddling his lap.

I slid my hands down his chest and under his shirt. My fingers automatically searched for and pressed against the symbol inked into his skin, only to jerk away when one of the doors to the theater room slammed against the wall.

"Jesus, been looking for you two for an hour."

I shot Diggs a look. "There aren't that many rooms in this house."

"Every minute is like an eternity when you're starving." He whimpered pathetically as he turned to leave. "Would it kill you to stop screwing each other for five seconds so we can eat?"

Neither of us bothered pointing out that we were fully clothed.

I just lazily climbed off the couch and reached for Maverick's hand—for that connection to him—and he followed.

We'd barely made it out of the theater room before Maverick had me against the wall with his mouth pressed to mine.

The kiss was slow and passionate and made my head spin.

"One day?" he asked against my lips.

"One day."

When Diggs shouted across the house, demanding we hurry up, I opened my eyes to find Maverick watching me. Dozens of emotions crossed his face before he pushed away, only to quickly lean back in for one last kiss.

He groaned when I traced his jaw with the tips of my fingers, the sound grating and intoxicating and full of yearning.

"We're coming," he bit out when his name tore through the house again. With a frustrated sigh, he intertwined our fingers and wrapped our joined hands around my back, tucking me close to his side as he led us toward the kitchen.

By the time we made it there, Libby was dropping her head into her open palm, and Dare was murmuring, "Christ, here we go again."

Diggs clutched his chest dramatically. "What do you mean you've never had cake?"

Lily scoffed. "I've had cake. Just not . . ." She shrugged and gestured to the cake in front of the boys. "Birthday cake?" She posed it as a question. "I don't understand the point of it."

"The point of it is to be delicious and bring joy!" Diggs

looked almost offended on the cake's behalf. "Why was your childhood so depressing? Why do your people want nothing more than to steal joy from lives?"

I bit back a laugh and hugged Maverick closer to me. When he tightened his own hold, assuring me he was holding me as close to him as possible, my chest warmed and threatened to burst with contentment.

Lily, who was watching Diggs whisper soothing words to the baked goods, let out a soft giggle as she rubbed her swollen stomach. "Oh yes, us Irish folk really want nothing more than to steal joy."

Diggs's focus shifted back to Lily. "You know what I mean. You didn't know what a fort was. Or what a sleepover entailed. You never had a grilled peanut butter and banana—"

"Still think that's gross."

"Blasphemy!" Diggs yelled.

"Can you just cut the damn cake?" Libby asked impatiently.

Diggs slammed his hands onto the counter, narrowly missing the massive cake he demanded every year for his and Maverick's birthday. "I want to know what the hell they did for birthdays if they didn't have cake."

Lily sighed and pretended to think about it as she rested her head on Dare's shoulder. After a few seconds, she shrugged. "Tried not to draw attention to ourselves so we didn't die."

Considering *we* were the people who would've done the killing, you would think the mood in the room would dip with her words.

It didn't.

Diggs grinned mischievously and a wicked laugh built in Maverick's chest.

Dare's smile was wide before he pressed a kiss on top of her head. "And, yet, you still managed to die before ending up in my arms."

"Yeah, well, sacrifices had to be made. Plus, you have cake."

Dare pinched her hip. Diggs shouted, "Hell yeah! My girl knows what's up." When Dare narrowed his eyes on him, Diggs held up his hands in surrender. "I'm just saying that she knows cake's important. Maybe more important than you."

In a move so fast Diggs didn't have time to prepare, Dare leaned across the counter, grabbed a fistful of cake, and smashed it against Diggs's face.

His mouth fell open in horror. "What did you do to my precious?"

"Call my girl yours again, see if I don't do more than that."

"It isn't my fault you didn't give her a cake on her birthday."

Dare huffed a laugh. "I gave her a baby."

I dropped my head back to look at Maverick and rolled my eyes.

"I saw that," Dare snapped.

A second later, Diggs was yelling indecipherable words just before I was smacked in the side of the head with something heavy, dense, sweet, and sticky.

Maverick's eyes widened in surprise just before a chunk of cake hit him full on.

"Are you fucking kidding me?" He tried to sound angry, but he hadn't gotten the entire question out before a smile was breaking across his face and a laugh was weaving between his words. He swiped his hands down his face and looked in Dare's direction. "I'm gonna kill you."

I turned in time to see Dare drum his hands on the counter and back away, his body being used as a shield so Lily didn't get caught in the crossfire. "Nice try. Pregnant wife means I'm safe."

Maverick's chest heaved with a laugh. "Asshole."

Dare stuck one of his fingers into his mouth, nodding as he did. "Damn, that's good cake though."

Lily broke from behind her husband and reached for the counter. "I wanted cake."

Dare whispered something in her ear, and she quickly dropped her arm and turned without another word, a secret smile crossing her face as she did.

I looked to Libby and Diggs, who were hunched over the cake with forks—a scowl and gobs of frosting on Diggs's face as he ate—to Maverick, who was still smiling.

He took one look at me and burst out laughing before picking chunks of cake out of my hair and off my shoulder and tossing them into the sink.

"I'm glad you find this funny."

He pressed his cake-covered mouth to mine and whispered, "Hilarious." His frosting covered fingers slid down my throat to my chest. "Shower."

One word.

That was all it took for my heart to take off in a stampede.

Heat swirled in my stomach and an ache built low in my core.

I stepped back, the corner of my mouth tilting up and

giving away everything I was thinking and wanting in that moment.

Clearing my throat, I patted Diggs's shoulder before swiping some of the frosting off the massacred cake. "Happy birthday, Diggs."

I kept my eyes on Maverick's as I licked the frosting off my finger and brushed past him, my smile widening when I heard the groan he tried and failed to suppress.

As soon as I was out of the kitchen, I ran for my bedroom in the Borello house, where we held most of our major events—like birthdays. Before I reached the door, Maverick was there, locking one arm around my waist and banding the other around my chest. He led us through the room and into the bathroom, keeping me tight against him as he kneaded my breast roughly while his lips and teeth sweetly tortured my neck.

I pressed my bottom against his growing erection, my breath catching in my throat as he ground himself harder, making me ache more and more.

I reached back, securing my fingers in his hair, silently pleading with him to take care of me—of us—to make the ache go away.

As if he could hear my thoughts, his hands moved, gripping and teasing as he tore at our clothes and underwear until we were naked and stumbling into the ice-cold shower.

The shock of it stole my breath. His kiss muffled my scream as I hurried away from the water, nearly falling in the process before he caught me and pressed me against the wall.

His breaths were mine, and my laughter was his, but soon, I forgot why we were laughing. All I knew was his kiss and his hands and the feel of him pressing against me.

I wanted the pressure.

I wanted the pleasure.

I wanted the high only he could give me.

Every touch as we cleaned the pieces of crumbled cake and streaked frosting off each other only served to bring us closer to what we were both craving.

Chests heaved with ragged breaths.

Kisses grew frantic.

Touches turned pleading.

He turned me and roughly pressed me to the wall of the shower, his thick length pressing against me, begging and seeking entrance.

The cold tiles contrasted with the warm water, making my head spin and my body feel as if it were climbing higher and higher.

I pressed my breasts to the cold wall and arched against him, moaning when he slid his cock between my legs, teasing my clit over and over and again.

And then he was pressing into me, filling and stretching me.

Trembling.

Whimpering.

"Oh God, Maverick."

He slid out just as slowly, only to push back in.

Once.

Twice.

He gripped my hips tighter. His fingers twitching with barely contained need.

"*Fuck.*"

He was gone and the water was off. Before I could cry

out, beg him not to stop, I was in his arms and we were out of the shower, leaving little pools of water as we went from the bathroom to the room.

His mouth fused to mine for one short, demanding kiss before he was dropping me to the bed, completely soaked, and then he was grabbing his pants and searching through his wallet.

Less than a minute later, he had a condom on and was flipping me onto my stomach and pulling me onto my knees.

I cried out when he pushed into me. Hard. Unrestrained.

His fingers dug into my hips, slipping and struggling to find their grip against my slick skin as he fucked me quickly, roughly.

And in that moment, I didn't want it any other way.

The heat in my stomach built like never before. My legs shook. My mind emptied except for one word on repeat.

More. More. More.

My orgasm ripped through me without warning, forcing a scream from me that I tried to muffle in the comforter. Every part of me trembled with the impact of it.

My body.

My soul.

I'd never felt more alive.

This was some form of heaven I was never supposed to touch, and I wanted to bask in it forever.

Nineteen

Maverick
TODAY

"We've been trying to get in there for the last couple of days," Conor said. "We've tried everything we could think of."

I scrubbed my hands over my face before slanting my head to look over my shoulder. "You've been trying to get in here for days? But you didn't think something might be wrong until today . . ."

Kieran, Jess, and Conor all gestured to the laptop and spoke at the same time.

"The emails—"

"Sutton—"

"A client with a highly delicate case emails every day." Kieran looked pointedly at the computer. "Einstein missed the email on Saturday because we were trying to figure out what was wrong with her. Now we've missed the last two days as well."

I faced the screen again. "So email the client from one of your computers."

"Can't," they said in unison.

This time, I turned fully in the chair to look at them.

The rest of my family was staring at them with varying looks of confusion as well.

"She only emails Einstein," Jess explained, exasperation leaking through her tone. "She emails every day just before noon and from a different email address every time. We can get a few minutes of responses before she has to go. She deactivates the accounts immediately following."

I looked to Diggs and then Dare.

Both were staring at Jess as if she'd lost her mind.

I was glad they were, because it was taking everything in me to refrain from reacting since Kieran was watching my every move.

I swallowed and waited until I thought I could speak evenly. "And that—" An edgy laugh climbed up my throat. "That never seemed suspicious to you? Before . . . or especially now that Einstein's gone?"

My chair was knocked back into the desk.

In the next breath, Kieran was bent over me, a hand on the desk and another by his side.

The air surrounding us seemed to drop a few degrees.

My heart started racing in response to it and the cold, lethal look in his eyes.

Knowing him and with the way Dare and Diggs were shouting, I had no doubt he had a knife in hand.

"I'm tired of the way you're talking to my wife. Understood?"

I slipped the gun out of my jeans and racked the slide. "Put Jess in Einstein's place. Then ask if I understand."

His jaw tensed and eyes flashed with a memory that he clearly didn't want to relive. "Been there."

"Then put your fucking knife away."

After a few seconds of staring me down, he pushed from the desk and stepped back.

I racked the slide again, caught the unused round, and turned to set both it and the gun on the desk before slowly releasing my pent-up breath.

Jesus Christ. That guy is fucking terrifying.

"It did . . . to answer your question," Kieran said from directly behind me. "None of us were sure if she was legit—Einstein especially. Sutton was unreliable and vague. It took some tests before we believed her."

"But our entire case with her relies on these daily emails and responding to let her know our progress," Jess added.

I knew this was what they did.

Helped women.

But at the moment, the lady behind the emails meant nothing to me. Not when Einstein needed me.

I stared at the space for the password again, and then glanced to her user picture, quickly disregarding it when it looked like a photo from the laptop's stock.

After a second, I looked back at the picture, my eyes narrowing as I studied the trees in the picture.

Oak trees.

"Those are oak trees," I said as my mind raced.

Everyone crowded around the chair and desk, trying to see the small picture.

"It's just one of those pictures that come programmed on all computers," Dare murmured, voicing my earlier thought.

I shook my head but didn't respond as I typed in the code we'd always used before emojis became a thing.

04K7R33

Jess pushed through everyone, getting as close to the laptop as possible when the password accepted and everything began loading. "How'd you do that?"

"You don't know her the way I do," I whispered, repeating my earlier words.

I opened up her email and typed Phoenix into the search, but nothing appeared.

A dozen or so unread emails did, though.

Jess murmured curses under her breath and pointed at two that looked like junk. "Those are from Sutton. We need to see those."

I lifted my hands from the keyboard and shot her a look. "We need to find Einstein."

"I know that, Maverick. But Sutton is in a situation with bad people. Einstein's been emailing with her for the last three months—at least. What if this is bleeding over onto Einstein because she was the one helping her?"

"She's right," Conor said. "They've been following Sutton's every move. It's why she started deactivating the email accounts once she began telling us her locations. We need to see those to find out where Sutton currently is."

I went to the first one, tilting my head in Jess's direction as I did. "Bad like what?"

"We don't know," Kieran murmured.

From the tension filling the room and pressing in around me, not knowing was a frustration for them.

"She's been vague," he continued. "One of the reasons we struggled with her in the beginning. Think she's afraid of what she saw and who they are."

"What'd she see?"

"We don't know." His tone was equal parts frustration and anxiousness.

Diggs snorted.

My chest jerked with a muted laugh, but I ground my jaw to keep from voicing my thoughts on the matter.

The whole thing sounded like the biggest bullshit I'd ever heard.

Sorry if you tried to respond yesterday. I waited as long as I could.

I'm worried if I make a big move by bus or something similar, they'll know.

I'm anxious. I can't sleep. I have this feeling they won't let this go on much longer.

Same place. Come.

"You guys aren't worried about walking into a setup?" Dare asked, disbelief weaving through his tone.

Exactly.

"Stop."

My head snapped up. I turned in the chair in time to see everyone else look at where Lily was playing with Beckham in the middle of the floor.

She was looking at Dare with so much disappointment that I cringed for him.

"Maybe she truly is terrified. Or maybe she—" Her ice-blue eyes drifted to Kieran and held for a moment. "It's possible she's in a situation she wants out of and saying anything would only reveal things better kept hidden."

Like when the families in this room had still been at war.

When Dare had wanted Lily dead simply because of who she was.

When Kieran and Lily had still been together because they'd had no other choice, and Lily had pretended to be someone else entirely to get away from her life at Holloway.

When she'd kept secret after secret from all of us to keep herself alive after realizing who we were.

Diggs turned, his eyes wide. "Yeah, this got awkward really fucking fast. Next email."

I waited as long as I could again.

What's the point of emailing every day if you don't respond?

New place. Come . . . or don't. We've made it this long without you.

There was an address at the bottom.

"Look up the address so Jess can call and see if she's there," Conor demanded.

"The fuck she will," Kieran bit out.

"We don't have a lot of options right now."

"I'll call," Jess said over them before lowering her voice. "It's just a call, Kieran."

A motel popped up when I searched the address, and after I gave Jess the number, I pulled up the computer's finder and searched *Phoenix*.

Tons of shit came up that had nothing to do with anything until I finally stumbled upon a folder labeled the same name.

I hurried to open it but was stopped from opening any of the files by a password lock.

When 04K7R33 didn't work, I sat back and drove my hands into my hair, groaning a curse.

"Numerical, Mav," Diggs said, smacking my arm, and then gesturing to the password box which read: These files are protected. Please enter the numerical code.

"I don't know a number that means anything to her that she would use." When he opened his mouth, I quickly added, "Birthdays are out."

I sighed, my head shaking as I tapped out the numbers from the original password.

04733

I bolted upright when that let me in. "No fucking way."

"How the hell?" Conor whispered behind me.

I scanned the first file, my stomach dipping with echoing pains from a year's worth of hurt. "Phoenix isn't a place. It's a guy."

Phoenix Nicolasi. Previously known as: Phoenix De Lange.

Head of Nicolasi family. Chicago, Illinois.

"He's from Chicago." I turned, looking from Dare to Libby. "Any way he's connected to Moretti? Last name De Lange or Nicolasi."

Libby's eyes were wide with old fears.

The Moretti family had ties to ours that went back a century—severed and repaired by a contract that relied solely on Libby.

A bullshit contract. One that was voided when the Morettis tried to take what they felt was theirs.

"Doubt it. I would've heard that name before. But if he is, this has nothing to do with Moretti," Dare said confidently.

I knew he was right.

Besides, Dare and Kieran had gone to Chicago a month ago to make sure the Moretti family knew what would happen if they came after one of us again. And they wouldn't. They couldn't afford more losses like the ones they'd already suffered.

I looked back to the screen, quickly skimming through the rest of the file Einstein had built on the guy, then opened the next file after entering the password again.

It was a scan of her coded writing.

I exited out without bothering.

The next and last was scans of emails between Phoenix and Einstein.

"These weren't in her email," I whispered as I scrolled through them, wondering why she would've needed to delete them.

The first email was from Einstein to Phoenix about three weeks ago.

Mr. De Lange, or is it Mr. Nicolasi now? Kind of hard

to keep up with you when you decide to kill off your surname. This has turned into a long intro . . .

Phoenix,

Don't bother asking how I found you or this email address, I usually find what I need to know.

Including all kinds of information about your wife, your friends, their families. Quite a thing all of you have going on in Chicago.

Not a threat. Just an observation.

As I said, I usually find what I need to know. For the first time, something is eluding me. Then again, it might not be there at all. Which is why I'm contacting you since you know everything there is to know about everyone.

Don't get a big head. No one likes cocky mafia guys.

I have something happening in or around Brentwood, TN.

From what I've heard, there has to be a family or a street gang. But there's no trace of anyone at all.

I need to know what I'm up against, if anything.

You might as well tell me your findings. I'll be checking your system anyway.

At least I'm honest.

Your new favorite Borello,
Einstein

"Brentwood where Sutton started out?" I asked as I scrolled to the next page where Phoenix's response was.

Kieran made a confirming sound in the back of his throat.

Einstein, or may I call you Avery?

I don't keep favorites in other families.

I also wouldn't have asked considering I already know who you are and what you can do.

Quite a thing your blended family of rivals has going on in your small town.

Take that as a threat or don't.

As for Brentwood. I have nothing on the city or surrounding areas, and as you already know, I have everything on everyone.

So I dug.

If I'm right, this is an old-school, hidden-in-plain-sight kind of organization.

Rich bastards who are never connected in any way. By the crimes. By the money. But they make all the decisions. The street gangs in the surrounding areas are controlled and paid off by them.

All the money bounces around and splits to offshores, but eventually, it comes back to their charities and businesses. Eventually. Too far out to trace unless you know what you're looking for.

You only received this response because I had no doubt you would hack my system if you didn't. I also respect your boldness.

But I worked around you.

You want the information?

Folders containing it all are waiting here in Chicago.

Phoenix Nicolasi

"Awesome," Diggs murmured, sarcasm dripping heavily. "So now our leads are Alex or literally anyone within throwing distance of Brentwood. Or she's just out getting folders while playing in the wind."

Twenty

Einstein
TODAY

I THREW MY HANDS OUT, slamming them against the walls of the air duct, and inhaled so sharply and suddenly it sounded like an inverted scream.

My heart faltered and then took off in a dead sprint.

So forcefully that I gripped at my chest, trying to keep it from bursting through.

I *ached*. My lungs, my chest, my throat . . .

I wanted to lay there. To never move again.

It couldn't have been a minute without oxygen, but it'd felt like hours.

I was worn out in a way I'd never experienced. As though I'd gone ten rounds with Johnny and lost.

But the fear of experiencing that suffocation again had me shifting onto my stomach again and forcing myself forward, one inch at a time.

Pure oxygen blasted me in the face, and I sucked it down greedily.

The taste of metal lingered on my tongue, nagging me. Prodding at the back of my mind. Trying to make me remember . . . *understand.*

Get out. Get out. Get out.

I have to get out of here.

I followed the faint light at the end of the duct I was in, determined to get wherever it led. Determined to just get *out.*

As the light grew brighter and brighter, the air blew harder, and something began to change.

The sweet taste in the air.

The way my body slowed and relaxed.

Air shouldn't taste like anything.

Sweet air.

Metal on my tongue.

My stomach dropped, and my chest heaved against the bottom of the duct. Anger swirled through me but faded just as abruptly as it formed.

Because I felt so at ease. Like nothing could touch me.

When had I started smiling—

Nitrous.

I slammed my hand against the metal and screamed in frustration.

Frustration that swiftly fled my mind and body because I just didn't have it in me to hold on to my anger.

Not when I couldn't stop smiling.

Not when I felt so damn good.

That voice in the back of my mind urged harder, louder.

Get out. Get out. Get out.

And I knew she was right.

I knew, I knew, I knew. Because my head was light, and I knew the reason behind it.

I'd been drugged over and over and over today.

At the restaurant.

By the water.

Through the IV.

Through the damned air.

And I didn't know how much more I could take. My shoulders shook with laughter, but I pulled myself forward until I only had two options.

The giant fan in front of me, which was still blowing tainted air at me, or the large grate above my head.

"It's been fun," I murmured to the fan and flipped it off before turning to my back and placing my hands on the grate.

With a slow exhale, I shoved with all the strength I had, cringing when it went flying up, only to come slamming back down.

I stared at the grate above me, mouth wide open. "I'm a superhero."

Pressing the tips of my fingers to it, I lightly pushed up. Awe pulsed through me when the grate lifted easily.

"Holy shit, he turned me into a female Captain America."

I lifted myself out of the duct and wiggled onto the floor of the room, letting the grate fall with a loud clang behind me.

The momentary feeling of awesomeness faded slightly when I looked around at the impressive setup of screens filling the room.

In everything that had happened since the air had

kicked on, I'd forgotten my suspicion that getting out of the room wasn't the true test.

But I had been right, because directly in front of me was a chair with a Post-it.

Let's see how good you are, hacker.

The mass amounts of nitrous oxide in my blood had me laughing. "Oh, it's on. I'm a motherfucking genius, and you gave me superpowers."

Twenty-One

Einstein
EIGHT MONTHS AGO

I STARED AT THE DOCTOR blankly. "No, see, that isn't possible. I mean, it is. But it isn't probable." I blinked quickly. "I mean . . . it can be, but statistically—"

"Oh gosh." She laughed. "Statistics mean nothing with this kind of thing."

"It was one night. Morning," I quickly amended, shaking my head and stumbling over my words. "It doesn't matter what time it was. It was one span of time."

"Do you know how many *one nights* have ended up in that chair? Or even, *we used protection* or *the pull-out method*? Miracles come on their own time."

Miracle.

I wasn't sure what word I would use to describe what was happening. But I didn't think *miracle* was it.

My brain wasn't functioning the way it normally did. I

couldn't process what was happening or think of which emotions were coursing through my body.

It was a miserable feeling. I felt—God, I felt normal.

Pregnant.

I just . . . I couldn't be.

Maverick and I had sex whenever we were near each other.

We were in that stage where I was sure if it were anyone else, I would be incredibly disgusted with us. It didn't matter where we were or who was near us, we found a way.

I knew condoms weren't one hundred percent effective. I *knew* that.

Just as I knew having sex could produce children.

So I knew physically I *could* be pregnant. I just . . . I *couldn't*.

This wasn't supposed to have happened.

"What do you say we take a look at the baby and hear the heartbeat?"

My head snapped up, my eyes widening. "What? No. Why the hell would I want to do that?"

The doctor looked at me, her expression turning careful. "Were you planning on keeping the baby?"

"What kind of question is that? I'm not giving it to you."

She pressed her lips into a thin line and swallowed, her throat moving slowly with the action. "I wouldn't ask for your baby, Avery. But I meant, were you considering the abortion route?"

I stared at her blankly. "Again, what kind of question is that?"

"Forgive me." Her head dipped to the side in practiced

shame. "I was confused by your determination not to do an ultrasound. However, we do need an ultrasound to make sure the baby is healthy and to see how far along you are."

"Oh."

I felt like an idiot. I never felt stupid.

Being pregnant made me stupid, or maybe it was the idea of a baby.

I know everything about locks and codes and puzzles. I know electronics like I know the ins and outs of my brain. I know numbers like a nerd knows Star Wars lines.

The one thing I know nothing about? Babies or being pregnant or becoming a mom.

Lily was due any day, but I'd hardly paid attention to her pregnancy. Clearly, I wasn't winning the Friend of the Year Award. I just hadn't seen a need when I'd been the first to have the guts to ask her, *"Who would willingly bring a baby into this world?"*

Our world.

A world of death and despair and destruction.

"I feel stupid," I blurted out.

A light laugh bubbled from the doctor. "You shouldn't, but why is that?"

"Does being pregnant make you stupid?"

"Not this early in the pregnancy." She sent me a mischievous wink as if she hadn't just stolen every ounce of oxygen from the room.

"Jesus, you're serious."

"They call it pregnancy brain, and later, mom brain. But it's more about being forgetful—not *stupid*."

"I don't think you understand. My entire life is based around being smart. My jobs are mine because I'm smart. I can't afford to have some mutant inside me stealing my brain and making me forgetful. And I don't know how to be pregnant or how to mom. And why would anyone ever choose to mom? And why the fuck am I crying? Who decided to give me so many goddamn emotions? I don't do emotions. Libby does. Make her be pregnant and stupid and crying."

"Okay, breathe, Avery," the doctor said soothingly as she gripped my hand in hers. "You just need to breathe and calm yourself."

I sucked in a stuttered breath and stood. "You know what? I think I might've just had a momentary lapse in sanity. I'm not pregnant."

"That won't—"

"No, see, you don't understand. I'm here for an IUD. Not a damn baby. You're supposed to put something in my uterus to prevent me from having babies. Not tell me there's one already growing *in* my uterus."

"Avery . . ."

I stood there, staring wide-eyed at the doctor's unwavering, yet, sympathetic face.

"I've had patients who wanted absolutely nothing to do with a baby come out on the other side, thriving in motherhood. Right now, you're just afraid. And it can be scary, especially when you weren't expecting it, but let's just take a few breaths, do the ultrasound, and take this a day at a time. Do you think you can do that?"

I swallowed past the tightening in my throat and moved my head, whether I nodded or shook it, I wasn't sure.

"If you're as smart as you say you are—and I don't doubt you are for a second—then you'll pick up everything you need to know in no time. That will help with your anxiety. Also, maybe telling the father . . ." She lifted a brow in question.

"*Why the hell would anyone bring a baby into this life?*"

Maverick's words that closely echoed my own rang through my mind on repeat. "Uh . . . I'm not sure about that. Right now anyway."

"Okay." Again, she gave me a cautious smile. "Why don't you undress from the waist down, and I'll be back in a second so we can start this."

Before I knew what was happening, I was lying on the table and the room was dark, and there was a thing up in me that I was pretty sure I hadn't signed up for.

I was going to kill Maverick.

I studied the screen as she softly called out everything we were looking at, committing it to memory. That way, when I had to be put through this torture again, I would know exactly what we were looking at.

That way, if I ever decided to tell Maverick, I could give him every single detail so he could go through the pain I—

My heart stalled when a little mutant appeared on the screen.

"That is your . . . well, wait."

I tore my eyes from the screen to look at the doctor and then quickly looked back to the black-and-white image.

Everything shifted, and the mutant changed.

Exactly like a freaking mutant.

"What just happened?" I asked quickly.

"Are you breathing, Avery?"

If it weren't for the smile in the doctor's voice, I would be yelling that I was on the verge of a heart attack because she was scaring the shit out of me and she still had a machine wand jammed up my vagina.

I cut her a hard look. "Might not be for long if you don't tell me what's happening."

She smiled gently.

I was no longer a fan of gentle smiles.

"Breathe and look at the screen while I zoom out."

"Of my vagina?"

She laughed but didn't respond. She didn't need to. The grainy picture on the screen said everything.

Everything.

Not one mutant. Two.

Of course there were two.

"Avery, those are your babies."

I nodded numbly, unable to take my eyes off the screen. Soaking up the picture in front of me. Devouring.

And then a noise filled the room, and it was unlike anything I'd ever heard before. A rapid, muffled *whom-whom-whom*.

It was beautiful. It was life. *My* lifeline.

And I broke.

My heart completely burst open as tears fell unchecked down my face.

"Both heartbeats sound great," the doctor said minutes later. "Babies are measuring right around eleven weeks."

I nodded and shut my eyes when I could no longer see anything in the room. "Emotions are so pointless."

The doctor laughed and placed something into my hand. "There are some pictures for you. I'll let you dress, and then I'll meet you back in here to talk some more."

I was still trembling with excitement and fear and some

other emotion I couldn't place or begin to describe when I reached my tree an hour later. I didn't know what to think or feel, or how to tell anyone—or who to tell.

I just knew something was happening inside me. Something I never wanted for myself and something I wanted to cherish forever.

After another couple of hours had passed, my excitement had drained with the setting sun.

I was about to have a beach ball protruding from my hips. Lily had voiced how uncomfortable she was the last couple of months, and she was only carrying one baby. I had two. Two mutants that would soon be fighting for space inside me.

I took it back. I wasn't going to have a beach ball, I was going to be a damn cow.

And the money . . . I took care of all Borello-related finances, so I'd seen the receipts for Dare and Lily's nursery alone. I'd been the one to put them in the books. I saw the price of a package of diapers.

And college? Fuck that.

Maybe they would get my mind and wouldn't need college.

Oh God, what if they're both girls and want actual weddings instead of mob-style weddings? I don't want to pay for that.

Who willingly had children? This was stressful.

It'd been all of three hours since I found out, and already, I was thinking of ways not to have to pay for their futures. And I was lucky enough to be sitting on an unreasonably large amount of money that only continued to grow since I had almost no expenses.

But that money was for fallback. That money was for the off chance the businesses disappeared or I ever needed to bolt and start over. We all had reserve money for those exact reasons. Not for freaking kids.

Mom of the year. Right here.

I sucked in a sharp breath and dropped my hand to my stomach.

Mom. I was going to be a mom.

How had this happened?

I jolted when a hand landed on my back and looked up to see Maverick staring at me. His expression a mixture of worry and irritation and urgency.

"Are you okay? Where the hell have you been?"

"What? Yeah, I've been—"

Going through a roller coaster of emotions.

Receiving news I never wanted, and somehow, news I feel like I've been waiting for my entire life.

I shrugged weakly. "I've been here."

His light eyes searched mine before they fell to the ground where my bag sat untouched. "Everyone's been trying to get ahold of you for hours."

My stomach dropped. My heart skipped painfully as I held my breath. Without asking, I grabbed for my bag and searched for my phone.

"Libby's freaking the fuck out," Maverick went on. "That Maxon guy she's always sort of been with? He got someone pregnant and they're getting married. When Libby found out, she lost it. No one can get her to calm down."

The breath I'd been holding rushed from my lungs as if he'd punched me.

"But we have to go. Dare called; Lily's in labor."

I nodded stiffly and scrambled to my feet, letting him lead me to the cars while I tapped on my phone, pulling up the browser and ignoring the missed calls from everyone. "We can leave my car here," I murmured, not once looking up from the screen as I scrolled through celebrity news sites.

It was everywhere.

I tapped on one of the many headlines that boasted Maxon's name.

"Maxon James has Been Rocking More Than Just the Stage. Henley's Mysterious Bad Boy to be a Dad!"

Picture after picture after picture littered the article.

Maxon holding a very pregnant girl to him. Maxon kissing her cheek. A close-up shot of the ring on her finger.

Not just an engagement ring. But a wedding band . . .

My brows pulled together tightly as I looked back at the girl's face and then zoomed in on it.

"I know her."

"Who?" Maverick asked, his voice gruff and irritated as he rushed through traffic.

"The girl in these pictures with Maxon. I know her."

Maverick reached over to tenderly grip my thigh. "You know something about everyone. They're in Los Angeles, though, so maybe she's an actress or model or something."

I usually *did* know something about the people I came across.

The line of their jaw. The shape of their eyes. In Lily's case, her lips, which was how I figured out she was Lily O'Sullivan and not *Elle* as she'd originally pretended to be.

People are nothing more than puzzles—their minds and bodies and features.

And I kinda had a thing for solving puzzles.

I glanced through the article again, my head shaking as

I did. I went to two different articles, but only found more of the same. There was no name for the girl.

If she'd been famous in some way, her name would've been in the articles.

"No, that isn't it," I murmured and then pulled a chunk of my hair into my hand, twisting it through my fingers as I went back to study the clearest picture of her face.

After Maverick pulled into a parking spot, he placed his hand on my cheek—his silent way of asking for my attention. Dropping my phone to my lap, I let him tilt my face toward him.

I pulled my bottom lip into my mouth and wondered if he could hear the way my heart thundered, threatening to burst from my chest.

Words gathered in my throat and pooled on the tip of my tongue. Begging . . . *screaming* to be voiced.

It would be easy to tell him. So easy.

And easily the hardest words I'd ever said.

I'm pregnant.

With twins.

We're going to be parents.

You should've heard their heartbeats. Nothing in the world will ever compare to that sound.

I'm pregnant, I'm pregnant, I'm pregnant.

"Why didn't you ask me to come sit with you?"

It wasn't until he spoke that I noticed the worry in his eyes, the way his brows were drawn together in frustration.

I hadn't once gone to our tree alone after the first time I'd asked Maverick to meet me there so many years ago. Not until this afternoon.

And he'd found me there after no one had been able to get ahold of me.

I needed to gather my thoughts. I needed to be able to cry without any of you seeing me.

I stared into his eyes and gave him the only truth I could. "It was a last-minute trip, I didn't think I would be there long." I studied his expression carefully and thought back to his tone. "Is that why you're mad? Because I went without you?"

He huffed out a semblance of a laugh and dropped his head, shaking it as he did. "No—I don't know. I went to the tree first when Libby said you'd just taken off, but you weren't there. When hours went by without word from you, I started getting worried, so I swung by again, and there you were. I was a little pissed that of all days you decide to put your phone away, it's a day when everything seems to be going crazy. But I was also already on edge because I'd left Diggs to deal with Libby after letting her cry and scream at us for what her boyfriend did. Now this shit is happening."

I looked out the window when he gestured to it with his head, but only gave the hospital a glance before bringing my attention back to Maverick. "You mean a baby . . . being born. That shit?"

He lifted his brows and sat back in his seat. With a slow breath out, he stared at the hospital as if he could see Dare and Lily through the walls. "Why didn't they think this through? An attack will come, and they'll go right for that baby."

All I could see was the fuzzy screen in the doctor's office that showed two perfect mutants. When I spoke, my voice was a strangled whisper. "You don't know that."

"Whether or not we're active, other families and enemies haven't forgotten us or what we did in the past.

They've been waiting for an opportunity. Dare and Lily are giving them the perfect one."

We'd had this conversation more times than I could count since Lily and Dare first told us they were expecting.

Maverick and I had been of one mind throughout it all. But after this afternoon? I couldn't imagine wanting anything more than to be right here in a handful of months, welcoming our babies into the world.

Not just *our* world.

I blinked slowly and looked at Maverick, studying his profile. "Maybe a baby is what our world needs. Maybe it's what our family needs."

He shifted toward me, confusion and shock warring on his face. "It's the last thing any of us need."

I knew. I'd known. But his words felt like a physical blow.

Those words that had been begging to be freed were nothing more than a strangled whisper in my throat. Like a deep, dark secret, never to see the light of day.

Each thought was softer than the last, like a flame dying out.

I'm pregnant . . .

With twins . . .

We're going to be parents . . .

You should've heard their heartbeats. Nothing in the world will ever compare to that sound . . .

I'm pregnant . . . I'm preg— . . . I'm— . . .

I stared straight ahead and swallowed past the knot in my throat. Then again. "Yeah," I managed to choke out. "Yeah."

I opened the door and slid from the car, not bothering

to turn when Maverick's voice sounded behind me, muted and warbled through the glass and metal.

When his own door opened and closed.

When his hurried footsteps worked to eliminate the distance between us.

He gripped my shoulder and turned me just before I made it to the entrance of the women's center, his eyes wide and filled with wild confusion. I watched as his lips moved but was unable to make anything out.

"What?"

My bag slipped from his hand and hit my feet just before Maverick was cradling my cheeks and pulling me close. "What's going on?"

"Our friends are having a baby. I'm going in there. Thought that was obvious."

"You were gone for *hours* today. No one could reach you. And now you're acting like—shit, I don't know. What the hell happened today? Where were you?"

"Clearly, I was at the tree since you found me there."

The muscles in his jaw worked. "Don't do this. Not to me."

I wanted to beg the same thing of him.

Please don't do this.

Please see how you're breaking my heart without realizing it.

Please don't make this day harder when I already feel like I can't handle it.

"Where were you?" he begged, the way his plea mixed with his frustration nearly undid me. "And why *did* you go to the tree without me?"

I pointed to the hospital and gritted my teeth. "If that was me in there, what would you do?"

"In where—" Maverick's eyes flashed to the side and then darted back to the entrance that sat a dozen feet away.

Horror covered his face so quickly that my chest heaved with a sob I refused to let out. I gripped his wrists to remove his hands from my face . . . or to steady myself. I wasn't sure.

But he didn't budge.

His eyes closed slowly and his head lowered. "Fuck . . . fuck, Einstein, no. You can't—no. For the love of God, tell me you aren't."

Maverick's words slayed me so deeply it stole my breath. When I was finally able to speak, I begged, "I'm asking what you would do."

"I wouldn't do anything because I won't let us be in that situation," he nearly yelled, his eyes flashing open. He rested his forehead to mine, his body trembling. "Avery, please tell me you aren't."

I swallowed past the pain and whispered, "Of course I'm not."

The relief that flooded him crushed me. Grasped the pure joy from my heart and tore it out. Swiftly. Brutally. Unapologetically.

When he pressed his mouth to mine, I didn't move. I couldn't. If I did, I would lose the death grip I had on the sob still stuck in my chest and there would be no getting it back.

My eyes were narrowed into slits when he leaned back, catching him off guard. "That's why I went without you."

"What—*Avery*," he said desperately when I forced his hands from my face and stepped away.

"I needed to think about things. Alone."

"What things?"

I looked at him standing there in stunned confusion, worry and fear filling his eyes. And all I could see was the man I loved. The man who had just shattered my heart with a few words.

With a quirk of my brow, I said, "My future."

I started for the doors, but I only made it a couple of feet before Maverick was pulling me into his arms, his breathing rough as his eyes wildly searched mine. "Your future? Before this afternoon, your future was *mine*, and mine was *yours*. What the hell does Lily having a baby have to do with our future and what did it change?"

"It has nothing to do with our future," I said honestly. "But today changed everything."

When I pulled from his grasp that time, he let me walk away.

Lock it up.

Lock it up.

I sucked in a steeling breath when I found Libby and Diggs sitting in a waiting area not far from the entrance.

Diggs stood, relief nearly drowning him when he saw me walking toward them. But his expression shifted into confusion when he looked past me and didn't see his brother. After a moment's hesitation, he started my way.

"You good?" he asked, his eyes darting back toward the entrance, to where I'd left Maverick.

"Of course."

"Right," he said, drawing out the word. "Uh, well, Libby isn't. She needs you."

I slanted my head in a nod and kept walking to where Libby was staring vacantly ahead while Diggs went to his brother.

As soon as I sat, Libby rested her head against my

shoulder and a tear soaked into the fabric of my shirt. "Did you see?"

"Yeah."

"I don't know how to do this," she murmured, her voice thick with emotion. "I don't know how to be happy about a baby when a pregnancy is ruining my life."

Everything in me lurched, and my hand automatically fell to my stomach.

I looked up when the twins came walking into the waiting room and sat. Diggs was shooting daggers at me. Maverick was holding my bag and looked nearly as wrecked as I felt.

My throat felt tight as I slowly moved my hand to the armrest.

It felt difficult to breathe.

I didn't know what would happen if I opened my mouth, if I'd be able to get words out or if I'd turn into a crying mess with Libby.

So I sat there instead, letting her cry for a few minutes.

"I don't know what, but something about the Maxon articles feels wrong," I finally whispered. "I'll figure it out. But right now, this isn't about what may or may not have happened in California. It's about Lily and your brother. Don't let your feelings for their baby be swayed."

Don't let your feelings for my babies be swayed.

Twenty-Two

Maverick
EIGHT MONTHS AGO

I leaned back against the tree and slid my hands into my pockets. My eyes were on the rising sun, but my mind was on a girl a mile away.

Einstein and I hadn't spoken. Not once since she'd walked away and left me outside the hospital.

We'd sat across the room from each other all night and into the early hours of the morning, waiting for Beckham to come into the world.

When we'd all piled into Lily's room to see the new Borello, we'd stood close enough I could've reached out and touched her.

But the words that left her lips were never meant for me. The few people she'd given her attention to hadn't been me. Throughout it all, she hadn't once looked at a screen.

Of everything, that last one was something I hadn't been able to get past.

It was rare for Einstein to be seen without her face pressed close to a screen. And each of those rare occasions belonged to me. To our time together . . . alone.

If she was in a situation with others where she was unable to search or study or code, she lost her mind. Restless movements and fidgeting until it all became too much to handle.

But throughout the night, she'd remained utterly still.

After she and Libby left the hospital, I took Diggs home and came here. She'd already picked up her car and was gone by the time I arrived, but it didn't matter.

I needed to see what she'd seen. I needed to feel what she'd felt.

Because hours alone at this tree had transformed her into a girl I didn't know.

Yet, the longer I stood there, the more confused I was by her reaction yesterday.

All I felt, all I saw, all I wanted was Einstein.

Forever.

I'd fought silently for her for years. I wouldn't lose her, not to something I didn't understand.

I raced to the girls' apartment and used my key to let myself in. It was almost eight in the morning, but I doubted they were awake since we'd only left the hospital a few hours ago. I walked through the silent and still apartment to Einstein's room, only slowing long enough to step out of my converse.

As soon as I slid into the bed beside her, her eyes flashed open.

Beautiful green eyes, bloodshot and filling with tears, stared back at me.

"Avery." Her name came out twisted with grief, with confusion, with an echo of the pain I saw deep in her eyes. "Tell me what's going on."

Instead of a response, she shifted closer to me and lifted a hand to trace along my jaw. Her eyes followed her fingers with rapt attention as they moved over my cheekbone and lips as if she was trying to memorize the lines of my face.

When her fingers trailed over my jaw again, her eyes bounced to mine. Before I could beg her again to tell me what was happening—what had happened yesterday—she drove her fingers into my hair and pulled me to her, her lips meeting mine with a soft cry.

I curled my arm around her waist and brought her body closer, pulling her to me like I could keep her there. Like I could assure myself this was still real.

I bit back a groan when her hand slid down my chest and inched under my shirt, her fingers playing across my stomach in that shy, teasing way that drove me crazy. I wanted to push her onto her back and settle between her legs. I wanted to devour her until she was gasping for air. But flashes from yesterday were assaulting me, reminding me of the pain, of the confusion, of the tears she had tried to hide.

I dropped my forehead to hers and begged, "Talk to me."

She pressed her head harder to mine but then rolled away, her chest pitching with a silent sob.

I sat up and leaned over her, resting my hand on the bed so I was caging her in. "Avery, you're scaring the shit out of me."

She choked out a weak laugh. "Funny. I'm terrified."

"Of what?"

Her glassy eyes studied mine before shifting to the side. "Of losing you."

Assurances were on the tip of my tongue, bleeding into the air.

But she and I both knew I wouldn't leave her—not for fucking anything. So, I was lost as to why she would worry about it at all.

"You walked away." I fisted my hands into the sheet, forcing myself not to touch her, not to comfort her, when her eyes shut with pain. "You made me think you were reconsidering a life with me after spending an afternoon alone, or *claiming* to spend it alone."

My fear and suspicions deepened when she didn't deny anything . . . when she didn't try to convince me of what she'd actually been doing when no one could find her yesterday.

When she opened her eyes, a tear raced down her cheek. "I realized that someday something is going to happen that will tear us apart."

A disbelieving laugh punched from my chest. "Are you kidding? After everything we've been through, you think that's gonna happen?"

"I know it will."

Her certainty rocked through me, leaving me uneasy. I pressed the tips of my fingers to her cheek and turned her head so I could look into her eyes. "*What* will?"

"It doesn't matter."

"How could it not matter?"

"Because I already know the outcome." A sob wrenched from her body, and she vainly tried to mute it by covering her mouth with one of her hands. After a few seconds, she slid the hand down to grip at her chest. "I know that I won't choose you."

I sat back, stunned.

"I can't imagine my life without you," she continued. "I don't want to . . . I don't know *how* to. Just the thought of a future without you wrecks me. Makes me physically sick. But I already know I *will* choose a future without you because you don't want the life I do."

My mind raced, but I couldn't keep up with it or with what she was saying.

It felt like each word had stolen a little piece of me until all I knew was the overwhelming love I had for the girl on the bed and the pain slowly consuming me.

I didn't know if she was pushing me away, if she was preparing for something in the future, or what the hell this something even—

I hissed a curse. "Lily. The—shit, the baby. That *is* what this is about. Isn't it?"

"I told you—"

"For the first time in . . . God, since I've known you, you suddenly want kids? A family?" *Everything people like us shouldn't have?* I didn't finish the thought, but it hung in the air between us as if I'd shouted it.

And she knew. She'd heard every unspoken word. We'd had this conversation enough times.

Understanding filled her eyes and her lips pressed into a thin line.

She knew.

I clenched my teeth and tried to calm my thundering heart as I waited for a response. Because this? God . . .

It wasn't that I had never wanted a family, it was that I couldn't have one. Not in this life.

The shit we'd seen, not just within the Borellos but in other families as well. The way kids were always used first in retaliations. Fuck, Borellos had killed both of Lily's brothers. The Holloways had faked Lily's death to keep her safe. And then Lily and Dare had excitedly brought a new life into our fucked-up one . . .

I couldn't do that. Wouldn't.

"I told you, Lily isn't what this is about," she finally whispered.

Relief pounded through my veins so quickly, only to be overcome by my frustration. "Then what the fuck is this about? What the hell would you choose over us? What else don't I want? You and I have always been on the same goddamn page, Avery, so what could it possibly be?"

Tears continued to trek from her eyes to her temples to her hair as she reached up to place a hand on my racing heart. "I know you. If I tell you in this moment, when you're worried about losing me, you will say anything to make sure you don't."

I opened my mouth to deny it and then growled out a curse and pushed her hand away as I got off the bed. I paced the length of her room quickly, driving my hands into my hair and fisting the strands.

"Maybe I would, maybe I wouldn't," I yelled, turning on her and letting my arms drop. "But I wouldn't write off our future without giving you a chance. And that's *exactly* what you're doing. You're writing us off because of some hypothetical situation. You're so sure I'll disappoint you without giving me a goddamn chance to prove that I'll be there for you. Through everything. The way I've always been."

"Trust me that I have and will give you chances," she said after a few tense seconds. "Trust me that I will never, under any circumstances, write us off. But if I were to tell you what I needed from you, you would alter your life and your wants to make sure I had it despite your thoughts on the issue. You wouldn't be *you* anymore. I lived that relationship with Johnny. It forms bitterness and resentment. And if you ever resented me? That would be worse than losing you."

My shoulders sagged. Grief twisted my words. "Nothing could be worse than losing you."

She tried to smile, but her face crumpled. No sound left her when she mouthed, *Terrified*.

I crawled onto the bed and pulled her into my arms, kissing her slowly, thoroughly. "I'll surprise you," I whispered against her lips. "I swear."

Twenty-three

Einstein
SEVEN MONTHS AGO

I woke suddenly, like someone had ripped me from my dreamless sleep. My sharp inhale resonated in the room like the crack of a gunshot.

I stared straight ahead, waiting for whoever had woken me to make themselves known.

*What*ever.

And then pain.

Low in my abdomen.

Spasming and contracting.

Seizing my body for a second that felt like lifetimes.

Stealing my breath and flooding my eyes with stinging hot tears.

I rolled onto my back, my hands immediately flew to my stomach. My heart lurched when another tremor of pain ripped through me. Because I knew—I *knew*. God, I knew.

That hope and life and joy that had been coursing through me the last three weeks . . . it was painfully absent. A dark hollow of heartache rested in its place.

For the first time in my life, a prayer left my lips.

Praying to anyone. Anything. Praying to a God I'd never given much thought to.

"Don't let this be happening, don't let this be happening. Don't take them from me," I sputtered out on a sob.

I shakily lifted back the covers, my chest heaving with a soundless cry when I looked down and saw the blood-soaked sheets.

I moved in slow-motion as I crawled off the bed. I might as well have been crawling through wet cement. I couldn't get away from the nightmare in front of me fast enough. All I wanted was to run. To sprint.

To wake up.

Please, God, let me wake up.

Once I was finally standing on unsteady legs, I pressed my hands to the small bump that had only just started to form between my hips and choked out, "You're okay. You're . . . oh-okay."

I didn't know what to do. I didn't know how to get through this.

I didn't know how my heart was supposed to survive this.

I reached for the corner of my sheets to strip the bed but nearly crumpled to the ground when the next tremor rocked through me. Buckling my knees and forcing a pained cry from my chest.

I looked around the room . . . for something, anything, as my body tried to take from me what I'd come to love most.

When another spasm pulled deep inside, I turned to leave the room. At the last second, I slapped my hand over my phone, sliding it off the nightstand.

I just needed to make it down the hall. To my bathroom. To the tub.

That was all.

But for how simple something should have been, it felt impossible.

To move when I was weighed down by grief so crippling that I wasn't sure I would ever get back up.

To continue forward when each ripple of pain was a reminder of what was happening.

What took less than a minute felt like hours. By the time I stripped out of my shorts and underwear and lowered myself into the dry tub, I wasn't sure how much of my heart was left unscathed.

Over the next hour, I wished I didn't have a heart at all.

Maybe then, I wouldn't have fallen in love within an instant. Literally within a beat of a heart.

Maybe then, it wouldn't have hurt so much.

Physical pain I could handle. This overwhelming, devastating grief that was suffocating me . . .

That . . . I couldn't handle that.

I leaned against the wall of the tub, tears endlessly streaming down my face. My bloodied hands resting in the tub beside me.

"I'm sorry. I'm sorry. I'm sorry." It was a whisper wrapped in torment. And it was all I had to offer them.

I looked at my phone again. And once again, I didn't know what to do.

Libby was closing at The Jack and would be gone for another couple of hours.

Maverick . . . I couldn't do this to him. Couldn't tell him like this.

I'd spent the last three weeks trying to figure out what I was going to do when I no longer looked just bloated. I'd spent the last handful of days not letting him near my small bump that had very clearly formed out of nowhere.

Every day I had the conversation with him in my head.

Every time I saw him, I vowed to tell him.

Then every time, he'd say something about Beckham or Lily and Dare that had me choking back the words.

Another echoing spasm. Another tremor.

I grabbed my phone and opened the messages. Then quickly sent one off.

Me: *I need help. My apartment. Tell and bring no one.*

I laid my head on the edge of the tub and shut my eyes.

I wasn't worried about her finding a way in. She could get in anywhere.

My hands fell back to the tub, and my lips trembled. "I'm sorry. I'm sorry. I'm sorry."

By the time she appeared in the bathroom next to me, my words were no longer wrapped in torment. They sounded the way I felt. Lifeless. Cold.

I glanced up at her, not caring that I was naked except for my shirt or that I was covered in blood or that my face was still wet from my tears.

I didn't know how to care anymore.

Jess's face was white with horror. "What . . ." Her eyes darted around the tub and my body. "Einstein . . ."

"I don't know what to do."

Her head snapped up at my admission. Shock and pain flared in her eyes. "What are—you're pregnant?" Her voice was a breath. "When—we didn't—I didn't know."

"I don't know what to do."

"Where the fuck is Maverick?"

"Jessica," I yelled, my voice cracking. "I don't know what to do. I need your help."

She swallowed, her throat moving slowly with the motion that seemed difficult. With a stuttered breath, she ran her hands through her hair and then nodded. "Yeah. Yeah, okay."

She twisted and searched through the drawers of my bathroom until she found a tie to pull her hair up in a bun before she squatted down so her face was next to mine. "Who knows?"

When I only stared pointedly at her, she nodded.

"Libby will be home in a little over an hour. I don't . . . I don't want her to see this. I don't want to be here when she comes back. She'll know something . . . and my bed—"

"You can stay with me and Kieran, he won't say anything. And I'll take care of your bed." Her eyes darted to my legs before meeting mine again, concern filling them. "We need to clean you up first."

A lump lodged in my throat. Somehow, impossibly, there was one last piece of my heart left to shatter. "I need to bury them."

Jess mouthed the word *them* as I lifted my hand from the tub. Her shoulders jerked and her eyes brimmed with tears, but she didn't let them fall. Her mouth trembled as she nodded quickly.

"Okay. Okay, okay. I, uh . . . Jesus." She leaned back and

slowly stood, her frantic expression was slowly replaced with determination. "All right. Let me go start on your bed and find something for them. Then I'll help you get cleaned up and dressed. And we'll . . ." She blinked slowly, then focused on me. "Where?"

She didn't need to say anything more. I already knew what she was asking.

I already knew *where*.

"There's a tree. I'll show you."

My mom told me long ago that showing emotions was weak.

Pains and failures needed to be kept private. Silent.

My parents were assholes.

Even though I'd never agreed with them, I somehow took on their lifestyle and habits.

So had my late sister.

I just hadn't realized it until I found out too late that her boyfriend was abusive. Until I found myself in a similar relationship and had already perfected a façade so no one would ever know anything was wrong.

Then again, people learned by example. And my mom was the perfect example of keeping a smile on her face and pretending life was normal after being beaten down.

I hadn't realized I'd held true to my mom's words until Maverick came into my life and shifted something inside me, making me want to pour out my heart to him.

But even after realizing this, even after learning to open myself to Maverick, I couldn't shake those lessons she'd engrained in me.

Whenever my pain had manifested in tears the last two weeks, I heard her voice in my head, quickly followed by my own.

"Emotions are weak."

Lock it up.

"Pains and failures need to be kept private and silent."

And this was the most excruciating pain and the biggest failure of my life.

Lock it up.

Lock it up.

Lock it up.

I blinked.

Slowly at first. Then rapidly, trying to pull myself from wherever I'd just been.

I wasn't sure if I'd fallen asleep or had been daydreaming or had just zoned out so badly that I'd completely forgotten where I was, but I flinched when I saw Kieran standing directly in front of me.

Shirtless.

Arms crossed over his chest.

Knife peeking out beneath one of them.

Jesus, the guy would never not be anything less than fucking terrifying. Constantly armed to the teeth with blades and wearing a look that said he was imagining a new way to kill you every time your heart forced another painful beat in his presence.

I didn't know how Lily had done it. How she'd been with a guy like him.

I didn't know how Jess did it.

Sure, attraction. I could see that. But, like I said, terrifying.

Assassins usually were. Unless they were Maverick.

I opened my mouth to speak, but my throat and mouth felt dry and rough and scratchy.

I forced a swallow, and then I forced another. "Can you, uh . . . don't you wear shirts? You know, when you aren't out with the rest of the world? Which I happen to be part of."

"You're worried about a shirt." It was a statement wrapped in that gritty growl that was pure Kieran.

"Well, yeah."

He slanted his head to the side, his eyes following on a delay. "Your priorities are skewed."

I shifted to look in the direction and jerked back from the handle of the knife sticking out of the wall, at exactly *my* eye level.

I whipped my head back to him. "Did you throw that at me?"

"You didn't notice."

The asshole didn't even have the decency to look apologetic. Or . . . well, anything other than *Kieran*.

"What if it had hit me?"

His eyes rolled. "I'll only ever hit you if I want to."

I gripped the handle and pulled, giving up when it didn't budge from the wall. With a huff, I glared at the man in front of me. "Want to tell me why you're maybe, maybe *not* killing me?"

He leaned forward and pulled the knife from the wall with nothing more than a flick of his wrist. "Want to tell me why you're here?"

My stomach dipped with unease and worry and the slightest bit of panic. "I was told I had a room here whenever I needed it."

Over the last two weeks, I'd needed it a lot.

I wasn't ready to face Maverick alone—not yet.

"You do," Kieran responded immediately, assurance leaking through his words. "But I never see you outside the office, and now you're here. Not just once, but every couple of nights."

When Jess brought me here after helping me bury my twins beneath my tree in a shoebox she'd wrapped in ribbon and a blanket, Kieran had met us at the door.

The only thing Jess said was, "She's staying. Don't ask questions. That's the end of it."

And he hadn't.

Not a word or curious look for two weeks.

I steeled my jaw and lifted my chin, staring him down even though I was sitting and he towered over me. "You want me gone, I'm gone and won't be back."

His piercing green eyes narrowed on me. "Is that what you heard?"

"That's what you're getting to; I'm skipping the conversation."

"You need somewhere to go, you have a place here. You need help?" He raised his arms out to the sides, both knives in clear view. "You really think Jessica and I aren't gonna be the ones to help you? That's what we do, Einstein. But right now, I want to know why you're hiding out here, so fucking spaced that you didn't notice when a knife passed within an inch of your face."

That last part was embarrassing.

Or worrying.

Depending on how you looked at it.

When I spoke, the bite I tried to fuel my words with was absent. "Your wife said no questions."

"That was two weeks ago."

My stare fell to the floor.

"Look, you don't want to tell me, that's fine. Obviously, it's bad. But whatever it is, you now have my wife keeping shit from me."

A knot formed in my throat, making it hard to catch my breath.

I swallowed thickly, trying to dislodge it. "I didn't . . . I didn't think of it like that. I don't, uh . . ." I stood and looked around the room, not really seeing anything. "I have to go."

Kieran stopped me with a hand to my shoulder, blade still securely in his grasp. "You don't have to go."

I nodded, my head bouncing all over the place as emotion threatened to consume me. "I do. I don't want to put anything between you two, and I have no intention of telling you." I sidestepped him, but only got a step away before I stopped. Turning toward him, I kept my face toward the floor as I silently begged, "When you find out—when Jess tells you—I don't want to know. I don't want to see it on your face or in your eyes. I don't want to hear it in the way you speak to me. Understand?"

A rumble of assent sounded in his throat, and it was all I needed.

All I expected, really.

I turned and made my way to the room I'd been sporadically staying in and sluggishly grabbed my laptop and jacket, shoving them into my bag as quickly as my arms allowed.

I turned to leave and ran right into Kieran's chest.

Before I could stumble away, one of his arms wrapped around me, holding me tight.

A sob bubbled up my chest and fell from my lips. "You promised."

"I *agreed*. But I haven't found out yet."

I dropped my bag and wrapped my arms around his waist, letting my tears fall and sobs build.

I was screaming at myself to rein it in, not to let him see a thing.

But the tears had begun, and I couldn't make them stop.

Soon after, Jess's arms wrapped around me from behind.

I was in the oddest hug. And it was exactly what I needed.

"I can kill Maverick before he knows I'm there," Kieran murmured when my cries quieted.

Horror and panic raced through my veins so quickly that I tensed, unable to move or speak.

My response sat on the tip of my tongue, thick and heavy.

No, no, no.

Jess tsked and smacked his arm.

"No?" he asked, confirming Maverick wasn't the problem.

"No," she hissed.

I tried pulling away from him, and they let me move out of the sandwich I'd become. I took a shuddering breath and kept my eyes on the floor.

Just kept them down.

Straight down.

Where my belly was supposed to be growing but wasn't.

Lock it up.

"No," I finally whispered. "He's innocent. Well, not completely. But he doesn't know anything. I didn't—he's fine."

I murmured my thanks when Jess grabbed my bag off the floor and hefted it onto my shoulder.

"You don't have to leave," she said, soft enough to give the illusion that her words were only for me. We both knew that Kieran could hear them too.

"She's right," he added.

"I do. I don't want there to be secrets between you because of me. And I . . ." I shrugged. I had to go, but I didn't know what I was going to do when I did. Where I was going to go.

I wasn't strong enough to handle this yet.

I still broke down every time I thought of telling Maverick.

I wanted to die whenever I thought of the betrayal he would feel because I'd kept something of that magnitude from him.

I wanted to go back in time and tell him that first day. Hour. That first second when I heard the first heartbeat.

I wanted us to be living different lives so he would've *wanted* this.

But it wouldn't have changed anything.

I'd still be here.

And they'd still be in the ground.

Twenty-Four

Maverick
ONE MONTH AGO

Diggs shoved me toward Dare's car with one hand and gestured toward me with the other. "Eh? Eh? Look at the boy getting out on his own."

My eyes narrowed into slits, but I didn't look away from Dare. "I'm being forced. Literally."

Dare shrugged where he leaned against his car, as if to say I'd left them no other choice. "You can't stay in your apartment all the time."

I pushed Diggs away when we neared Dare and took the last couple of steps up to him on my own. "I don't. I leave almost every day. I work. I show up for the meetings—"

"But you've been avoiding family time," he said with a knowing look. "No one avoids family time. So we're going out."

I didn't remind him that Einstein had been avoiding us completely.

I didn't bring up that Libby always skipped out on family time, which had only gotten worse since she and Maxon had gotten engaged.

I just slanted him a grin. "Going out, huh? You have a kid and wife at home, maybe we should rethink that."

Dare pushed from the car and opened the passenger door. "It was the *wife's* idea. Get in."

Before I could move, my phone rang.

Considering the only two people who ever called were standing right in front of me, we all stopped moving.

I grabbed for the phone and just stared for a second, sure I was seeing things when Einstein's face covered the screen, before scrambling to answer. "What's wrong?"

Funny that I knew before hearing her voice that something *had* to be wrong.

But not only did Einstein and I not talk anymore, she also never called. *Period*.

When she spoke, her tone was direct and held that slightly wild edge, the way it got when there was a puzzle right in front of her, taunting her until she was able to solve it. "Need you and Diggs to get Dare."

I looked over at Dare. "They're with me at my place."

He gave me a look, silently demanding to know what was going on.

I put the call on speaker just as Einstein said, "Okay, then pick me up. I'm at the tree."

I was already reaching for the passenger door, ready to slide into the car. If Einstein needed me, I'd always be there. "Coming. Tell me what's going on."

"Don't know. Libby called, yelling. Said Maxon was in danger." Everything was said distractedly, as if she were already working on it. "Just get over here. I need to find him."

I looked between Dare and Diggs when the call ended.

My hand was still on the door, one foot was on the pavement. Dare had his hand on the keys, ready to start the car. Diggs was eerily quiet.

Tension quickly built.

"Is there any way your trunk is still loaded?" I asked Dare, silently hoping he hadn't emptied it out.

All our cars had at least a gun in them at all times, but we'd kept Dare's stocked.

"Always," he said on a growl as he cranked the engine, peeling out of the lot as soon as I had the door shut.

I gave him quick directions to a place I'd sworn to never tell anyone about, my knee bouncing as the short drive seemed to drag on.

"Funny that a guy who stripped his title and dissolved our family's mafia ties still has his trunk loaded a year and a half later."

Diggs sat forward so he could look at Dare, who was slowly shaking his head.

"I know it's coming. I *know* families will come and attack. I knew when I dissolved the ties we would never truly be clear of the shit."

"Then why do it?" I asked.

"Because I vowed to the minute I was forced to be boss, and I keep my word. I know it doesn't matter what happened then or what happens now, enemies have long memories. They'll be back. But we'll be ready, and they won't be expecting that."

"We'll be ready with five of us," I said drily. "Three, if Libby and Einstein keep disappearing."

He cut me a sharp look, telling me that I was pushing it. "They will always be there when they're needed. And you're forgetting four people."

A huff pushed past my lips. "Uh . . ." Considering most of the older generation had left in search of other families or a normal life when we disbanded, there was no one else.

"We went through a lot of shit with them, but Kieran, Conor, and Jess are in this with us." He pulled up to where Einstein waited and smacked me. "And don't ever forget my wife again."

I opened my mouth to argue that Lily and fighting enemies didn't mix, but then I decided against it.

Lily had fought Johnny twice and survived. She had the scars to prove it.

"Right. Sorry."

"Holloway," Einstein said as soon as she was in the car, and before any of us could ask, she clarified, "Maxon's at Holloway estate, let's go."

She never once glanced at us, just continued swiping at her tablet before dropping it into her lap and digging into her bag for her phone.

"So he isn't in danger," Dare said, drawing out the last words.

"I don't know," Einstein said, her voice filled with frustration. "I thought Libby was just freaking out at first. You know, being Libby. But she sounded scared. Told us to find him and stay with him."

Dare was speeding off toward the old Holloway estate before Einstein finished talking. "Does he have a reason to be there? Did the Henley guys move in there already?"

"Yeah, about a week ago," she murmured.

I looked into the backseat when I heard a loud ringing and found Einstein holding up her phone. Libby's name was splashed across the top, the speaker button was highlighted.

"Where is he?" Libby asked in way of greeting.

Einstein wasn't fazed, just grabbed her tablet and looked at the map on the screen. "At Holloway."

Something similar to a cry or a moan sounded through the phone.

"I told you," Einstein hissed, her eyes never moving from the tablet's screen.

"Was that happy or sad?" Diggs asked.

I looked at Dare. "She crying?"

Dare reached behind him and snatched the phone from Einstein's hand. "We're headed there now. Tell me why. Tell me *everything*."

"I don't have time," Libby said, her voice thick. "Moretti. Dare, it's Moretti."

Dare's head shook in denial.

Moretti . . . I know that name.

"They're here—they've been stalking me," she continued. "They've killed guys I've slept with."

Dare's face fell as he smacked the steering wheel. "*Fuck.*"

I listened to their back and forth, taking in everything Libby said as I tried to figure out how I knew the name Moretti.

It was there, teasing my mind, but I couldn't grasp the memory.

"They were at the bar with me tonight. They did something to my car. My gun's gone."

"Where are you?" Dare demanded over Libby's crying

as he took a sharp turn to take us toward The Jack instead of Holloway estate.

"My car."

"Lib—*fuck*. Are you kidding me? Get back in the goddamn bar. We're coming to get you."

"I have *nothing*," she cried out.

"Damn it, Libby," he yelled. "Run. Run to the bar. Now."

Diggs leaned forward and tapped my shoulder. "Moretti . . . wasn't that the family they were dealing with when they found us at the black site?"

I bit out a curse when it all came rushing back. "*Yes.*" I turned in my seat to face Dare. "What the hell are they doing back now?"

His head was shaking in quick jerks. "I took care of them. Libby told me they would come back for her, and I didn't listen because I took care of them eleven fucking years ago."

Libby suddenly cursed, her voice far away from the phone.

"Libby?" Dare called out.

When there was no response, he yelled her name until she shakily said, "I'm here."

"What the hell happened?"

"I-I fell."

Deep voices sounded near her, too far away to make out what they were saying.

"Of course," she whispered. I'm—"

"Libby?" Dare asked, his voice low and tense. "Libby what's going on? Who's there with you?" When she didn't say anything, he pressed harder on the gas, weaving through the light traffic faster than before.

"Oh God, Gabe," Libby said, horror dripping from her words.

Dare flashed me a confused look, then yelled, "Who the hell is Gabe? *Libby*."

"Meet me at Holloway," she said quickly.

Dare, Diggs, and I all yelled that we were just down the street from her, but the call ended.

By the time we made it to The Jack, Libby was already gone.

As soon as Diggs and I checked the bar and slid back into the car, Dare took off toward Holloway. "If they're in town, we need to all be in the same place until we know what's going on and have a plan—even if that place is Holloway. Lily's headed there now. And Einstein knows who Gabe is."

"Might," she said from where she was curled over her tablet. "Libby slept with a Gabe during the times she and Maxon were *off*. It could be the same one and most likely *is* considering her tone."

"So, not a Moretti?" Diggs asked.

"Don't know yet. The only living Moretti any of us has met is their boss. But I doubt it's them, because I've been hearing Gabe's name for years. If he were a Moretti, he would've done something a long time ago."

The Morettis were a family from up in Chicago. In the early 1900s, the Borellos, Morettis, and a third family made up the Willow Gang.

Things went bad fast and the rebellion against the Moretti family began.

Of the two rebelling families, only three Borello brothers made it out alive and finally stopped running in Wake Forest.

For a while, they stayed under the radar, but eventually, the Borello family became more notorious than the Willow Gang ever was.

In trying to establish peace with them nearly a century later, Dare and Libby's dad gave Libby to the Morettis in a secret, blood-binding contract. Per the contract, Libby was to be married to one of the Morettis by her twenty-first birthday.

They found out when he died and Dare became boss.

When the Moretti boss died a year before the deadline, Dare offered the new boss everything he had to release Libby from the contract.

That was when Einstein, Dare, and Johnny found Diggs and me sitting in the black site.

And the last any of us heard from them, they'd allowed the change.

"She said they've been stalking her. If they've been here, watching her, how did we not know?" Dare asked as we pulled up to the Holloway mansion.

I turned on Einstein when a thought hit me. "Your computer. The systems."

She slowly looked up at me, her eyes slightly narrowed. "Excuse me?"

"Last year, someone got into your system at ARCK, remember? The paperclip."

Her eyes filled with fire.

"When the hell did this happen and why didn't I know?" Dare demanded, and Diggs slowly leaned back in his seat as if that would save him from the anger coming off Dare in waves.

"Because it had nothing to do with you," she said through clenched teeth, her eyes never leaving mine.

Dare started to argue, but I hurried to ask, "Did it happen anywhere else? Could it have been the Morettis looking for information?"

"Don't you think I would've told Dare if I thought Morettis were sneaking past my security?"

"You're supposed to tell me if someone is getting past your security regardless," Dare ground out.

Her eyes rolled and focused back on her screen, her fingers quickly moving across it.

"Einstein," Dare snapped.

"It was ARCK, not Borello. Sorry for not telling you. But at the moment, we have more pressing concerns, like the fact that Morettis are apparently in town and killing people Libby slept with, and one of those people happens to be in that mansion. So, why don't we go protect him the way your sister asked us to and see if she's already in there while we're at it?"

She didn't wait for any of us to respond or question her. She just shoved her door open and stepped out of the car.

Lily pulled up next to us as we followed Einstein out and hurried to Dare's side, her face paled when she looked at the intimidating house. "I never thought I'd be here again."

"Where's Beckham?" Dare asked, his tone holding a hint of panic.

"I left him with your mom."

Dare dragged a hand through his hair and hissed a curse. When dread washed over Lily's face, he hurried to say, "It's okay. That's probably better."

"I didn't want him in this house," she said on a rush, her tone frantic.

Dare pulled her close and pressed his head to hers. "It's fine, Lily. He'll be fine. My mom will keep him safe."

So, they did know he was a target . . .

But the Moretti family had only ever had one interest.

And that was Libby.

I turned and headed toward where Einstein was walking up the porch steps and digging in her bag.

When I came up beside her, she was pulling out her set of lock picks, "Did you have to bring that up?"

"It was an honest question. Is it still happening?"

Irritation leaked through her words when she said, "How about you do your work and let me do mine."

I clenched my jaw to keep from saying anything else and reached for my gun when she dropped the picks back into her bag and grabbed the handle.

"We expecting anyone on the other side of the doors?"

"I just didn't want to wait for someone to answer," she said and shoved the doors open before I had a chance to stop her, walking into the house as if she owned the place. "Hey, there's our favorite rock star. Safe and sound."

I followed her in with everyone else close behind me, my steps slowing when I noticed Maxon and Lincoln standing in the middle of the massive front room staring at us with wide eyes.

Lincoln, who I knew Einstein had a weird history with.

Lincoln, who—of the four of them—had dared to talk to Einstein while she was still with Johnny.

Lincoln, who was slowly raking his eyes over her.

Diggs hit my back and yelled, "Food!" and headed toward the smallest of the three kitchens in this mansion.

I quickly took in the space and wondered if the Henley guys knew how much blood had been spilled in this room during the parties the Holloway gang had held over the years.

"What are you doing here?" Maxon asked, pulling my attention back to him.

Einstein lifted her shoulders and grabbed the tablet from her bag. "We go where we're sent, rock star."

"Have you talked to Libby?"

Maxon's face twisted with a mixture of frustration and grief at Dare's question. "Not for a couple of days."

I looked to Einstein, but her eyes were wide with surprise.

Then again, she'd been pushing all of us away, not just me. Maybe she would've known this if she'd been around.

"Want to tell me why you're here and not talking to my sister?" Dare's tone was low and threatening, and demanded an answer.

"You think I want to be here?" Maxon laughed, the sound pained and aggravated. "I want to be with her. I want to still be engaged to her."

My stare returned to Einstein.

That familiar ache in my chest flared because this all sounded so familiar.

"Your sister changed the locks on me and then tried to give me my ring back. Apparently, there's some other guy who won't leave her for California like I do."

"Right," Einstein said as she lifted her tablet and started swiping across it. "That would explain the zombie dark circles under your eyes. Don't worry. It's all part of the life."

A huff punched from my chest and was echoed by Maxon.

"The hell does that—"

"Dare, get Libby on the phone," Einstein demanded, ignoring Maxon. "Rock star boys, get me a workstation."

Frustration laced each word when Maxon asked, "Wait, what are you all doing here?"

"Apparently helping your maybe, maybe-not fiancée protect you from some bad people. Sit down. We'll tell you all about it."

"What'd you just say?"

Einstein lowered the tablet enough to look at Maxon and then spoke very slowly, which had me biting back a smirk. "There are bad people here. People who want Libby, and I *would* say I'm guessing, but I'm me, so I *know*, that you went through a breakup so she could protect you from them."

"You mean Moretti?" The question was lifeless coming from Maxon. "The pictures are from them, aren't they?"

The room immediately filled with tension.

"What pictures?" Einstein asked carefully.

"It keeps going straight to voice mail," Dare said before Maxon could answer, his words weighed down with apprehension.

"Shit," Einstein whispered. "Rock star boys . . . workstation. Now."

None of the Henley guys moved.

I was already headed toward the kitchen with Dare, who snapped, "Computers. Tablets. Anything."

By the time we had all the food and alcohol cleared off the breakfast bar, three of the guys were jogging toward Einstein, who had taken up post on one of the stools, still swiping on her tablet.

"Someone seemed to think I would've found you at the

house you just bought," she whispered to Maxon as the laptops were set in front of her.

He looked to her and then asked "Me?" His eyes widened when Einstein logged into each of the laptops without ever asking the passwords before dropping her attention back to the tablet.

"Not talking to anyone else, rock star."

I slid in beside her to start pulling up site after site on the laptops.

I didn't know how to access any of them or how to use them once in there, but I'd watched her enough to know most of what she needed. To know how to set up the computers in a way for her to immediately start working.

"I bought that house for Libby and me," Maxon finally said. "I don't want to be there without her."

"Fair enough—shit," Einstein hissed. "Problem."

Dare was suddenly there, pushing through Maxon and grabbing the tablet. "Is this the last one?" When Einstein made a sound of confirmation, Dare threw the tablet onto the bar. "Fuck!"

I gripped Dare's shoulder and pulled him close, dropping my voice so it wouldn't carry. "We don't lose people this way. We'll find her."

"What's going on?" Maxon asked.

Dare turned on him, his breaths harsh and expression feral. "Moretti were at The Jack. Tonight." He threw his arm out toward Einstein. "Libby's phone's off. Last tower it pinged off has her headed out of town."

Maxon's face paled with denial and worry and anguish.

His head shook slowly, as if he could push Dare's words from his mind.

When Dare spoke again, I watched as the floor was ripped out from beneath the man in front of me.

"They have her."

The last half hour had been a shitstorm of stress and frustrations.

Maxon had continued to call Libby, hoping in vain her phone would be on.

The thick tension between him and Dare finally snapped and would've resulted in blows if the other Henley guys and I hadn't forced them away from each other.

And whenever I glanced at him, Lincoln was staring at Einstein in a way that made me want to hit something.

Then everything went downhill fast after Einstein had me call Conor. I got to be the one to tell Dare that not only had his mom known about the stalking and pictures but so had Conor.

He'd been helping Libby try to figure out who was behind it all.

The only good thing to come from that was he'd done some of Einstein's work for her, including just having finished compiling a list of all the Moretti men and finding the contract, which he had sent to Einstein before headed this way.

The same contact that had been signed in Borello and Moretti blood.

The one that *still* said Libby belonged to them.

That said whether or not she willingly married a Moretti by her twenty-first birthday, the union would still be seen as lawful in the eyes of the State the day after her birthday. And lawful in the eyes of God once the union was willingly consummated.

And among the pictures of Moretti men . . .

Gabe.

Einstein sucked in a sharp breath and sat straighter. "I've got something. There's nothing for Moretti, but Christian Daniel and Gabe Anthony—both partial names of a couple of our Moretti boys—have a firm in Raleigh. They also have apartments, and Christian has a warehouse on the way there in a very secluded place. Not sketchy at all," she said drily.

Dare pointed from me to the line of laptops. "We're hitting that first."

Diggs and I went to look at the satellite map Einstein had pulled up of the warehouse in question.

I'd barely glanced at it before Einstein's tapping on the keyboard stopped. "Sloppy, sloppy, sloppy . . . not even checking the property first." She tsked. "Someone's trying to sneak up on us, Dare."

My attention darted to the live feed she had of Holloway estate just as Dare came up behind her to study the screen.

"One of ours?" he asked.

"No. Looks like he was sent to keep us here," she murmured. "Walked on too. Guess he didn't want us to hear the car or see headlights."

I dipped my head in the slightest nod when Dare slanted a cold, demanding look at me.

With a growl, he turned to face the Henley guys. "Are you expecting anyone? Food, friends, manager? Anyone?" As soon as they all muttered hesitant *nos*, Dare looked back at the live feed. "Maverick. Diggs. Take care of it."

Diggs smacked his hand onto the counter and pushed back, headed away from the kitchen. "Hell yes. Wait," he said, turning back to Dare. "This is the first time without bandanas. Should we have a moment of silence? This is huge and kinda sad."

A huff pushed from my lungs.

"Jesus, Diggs," Dare groaned. "Go."

I grabbed Diggs's shoulder and turned him toward a hall when he went for the front door. "He's walking toward the door."

"Yeah . . . open. Shoot. Done." He lifted his hands out dramatically. "Ta-da."

I glanced over my shoulder to where the band was standing out of hearing distance from us. "At least three of the Henley guys would call the cops. I'd say that's a bad idea."

We opened the second door we came across and hurried through the space, which was littered with instruments.

My brother and I had never been in the mansion, but we knew everything about it.

The exact distance from one house to another on the property.

Every secret passageway.

Where every hall led, what every door concealed, and every window that opened.

Like the ones in this room.

It had been our job to know.

"This doesn't feel real." Excited energy poured from Diggs as he bounced on the balls of his feet. "My face feels naked."

"Get over it," I whispered before easing open a ground window. "Right now, we have a job to do. No guns."

Diggs punched my shoulder. "Why do you suck the fun out of everything?"

I cut him a hard look as I folded myself onto the windowsill and placed one foot outside. "I don't have my suppressor . . . do you?"

"Do you?" he mocked as he pushed me the rest of the way outside.

I stumbled, barely catching myself on the grass. When Diggs followed, I shoved him and lowered my voice. "Not the time. Go. Make sure there's no one else."

He rocked back before leaning forward to grip my shoulder. "You alive?"

My mouth twitched into a smirk. "I'm alive."

"Keep it that way." And then he was gone, disappearing into the night to hunt.

I took off in the opposite direction, toward where the man stood just before the porch, checking the gun in his hands.

Something he should have done before he took his first step onto the property.

I slowed as I neared the man, making my steps as silent as possible and trying to match my breathing to his.

Diggs was right. This felt *off*.

For generations, Borellos had worn black bandanas covering the lower halves of their faces. Ever since they'd picked us up, we hadn't done anything on the offensive or defensive without our faces partially covered.

Until tonight.

As I was passing the man, I said, "Nice night."

He turned, but I was already following through with his movements.

Gripping the hand holding the gun, I extended his arm

and thrust my palm into his locked elbow.

The gun fell to the gravel driveway.

His mouth opened and face twisted in pain and rage.

Before he could make a sound or react, I wrenched his head back and slammed my fist into his throat.

Gasping.

Wheezing.

Panic on his face and in his eyes.

I kept a tight hold on him so I could look him in the eyes when I asked, "You a Moretti?"

His eyes widened. A small spark of anger and determination flared before quickly dying out, answering for him.

He struggled to grab me.

My neck, my shoulder, my chest.

But his movements were sluggish and he was struggling to keep himself on his feet as he choked out blood.

"Getting harder to breathe?" I watched him for a few seconds and then bent close, my voice all grit and steel as I seethed, "You shouldn't have come after my family."

Headlights appeared at the beginning of the long driveway, coming quickly.

I let the man fall to the ground as I bent to pick up his gun.

Despite the fast approaching car, my movements were slow. I wanted to drag this out as long as I could in the short time I had left.

It wasn't that I enjoyed this.

But a quick death was a mercy, and mercy wasn't shown when the lives of people I loved were on the line.

I looked the gun over and then aimed it at the man. "Your family is about to find out what happens when they take people who don't belong to them."

I watched him struggle to breathe for another second . . .

Then pulled the trigger.

I ran for Dare's car, ready to take cover, but slowed when I heard Diggs yell, "Oh, *oh*. Look who I found."

The truck skidded to a stop on the gravel, and Diggs jumped out of the passenger side, pointing at me with a look of feigned betrayal on his face.

Conor rounded the front of the truck, his attention catching on the man lying in front of the porch. "That a Moretti?"

"Yep."

He nodded in my direction, his steps never slowing as he continued toward the front door of the mansion. "Good work."

When I focused on Diggs again, he hadn't moved. "You said no guns."

I lifted my arm to show the gun in question. "He had a suppressor."

His mouth opened and shut a few times before he said, "You said no guns, it's still cheating."

"It really isn't."

"I didn't make the rule, you did," he said, exasperation filling his tone. "So, when we go to this warehouse, I'm grabbing a rifle out of Dare's trunk, and you're not giving any rules this time. We're gonna walk in there like badasses with flames and doves and theme music and all that shit."

A disbelieving huff worked up my throat. "You're such an idiot."

"Yeah, and you fucking love it. Let's go save Libby."

Twenty-Five

Einstein
ONE MONTH AGO

I sucked in a sharp breath.

My muscles tensed in preparation. To run, to fight, to fall to the ground sobbing, *begging* for his forgiveness.

In preparation for anything.

I knew, without a doubt, who was walking up to where I sat against my tree.

Could feel it in the way my chest both eased and ached, smell his faint woodsy scent being carried to me on the breeze, and could practically hear his thoughts shouting at me.

Demanding answers.

Pleading with me for a life I could no longer give him.

I bit back all the words I might have said when he sat, my eyes fixated on where his leg brushed the exact spot . . .

"Figured you'd be here," he said after a few moments, his tone gruff, tortured.

My head snapped to face him, and I quickly blinked away the wetness gathering in my eyes.

Of course I was here.

I was *always* here. More so than I'd ever been before.

Did he know what he was doing to me by being here with me? Did he know that I wanted to fall into his arms and tell him everything? Did he know how desperately I needed him to leave?

Because I was standing on the razor's edge.

Yesterday, I almost hadn't been quick enough. We could've lost Libby, which was unthinkable.

I'd stayed strong throughout it all. Running on the knowledge that our family didn't lose people this way and that I was the only one who could find her. Functioning on pure rage because someone dared to try to take another person from my life.

And they'd almost succeeded.

It hadn't just been the Moretti family wanting to take what they thought belonged to them, it was a decade's worth of plotting and betraying. All coming down to this moment and two cousins who both thought they owned Libby, one ready to overthrow the other in the family.

Gabe killed Christian.

Libby risked her life trying to escape and killed Gabe just as we pulled up to the warehouse.

It was over, and all the adrenaline had fled my system.

I felt fragile.

Wrecked.

And so dangerously close to revealing things better left buried.

"Wanted to check on you."

I forced frustration and ice to seep through my words when I said, "I'm fine."

Maverick blew out a strangled sigh and rested his elbows on his knees, nodding as he did. "Yeah. Figured that too." He twisted his neck to look at me, his forehead pinched and eyes narrowed from his hurt. "Is it really that hard to be near me now? You can't just tell me how you're handling everything?"

"I said I was fine, because I am. I found Libby. We saved her. There's nothing to be *handling*."

Lie.

Lie, lie, lie.

A pained huff punched from his chest, and he looked straight ahead. "Jesus."

The truth was that, for the last seven months, I hadn't known how to handle anything that had been thrown at me.

I'd always prided myself on being smart. On knowing exactly what to say and what to do for every situation.

I'd never felt more lost in my life.

Being in the middle of the ocean without a way to get to shore or save myself didn't come close to explaining it.

I'd had help.

I'd been holding on to my lifeline . . . and I'd let go.

Every time Maverick extended it again, I hated myself a little more for shoving it away.

But I didn't know any other way.

With each passing day, I felt myself sinking deeper and deeper into the darkest depths of the sea.

Unable to reach out. Unable to call out. Unable to do anything but watch as I singlehandedly drowned myself.

I wasn't sure I would ever recover from failing him—

failing *them*. And I loved him too much to drag him down with me.

I stood from my spot at the tree and started to leave.

"This isn't you. You aren't like this. You don't have a heart of stone." He gripped my hand when I continued to walk away. "Avery—"

"*Stop*." I ripped from his hold and tried like hell to ignore the pain in his eyes. My voice twisted and wavered when I said, "I know I don't, Maverick. A heart can't be made of anything if you don't have one at all."

"What do you . . ." A frustrated huff left him. "What the hell happened, Avery? What happened to *you*. What happened to us?"

Lifeline.

I buried my heart.

It feels like my soul died.

It feels like this weight is slowly crushing me, reminding me of how I couldn't hold on to them. Reminding me of the pain.

And I don't know how to let you understand.

I don't know how to let anyone else in on my biggest failure—especially you.

Sinking.

I shook my head and clenched my teeth, willing away the threatening tears.

Lock it up.

Lock it up.

Maverick rocked forward when I stepped back, arm half-raised as if he wanted to make another grab for me. "Avery . . ."

I turned and hurried toward my car, ignoring when he yelled my name.

Deeper and deeper.

Twenty-Six

Einstein
ONE MONTH AGO

I WATCHED THE MAN BEHIND the bar as people came and went. As he chatted up the regulars and grunted to the women who flirted shamelessly with him.

I didn't *need* to study him. I already knew everything about his features and life.

I'd run everything I could on Zeke when Borellos first started coming to The Jack, only to do it again when Libby started working here. We spent so much time here, I could tell you when he was in a good mood by the way he grunted.

Who even grunts and still gets women to fall over themselves and crawl over each other to get to him?

Zeke. That was who.

I didn't understand it.

Hence, why I was scrutinizing him.

Sure, if I wanted to get technical, the man was attractive. Symmetrical face and bright green eyes. He had that big, burly, lumberjack thing going for him that women of all ages went crazy for lately. He was a lot like Conor . . . only without the sweet personality.

Zeke was also obsessed with being old without actually being old. I'd decided long ago that it was a complex from going gray early in life—again, something women seemed to go crazy for. That didn't stop it from being weird.

But he was no Maverick.

I took in a stuttered breath and let my stare drift in Zeke's direction again before calling out his name.

The few seconds it took for him to get to me felt like an eternity of torture, mocking me for what I was about to do.

I trembled when he stopped in front of me and laid his hands flat on the bar, eyebrow lifted in silent question.

With a steadying breath, I looked him straight in the eyes and said, "I think we should have sex."

His brows shot up. "The fuck you just say?"

I started to gesture to him but then hurried to clasp my shaking hands in my lap. "I've been listening to you grunt at people for the last hour. You're clearly frustrated."

"I always grunt at people."

"Not like this. This is your frustrated grunt. And what I'm offering will help with that."

He leaned forward to rest his forearms on the wooden surface separating us and narrowed his eyes at me curiously. "What exactly is it you would get out of this?"

"The pleasure of your company."

He barked out a laugh. "Bull fucking shit. You're pretty funny, kid."

"I'm serious," I hurried to say when he started pushing away.

He stopped, his amusement slowly fading. After a few seconds, he grunted at me.

"Yeah, I don't actually know what your grunts mean. Just tell me when and where we should do this." I gripped my hands tighter and hoped he didn't hear the tremble in my voice.

Pure shock covered Zeke's face for a moment before he leaned as close as the bar allowed. "I've never understood you, kid. You're weird and confident and say shit with no apologies. You're your own kind of woman. I like that. But there's no way in hell I'm touching you."

Relief flooded me so quickly that it took a second to realize I was being rejected.

I wasn't even hurt.

"Wait, what? Why not?"

"I don't touch women who don't belong to me." His eyes quickly raked over me. "Long as I've known you, you've belonged to one guy."

"Johnny's dead, in case you somehow missed that memo."

Zeke pushed from the bar and folded his arms over his chest. "No one in this town missed that memo. But I wasn't talking about him."

I clenched my teeth until my jaw ached from the pressure. "There's no one else I've ever belonged to, or ever will."

He tilted his head back and laughed long and loud. "Like I said . . . you're pretty funny, kid."

"I can prove it to you."

I can't, I can't, I can't.

He shook his head in disappointment. "Don't doubt that you would try. Still won't touch you."

The words *thank you* were on the tip of my tongue while another vain attempt was choking me. All I could do was slide off the barstool.

"Kid," Zeke called out when I turned to leave. "Don't know what happened between you and Mav, but this isn't the way to get back at him."

I swallowed back a sob and forced my steps to remain steady when all I wanted was to run.

I wasn't trying to get back at him.

I was trying to give him a reason to move on from me.

I walked in a daze. Not realizing where I was headed until I was already walking through the door of my favorite coffee shop.

I looked up when the aroma of freshly brewed coffee and warm pastries registered in my mind and walked numbly up to the register to order.

Every significant conversation and memory with Maverick rushed through my mind as I waited for my drink, only to be quickly overshadowed by all our recent arguments.

Sad that it was so much easier for Maverick and me when Johnny was still alive and we couldn't be together.

I would give anything to go back to that time. To have my precious stolen moments with him. To relive them again.

I was hit from behind and started stumbling forward, but was righted before I could smack into the drink counter.

"Shit, sorry. I'm sorry," a deep voice said. "I was looking at my phone and . . . well, I'm sorry."

I turned, already waving off the apology. "It's fi—" My brows pinched when I took in the man. "I know you."

"You do?"

"I know your jaw. And your smile. I know you . . ."

"That's specific," he said with a hesitant laugh.

"I'm good with faces."

His laugh deepened. "Sounds like it. Uh, well, I've actually seen you in here a few times." He glanced away, embarrassed. "I wasn't sure you'd noticed me. I just moved into town."

Doubt wove through my tone when I asked, "Did you?"

I would've known if someone new moved into town.

A little FYI to the man trying to lie to me, no one had.

"A few weeks ago." He pointed to the front of the shop. "Actually, just on the outskirts of Raleigh."

That was better.

"But I like the pace of Wake Forest, so I usually spend my days here. Don't tell my condo," he mock-whispered.

"And what is it you do . . ." I trailed off and slowly lifted my brows.

"Alex."

"Einstein."

He tilted his head, his expression twisted with a mixture of confusion and amusement. "Einstein, huh? Cruel parents."

"On-point friends."

"Ah. Well, I *could* tell you what I do for a living, Einstein, but then I'd have to kill you."

"Touché."

He shrugged and rubbed at the back of his neck. "It lets me work remotely and pays the bills. Can't complain."

I looked at the counter when the barista set my drink down and then offered him a brief smile. "Well, I'll let you get back to your top-secret business in slow-paced Wake Forest, Fake Name Alex."

His lips twitched into a flash of a bright smile. "I can show you my driver's license."

"Oh, there's no need. I know your face and your fake first name. I'll find you out soon enough."

"Or you can just find me here."

"I guess we'll have to see which happens first."

He searched my eyes as I stepped away. "Looking forward to it."

I committed everything about him to memory as I hurried to ARCK.

He had Kieran's build . . . so around the same weight. I'd give Fake Name Alex another five to ten pounds of muscle. Closely cropped dark hair. Blue eyes. No visible tattoos. Hint of a scar on his right eyebrow.

That jaw and smile . . . I knew them, just not from the coffee shop or Wake Forest.

As soon as I was in the office, I hurried to my desk and set my coffee beside my laptop. I had my computer on and a few sites that I needed open when Jess appeared beside me.

"I said hi, and you walked right by me."

"Busy."

She huffed. "I can see that. With what?"

"I need to know who this guy is."

She hunched down to have a better look at my screen. Her tone immediately dropped. "What guy? What happened?"

"Working here."

"*Bored* here. And you work for me." She pulled a long

chunk of my hair into her hands to play with it, not caring when I continued to swat at her.

"Say I work for you again and see if I don't have your husband kill you."

She let out a wild laugh. "I'd like to see him try. He can't even *sneak up on me*," she said, her last words nearly a yell.

I glanced up in time to see Kieran appear behind her, his arms curling possessively around Jess's waist. "What are we doing?"

"Still trying to work," I mumbled, exasperation leaking through my tone.

Jess gave a teasing tug on my hair. "She said she needs to know who a guy is."

I groaned and turned in my seat to face them, smacking at Jess's arm as I did so she'd drop my hair. "There was this guy in the coffee shop just now—"

"What'd he do?" Kieran demanded, his body tense and eyes full of fire.

Jesus. Mobsters.

"Nothing. Good Lord. You Irish—"

"You know, you say that a lot, but you look more Irish than I do." His words were all tease . . . well, as much as Kieran *could* tease.

I sliced my hand through the air, motioning for him to drop it. "Whoa, buddy. Let's not get crazy. Don't let the red hair and green eyes and freckles fool you." I paused when I realized what I'd just said. "Scottish by blood. Italian by choice. Anyway, this guy . . ."

I recounted the entire conversation to them and then sat there, waiting while they just stared at me before Jess burst into laughter.

"Einstein, please tell me you aren't really looking him up."

"Of course I am," I said as I turned back to face my screen.

"He was flirting with you."

I stopped and looked at the couple. "What?"

Jess dropped her face in her hands before peeking out the side to murmur to Kieran, "What is it with you ex-mobsters and not understanding what flirting is?"

He smirked in a way that left me feeling cold but had Jess blushing.

Ew.

"Thought you liked my version of flirting?" he countered softly.

"Oh, I do."

"Gross." I mock-gagged. "I'm sitting right here."

Jess giggled in that way only she could. In a way that sounded sultry and amused and a little crazed all at once.

She tapped her knuckles on my head and then pulled another chunk of my hair into her hands. "He was flirting with you. I'd also safely say you were flirting back."

A wave of heat washed through me, leaving me uneasy. "How the hell did you get that from anything I just told you?"

"In your defense, I know you're *you*, and you Einstein everyone you meet and tell them all the ways you think you know them. But you shouldn't tell a hot guy that. Especially about his smile."

"You think he's hot?" Kieran asked, his tone warning her the man's life could be at risk depending on her answer.

Jess rolled her eyes and didn't spare a glance at her

husband as she continued talking to me. "You were asking his name and job. You more or less told him you planned to see him again *after* you told him you were going to look into him. That's flirting. And stalking—but that's also just you being you."

"I was trying to get information. I was genuinely letting him know that I was going to search him because I didn't believe anything he told me."

"And this is why no one other than Maverick will ever be able to handle you," she teased and gave another tug at the braid she'd just woven into my hair.

I turned away before they could see my pain over just hearing his name.

I stared at my screen unblinking for a while before I finally cleared my throat and lifted my hands to my keyboard. "I don't need anyone to be able to handle me. And I don't need Maverick."

Jess jerked on the braid until I looked at her. Worry pinched her face. "Are you not . . ."

My expression must have answered enough.

After a few seconds, she nodded. "If you still haven't gotten back together with Maverick, then maybe you should go to the coffee shop and ask Alex out." She lifted her shoulders. "You never know, a night with him might be what you need."

Acid churned in my stomach.

Everything I'd done for the last seven months had only made Maverick fight harder for us.

I knew what I needed to do.

Clearly, or I wouldn't have just asked Zeke to sleep with me.

I knew, because my soul had cried and ached for his

with every fight we'd had. But it recoiled and thrashed at the thought of letting anyone else touch me.

I would always be his.

But all I had left to give him were pains and failures and an inescapable, consuming nightmare.

And he deserved more than that. He deserved everything.

"Or maybe whatever is making you look like that is telling you all you need to know about Maverick," Jess said gently, a knowing look on her face.

"You don't understand." The words were out before I could begin to force them back.

Jess and Kieran understood more than anyone. But they couldn't understand the constant turmoil. They couldn't understand the deep-rooted need to hide my pain from the world and to push anyone who got too close to see it away.

I was suffocating. Drowning.

And I would do anything to make sure Maverick didn't drown with me, no matter the cost. No matter how much he would hate me for it later.

There was already so much to hate me for anyway.

Just then, Conor called out from the front of the office. "Lunch."

I grit my teeth and took the sick feeling in my stomach and imagined it turning into the strength I would need to get through the next few minutes.

With a hard nod to Jess, I took my hair from her hands and stood, my steps strong and determined when I felt weak and wrecked and broken.

Conor smiled that boyish smile when he saw me. "Didn't know you were gonna be here. There's a ton, take what . . . you . . ." His brow furrowed. "Einstein?"

I grabbed his hand and turned, striding purposefully back the way I'd come.

"Everything okay?"

I didn't say anything. I wasn't sure I could yet.

I gritted my teeth and kept my eyes straight ahead, ignoring the dread covering Jess's face and hardened indifference on Kieran's as we passed them. Once we were in the back room, I shut the door behind us and released Conor's hand.

I paced a few feet away and mentally sang a code in the tune of "Twinkle, Twinkle Little Star" until I was sure I wasn't going to throw up or pass out, and then turned to him.

"I want you to kiss me."

Conor's reaction was identical to Zeke's. Eyebrows shot up, shock was pure and whole.

"I want you to kiss me and I want you to take me back to your place and-and-and I want you to sleep with me. I want you to have sex with me."

A sound somewhere between a cough and a choke caught in his throat.

Then, after what felt like an eternity, he nodded, slow and uncertain.

Pain washed through me like a wildfire.

When Conor stepped toward me, I wanted to scream that I took it all back.

But he was coming closer with a look of understanding in his eyes, his hand was on the back of my head and he was leaning in, and I was paralyzed.

I tensed just before his lips touched me but relaxed when they only lingered on my forehead for a second before he stepped away.

"There's your kiss," he said softly. "I'm not taking you back to my place. And I'm not sleeping with you."

I blinked quickly, trying to absorb the relief that threatened to consume me for the second time today. "Why does everyone keep rejecting me?"

A sharp laugh burst from his chest. "Don't know who the rest of *everyone* is, but I'm guessing it might have something to do with the blow to our pride we would suffer."

"Not following."

"When you scream Maverick's name instead of ours when we're inside you."

I felt hot and cold all at once. I felt sick.

"You're beautiful, Einstein. Anyone would be lucky to take you home, but we all know you don't want anyone but him to." His words were soft and kind and held no hint of desire.

Not that I'd expected them to.

Not that I wanted them to.

My stare dropped to the floor and I took an unsteady step away.

"Tell me why you're doing this."

"Because I don't want him," I whispered as I headed for the door. "I *can't*."

"Einstein—"

"I have work to do."

A half hour later, I was still so frustrated from my double rejection—and drained from the stress of attempting at all—that when I saw the contact name on the email that just landed in my inbox, my entire body halted.

My lungs pushed the air from my body in an annoyed huff.

My heart gave one last pitiful thump.

And my fingers stopped tapping on the keys.

Yeah. That frustrated. It stopped my fingers.

My heart started up painfully, and I sucked in a deep breath as if I were preparing to scream.

"You've gotta be fucking kidding me."

Over a month since I'd heard from her. Since I'd messaged her back and told her not to contact our company again.

Five weeks and three days . . . if you wanted to get technical.

And yet, here was another email from Sutton Larson.

"You've got some big ol' brass balls, lady. Or man. Robot. Whatever you are," I murmured, dragging my fingers across the mousepad to open up the email.

Please. We do need help. Genuine help, as you call it.

I'm afraid. Afraid for my daughter's life and my own.

I don't understand what you mean. Existence? I am Sutton Larson. Sutton Larson is me.

I'll find a way to get you a copy of my ID if that will prove it to you. But we need help. We need to get away, and I don't know if I can do that by myself.

I'm afraid they're watching us closely . . . if you understand what I mean.

That was why it took so long for me to reach out to you again.

We will be here as long as we can wait.

If you don't come for us, I'll write to you when I can. Please don't contact me. Just come.

At the bottom was an address.

I put it in a search bar and within seconds had a seedy-as-hell motel outside Brentwood on my screen. It screamed disease and bed bugs and all kinds of things I didn't want to think about.

My brow furrowed as I hurried back to the email.

Typing in a search for her name, the four emails I'd received from her pulled up. Every single one had come at the exact same time—two minutes before noon. Nothing was suspicious about the email address itself, it was just her name with numbers.

If I were trying to hide an email account from someone, I wouldn't have my name attached to it in any way.

If I were trying to convince someone I was legit, I wouldn't act so shady and send every email at the exact same time.

I tried to see where the emails had come from, but I only got as far as Brentwood, Tennessee, before it died off. And when I tried to reply, asking who *they* were, I got an immediate, automated response saying there was a delivery failure.

"Awesome." I pushed from the desk and wandered into Kieran and Jess's office, not bothering to knock. "How difficult would it be to see if there were people in, say, Tennessee?"

A shocked laugh punched from Jess's chest.

Kieran's brow furrowed. Or maybe it just stayed the way it always was.

"People who may or may not want to do us harm. Say . . . old enemies?"

"You tell me," Kieran said in that low, growling tone of his. "That's your job."

"Yeah, well, what if I already checked and came back with nothing?"

Kieran sat back in his chair far enough for me to see the small blade he was rolling along his knuckles.

From his silence, I had to assume he was thinking.

Jess looked from me to him. "If she didn't find anything, then there isn't anything. Right?"

Kieran shrugged. "You'd think."

"It is very wealthy there," I mumbled. "Very."

He caught the blade in his hand and used it to point at me, all the while his stare remained on Jess. "Then again . . ." He blinked quickly and sat forward, finally looking back to me. "Tennessee?"

"Well, Brentwood."

He watched me for a few seconds, his head shaking as he did. "I don't know of any families there."

And Kieran knew plenty of families because he hadn't just been Holloway's assassin, he'd been their underboss.

He also knew the places where greedy, corrupt politicians resided. Ones who turned a blind eye to the goings on in darker worlds in order to gain votes and rake in money and drugs and women.

Anything.

Everything.

All for a little taste of *our* world while riding high with clean hands in *theirs*.

"I can ask around—"

"No," I said, ignoring their curious looks.

I was sure I was being played by whoever was behind the emails.

But my gut twisted and heart raced at the thought of Kieran asking around—of *anyone* asking around.

It didn't make sense, but I knew I needed to keep this within ARCK.

I quickly told Jess and Kieran everything about the emails I'd received. The length between them, the times they'd come in, and what they'd contained.

"I'm positive it's someone messing with us or me. A woman or man . . . I don't know. But I have a feeling they're waiting to see what we'll do. At the same time, the thought of them knowing we're looking into anything she's said has me scared for her—or, well, the idea of this woman."

Kieran was nodding his agreement as I spoke. "Then we'll look quietly. No traces."

A breath of a laugh left me. "That isn't possible."

A wicked grin shaped his lips. "I wouldn't be so sure."

"The email today said she was afraid they were watching closely. It could be something they said to explain away why I would no longer be able to respond. It could've been real. Or it could've been a warning to us."

Jess sighed. "So complicated. Let's just go there, get her and the kid, kill anyone who tries to stop us or come after us, and be done."

The grin on Kieran's lips twitched, threatening a full smile. "Can't. Like any of our other special cases, it has to be treated delicately and executed at the right time. But from the sound of it, this one will be more difficult to complete if she insists on being impossible to communicate with. I can't trust that she's going to be in a motel, that could be a trap."

"It looks like one," I said under my breath.

Kieran blew out an exaggerated breath, his eyes glazing over as he thought. "She said she witnessed a crime?"

I nodded.

"Whenever her first email was, go back six months for the surrounding areas and look at all the major crimes. See if there are any where the suspects weren't caught. Start there."

I pushed from my position at the wall. "Done."

"Every day from here on out, be at your computer before noon," he continued. "If she emails you, respond immediately. Tell her we need a way to confirm she's real. Picture, video, call, something. I'd prefer video with this one."

I dipped my head in understanding and headed back to my desk, more than ready for something to keep my mind and hands busy.

Twenty-Seven

Einstein
TODAY

I wasn't the female Captain America.

I wasn't given superpowers.

As I found out when I tried to open the single door in this new windowless room.

There was no ripping it off its hinges.

Or punching it out.

Or kicking it down . . .

I was just Einstein.

Fortunately for me, the one thing I'd always had was my brain.

Unfortunately for me, my brain was a super hateful bitch after the crazy unknown trips I'd been on today and the constant stream of nitrous laced oxygen pumping into the room.

But I'd already looked, the only vent I could find was the one I'd come out of.

And as with the other room, this door only had a super pretty, old-fashioned dummy keyhole and a handle.

So there was nowhere to go but back, and I felt much more at home in a room full of super-duper high-tech screens.

Then again, with the way I felt at the moment, I would've felt at home pretty much anywhere. But this room had a toilet. Bonus.

They weren't total dicks—

My body lurched forward.

My mouth opened and shut, gaping, silently begging.

I was still so raw from before that my body immediately reacted.

Went up in flames.

Submerged in the deepest parts of the ocean.

I didn't feel the impact when I fell to my knees. Or when I fell to my side, landing on my shoulder.

I felt nothing and everything.

Screaming.

Inside.

That was me in my head.

I clawed at myself and the floor but felt nothing beneath my fingers.

Dark, dark, darkness gathered.

And then my chest was heaving as if I'd been shocked.

The screaming inside was reverberating throughout the room.

That burning deepened as I tried to fill my lungs with untainted air.

I wasn't sure how long I lay there as oxygen mixed with my blood and cleared my head.

Flat on my back. Trembling. Sobbing.

But I could no longer find the will to move as the weight of the day bore down on me.

As helplessness built within me and threatened to consume me.

It was as though this place had been built specifically for me. To torture me. To drive me insane.

Locks I couldn't open.

Drugs that knocked me out and had lingering effects. Others that impaired every thought and mood and would surely make it impossible for me to get out of here.

It all felt so personal, and I didn't even know them.

When Libby had been taken, there'd been a purpose behind their psychotic minds. They thought they owned her. They were taking what they'd thought was theirs.

It had also been well over a decade of fears and threats in the making.

This was none of those things, and I was not a fighter like Libby.

I was not a war mastermind like Dare.

I was not an unstoppable assassination team like Diggs and Mav—

My heart twisted. A sharp sob ripped through the room at the thought of Maverick.

This day had been nothing but hell after hell, and I wondered if he knew I was gone.

If anyone would notice before he left town.

Or how long it would take anyone to notice at all.

And I had no one to blame but myself.

I'd pulled back. I'd pushed away. I'd wanted distance between myself and everyone else—especially Maverick.

I'd *needed* it.

I'd needed everyone far enough away so they wouldn't see the pain sliding through my veins like broken glass.

I would give anything to go back.

To do it all differently.

Or to at least go back to that last moment under the tree with Maverick. To grieve with him. To beg him not to leave. To apologize for all the hurt I caused him.

If I ever made it out of these rooms, I knew we would never be the same. We couldn't.

I'd damaged too much.

But it would be enough for me to be able to look up and see him walk through a door.

To see that smile that always started hesitantly, as if he had a secret.

It would be enough to see him happy again . . . even if I wasn't the one behind his happiness.

"You fight for what you love. And I've never loved anyone the way I love you, Avery."

I blinked away the past when I tasted that now-familiar sweetness on my tongue.

It took only a second before I knew what was happening, that the oxygen was laced again.

"No. No, no, no."

I didn't want to relax. I didn't want my brain to be fuzzy. I didn't want to be carefree.

I *wanted* to hurt.

I *wanted* to know what was happening around me . . . to care that I was trapped in this place.

I wanted to care about my survival. I wanted to care that for the first time in nearly a year, I could feel my heart.

It hurt and ached, but it was there instead of buried in the ground within a box.

I scrambled to my feet and hurried to look at the screens covering the room, pausing when a little yellow paper caught my attention.

I'd been so focused on finding a vent or going for the door earlier, that I hadn't looked at the screens. I hadn't noticed another Post-it.

I stepped up to it, hesitation warred within me as my eyes darted to the screens surrounding it before reading the words.

I WANT YOU CLEAR FOR THE NEXT PART.
OR ELSE IT WON'T BE FUN.

I ripped off the note, read it again, then looked at the screen it had been on.

SYSTEM ON was highlighted in red at the top of the screen.

A list of words lined the right side—MAX was in bold. AIRLOCK and REVERSE were grayed out.

In the center were two large outlines of gas tanks, side by side.

Beneath each was a code.

N_2O.

O.

I tensed for all of two seconds before my hand flew to the screen, my fingers hovering over it for a moment to make sure I wasn't seeing things wrong.

To make sure I wasn't selecting the wrong one in my quickly relaxing state.

Tapping the tank on the left, I dragged the nitrous oxide all the way down until it was at zero and then waited.

And waited.

To see if they'd switched it on me.

To see if I'd made a terrible mistake.

But there was nothing. And the longer I waited, the clearer my mind became.

I tapped on LOG and quickly scanned the information.

SYSTEM: **ON**

BEGIN 10-MINUTE CYCLE

65% OXYGEN 35% NITROUS OXIDE | 6 MINUTES | MAXIMUM SPEED

55% OXYGEN 45% NITROUS OXIDE | 2 MINUTES | MAXIMUM SPEED

AIRLOCK STATUS: **SEALED**

FAN STATUS: **REVERSED**

0% OXYGEN 100% NITROUS OXIDE | 45 SECONDS | MAXIMUM SPEED

FAN STATUS: **NORMAL**

100% OXYGEN 0% NITROUS OXIDE | 75 SECONDS | MAXIMUM SPEED

AIRLOCK STATUS: **OPEN**

RESTART 10-MINUTE CYCLE

And then the cycle repeated, confirming what I'd already known and feared.

"Asshole."

Twenty-Eight

Maverick
ONE MONTH AGO

I SWUNG OPEN THE DOORS to The Jack a little harder than necessary.

I felt restless.

Anxious.

My chest felt tight. Making it hard to catch my breath.

I dragged my hand across it, trying to relieve the pressure there.

I wasn't sure why I thought applying pressure would relieve pressure, but at that moment, nothing was making sense. My head was fucking spinning, my gut churning.

They had been ever since I'd got the call a half hour before.

It'd been short. Direct.

"The Jack. Thirty minutes."

There'd been nothing in the way of explanations.

And that was why I felt ready to punch the next person who spoke to me and puke if I forced too deep of a breath.

I looked up, my narrowed eyes finding the guy easily.

Leaning against the bar with his back to me. A tumbler of whiskey next to him.

"You summoned me," I murmured when I slid up beside him.

The anxious twisting of my stomach warned me against drinking anything, but if he had a drink waiting for me, I had a feeling I was going to want it.

Probably gonna want a few.

I grabbed the glass and slammed the whiskey back. Letting the familiar burn coat my throat and attempt to calm my nerves.

"Another?" he asked when I set the glass on the bar.

Shit.

"Depends on why I'm here." I twisted so I was facing him and gave him a look that told him I was waiting.

But he didn't offer anything. Didn't explain away the meeting or deal the devastating blow I was expecting and dreading.

Instead, he stood there, staring at the worn wood of the bar, his throat moving with his forced swallows.

"If Einstein's still not showing up to work, I can't help you with that. She only shows up to our meetings when she wants to, and even then, they turn into a disaster."

Conor finally turned to look at me, his expression and tone hesitant. "No, she's there. When she wants to be." He shrugged. "Can't do anything about it, she still gets her work done."

I lifted my brows slowly. "Then why are we here?"

I normally liked Conor.

I did.

But he'd caused so much fear and grief and worry over the last thirty minutes with just four words, that I almost hated him.

"I want to know what you did to Einstein." His demand didn't hold any of the bite I knew he could put behind his words.

There was no intimidation.

He sounded exhausted almost. Or maybe sorry.

A huff flew from my lips as I dropped onto the barstool. "I'd like to know. I've been begging her to tell me for months. One day we were perfect, the next . . ." I held up a hand and then let it fall to my leg with a soft *slap*. "She just shut down and shut me out, and ever since, she's been acting like *we* never were."

He was nodding while I spoke, as though he was getting the answer he expected. "Not that I knew her that well before she started working for us, but she changed overnight. Then again, you could've done something, and I wouldn't have known, because it isn't like she divulges the crazy ins and outs of her mind to anyone."

She had. To me.

"There's something you should know." He cleared his throat, and if I hadn't been watching him so closely, I wouldn't have noticed how he tensed. How he seemed to be preparing for a fight.

God damn it.

"Whatever *did* happen between the two of you, I'm pretty fucking positive she's trying to end it by pissing you off." He looked to the bar before hesitantly glancing back at me, his face pinched in worry. "She asked me to sleep with her. *Told* me to."

I thought I was going to fall.

I *was* falling.

I could feel the seat below me and knew I was sitting just as I knew the entire floor was being ripped out from under me.

"I said no," he said quickly. "Obviously."

I couldn't meet Conor's stare. I couldn't even hold my head up.

No.

No, no, no.

It didn't make sense. That wasn't Einstein.

I'd been there for her for a decade. I'd been the one who loved her unconditionally and who she loved in return. And, even then, it'd taken months of slow, *slow* build before she'd been ready.

She would never let just anyone in.

Not after what she'd been through.

Anything less than someone she trusted with her entire body, heart, and soul would never be enough for her to give herself to.

If there was anything I knew about that girl, it was that.

I flinched and jerked away from Conor when he placed his hand on my shoulder.

He rocked back, hands raised as though I was aiming a gun at him. "Sorry. I'm sorry. I just—I just wasn't sure you were hearing me."

I shook my head in a quick jerk when I realized that meant he'd been talking.

A slow, steadying breath blew from his lips. "The way she was, it was weird. It was frantic. She might as well have built a steel wall around her the way she reacted when I mentioned you. I could see it. Hearing your name hurt her. Then she shut down and bolted. Hasn't talked to me since."

"You want me to apologize?" The question came out a snarl, making Conor jerk back.

"Man, I told you. I said no. You think I don't know about the two of you? Think I don't know that it's you for her and her for you? I'm not gonna go stepping between that."

I needed to be thankful.

But she'd gone to him. To fucking *Conor*.

The guy was my opposite. Blond. Full beard. Covered in tattoos. And had half a foot on me because he was a fucking beast.

It was hard not to hate him when the girl I loved was choosing him instead of me.

I dragged my hands over my face, pausing when someone cleared their throat near me.

Deep and gravelly and sounding annoyed as hell.

I knew that sound.

I looked over the bar to where Zeke stood. "Not the time, man."

He grunted something I couldn't understand and then nodded at Conor. "If we're sharing, and he's in closer range of your hands, then yeah, it's as good a time as any."

I spared a glance at the man next to me, but his brow was furrowed in confusion.

By the time I was looking at Zeke again, he was already talking. "Kid was sitting at the bar a couple of days ago. We had an identical conversation," he mumbled, nodding to Conor.

"She asked you." It came out more a demand than a question.

"Told me we should. And like the Hulk over here, I said no. 'Cause as long as I've known her, she's belonged to you."

"That's what she meant," Conor murmured.

I pushed the empty glass toward Zeke in silent demand but kept my head slanted in Conor's direction. "What the hell do you mean?"

"She asked me why everyone kept rejecting her. Now I know who everyone is."

Zeke put a shot glass in front of me.

I threw it back.

And then another.

When I stood and grabbed for my wallet, he held a hand up and shook his head.

"Well . . ." Something that sounded like a wheeze and a strangled laugh left me. I nodded, unable to stop or know what to say. "Fuck."

I tried to walk calmly out of the bar.

I stalked.

My rage and agony and disbelief pounded through my veins until I was shaking from the fatal combination.

I wanted to hate them. Hate *her*.

I wanted to say fuck it. That I was done.

But as I found myself walking to our tree, there was only one question going through my head on repeat.

Same one I'd been plagued with for months.

What the hell did I do to her?

That night, I was unlocking her apartment door and storming in.

I'd tried to talk myself out of this no less than a dozen times.

Each time, my anger had only continued to grow, and I'd found myself headed this way. Finally, I'd stopped thinking of every reason why I shouldn't and focused on all the reasons why I should.

Because I'd been there for this girl since the day she saved me.

I'd fought for her.

And I wouldn't give up so easily.

On any other day, I would've been positive Einstein would be in her room, lost in hours upon hours of work or finding some new code she had to figure out.

After my talk with Conor and Zeke today, I was terrified that I was about to walk in on something that could potentially wreck me for the rest of my life.

But it was a risk I had to take.

For Einstein.

For us.

I headed for her room since the only light in the darkened apartment was coming from that direction. My hands fisted and jaw ground the closer I got, but as soon as I turned the corner to the hall and saw her sitting at her desk with her headphones on, my frustrations eased.

Slightly.

I banged my fist on the corner of her desk so she would know I was there a second before I grabbed her headphones and tossed them away.

She jerked and whirled around in her chair to face me. "What the hell do you think you're doing?"

I gestured to her headphones. "What the hell are *you*

doing? You can't hear anyone walk up on you. You can't do that shit now that you live alone."

"I think better with them on."

"You're fucking clueless with them on."

For probably the first time since I'd known her, she seemed too stunned to speak. After sputtering for a few seconds, she said, "Are you really here to give me a lecture about my headphones? And what makes you think you can just walk in here?"

"Years of that being what we do, Einstein." I folded my arms across my chest and planted my feet firmly to the floor. I didn't plan on going anywhere until I got answers. "Tell me why you're doing this."

Emotions flickered across her face.

Pain. Defeat. Exhaustion.

When she answered, her tone was soft and sounded weighed down. "Maverick . . . we can't keep doing this."

"We can, and I will. Because you fight for what you love. And I've never loved anyone the way I love you, Avery."

She shrugged and tried to force a smile. "Well, I can't—"

"Save it. I've heard it all, and I don't believe any of it."

"That isn't my problem." She huffed, but it sounded strained and so unlike Einstein. "I can't make you believe anything, but you have to accept that we're over."

"I will when you do."

Silence filled the room, heavy and aching.

Finally, she whispered, "I accepted that a long time ago."

"No, you decided it and forgot to tell me why." I spread my arms out and looked around. "I've been here, begging and pleading with you to give me the slightest fucking clue as to what has been going on. But all I ever get is wall after wall after wall."

"You think you'd take a hint."

"You think you'd offer me a reason for shutting me out."

Her stare dropped to the floor. Her slender throat moved. After a moment, she turned back toward her screens. "We don't always get what we want."

"The world. I would give you the damn world. And you can't give me *this*?" When her hands reached out for her keyboard, I grabbed the back of her chair and spun her around. "Fucking *talk to me*."

"There's nothing to say," she cried out as tears filled her eyes and fell down her cheeks. "Maybe what we thought we could have was only ever there because it was unattainable. Forbidden. Once it was there for us to reach out and hold, it slipped away. Did you ever think of that?"

"Not for a second. What we had was stronger than ever." I snapped my fingers right in front of her face, but she didn't flinch, her eyes just held mine through her tears. "And like that, you took it away. *You*."

Her brows slowly pinched. Her face contorted in pain. "Did I?" she asked, disbelief coating her words.

I leaned forward so I was face to face with her and grabbed the arms of her chair. Gritting my teeth, I sneered, "I'm not the one telling people to fuck me."

Shock and shame flitted across her face before she was able to drop her head to stare at her lap.

"Yeah . . . yeah, Conor may be loyal to you, but he's coming to me because even they all know something's wrong with you. Think he had a clue when you told him to sleep with you. Think Zeke did." A forced laugh crawled from my throat. "Fucking *Zeke*, Einstein?"

I pushed away and dragged my hands through my hair.

She didn't respond.

I wanted to say I hadn't expected her to, but everything she did lately was so unexpected that I never knew what she would do next.

"Who else?" When there was no response, I asked, "Who else? Diggs?"

Her head shot up. Shock and disgust twisted her expression. "Oh, fuck you."

"Right now, I wouldn't put much past you."

There were three names on the tip of my tongue, nearly falling from my lips. Names I'd had my suspicions of ever since they'd rolled back into town and decided not to leave again.

After my talk with Conor and Zeke, I had a feeling all my fears were going to be confirmed. And I didn't think I could stomach it.

I clenched my teeth and ground out, "The Henley guys?"

Her eyes slowly lifted so she was looking at me from beneath her eyelashes.

Acid swirled in my stomach. My legs felt unsteady.

"Ledger? Jared?" My chest rose and fell in quick jerks when she only continued to watch me after each name. I ground my jaw until I was sure it would shatter. When I asked the last name, it came out low and threatening. "Lincoln?"

Einstein straightened her spine and squared her shoulders. Her chin lifted just slightly. But she would no longer look me in the eye.

Fuck.

"Why?"

I was trembling.

My heart was limping in the middle of a sprint. Pounding. Threatening to burst from my chest. And every few beats, it faltered.

Wounded.

Bleeding out.

Dying.

That was what this felt like.

I slammed my hand against the wall closest to me. *"Why, Avery?"*

She lifted her brows and sighed. "This is where I tell you I'm sorry you had to find out this way," she mumbled as she reached for her tablet where it sat at the edge of her desk. She folded her legs in the chair, her fingers already flying across the screen. "Except, you know, I'm not."

Lie.

The slight hitch and waver in her tone. The way she was hiding from *me* behind her tablet.

All of it screamed she was lying.

Einstein and her fucking walls.

"Bullshit."

Before I knew I was moving, I had her tablet in my hand and had smashed it against the wall.

"Are you insane?" she yelled. "I can't just go buy another one like that. I built—"

"I don't care about your damn tablet."

She swung her hand out to gesture to where it lay on the floor. "Obviously."

"I care about what you're doing and why. This isn't you. After everything you went through. After everything we went through together to get you to a place where you felt safe and comfortable with me. You wouldn't just—"

"Or maybe I would," she snapped. "Maybe I would sleep with all of Wake Forest if only to *finally* get it through your head that we're done."

I rocked back.

The air rushed from my lungs.

"Whatever did happen between the two of you, I'm pretty fucking positive she's trying to end it by pissing you off."

"So that is it?" I laughed but it sounded sad, strangled. "You're just doing this to make a statement."

Her silence was confirmation enough.

I nodded slowly, almost absentmindedly, as my hands curled into fists and then relaxed.

Before I could talk myself out of it, I moved forward, hauled her out of the chair and against my chest, and crushed my mouth to hers.

She gripped my shoulders and put the slightest pressure against them.

And then her body melted.

Her mouth opened with a sigh.

Her tongue met mine in that familiar dance.

A whimper mixed with a cry slid up her throat and got lost in the kiss.

And then she was gripping me and wrapping her legs around my waist; her fingers were sliding up my shoulders and curling into my hair.

And my heart . . . that sprint was coming to an end.

That limp had turned into a crawl.

Because I could feel her love and her pain in the kiss.

I could feel her silently pleading for me not to let her

go. Begging. After so long of her doing everything to destroy us.

I ended the kiss as abruptly as I started it and studied the tears streaming down her face as I lowered her back to the chair.

I swallowed past the grief and heartache tightening my throat and stepped away from her. "Yeah. That felt like we're done."

A sob ripped from her throat, but she didn't say anything as I headed for the door.

When I reached it, I stopped and looked at her again.

Curled in on herself in her chair.

In pain.

Breaking.

And everything in me wanted to go to her and make it go away.

"You're a fucking coward."

She slowly lifted her head, a crease formed between her eyebrows.

"All of this time, all of this bullshit you've put me through, and now this? Lincoln, Conor, Zeke . . . and who knows who else. Just to prove that we're done?" My chest pitched, heart tripping frantically to find purchase on shattered ground. "All you ever had to do was talk to me. Tell me what happened. But what you're doing, what you've *done*? You're a coward."

Her chin shook before she could steel it.

I shrugged helplessly. "I've spent every day—fuck, every minute trying to figure out what happened. What went wrong. What I did. If I hurt you. Anything. I've gone over every part of our time together so many times I've lost count, but I'm more lost today than I was when you first shut me out. And for some reason, you've been punishing me for that.

"But I think I get it now. I've been fighting for us because I love you, and I knew you still loved me. That kiss proved it." I forced a smile, but it felt all kinds of wrong, because *this* was wrong. "And that . . . I'm pretty damn sure *that* is why you're pushing me away."

Jesus fucking Christ.

The way her face fell confirmed it all.

I wanted to beg her to tell me it was something else. Something that I could hate her for. Something that made *sense*.

"You'd think I would feel a little more at ease after figuring out what's going on in that head of yours. Knowing that what's been going on is simply the fact that I love you, and you love me. Not something horrible." Something like a laugh fell from my lips. "Right?"

She opened her mouth to say something, but then she paused when her lip quivered and clamped her jaw shut.

Good.

After all this time, I didn't want her to explain herself.

"You and I? We've loved each other for a long time. With the lengths you've gone to end us . . . I almost wish it had been something worse."

I left.

Stumbled out.

Texted Diggs and met him at The Jack.

When he got there, he didn't ask questions. He took one look at me and had Zeke bring an entire bottle over.

When I only sat there holding my first shot in my hand, he sighed and grabbed it from between my fingers to set it on the bar.

"E?"

Like he had to ask. Everything lately was about Einstein.

"You see her?"

I shifted my head, grabbed the shot glass, and pressed it to my lips.

The warm liquid was still burning a path down my throat when I poured another to throw back.

I set the glass down and slid it across the worn wood, back and forth between my hands as I recounted the entire day to my brother. Starting with the call from Conor and ending with somehow forcing myself from Einstein's apartment.

He didn't say a word.

Not while I spoke. Not for long minutes after I was done.

Just sat there beside me.

Finally, he cleared his throat and said, "I've been there with you every day, every *year*, of this mess with her. I hurt with you and for you. I always knew what she meant to you. And I . . . damn it, man, I always wanted a day to come when you could be with her. But now?"

"Don't." I curled my hand around the shot glass and then slowly released it, watching it clatter to the wood. "Don't go there. I can't. She's . . ."

"Look what she's doing to you."

"I have, Diggs. I see it. I feel it." I twisted my neck to look at him. "But she's everything. She'll always be everything."

"All right, Mav." He nodded and tipped back another shot. "All right."

Twenty-Nine

Maverick
ONE MONTH AGO

Focus.
 Focus.
 On anything other than the girl in front of you.

I shifted my stare away from Einstein for what had to be the tenth time in the last minute. But as soon as my gaze settled on the book that rested on the table in front of Dare, I felt my attention being drawn toward her.

A magnet pulled.

That was how it had always been between us.

That was how it would always be.

I ground my teeth when she flashed me a hard look and tried to focus on the book again. At Dare. At Diggs. Fucking anything.

I lifted my brows and slanted my head in Dare's direction when he said something to me.

Maybe asked.

"Hmm?"

He blew out a harsh breath through his nose. His eyes narrowed into a look nearly identical to the one Einstein had just given me. Only his frustration wasn't directed at me.

It was directed at her.

He didn't know what was going on with her or what had happened between us—shit, none of us did—but he knew all my hurt and heartache and distractions came down to the girl sitting across from me. The one who looked as if she didn't give one single fuck.

The muscles in his jaw worked. When he spoke again, his tone was laced with venom he was trying to suppress. "Asked if you checked in with the owner across the street."

I cleared my throat and nodded to my brother. "Diggs did."

Diggs glanced up, his eyes wide as he shoveled a whole pancake into his mouth.

"She's interested in selling to us," I said, trying to loop him back into the conversation.

Diggs pointed in the direction of the store in question. "Her?" he asked through his mouthful of food. When Dare nodded, Diggs huffed and stabbed at another pancake. "Oh yeah. She's down. Wants to move. Be near her hot-as-hell daughter."

If it were anyone else, I never would have understood a word he'd said.

But Diggs talking with his mouth full of food was as common as the sun rising and setting.

A laugh rumbled in Dare's chest. "She add that last part in?"

"She showed pictures." Diggs smiled wide. "I'm pretty much family now."

Dare tossed his pen at him. "Good. They can deal with you then."

Diggs feigned offense and shoved the second pancake into his mouth. "You'd miss me."

They continued on, but their words were drowned out by Einstein again. Ignoring them and me as she tapped away on her new tablet.

I watched her. Not really seeing what she was doing, just looking at *her*.

The permanent furrow of her brow.

The dark circles under her eyes.

The way she continued to torture her bottom lip.

The subtle shift of her arm every minute or so as she brushed it across her chest, as if I wouldn't realize she was rubbing it.

But that was it. I'd always prided myself on knowing her, knowing what she was thinking. And no matter how hard I studied her, I couldn't hear a damn word.

Something pulled at my subconscious, begging me to look. To *see*.

With a quick flick of my eyes away from the only girl who mattered, I took in the rest of Brooks Street Café.

Like every other morning, people filled the booths.

Some couples, some families, all different ages.

Magnet.

Pull.

Need I couldn't resist.

When I looked back at her, her green eyes were on mine. Wide, pained, confused.

I wanted to scoff at her pain. I wanted to yell that if

anyone should be confused—had the right to be—it was me.

Before I could contemplate saying anything, my attention snapped back to a booth across the aisle and down a few. To a slightly familiar man staring at Einstein as if he knew exactly what he was looking at. Who.

As if he'd found what he'd been hunting.

Only she wasn't prey, and I would kill anyone who tried to capture her.

The man looked at me. A slow, knowing smirk covered his face.

I shifted, my body tensed and my hand dropped to my gun at my side.

"Whoa, whoa," Dare hissed, gripping my forearm and stopping me from moving. From going after the man who was damn near laughing at some fucking joke he alone was privy to. "Calm down." When I didn't relax, Dare dug his fingers into my wrist until I lost control of my hand. "I said calm down."

Diggs looked between us, fork paused halfway to his mouth.

"That guy," I said through clenched teeth. "I keep seeing him. Few times here. A few at The Jack."

Dare yanked on my arm so hard that I nearly toppled over into the booth. He slanted his head against mine, his words harsh. "You don't make a scene here. Got it?" Once I stopped struggling against him, he said, "It's fucking Wake Forest, Maverick. Who cares if you see someone a few times?"

I stared at Einstein, whose face was fixed into a carefully composed mask of disapproval and annoyance, and then said to Dare, "I've only seen him the last few weeks and always after Einstein shows up. If she isn't here or wherever we are, he isn't there. And he was looking at Einstein like she's who he was looking for. Who he's after."

I felt the shift in the air immediately.

Diggs went so still it was eerie. Taking in all his surroundings without ever having to turn or shift.

Dare's body was as tense as mine, his chest was moving with uneven, ragged breaths as he glanced in the direction I'd been looking.

Even though Einstein huffed in annoyance, I knew she was waiting. Knew she was worried. Her stare had fallen to the side in the way it did when she was listening intently, and her hand was still above her tablet.

"Gray shirt? Buzzed hair?" Dare asked on a breath.

I made a sound of agreement deep in my chest.

Einstein's head snapped up a split second before she turned fully in her seat to look at the guy. "Oh my God, you guys," she said loudly when she twisted back around, the words all groan and irritation. "That's Fake Name Alex."

None of us moved or responded.

But the energy between us was so thick and ready to blow, I knew it wasn't long before one of us snapped . . . and with my current standing with the girl I loved, I sure as hell didn't want it to be me.

"Explain," Dare demanded.

She gave him a dry look. "I did. Fake Name Alex."

His next intake of air sounded like a hiss. "Maverick thinks he's stalking you. You somehow know his name but tacked *Fake Name* in front of it. That doesn't comfort me. So *explain*."

"I thought he was giving me a fake name. Turns out he wasn't. End of story."

"When was this?" Pure demand mixed with my worry and ache for what we'd lost.

"Now you deserve to know where I am and what I do and who I talk to?" She scoffed. "No. That was never us before and that sure as hell isn't us now."

It felt like her words slammed my body back into the booth. The air rushed from my lungs on a pained wheeze.

What the hell happened to us?

Diggs threw down his fork so hard it clattered off the plate and bounced across the table. His brows were pinched tight in anger when he slanted his head toward her. "You're one more comment away from being on my shit list. Got it? Whatever the fuck's going on with you, I'm over it. We all are. Get your shit together and get over it."

I slammed my foot into his leg. "That's enough."

He barked out a sharp laugh. "Yeah, no. It's not." He twisted so he was fully facing her and growled, "Stop punishing everyone for something that none of us had anything to do with. Stop being a bitch to Mav. He doesn't deserve any of the shit you keep throwing at him, and I'm fucking tired of watching you beat him down day after day."

Silence.

Loud and deafening and too much to handle.

Einstein's face wavered between shock and pain, indecision and worry.

"What?" Diggs snapped. "Surprised I called you out on your shit?" He laughed low and aggravated. "Yeah, see, I know you, E. Maybe not as well as Mav, but I know you. You're snarky and blunt and your humor is different, but it's funny as hell. *You're* funny as hell. This Einstein we've been dealing with for months now? She isn't funny. She isn't snarky. She's hateful. It's like your purpose in life has shifted to trying to hurt everyone in your path, Maverick most of all."

I couldn't find it in me to tell him to stop.

I wanted him to. I could see he was hurting her and that wrecked me.

But everything he was saying was true. I knew it. Dare knew it. Einstein knew it.

You could see it in her eyes.

They were all words, or variations, that I'd been telling her for over half a year. But she'd been so set on pushing me away, that she never listened.

She didn't hear me.

Not anymore.

Diggs looked to Dare. "Meeting over?"

Dare lifted a hand off the table before letting it fall. "Sure."

Diggs stood where he was, climbed over Einstein, and dropped out of the booth. He took one step away before turning around and leaning in close to her.

"My brother would shift the world for you." His voice was all grit and steel. "He would fucking die for you." Looking to me, he pushed from the table and said, "He deserves someone who would do the same."

And then he was gone.

Walking toward the front door and passing by the guy who had caused this shitstorm, staring him down as he did.

And that piece of shit Alex just smiled to himself the entire damn time.

Before I could look back at Einstein, she was slipping

out of the booth and hurrying away.

It was instinctive to go after her.

But I hadn't gotten off the bench before Dare gripped my shoulder and forced me back down.

"There are times you run after the girl. This isn't one of them."

"I'll always run after her."

Because that was my heart, my soul, running away from me.

"She isn't just pushing you back to see what you'll do. She's pushing us all away, hiding behind a fortress, and burying herself so we can't find her. Going after her is only gonna make her dig faster."

When he was sure I wasn't going anywhere, he released me and let out a long, slow sigh.

I stilled, then slowly reached across the table and grabbed the tablet sitting there, forgotten.

Einstein never left any of her electronics behind.

Dare murmured a curse when he saw it and sank back in the booth. "I hate to say this, but Diggs was right."

"I know."

"About the last part."

My chest wrenched open. The ache residing there lately magnified. I struggled to take a breath but couldn't figure out how to make my lungs work.

I dipped my head shakily. "I know."

"I don't know what happened to her or what's going on with her. I talked to Libby, but she can't get through to Einstein either. She's worried, we all are." He turned to look at me and gripped at his chest. "I love Einstein, she's like a sister to me. She had been in my life long before she ever joined our family. I've seen her go through the worst shit anyone ever could, and I've never seen her like *this*."

I think I nodded.

Or maybe I crumpled.

I wanted to ask *then why*.

All I wanted was for someone to give me answers.

I wanted my girl, *my* Einstein back.

Dare set his hand on my shoulder. "You're fighting for someone who doesn't want you to fight. And you deserve better."

I swallowed thickly, past the pain and hurt and utter devastation.

I nodded and held up the tablet before dropping it on top of his folder.

I shakily stood from the booth and tried to walk away, but I couldn't make my feet move.

Drowning.

I was drowning.

Looking to Dare, I said, "I don't know how to live in a world where she doesn't love me."

His mouth twitched into a frown. "I know, man. I know."

Thirty

Maverick
TODAY

I PULLED UP THE SEARCH on Phoenix and scrolled to his number. "Someone call Phoenix while I find the search Einstein did on Alex. See if she's there or if he knows where she is."

Before anyone could move, Dare's phone rang.

I stared at the computer as if Phoenix Nicolasi was listening to every word we spoke.

"Yeah?" he answered gruffly and then quickly hit my shoulder three times in rapid succession. "Got it. Let me know if he leaves."

I didn't wait for Dare to explain, I already had my gun and was out of the chair, following him as he hurried through the office.

"They think Alex is at the coffee shop," he said when we were in the main room and headed for the door.

I turned to snap at Diggs to come with us, but he was by my side.

Looking at everyone piling into the main office, I met Kieran's hardened stare and pointed toward the room we'd all just been in. "Search for anything on Alex. The password is 04733."

Within minutes, we were pulling up to the coffee shop.

Before I could throw open my door, Dare slammed a hand down onto my arm, keeping me where I was.

"Calm. If he has something to do with this, we don't need him running."

Diggs leaned forward, a shit-eating grin on his face. "I could find him."

"He won't be able to run if I shoot his kneecaps," I murmured.

"Calm," Dare reiterated. "If he *doesn't* have anything to do with it, we don't need that attention brought on us."

I dipped my head in a reluctant nod, pushed open the door, and stepped out.

My muscles were twitching.

My blood was pounding in my veins.

But I walked in slowly, my hands curled into fists to keep from doing something stupid.

Like shoot him before he could answer our questions.

It didn't take long to find him where he sat at a little table on his laptop.

I'd seen him too often lately. I'd started watching for him whenever Einstein was out somewhere too.

He glanced up when I took the seat opposite him, confusion and surprise flashing across his face before his mouth slowly spread into a smirk.

It was the same smirk he'd worn that day at Brooks Street.

The one that told me he'd known he was on my radar and was setting off alarms. As if he'd known Einstein was going to choose him over me.

I wanted to kill him.

A threatening grin pulled at my lips when I visualized it.

I grabbed his laptop and handed it off to Diggs, my grin widening when Alex reached for it, his face falling.

"The fuck? Don't—*shit*." The hand he'd had outstretched to try to stop the handoff formed into a fist. "Those are spreadsheets for work. Swear to God, if you alter anything . . ."

"I don't know what I'm looking for," Diggs murmured to Dare and me.

Dare blew out a sharp exhale. "Why do we bring you?"

"Cause I'm so purdy."

I resisted an eyeroll and kept my stare on the man in front of me.

Alex stood when the guys walked away but froze in place when I slid my chair around in front of him, close enough for him to see the gun pointed at him.

"I think you should sit. They'll be back."

His throat bobbed as he slowly sank back into his chair.

Not a second later, the guys came back, dragging chairs to the table that was too small for the four of us.

Dare dropped the laptop onto the table then went to work on it again.

I doubted he knew what he was looking for, but him going through it was more of a mind-fuck than anything.

"I can lose millions for my company if anything on

those sheets is inaccurate," Alex said in a low, pleading voice.

"Didn't touch the sheets." Annoyance leaked through Dare's tone and expression, but his eyes never left the screen.

Diggs laughed. "Speak for yourself."

Alex's jaw worked, and he looked seconds away from lashing out.

"You took Einstein on a date Saturday."

His furious stare darted to me. A huff punched from his lungs. "Is that what this is about?"

"Considering she's been missing since. Yeah, I'd say so."

Alex leaned close, his lip curling as he did. "You're real tough coming here with your boys and trying to make me do what you want by waving around that fake piece of bullshit in your hand. Go look for her somewhere else."

Dare lowered the lid of the laptop and leaned over it, a cruel smile on his face. "You don't seem surprised or concerned. Truth or dare."

Alex's eyebrows drew together in confusion, forming a crease between them. "Fuck you."

"Now, you see, that's the wrong choice." The smile fell from Dare's face, until all that was left was an unforgiving coldness.

Within seconds, I heard the distinct sound of a round being chambered. And then another.

Tension grew, forming a bubble around us that drowned out everything else in the coffee shop.

Alex's eyes widened and darted between the three of us.

"Truth or dare," Dare murmured again.

Alex tried to answer a few times before he finally stuttered, "Truth."

Dare clicked his tongue and cocked his head to the side, showing his displeasure with Alex's choice, but asked, "Do you know where Einstein is?"

"No. No, how the hell am I supposed to know? She left before the food ever got to the table."

I cut a look to Dare to see what he was thinking.

No one could lie to Dare without him knowing.

But he was just staring Alex down with a look prompting him to continue.

"We ordered, and a few minutes later, she said she'd be back." Alex lifted his hands out to his sides as if he were helpless. "She never came back." A defeated laugh sounded in his chest. "Should've known she wasn't going to when she took her bag."

"Her car's still in the parking lot," I said, telling him things he likely already knew. "Her phone was found under the restaurant table after your date. The manager gave it to friends of ours *today*. She doesn't go anywhere without it."

"I don't know what you want from me," he said exasperated. "I sat there like an asshole for twenty minutes before I realized she'd ditched me. She took her bag and went to the bathroom, which was in the same direction as the front door. Before that, she barely said ten . . . *fifteen* words and almost started crying. If you think she's gone, maybe she just wants to be alone right now."

My head was shaking, but I didn't have a chance to speak before Dare shoved the laptop toward Alex.

I looked to him in confusion, but he was standing, gun already secured.

"Let's go," he said in that tone that left no room for discussion.

I wanted to stay.

I wanted to demand more answers.

I wanted to beat the shit out of Alex simply for being the last person to have seen Einstein.

But I slid my gun into the back of my jeans and stood, watching Alex's expression as I did.

That smirk never reappeared.

He never looked like he'd just won.

But there was something I didn't trust about the guy.

As soon as we were all outside, I said as much to Dare.

He rubbed at his jaw and then dug in his pocket for his keys. "Gut instinct, or because Einstein went on a date with him? Because, unless he's a sociopath, I never caught a lie."

A reply was on the tip of my tongue, but I didn't know if it was the truth or not.

It felt like an instinct.

It felt like there was something screaming inside me, pulling me back toward the coffee shop.

But I'd wanted to kick his ass for weeks.

"I don't know, man." I blew out a ragged breath and headed for the car. "I don't know."

Thirty-One

Einstein
TODAY

I'D WORKED MY WAY THROUGH all the touchscreen computers and devices in the room and had pulled the chair over to a cluster near the one that controlled the oxygen.

All but the four in front of me were nothing more than keyholes.

Shiny.

Begging me to touch.

Taunting me with all the ways they could help me escape.

Fake.

Very impressive forgeries.

Whoever set them up really knew what they were doing.

The ones with codes on them had hidden messages

within them, such as my phone number and date of birth intertwined with the messages left on the Post-its.

There were others with satellite maps and random sites pulled up.

I bet whoever built this thing thought they were so clever when they left up the search about where to buy Post-its . . .

I didn't find it amusing. None of them responded to touch either, and there wasn't any way to control anything in the room but by touch.

The small cluster in front of me that *did* work had a feed of the room I'd managed to crawl out of.

Mirrors of my tablet and laptop, down to the very last app and folder placement, including the new folder I'd added the last time I was at the office.

And there was a black screen in the very center.

I'd never wanted to touch a screen more in my life, but memories of nearly suffocating had me hesitating.

Then again, it might be the best one to touch in this entire room.

Something about the clones had red flags raising, but I didn't have any other options at this point.

Bringing my hand up to the clone of my laptop, I clicked open a folder that held random, mostly meaningless files, and waited.

I hadn't realized I'd been holding my breath until my lungs screamed in protest. I quickly released the breath and forced my lungs to move in measured inhales and exhales as my eyes darted over everything and I waited to see if anything changed.

When nothing did, I laughed.

A short, breathless sound.

Because this was incredible. Unbelievable even.

I hurried over to the mirror of my tablet and opened the texting app. I didn't think, just tapped out a message to Maverick and hit send.

Nothing.

The message stayed in the preview box.

The send button stayed highlighted, mocking me.

"Are you fucking kidding me?"

I opened the FaceTime app and tried to call him. And then Libby and Dare and Diggs before I slammed my hand against the screen and yelled in frustration.

I ran my hands through my hair and closed my eyes, blowing out a slow breath as I did. "You can do this. You can do this."

Going back to my "laptop," I pulled up an email and tried to send it . . . but got the same result as the text.

I could type but not send.

I opened folder after folder until it finally hit me to open a file, but I wasn't even able to highlight it.

Once again, an illusion.

Another keyhole.

Only this one more elaborate.

And the brief glimmer of hope that had begun to form in my chest that I might be able to contact my family abruptly vanished.

I sat back in the chair and pressed the tips of my fingers to my head, trying to force myself to think.

My gaze shifted to the black screen for the umpteenth time since I'd sat.

"Okay." I blew out a quick exhale and reached forward to tap my fingers on the screen.

A computer.

Literally. Just a computer.

Not mine . . . nothing identifying on it.

Just a computer.

I started searching for the IP address, my head shaking as I did. "*Why* haven't I taught any of you to do what I do?"

I searched through what I could in a few minutes before I realized I wasn't going to get any real information—not that I actually expected to find any considering the lengths these people had gone to.

And it had to be *people*. This couldn't have just been the work of one person.

Once I was sure this computer actually worked, I wasted no time trying to slip into mine.

And ran right into a wall.

"What . . . that isn't . . . mine."

My eyes scanned the screen, looking for any familiarity, but there was none.

I knew my system like the back of my hand. This wasn't my firewall.

Hack your way out of this.

"Seriously?" I asked with a laugh when it started to make sense. "Someone didn't do their homework. I do this for fun."

Minutes later, the corners of my mouth curled up as I slipped through, only to run into another wall.

Different, none of the same characteristics. And once again, not mine.

But this time, as soon as I started getting close, everything changed. The entirety of the firewall disappeared in chunks and was replaced by a third one.

"*What?*"

And a fourth.

And a fifth.

By the time the sixth firewall appeared, I kicked the chair away and yelled in frustration.

Because I didn't know how long this would continue.

And I knew I *would* continue, because it was the only option I had.

I was so irritated and focused and driven that I didn't notice the sixth system I was starting to hack into was mine until a few seconds in.

I froze and stared at the screen, trying to make myself believe that it was really there. And then I was rushing.

My fingers flew faster and faster the deeper I got without being stopped. My mind raced with the possibilities of what I could do and what I *should* do to let my family know where I was.

It needed to be as cut and dry as possible for them.

And it needed to be convincing.

I opened the webcam and tried not to take note of the way I looked—like I'd been to hell and back several times. I snapped a picture and saved it as the desktop background just in case.

Then I pulled up the internet, searched for my current address, and watched in horror as everything began rapidly disappearing from the screen until there was nothing left.

"No, no, no, no. *No.*"

When it was only my face, silently pleading with them to find me, the picture disappeared and the screen went black.

I didn't move.

I *couldn't*.

This was a game, and they were laughing their asses off.

I flinched when the screen changed to a blinding white

before shifting, slowly, slowly, slowly until a picture of a Post-it formed in the center.

Try again.

I ground my jaw, trying not to scream at whoever was behind this. Whoever might be listening.

Trying not to give them any more reasons to enjoy my torment, I tapped the screen and slid into my system again as naturally as breathing.

No firewalls.

No nothing.

Only to realize that wasn't what they meant by *try again*.

This wasn't a video game where the game regenerated back to the original settings every time the player died.

Because my computer was still wiped.

I dropped my head into my hands, peeking out just above the tips of my fingers. It was like a car wreck I couldn't look away from.

Except there was literally *nothing* right in front of me.

My nothing.

Anger pulsed, making me tremble.

"It's backed up," I whispered, trying to soothe the phantom feeling of being gutted. "It's backed up. Everything I have is backed up. I can fix this. I can fix this . . ."

If I can just get out of here.

My lips shook when I exhaled, slow and steady when I felt anything but.

Grabbing the chair, I pulled it up to the screens again and lifted my hands to the main one, quickly exiting out of my system as my mind raced for what to do next.

If I was looking for someone, for *me*, I would track

them. The same way I'd attempted to track Libby. Phone, tablet, any electronic—since I had every one of our devices set up for tracking in the event of this exact situation.

But *I* wasn't looking for me. My crew was . . . hopefully.

And I'd just caused the assholes behind this fucked-up game to wipe my computer, so I knew what they were doing by offering up mirrors of my devices.

Those mirrors made your mind want the comfort they offered.

They tricked you into taking the easier, more familiar road instead of the harder path.

And I wasn't falling for it again.

I cut a glare to the screen closest to the grate where I'd left the Post-it

I want you clear for the next part.

Or else it won't be fun.

"If wiping a computer is all you have up your sleeves, you're going to be disappointed in my reaction." My brow furrowed. "And what's with this *I*? Is it the collective *I*? Either way, *I* would like to inform the collective *you* that you're all dicks."

I sucked in a quick breath when the next idea hit me. Because I knew they were watching my every move.

I could feel it. And I was counting on it.

I hurried to my next system and found another firewall that wasn't mine.

Not a surprise.

After pushing through only four that time, I slipped into every single ARCK desktop in rapid succession, starting with Conor's, and turned their music on full volume.

"Let's play, fucker."

Thirty-Two

Einstein
THREE WEEKS AGO

I was sitting at my computer at two to noon.

Just as I had every day for the last week and a half.

But I wasn't waiting around for a robot. I was only here because Kieran told me to be right here.

In this seat.

At this exact time.

I'd already searched all of Tennessee going back the last year because the last six months hadn't come up with enough for me.

I checked anything and everything I found. Even petty crimes.

If there were gang affiliations connected with the crimes, I looked into them.

If there were ties to the mob, I found them and looked into those too.

I got into such a twisted web of who people may or may

not be connected to that I was searching everyone from the county jails to dating apps.

When that came up with nothing, I started searching schools.

But there was nothing.

Nothing with the name. Nothing with a kid who might've been pulled or had suddenly missed a lot of school.

Just nothing.

I'd even resorted to *calling* the damn motels in the area that had sketchy bookkeeping and cameras that didn't work and asking if anyone had paid for a room with cash.

I'd never been more sure I was dealing with someone trying to mess with us. Trying to catch us and harm us in some way.

Yet, I didn't stop looking.

Each day, when noon came and went, anxiety twisted at my gut. Making me feel as if I were failing Sutton and her daughter by not finding all I could about them. As if I were the one putting them in danger by not sending Kieran or Jess to retrieve them.

A chime sounded on my laptop.

My stare swept up to the corner of my screen, and I froze for all of two seconds before I hurried to respond to the email that had just come through.

I didn't read what she'd written.

I just sent a reply.

Don't leave. Need to talk! Can you call?

I sat stiffly in my chair, reading her email and checking the new email address as I waited for a response that might never come.

We had to leave the last place. Will you come? Can you help?

Do you even care, or is this really some bullshit place that laughs when people finally reach out and seek help?

Once again, there was another address at the bottom.

This new motel didn't look much different from the other and it was only about fifteen minutes away from the previous one.

Just when I was about to send another probably useless email, one came in.

I don't have a phone.

I can't afford to have a way they can track me.

"Well, I can't afford for you to be a trap," I murmured to myself as I tapped out a response.

> We care. We want to help those who need help. We've never had someone try to remain so hidden from us.
>
> If you stop to think about it, you'll see why that can raise red flags.
>
> In one minute, I'm calling the front office of that motel.
>
> You can get there or you can't. Simple as that.

I hit send and sat back, letting a mental countdown begin.

"See? I can be nice and polite and direct all at once. Sort of." I picked up my phone, punched in the number to the motel, and waited. Just before I hit the green button, I whispered, "The person working the front desk better answer before you do."

The phone rang once.

Twice.

Three times.

I rolled my eyes. This might not work at all if it was such a seedy place they didn't bother answering their phone.

"Sleepy Inn," a woman said in way of answering. Her voice was older and hoarse and raspy. "We got vacancy by the hour or night. Cash only. Don't even think about checks, you little shits with your bouncing checks."

My mouth curled into a smile. "That sounds just great, and you seem nice," I said with all the sarcasm I could muster. "So, this is how this is gonna go. I'm going to ask you a question and you're going to answer. If you don't, I have a very, *very* scary friend who would love to come and pay you a visit. Are we feeling each other?"

There was a pause before she sighed. "The question?"

"See, I knew you seemed nice." I drummed my fingers on the desk and kept my stare on the last email from Sutton. "I need to know if you have a woman and her daughter in there. Woman is . . . oh, say, twenty-seven."

"Tell me what's in it for me."

"You don't die," I said honestly.

"Well, I ain't a snitch."

My eyes rolled. "That's a big word to be throwing around where you are."

She wheezed a laugh. "Doubt a little thing like you knows anything about that."

I smiled.

"Anyway. This mom and her kid came in about an hour ago. They—"

A woman's frantic voice suddenly sounded. Faraway, but clear as day. "I need that phone. I need—*please* I need that phone."

Before the woman I was talking with could respond in any way, I said, "You've been *super* helpful. Now, I need you to give her the phone."

The woman clicked her tongue and drew out a long sigh. "Disrespectful. That's what people are."

The phone changed hands, and after a few seconds, there was a hesitant, "Hello?"

I pulled the phone away from my ear when a shuddering breath ripped from me.

Because I was questioning everything I thought I'd known about this woman and this case. If I'd been wrong . . . God, I wouldn't be able to forgive myself if anything happened to her.

I pressed the phone to my ear. "Sutton?"

"Yeah. Yes. Yes, hi." She sounded out of breath and panicked. "I was on the other side of the motel. I got here as fast as I could."

I understood that. I hadn't expected her to be in the office within a minute.

Clearing my throat, I got right to the point. "With what we do, can you understand the red flags?"

"Of course I can." Her voice dropped to a whisper. "But I can't give you more than what I have. Do you know how long, and what it took, for us to be able to run? I can't sleep. I can't afford to be in one place for long. I can't afford to move without constantly looking over my shoulder. They're everywhere."

I replayed her typed words and what she'd just told me, trying to come up with a mental image of her.

And failed.

There were moments of strength. Of tenacity.

But the fear was there and real.

It sounded like fear had become her life and was burying the person who she used to be.

"Helping people in these situations is all we want to do," I finally said. "In this kind of situation . . . when they're *every-*

where, as you said, it's tricky. We need to be in contact with you and get any information we can so that, when we come in to get the two of you, we don't walk into an ambush."

"I wouldn't—"

"But if they're watching you . . ."

There was a pause before she said, "I understand."

"You said you were on the other side of the motel just now, how have you been emailing me?"

"Internet cafés at first, but going out was too much of a risk. I bought a laptop the last time we changed locations. With cash," she hurried to clarify.

I worried for a moment over how to say this next part without scaring her. "Depending on how you set up your laptop, with your name and logging into old accounts, they can track you through it."

Her exhale ripped through the phone. "I didn't—I haven't—it's not on there. Nothing is. Everything is new. All the accounts, the name, everything."

"Okay good, that's good," I tried to assure her. "What isn't good is not having a reliable way to contact you. You can't deactivate your email accounts anymore."

"I'm not comfortable with that. Not now that I'm telling you where I am."

It took everything for me not to sigh in frustration. "Then I need you to continue emailing me every day until we are able to get you. That way, we know where you are, and we know you're okay. Give us whatever information you can, the more we know, the better."

Another pause. I could feel her hesitation like a living thing trying to crawl through the phone. "I'll . . . if it means you'll come, I'll do it."

"We will come. Now I know you don't have a phone,

but I need you to write down my number so you and your daughter can memorize it. That way, if something happens and you can't email me, one of you can find a way to call me."

After she hesitantly agreed, I waited for her to get a pen and paper from the super helpful clerk and then gave her my number.

"I need to know one last thing. How did you find out about us?"

"My mom." Her voice wavered and dipped when she continued. "She knew small things. No details, only that I was scared and felt like I needed to get us away. She led me to you."

We weren't impossible to find.

Easy to find if someone was looking for your everyday private investigators. But these cases were different. A person had to dig if they wanted to find out about our services for what Sutton needed. There were hints left on sites all over the internet that led to us, but we didn't advertise for safety reasons.

"All right," I said, accepting it. "From now on, stand by for a little while so I can email back and forth with you like I did today. And when you create new accounts, stop putting your name in them."

"Right," she said with a sigh, as if she should've known that.

"I'll talk to you tomorrow."

As soon as I ended the call, I pushed out of my chair and hurried into Kieran and Jess's office to update them, calling for Conor as I went.

Over a week later, I was standing in line at the coffee shop when a low chuckle sounded from in front of me.

I wasn't sure why I heard it, why it stood out to me so much—people were talking all around me, the espresso machine was singing a beautiful song, music was pouring from the speakers a little too loudly—but it did.

I glanced up for the briefest of seconds.

The force of dragging my attention away from the site's code I was studying felt like dragging myself through mud. But in that split second, I saw the man in front of me, the one who'd laughed.

Saw his build and his hair.

Closely cropped, dark hair.

Lean, fighter's build, easily recognizable through his tight-fitting shirt.

But the observations were nothing more than nagging thoughts in the back of my mind. My focus was already back on the code, trying to find the weakness.

Because there *had* to be a weakness.

"I'm beginning to think you're stalking me."

The moment he spoke, my head snapped up, the elusive weakness forgotten. "Fake Name Alex."

He glanced over his shoulder, a smirk shaping his lips. "Still on that?"

"Are you still showing up everywhere I am?"

Turning fully to face me, he spread his arms wide to indicate his position in line. In front of me.

It was the only response he needed to give.

I lifted an eyebrow. "Who's to say you didn't sneak in before I could? We all know I was focused on what was in my hands and not on men who may or may not be stalking me."

"Men?"

"Man," I corrected.

That smirk widened into a wicked smile that rivaled Kieran's. "Then who's to say indeed?"

He stepped back, moving forward with the line at the exact time the others moved, without ever looking over his shoulder.

I made a mental note of that.

"Are you headed anywhere?"

I shot him a challenging look. "At the moment, or in life?"

His eyes flashed with amusement, and for a second, he just studied me. "I want to know both, but answer for this moment."

"I'm sure my boss would appreciate it if I showed up at work. I'm also sure people will come looking for me if I don't."

His chest shook with a silent laugh, and his face scrunched in bemusement.

It was annoying that it made him look kind of adorable.

He took another step back, effortlessly moving with the line again without ever needing to look. "Uh, well, do you have time to let me buy you coffee? Or will the cavalry come?"

My chest seized.

I forced my expression to remain neutral, but inside, I was trying to figure out how we had gone from talking about him possibly stalking me to him buying me coffee.

I knew that if I relayed this to Jess, she would see it differently from how I saw it.

She would say he was flirting with me.

But, if asking someone if they were stalking me and

warning them people would come looking for me if I were to go missing was flirting, then I didn't understand it.

At all.

Unable to handle it any longer, I tilted my head to the side and dropped my voice to a whisper. "Are we really not talking about you stalking me?"

The shock that covered Alex's face had humiliation swimming through my stomach.

"No. No, we're not." His eyes darted around the shop, and he lowered his head so he was closer to my level. "Are we?"

I'd never been more confused. Or mortified.

And it was making it incredibly difficult to come up with any form of response.

Yes. No.

Anything would be better than just standing there staring at him, but for long seconds, that was all I seemed to be able to do before my brain restarted.

I lifted a shoulder in a hint of a shrug. "Whether we were or weren't, you've kind of earned the title of my stalker in my family. And if you aren't, they're going to be highly disappointed."

The corners of his lips twitched into a smile. "I think I might disappoint them. But maybe now you'll let me buy you coffee?" He drew out the sentence, leaving it open to me.

I tilted my head toward the counter, where the barista was waiting to take Alex's order.

It was the first time he hadn't stepped back.

"I'll *let* you. That doesn't mean I have time to stay here and drink it or that I've made up my mind about you."

His laugh was full and smooth as he turned and stepped

up to the counter, quickly ordering a black coffee before looking to me expectantly.

I loosed a sigh and stepped forward, ordering a caramel macchiato—something I never ordered—all the while keeping my eyes on Alex, waiting to see if he reacted in any way.

After all, a stalker would know my drink was a cinnamon dolce latte.

But the only shift in his expression was the mixture of relief and victory that filled his eyes when I finally ordered.

And, once again, I was left a disordered, embarrassed mess.

"So this *fake-name* thing," he said when we got to the drink counter, pulling me out of my internal meltdown.

I blinked quickly and looked at him. "Hmm?"

"I *will* show you my license, or anything you want, just to prove it to you."

"Oh. No. No, I believe you."

I had to. I'd looked him up.

Alex Kincaid.

Leasing a condo just out of Raleigh that showed exactly how much money he had and made. Moved here from Georgia. And since I'd found out he was a software engineer all on my own, he wouldn't have to worry about killing me.

Not that I could tell him any of that.

I shrugged. "Just haven't talked to you since that day. *Seen* you, haven't talked to you."

He blew out a slow breath that ended on a laugh. "Yeah, the other week was—"

"Ridiculous."

"Intense?" he offered. "Those guys . . ."

Brothers. Best friends. The love of my life.

"Family." The word came out strained.

He nodded in understanding. "Ah, your family that thinks I'm stalking you. That would explain the looks like they wanted to kill me."

"What can I say? You came into our place and tried to have breakfast."

He feigned shock. "*Your* place. I may have just found that joint, but I'm claiming it as my own. Best breakfast in town."

I tsked and gave him a pitying look. "Oh, nice try. But that isn't how this works."

"Pretty sure that's how it's worked since kindergarten. You claim something, and it's yours. I've licked a plate."

A surprised laugh climbed up my throat, and he smiled widely in return. "While that's good and weird to know, that's really not how it works with that café. Our family owns it."

I kept Dare's name out of it.

That was how he'd always wanted it.

That was how we kept Brooks Street Café free from enemy attack or retaliation.

Alex looked defeated. "There goes my plans to take over the place one plate at a time." He shifted, his face morphing into something a little more Kieran-like. "So, what you're saying is that I should stay away? Based on the warm welcome I got."

Tears burned the backs of my eyes and tightened my throat at the mention of the meeting that had gone to hell.

I know it had been my fault.

Everything was lately. Nearly all of it on purpose in order to separate myself from the people I loved.

But that day . . . that day had been different.

Having Diggs unleash his thoughts and frustrations on me—all deserved.

Hearing Maverick initially try to stop him, try to stand up for me, even after I'd hurt him so much.

Seeing Dare's look of agreement as Diggs spoke.

Knowing everything I'd been doing was finally working and panicking about it.

Wanting to scream that I was sorry and confess everything. Take it all back. Go back to how it had all been before. When we were a family. When I was deliriously in love with Maverick and we were happy. When I wasn't ruining us all.

Then remembering why I'd started on this journey in the first place. Swallowing the words begging to be freed and forcing myself away before I could crumple.

I stamped down the emotion threatening to choke me and forced something that felt like a smile onto my lips. "No, you should go there whenever you want. The guys . . . I mean, you're going to run into them. Especially if you plan to stick around here and not in your condo. Or around the Raleigh area."

"Are we sure you aren't stalking me?"

I forced myself to look at Alex when the playful hint in his tone broke through the suffering I was trying so hard to suppress.

"You told me where you were living the last time we were standing here."

He made a face, as if he were considering my words, and then offered me a soft smile. "Who knows what I'll tell you next time we're here? Maybe I'll even tell you what I do for a living."

"And then kill me?"

He paused and studied me, giving me another look of contemplation. "You're funny. I think I might just let you live." The words were all a wicked tease.

I tried to smile.

Really, I did.

Except this time, I knew Alex was flirting.

And after skipping this morning's meeting because I'd finally succeeded in pushing the suffocating Maverick pain to the very back of my mind, it had just come rushing back. And it was all I could do to stay standing.

I dipped my head in thanks and cleared my throat. "The guys, though, they're always everywhere. They've seen you at the bar, at the café . . . just around. There's no avoiding them. They flipped out. They'll get over it. Don't let them bother you."

"It takes more than some overprotective brothers to scare me off."

Right.

Right . . .

My drink was set beside us, and I was thankful for the distraction so I could turn away from Alex's stare.

I thanked the barista and then Alex.

When I turned to leave, he grabbed my arm. His hold gentle, and his expression full of confusion. "Whoa, what? You're leaving?"

Shaping my mouth into what I hoped was sly grin, I said, "I told you I didn't have time to stay here with you."

Disappointment wove through his words when he asked, "Well, have you made up your mind about me?"

No.

I don't want to.

You aren't Maverick. You never will be. No one ever will be.

"About you as a person or about whether you're stalking me?" The words sounded strained, and my voice cracked at the end.

I needed to get out of here.

His amusement was palpable. "Both."

I glanced around the shop. "Guess we'll find out next time you stalk me." I lifted my drink in parting and turned to leave.

I didn't make it a step before he was in front of me, his expression pleading and vulnerable. "What if we planned to see each other?" He cleared his throat, his head shifting in a barely imperceptible shake. "What if I wanted to take you out? To coffee or breakfast at a place you apparently own or dinner."

My tongue darted out, wetting my suddenly dry lips.

The word *no* crashed through my mind so loudly it made me a bit lightheaded.

No.

No, no, no.

Thoughts of Maverick filtered in.

Of when he stood patiently by when I was with Johnny.

When he helped me after Johnny died.

When we were finally, *finally* together.

And lastly, of the gut-wrenching look permanently etched on his face lately.

I wanted to scream no just as badly as I wanted Maverick to move on and have a normal life.

That life he'd told me he would be living if he'd never joined the family.

He could still have it.

But not with me.

I nodded, the movement slow and shaky. When I spoke, my voice was barely audible. "Yeah, okay." Surprise and excitement lit in Alex's eyes. Before he could respond, I shifted past him. "Let me know. You know, next time you stalk me."

He was smiling when I turned and left the coffee shop.

I didn't make it to my car before a sob ripped from my chest, nearly sending me to my knees.

Lock it up.
Lock it up.
Lock it up.

Thirty-Three

Maverick
TODAY

I SMACKED THE DASHBOARD OF Dare's car. "Alex said Einstein took her bag." When he looked at me, I said, "Her tablet isn't at the office or at the apartment. It has to be in her bag."

He snapped and took the last corner quickly to get us back to ARCK. "We can track it."

"Do any of us know how to track—" Diggs hesitated when we all saw Lily standing outside with Beckham.

Relief visibly poured from her when she saw us.

Dare didn't bother with a spot. He parked in the street and flew from the car.

Diggs and I were right behind him.

"The computers are going crazy." Lily's eyes cut to me. "Einstein—"

Lily was still talking, but I was gone, running past her

with Diggs on my heels and bursting into ARCK and fucking chaos.

I jolted back and glared at Conor.

Music was blaring from his computer.

"What the hell? Turn it down."

Conor held up his hands. "It isn't me, man. It's happening to all of them. They keep—" His shoulders sagged when the music abruptly turned off. "They keep turning off and then turning back on."

I looked to my brother, hope and fear swirled in my chest. A lethal combination.

"She's trying to get our attention. She has to be."

Conor pointed behind him when music started blasting from one of the back offices. "Jess's. Kieran's will be next. Did, uh, did Lily tell you?" he asked, his voice grim.

I shook my head, my mouth opened to beg him not to tell me when his lips tightened into a thin line.

I didn't want to know.

Not if it caused this reaction.

"Einstein showed up on her laptop. Like she hacked into it and was taking a picture of herself just before her entire computer wiped clean." He cleared his throat and struggled to hold my stare. "Maverick, she . . ."

The floor tilted.

I staggered back a step.

"Someone has her," he finally said, confirming what we'd all feared. "And she doesn't look good."

Thirty-Four

Einstein
TODAY

Every movement I made was deliberate and to the point, easy to follow, even easier to replicate.

If no one was in the office, this was all going to be for nothing.

On the third round, I hit Conor's system and turned the music on once again, not knowing if someone in the office or the people shadowing me had been the one to turn it off again, then I did the same to Jess's.

It was then that I was finally met with resistance.

Every time I hit play, the song was stopped.

I had a war over the play / pause button for a few seconds before mumbling a prayer under my breath that my plan was working and easing out of Jess's computer.

Then I reversed.

I went back to Conor's and hoped my shadow was

already going into Kieran's using the simple steps we'd taken every time before, expecting me to do the same.

Every nerve ending was trying to take over, to secure the firewalls. But I knew I didn't have the time.

I opened the FaceTime app and hoped like hell that someone was there, watching, because I had a feeling I wouldn't have the time it took for someone to answer.

As soon as the app loaded, I clicked Kieran's name and started talking before he could answer, knowing if anyone was near Conor's computer and it was on, they would see me.

"Please, *please* someone be there watching this." The plea was so rushed and frantic, I nearly tripped over the words just trying to get them out. My lips were still parted, but only my ragged breaths left them.

Because with the video up, I could no longer think of anything to say.

I didn't know where I was.

I didn't—

A pained laugh caught in my throat, and I shoved my hand into my hair. "God, do you even know I'm gone? I-I . . . someone took me, and I—*Kieran*," I shouted when the call was accepted.

A sob burst from my chest, and I was barely able to stay upright as bone-shuddering tremors wracked my body.

Because Kieran wasn't the one who answered.

I forced back a strangled cry of relief.

"Where are you?" Maverick demanded, as though he'd already said it a couple of times. "I need you to help me."

"I know," I whispered through the tears tightening my throat. "I'm trying. Maverick, I'm so so—"

"Avery." The calm determination of his tone stopped me.

His gray eyes were searching my face, studying me, looking at me as if to pour all his courage and strength through the screen to me.

I could still see what he was trying to hide. His agony. His terror.

"We don't lose people this way." He clenched his jaw, the muscles twitching under the pressure. "And I refuse to lose you. Breathe and help me find you."

I nodded, my chin wavering as I dragged the FaceTime window to the side of the screen and opened the search engine, rambling breathlessly as I did.

"I tried checking the IP, but whoever's doing this is trying to throw me off. The network host changes every few seconds. And everything in here has been a dummy, so I think those are too."

Just before I could search for my current location, Maverick said, "Your phone was in the restaurant."

I flinched, my mouth opened to apologize for what the phone's location had meant.

For all the hurt I'd caused him.

For going on a date at all.

But he continued before I could speak. "But your bag is gone and so is your tablet. It has to be with you somewhere. Turn on—"

My finger was still hovering over the search button when the internet browser disappeared along with the FaceTime window. Everything on Conor's desktop disappeared right after.

I reached for the screen, a cry of shock and defeat falling from my tongue.

My hand formed into a fist.

I wanted to hit something. I wanted to scream. I wanted to continue crying.

I didn't have the time for any of those things.

Before they had a chance to stop me, I rushed to the next system and was met with three sets of firewalls.

I alternated between hiccupped sobs and cursing with each new one.

But as soon as they were all down, I hurried into Maverick's computer.

I'd been slipping into his computer undetected for months to get statements and reports for Borello financials, and I could do it in my sleep.

As soon as I was in, I hurried to pull up the link to track my tablet and the tracker in my bag and then sent them to Maverick, all while I had the FaceTime app open and was trying to connect to my phone.

I could hear Dare and Kieran shouting orders in the background when Maverick answered. "You track your bag?"

"It's a child tracker," I explained, my words hesitant.

Easy.

Too easy.

Why go through all of this, only to leave me a way to track myself?

"Of course it is." All his pain and anger and worries ripped across his handsome face. "I'm coming. I'm going to bring you home. And I'm going to kill whoever tried to take you from us."

"Alex." I swallowed thickly as my unease grew. "It was Alex—the guy from Brooks Street. But he can't be the only one behind this."

Maverick's face fell before denial and horror set in. "What—"

I jumped and looked around when an alarm sounded in the room.

"What is that?"

"I don't—I don't know." I looked wildly, trying to figure out where the piercing noise was coming from.

And then I saw it. Not far from where I sat. The flashing red coming from beneath the Post-it.

The air punched from my lungs. "Oh God."

Maverick was yelling my name, but I'd already pushed from the chair and was running for the screen that held the outlines of the tanks.

On the list on the right side of the screen, both MAX and AIRLOCK were bolded. REVERSE was a darker shade of gray than it had been and was slowly blinking.

The oxygen and nitrous oxide tanks were flashing red. A question mark filled each tank where their percentage levels used to show. Beside them, in large, bold numbers, a timer was counting down.

With less than ten minutes left on it.

9:46

9:45

I tapped on the screen over and over again. Trying to do anything.

Alter the fan. View the log.

But the entire screen was locked.

9:41

9:40

My chest heaved with a muted sob as I stumbled back to the chair.

"What is—"

"How far are you?" I asked, begging with my voice alone for them to be close, for them to already be here.

But Maverick was just sliding into a car and shutting the door behind him.

He looked to the side, and after a muffled response from one of the guys, said, "About fifteen minutes, maybe less."

My spirit crumpled in a few, simple words.

Because I could see that countdown in my head as though it was still right in front of me.

9:26

9:25

"Hey," he said, his voice so warm and so gentle that he nearly succeeded at hiding his panic. "We're coming. Even if they find out we're tracking you, we have the location locked. It'll be okay."

They already know . . .

I want you clear for the next part.

Or else it won't be fun.

I got it.

A race to beat them at their own game, where they were always one step ahead because they were the damn puppet masters.

There had never been a way for me to win.

Every time I came close to revealing where I was, I'd been blocked.

Just when I thought I might've won, they gave me a few moments to bask in the relief before crushing me.

Because they'd given me a way to find myself, only to make sure I wouldn't live long enough to be rescued.

That was, *if* my bag was even around here somewhere.

They very well could have stashed it somewhere in the opposite direction, leading the guys away from me.

"Hey," I said, my voice strained and barely able to be heard above the alarm. "Remember that time we snuck into the theater room just to talk?"

Hesitation settled over Maverick's features, but he attempted a smile. "Which time?"

9:06

9:05

Instead of responding, I voiced the words I'd wanted the chance to say one last time. "I'm sorry, Maverick. For everything."

His head shook roughly as the FaceTime connection started breaking up the farther they got from the building. "No. We aren't doing that right now."

We don't have a later . . .

"You need to know that you're the best—" My head dropped. My shoulders shook with my silent sobs.

Maverick was yelling at whoever was driving to go faster.

Was yelling at me not to talk the way I was.

Was telling me they were coming.

8:46

8:45

When I was finally able to look at him again, he was staring at me with absolute devastation. "You're the best thing to ever happen to me. And I never deserved you."

The connection cut out for a few seconds before coming back. Maverick was biting out curses at the driver.

When he glanced at the phone, he yelled, "Don't do this. Don't say shit like that. What the fuck does that alarm mean?"

I forced the corners of my mouth up. "That day in the theater room . . . you promised to bury me under the oak tree."

I felt his shock and pain and denial and rage as if they were my own.

As though we weren't miles apart.

"No."

"You promised."

"Avery—"

I placed my hand over the screen when it went dark.

Just as it had looked when I first entered the room.

8:04

8:03

"Death won't be the end of us," I whispered and then sank back into the chair and let the alarm drown out my cries.

Thirty-Five

Maverick
TWO DAYS AGO

I'D TRIED.

All week I'd tried to picture a life without Einstein in it . . . and I'd failed.

It wasn't that life didn't make sense without her, it was that I just couldn't see it.

I knew I was putting myself out there, only to have her beat me down time and time again.

To have her shred my heart one more time.

But I didn't know how to accept defeat and step back.

Not from her. Not after that kiss.

And it didn't help that I *still* had to work with her. That even if we stopped calling ourselves a family, we would always be one.

Dare. Lily. Libby. Einstein. Diggs. Me.

I walked slowly to where she sat near the tree, telling

myself I was only there for business while preparing myself for the fight that was sure to come.

She glanced over when I was nearly to her, her body sagging when she saw me. "What, Maverick? What do you want?"

A huff of frustration worked up my throat as I scratched at my jaw and sucked a breath in through my teeth. "Yeah, see, the business can't run if we don't talk. And you've been ghosting me."

"Then take a hint."

I folded my arms across my chest. "What hint is that? That you want to be done? That you want someone else to take your position?"

"Done with you? Yes. And no one is taking my position until I'm buried under this tree."

Her words held none of her usual bite.

She sounded broken and defeated. As if she didn't have the energy or will to continue this bullshit game she'd been playing. As if she knew the words to say but didn't have the strength to put behind them.

"You still have to talk to me."

She looked at me, sadness and pain etched in her eyes. "Text me what I need to know if you feel so inclined. We don't have to talk."

I laughed, but it sounded like a snarl. "And Dare and Diggs? Is that what you're gonna make them do too? From what they've told me, you aren't talking to anyone. You didn't show for the meeting today. Again. This isn't ARCK, Einstein. You need to talk to us, get information from us, in order to do your job."

"I'm doing my job just fine. You should know me well

enough to know I don't need to talk to anyone to get information."

My brow pulled together for a few seconds before my body tensed. "You've been hacking me? Are you fucking kidding?"

"Why, have something to hide?"

There was nothing—not one goddamn thing—that Einstein could see on any device I owned that I wouldn't show her myself.

But the thought of her slipping into any of my shit to get information she needed pissed me off. Mostly because, as much as I hated to admit it, I could no longer trust her not to destroy my computer in some way.

Or me.

She'd been trying so hard to push me away, and she had it in her arsenal to take it a step further.

Diggs and I had only remained untraceable from FBI and CIA this long because of Einstein. She could reverse it all if she wanted.

One thought. One swipe of her finger. One breath, and it could be over for us.

There'd never been a time where the thought had entered my mind that she *might* . . . until recently.

She rested an elbow on her knee and dropped her head into her hand. Before I could figure out a way to respond, she mumbled, "Calm down. I get the information from all the businesses. Probably before you do."

My chest pitched. I loosed a ragged breath.

"So, what, you're making me irrelevant? And Diggs? Tell me how that's supposed to reassure me."

"Never said I was doing that."

"You said no one was gonna do your job until you were

dead. But you just informed me you're also doing ours *before* we can. We all know we don't need multiple people doing the same thing."

She lifted her brows knowingly and repeated her earlier words, "Take a hint."

A harsh laugh punched from my chest. "Jesus, what happened to you?"

She stood and gave me a warning look as she started toward the lot. Back stiff but head dropped low and chin tucked against her chest. "Don't. I'm not doing this with you again."

"What happened that being with someone as sadistic and abusive as Johnny was so much easier for you?"

"Maverick, stop." She turned to face me and pleaded, "Stop doing this to yourself and to me."

"Fine."

The word was out before I knew what I was saying.

But I knew I wouldn't take it back.

I didn't know how to step back . . . but I knew how to walk away. For good.

A soggy laugh wrenched from my chest. "I guess you're finally getting what you want, because I can't do this anymore, Avery."

If I hadn't been watching her so intently—as I had been for nearly eleven years—I wouldn't have seen the way her body jerked and her mouth parted with a shuddering breath. The panic and crushing pain that flitted across her face before she could school her features.

But it didn't matter if she tried to hide it.

I saw every reason why she didn't *want* to be apart, to be pushing me away, in that flash of pain, and it gave me every reason to keep fighting.

I would always see that pain, and I would want to fix it.

But tomorrow and the next day and the next, we would be right here. She would make sure of it.

All this time, that was what I hadn't been able to grasp.

That was what I couldn't begin to accept until I'd found out she propositioned Zeke and Conor and Lincoln as a way to shut the final door in my face.

"You've been pushing so goddamn hard, but you had to know I wouldn't stop fighting for you." I struggled for what to say for a few seconds, my throat tightening and straining my words when I finally said, "I can't live with you right here and not do something. But all I'm doing is hurting both of us more in the process. Clearly."

I lifted a hand and let it fall.

My chest wrenched open.

A twisted sound of torment climbed up my throat.

"So you want me to stop doing this? Then I'll stop. I'll leave. You. The family. Wake Forest. I'm gone."

Her face fell in horror. "Maverick, no."

"That's the only way," I nearly yelled. I grit my teeth and struggled to calm myself. "Don't you see?"

Her chest rose and fell quickly. One hand gripped at it and the other drove into her hair. "I nev—I never wanted this. I don't want this. I just . . . God," she cried out and turned, taking a few steps away before facing me again.

My body tensed when I saw the tears streaming down her cheeks.

The only thing in the world I wanted in that moment was to go to her and to pull her into my arms, but I fought against the instinct.

I'd been fighting the instinct for nearly a decade, so I could fight it for a few more minutes.

"Just tell me before I leave why being loved by me was so damn terrible."

Pain wove through her voice when she forced out my name. "Maverick . . ."

"You owe me that, Avery." When she just stood there shaking her head, a frustrated huff fell from my lips. "Figures."

I made myself take that first step that felt so damn impossible.

And then the next.

I knew once I got in my car, that would be it.

No more nights spent talking at this tree. No more secret conversations. No more hours wrapped up in each other.

Done.

I slowed when I neared her but couldn't force out the words.

Goodbye. Goodbye. Goodbye.

I love you.

I love you.

I will always love you.

I swallowed back the emotion threatening to choke me and pushed on.

Each step felt heavy.

Wrong.

I felt myself crumpling. Felt my soul pulling back, yelling for me to turn.

Felt the best parts of me dying.

"Being loved by you will always be the only time in my life that truly mattered. When I truly felt alive."

I'd stopped walking as soon as she started speaking, her voice cracking with emotion and pain.

"But I buried my heart, and the absence of it changed everything. It destroyed me. Shattered me. And it formed this chasm between the two of us that can never be repaired."

I turned, already stammering over my words. "What—I don't—*why?*"

"All I wanted was for you to move on and have a life you deserve," she continued as if I hadn't spoken. "All I wanted was for you not to get caught in this nightmare with me. But I never wanted you to leave."

"Nightmare? Avery, what nightmare?" I begged when she only looked at me helplessly.

She opened and shut her mouth a few times, her hands moving from her chest to her stomach and back again. "I feel like I'm constantly screaming and no one hears me. And the thing is, I don't want them to."

I stepped toward her without thinking but stopped when she held a shaking hand out.

She choked on a mix between a sob and a laugh. "I don't want anyone close enough to see what they shouldn't see. So I've been struggling to be the person everyone expects me to be . . . but I feel like I don't know her anymore. And all the while, you were there, fighting and fighting, unable to see that what was best for you was to walk away from me."

Heat pulsed through my veins like flash fire. "Of course I couldn't see that! Damn it, Avery, you were my life. You *are* my life."

Grief dripped from her when she said, "Staying with me would only ruin your life more than I already have."

My head shook subtly. "I don't . . . I don't understand."

Her words.

Her actions the last year.

How something so bad could've happened to her without my knowing—without her telling me.

"Why? *Why* won't you tell me what happened to you?"

She watched me for a few moments, a watery smile playing on her lips. "Because it's too late," she finally whispered. "When it happened, the last thing I felt like I could do was tell you."

I rocked back from the blow of her words and pressed my fist against the aching in my chest.

"After, I didn't know how I was supposed to."

"Avery," I whispered, her name wrapped in uncertainty and pain. "Did someone hurt you?"

Her head shook slowly but firmly. "I wish I would've told you when it first happened. But it's too late, and it won't change anything; it will only bring more pain. It won't change the irrevocable damage I caused us. It won't help me find my way back to who I used to be. So, what's the point?"

"The point is that I'm right here. I've always been right here, loving you. Unconditionally. And I want your hurt. I want your pain. I want to bear the weight you're struggling under. If you would trust me enough to let me."

"It's too late."

"It'll be too late when I get in my truck and drive away." I gestured to her weakly before letting my hands fall heavily to my sides. "You said you wish you would've told me when it happened. One day, you'll wish you had told me now."

She was silent for so long that I was a second away from leaving or begging her one last time—I couldn't figure out which—when she said, "I already have."

My shoulders sagged when the breath I'd been holding rushed from me. "What?"

"I buried my heart."

I drove a hand into my hair and rolled my eyes. My chest heaved with a laugh that lacked any humor. When I rocked back to leave, my stare fell on her again.

The way she stood . . .

Broken.

Crying.

Hands gently and protectively placed on her flat stomach.

Avery . . .

I wasn't sure if I said her name or if I was yelling it in my head.

A brick settled in my stomach.

The air fled from my lungs.

It felt like the world stood still around us and moved in warp speed all at once.

No.

No, no, no. I would've known.

Confusion and grief and anger formed a lethal combination in my veins, making my heart race and falter.

Making my chest heave.

Making my body tremble until I didn't know if I was going to yell or fall to my knees.

She wouldn't.

She wouldn't go so far to ensure she didn't bring a baby into this life . . . would she?

". . . what was best for you was to walk away from me."

"Staying with me would only ruin your life more than I already have."

What did you do, Avery? What the fuck did you do?

The question was bouncing around in my skull, growing louder and louder until it was all I could hear.

I stared, unseeing as her words played again and again, ripping a sob from my chest, bringing me back to the present.

I blinked, trying to see through my pain, to where Avery stood, trying to hold herself together as she quietly cried.

"What did . . . why didn't you tell me?" I choked out, throwing the accusation at her.

"You didn't want them," she yelled, her words twisted in grief.

"I'm not the only one who didn't want a baby, Avery. You, you, you never—*fuck*." I tried to calm my erratic heart. Tried to gather my thoughts. But everything only seemed to get worse. "I told you. I *told you* if you ever ended up pregnant, it would be something that was *our* situation. Not *yours*. And you made it yours. You kept me out of it."

"You didn't want—"

"Don't put this shit on me. You told me having kids was stupid and selfish. You said you refused to bring kids into this life." I slammed my hand against my chest. "I know what I said. That doesn't mean I wouldn't have fucking *been there* every goddamn minute if I'd known. That doesn't mean I wouldn't have—" A choked cry escaped me. "That doesn't mean I wouldn't have stopped you."

I scrubbed my shaking hands down my face.

I sucked in a breath to yell at her or roar in frustration and agony. Something. Anything.

When everything suddenly halted.

"I buried my heart."

"Maybe a baby is what our world needs. Maybe it's what our family needs."

"If that was me in there, what would you do?"
"I buried my heart."
"I buried my heart."
"Oh God."

My legs gave out.

I fell to my knees.

I looked to Avery, who was shaking so hard her body was moving with little jerks. "Stopped *me?*" She shook her head. "You did not want them."

"You never—" The rest of the words caught in my throat when what she said finally registered in my mind.

"Told you?" she asked. "I know, Maverick. I'm aware. But I didn't know how. You wouldn't stop going on and on about Dare and Lily's baby and how much of a mistake it was to get pregnant."

Them.

"I found out the day Lily went into labor," she cried out. "How was I supposed to tell you when every word out of your mouth was how babies in our world were a mistake?"

Them.

"How was I supposed to tell you when the first time I tried, you said, 'For the love of God, tell me you aren't.' And I'm pretty sure there were a few 'fucks' and 'nos' in there too."

Them.

"Avery." I sought out her eyes and swallowed past the thick knot in my throat. "Avery . . . did you say *them?*"

Her chest seemed to cave in.

Her face pinched with a grief I couldn't even begin to comprehend.

When she was finally able to speak again, she said, "Twins. I was fourteen weeks when I lost them."

Lost them.

Not gave them up.

Not made a choice.

My open palms hit the earth, arms shaking with the effort it took to hold me up.

The world was spinning.

I was going to throw up.

Emotions were overwhelming me and trying to drown me.

Fighting for dominance inside me.

Tripping up my mind.

Anger.

So god damn angry.

With Avery for keeping this from me. At her thinking I didn't deserve to know and pushing me away for so long *because* of this.

Grief for what Avery had gone through alone, for our loss.

Agony from knowing what could've been and what wouldn't be.

Most of all, I hated myself.

For not realizing. For making her think she couldn't come to me during the worst time in her life.

Five minutes ago, I would've said I never wanted kids.

But that was then.

My chest ached, felt as if a hole had been punched straight through it. The pit was so wide and so deep that I doubted it would ever be filled again. And I hadn't even known.

I wanted to hold Avery. I wanted to hate her for keeping this from me, for putting me through nearly a year of heartbreak and confusion. For not giving me a chance to show her that I would've been there. That I would've been everything she needed. They needed.

"The tree," I said, my voice strained. "You buried them under the tree, didn't you?"

She nodded, a faint, quick movement, and I somehow pushed myself to standing.

I felt unsteady.

But I just needed to make it there.

And I knew . . . I fucking knew, because every time I'd found her here since she first shut me out, I'd found her in the exact same spot.

I should've known all along.

I made it to the place where she always sat and looked at either side. Gritting my teeth, I demanded, "Where?"

A few moments later, she appeared between me and the tree and gestured to a spot near my feet. "Right there."

I nodded and dragged a hand through my hair, gripping the strands as I did.

How many times had I sat here since then and not known?

"Leave."

Her voice was a breath. "What?"

I slanted a glare at her. "Leave."

Shock and pain flitted across her face.

And for the first time, I didn't know how to care.

"I'm sorry, Avery. For what happened. I'm so damn sorry. But you never gave me a chance. If you would've . . ." A sad laugh left me. "This all would've been different."

Her expression hardened. "You don't know that."

"I do. Because my first thought wasn't *thank God*. It was *what did you do?* I didn't feel relief. I felt pain. I was fucking terrified that you had gone to extreme lengths to make sure you didn't have a baby."

Hurt flashed through her eyes. "I would never—"

"I know that now, but if you had told me then, back when you first found out . . . God, Avery, you should have told me."

"You didn't want kids." Quiet. Her voice was so quiet, so broken. But, still, I didn't care.

"Of course I didn't want a kid. But you didn't either before you found out. Right?"

Her mouth formed a tight line and a shadow passed over her face.

"That changed for you. You didn't have the right to decide that it wouldn't have changed for me too." My voice cracked when I continued, "You didn't have the right to punish *me* for something I was ignorant of."

"I know. I know, I'm sorry. I—"

"You told me. You explained. Think it's safe to say that you made your point. You successfully beat me down. You successfully destroyed my heart. I'll be gone by the beginning of the week, but right now, I want time here."

"I don't want you to leave," she cried out.

"One of us has to leave, Avery. I told you I can't live here with you treating me like I'm nothing. Like you don't love me. With you placing blame on me for something I had no knowledge of. That hasn't changed now that I know why you pushed me away." I grabbed at my chest and choked out, "I'm fucking sorry. I'm sorry that you felt alone. I'm sorry that you went through that at all, and I wish—God, I wish I could take it away. I do. More than anything in the world. But your feelings won't change. So my decision can't."

She started to talk, but I held up a hand to stop her.

This would only continue to go on and on.

And I didn't have the fight left in me anymore.

"You robbed me of time I should've had. Time to be excited. Time to grieve. Everything you've had nearly a year to do, I've had *minutes*. So give me time to be here. Alone."

Avery looked at me, indecision and pain wavering in her eyes.

A dozen things begging to be said.

A dozen things left unsaid when she finally turned, her body curling in on itself as she took the first step away from me.

It was better that way.

Once she was gone, I dropped to my knees, pressed my forehead to the earth where our twins were buried, and cried.

Thirty-Six

Einstein
TWO DAYS AGO

I BURST THROUGH THE DOORS of ARCK, ignoring Conor's questioning stare as I passed him on my way to the back room where my desk and laptop waited.

I heard him calling my name.

Heard him asking if I was okay.

All I could focus on was Maverick's voice in my head.

Pleading with me to talk to him over the last year. Begging me to wait. Stripping away everything until he bared his bleeding heart, over and over, so I would know he loved me despite it all.

Until today.

I succeeded—as he'd said—and I'd never hated myself more.

I wanted to lay there with him, under the tree, by our babies. I wanted to apologize for failing them and him. I wanted to . . .

A sharp sob tore through my soul the instant the thought flitted through my mind.

My knees threatened to give.

I wanted to go back in time and never find those two brothers.

Life would've been cold, loveless, meaningless . . .

But it would've been easier.

I stumbled to my chair and dropped into it four minutes before noon. I hurried to pull everything up and didn't turn when I heard them shuffling in.

"Einstein."

"She still has a couple of minutes," I mumbled, trying to hide the tremor in my words.

"Einstein," Jess repeated, this time her voice was a bit firmer than before, gently demanding my attention in a way only Jess could accomplish.

I blinked quickly, making sure the tears stinging the backs of my eyelids didn't betray me, and turned to face them. "Yes, I've seen the time. Meant to be here a while ago. You can dock my pay."

I knew I didn't fool any of them when they all continued to stare at me instead of coming back with a retort.

Kieran's face was in that impenetrable mask of frustration, not that it was any different for him.

Jess looked worried and saddened.

Conor looked confused and a little taken aback.

It hit me then that I'd never once checked to see what I looked like before I walked in here. I'd driven over straight from the tree.

From my argument with Maverick.

From my confession.

It had to be written all over my face that I'd just spent the last fifteen minutes sobbing.

Puffy, red eyes. Streaked mascara on my splotchy cheeks.

Fantastic.

Jess's eyes flicked to Kieran before meeting mine again. "What happened?"

I forced a sarcastic sound in the back of my throat. "Well, I was getting ready to wait for Sutton's email when the three of you came at me like you'd planned an intervention. So, why don't you tell me?"

"Einstein," Kieran murmured, his tone soft and disapproving.

My head shook quickly. Firmly.

No, no he couldn't do this to me.

He promised. He *promised* he wouldn't treat me differently.

I looked at Conor as panic made my heart thunder in my chest.

His stare was bouncing between the three of us, confusion still marring his features. "Am I missing something?"

"No." It was harsh and too loud to be believable. I knew it the moment it left my lips.

Conor's eyebrows lifted, but he didn't ask.

Kieran cleared his throat and nodded toward the door. "Conor, you should go."

He huffed. "No."

Kieran's surprise was palpable. The temperature in the room felt as if it dropped a few degrees.

Every cell in my body was telling me to run. That I was in a room with something dangerous.

Jess just rested a hand on her husband's forearm, and

Conor folded his arms over his chest. "Fuck that," he said, not backing down. "If Maverick did something to her, I want to know."

"He didn't. He *wouldn't*." I tried to put strength behind my voice, but I was still trying to press myself into my chair, trying to become invisible, to hide in a room full of people.

Conor's expression only seemed to become more frustrated when he turned his attention back on me. "Yeah, see, I might have believed that before you came in looking like this."

"Conor." Kieran all but growled his name.

When I risked a glance at him, his chest was heaving and his jaw was locked tight.

Fucking mobsters.

Kieran's throat moved with his forced swallow before he moved his head in some combination of a nod and a shake. "He wouldn't. Go."

"Man, I love you, but we're partners. You aren't my boss anymore." Conor made a face that clearly said he didn't plan to go anywhere. "If she tells me to, I'll leave. For now, I plan to stand right fucking here until I know who I'm gonna beat up."

"No one. Jesus." I scrubbed my hands over my face and tried not to cringe when I felt the dried streaks on it. "And I'm not gonna make anyone leave because we need to be here for a reason anyway." I started to turn, but Jess stopped me with a foot on my chair.

"You and Maverick fight?"

I tried to shrug. I tried to laugh. I didn't think I accomplished either. "Would I care?"

Her face twisted with doubt, probably because the last

time she saw me cry was a couple of weeks after she'd helped me bury a box.

She opened her mouth, only slightly, and then let it shut.

She knew Maverick and I fought. She knew everything I'd been doing.

"This is different," she whispered so softly it was nearly inaudible. "Did you talk to him . . . about something in particular?"

My chest twisted.

My lungs constricted.

I bit my tongue to keep from crying out and shrugged. "Like us being over?"

Her body sagged. "Einstein . . ."

"I have work." I turned around and was thankfully not stopped this time.

I took in deep, shuddering breaths and focused on my screen.

On my email.

On the new email that *wasn't* there but should've been. Because it was currently six after.

I jerked forward, my hands flying over my keyboard and mousepad as I frantically thought.

Sutton had been emailing us every day. Just small updates to let us know where she was or if she was in the same place. A few times she slipped in just how terrified she was of these people she felt surrounded by, but never shared their names.

Never gave us enough information.

But every email had continued to come at the same time without fail. Until today.

"She missed the time," I whispered.

Less than a second later, I was crowded by all three of them.

"Do we give her a few more minutes?"

"No," came back at me from the three of them, making me flinch.

I didn't have a way to contact her until she emailed me first since she continued to insist on deactivating her account after every short conversation.

So I pulled the number from the last motel she'd been at and had Jess calling it within seconds.

"Hey there, sweetheart," she said in her most seductive voice. "My girlfriend was supposed to be passing through there, and we're starting to get worried because we haven't heard from her in a while. Do you think you could maybe tell me if she's there?" After a few seconds, she made a dejected sound. "I know you aren't supposed to say, and people keep it pretty hush-hush around there, but you would really be doing me a *huge* favor."

Kieran growled.

Jess touched his jaw with the tips of her fingers but kept her stare on the floor. "Knew you wouldn't let me down. She would've come in a night or two ago. We're just so worried because it isn't like her not to check in, and she has an adorable little girl." She giggled, the sound low and throaty in a way that made me uncomfortable for Kieran. "What, baby, you want her blood type too?" She dropped the phone to her chest and hissed, "What's her hair color?"

I looked between the guys, but Kieran's focus was solely on Jess.

"I don't think we know," I whispered as I hurried through every email.

I should know this. I *would* know this if my mind weren't so muddled with emotions.

This was why emotions were bad things.

They took up too much space in my head. I didn't have room for this shit.

I'd only made it through three emails when a chime sounded from my laptop.

I hissed something that might've been a curse or one of their names or any number of things when a box appeared in the upper corner of my screen with a computer-generated email address on it.

I turned to Jess and bit out, "It's her. Hang up."

But Kieran had already taken Jess's phone and was tossing it aside, letting it clatter to the floor.

The energy in the room had changed while I'd been scouring emails, and I hadn't noticed until that moment.

But it was suffocating.

Well, shit.

I didn't know if I should try to disappear into my chair again or stand between them in an attempt to protect Jess. Not that anyone could stop Kieran. Not that I actually thought he would ever hurt her.

But the guy was terrifying and weighed down with knives.

It was instinctive to want to run or fight.

And I was caught in limbo, unable to breathe while I waited to see what he would do.

Then Jess pushed up onto her toes to kiss Kieran, breaking the tension in the room.

Super slow.

Super long.

Super gross.

It was entirely inappropriate considering Conor and I were both right there, and I didn't know how to look away.

"I think I'm vomiting," I mumbled.

Conor turned my chair so I was facing my laptop and then bent to stare at the screen with me.

I blew out a shallow breath, trying to ease my stomach. "Thanks."

He made some sort of affirming noise. "I've learned to leave the room. Except we need to be in here."

"Technically, we could take the laptop." I drummed my fingers next to the mousepad and clicked my tongue. "But we'd have to get around them, so I'll just pretend there's nothing weird going on behind me."

A low laugh built in his chest. "Email."

"Yeah, that."

I clicked it open and quickly scanned the contents a couple of times before sitting back in the chair.

I know I'm late, but I'm here, and we're okay for now.

Still in place. Not for long though . . . maybe, I'm not sure.

Any updates? Are you coming?

"Huh," Kieran murmured from directly beside my head.

I jumped, sucked in a sharp gasp, and clutched at my chest like the ditzy girls in horror movies who should die first but were somehow the only ones left alive when the credits rolled.

I turned on him and backed away as far as the chair would allow. "What are you doing?"

"Reading."

"In my ear? What is wrong with you? I can't even hear you breathe, you freak."

The corners of his mouth slowly tipped down into a frown.

I sighed and sagged in my chair. "I didn't . . . I didn't mean anything by that. I don't think you're a freak. I just meant that you're unnaturally quiet, but I guess I should've already known that. I just never realized how . . . quiet—"

His head slanted to the side, stopping my ramble. "You're missing things today. A lot. You've never been distracted like this before."

I forced a smirk. "Guess I need coffee."

He stopped me from turning toward the desk. "I just scared you by talking. You aren't remembering things like whether or not we know someone's hair color. You usually remember the slightest details after seeing it once. And I've never seen you try so hard to convince us or *yourself* that you're okay."

"What, because I don't want to watch you and Jess make out? Because I forgot a few things for the first time in my life? Sue me."

"Einstein . . ."

The second his worried tone registered in my mind, I shot him a glare, silently demanding he stop.

Stop talking. Stop looking at me like he pitied me. Just *stop*.

"Did you tell Maverick?"

"You promised you wouldn't do this," I said through clenched teeth. "So don't."

"We aren't going to ignore when you're obviously hurting, Einstein," Jess said, coming around Kieran to kneel in front of me. "And you can push all you want, but we push right back and we don't go anywhere."

"Just let me do my job and let that be the end of it."

She shrugged and offered me a sympathetic smile. "No."

I turned and reached for my computer and looked on in horror as Conor closed out the windows while Kieran held my arms down. "No. *No*. What are you doing?"

"We missed our window to respond to Sutton," Conor said as he closed the laptop and turned to sit on my desk so he was facing me.

"You just touched my laptop."

He gave me a placating look. "I didn't break it, and you don't have any work that needs to be done right now. Stop deflecting."

"I don't?" I asked on a laugh and pushed against Kieran's hold. "Then I guess I'll be going."

They all murmured my name pleadingly when I rolled my chair back and stood.

"Einstein, wait," Jess begged when I started for the doorway.

"I'm fine," I said with a saccharine grin when I faced them again. "If you don't mind, I have places to go. People to see. Men not to care about. Things not to discuss."

"Einstein," Jess called out when I made it out of my office. "Einstein, *talk to me*."

I whirled on her and cried out, "Why? *Why* do you want to talk? *What* do you want to talk about?"

The girl who was just as blunt and unapologetic as me stood there, hesitation and worry written all over her face. It was as if she wanted to help but was afraid of hurting me more.

I was so far past help.

"Because I know you need to talk about it," she whispered. "I can see it."

I laughed, but it sounded frantic and pained. "I don't need anything. You just want to ease your curiosity."

Jess's expression turned pleading and determined.

"He knows what happened, and he's moving away. All right?" I tried to make it all sound as if it hadn't destroyed me. As though it wasn't tearing me up knowing he wouldn't be here anymore.

As though their shock wasn't pressing down on me, making my legs buckle under the weight and nearly sending me to my knees.

Before Jess could say anything, I held up my hands and continued walking backward, toward the front door. "End of story. There's nothing more to talk about because we all know this is what I want."

Her brows drew together. "Is it?"

"Does it matter?" I steeled my jaw and forced a smile. "It's done. It's over. He's leaving, and I have a date I have to get to."

Jess drew back, a dozen emotions passing over her face before she hissed, "Wait. *What?*"

I paused with my back against the door. "A date. You know, the thing you told me to go on." I waved a hand at her and huffed. "Thought you would be proud or something. He was your idea."

She blinked quickly, her face betraying everything she was trying to figure out.

Like how she could have anything to do with my going out with someone who wasn't Maverick.

When the guys turned on her and demanded answers, she hissed at them to stop and then started toward me. "Who was my idea?"

"The guy from the coffee shop." I grabbed the handle of the door and gave her a knowing look. "I seem to remember you telling me to ask him out. Not that I did. Not that it stopped him from asking a couple of times, including yesterday when I made my coffee run."

"Einstein, *wait*. This isn't a good idea," she said in a rush when I opened the door and took a step outside. "Not today. Not when you're so . . ." Her eyes dipped over me and her face fell. "So heartbroken and in so much pain."

"You have to have a heart for it to break."

She grabbed my hand before I could let go of the handle. "Do you think this would hurt so much if you didn't?"

I forced a smile and shrugged. "Phantom pains. That's all."

She stepped closer so her head was nearly pressed to mine. "That's bullshit, and you know it," she whispered. "I know what it's like to hide pain this way. I see you pretending it isn't there. You don't have to do this."

"Try to move on with life?" I asked with a forced laugh. "It's a date, not marriage. I'm not agreeing to be his eternal love slave."

Her eyes narrowed into slits and her jaw clenched.

I wanted to crawl into a hole for carelessly throwing *that* at Jess when she'd sold herself to men for years in order to keep her and her mom alive.

I sucked in a sharp breath and stumbled over my next words. "I didn't mean it like that. Besides, it's lunch. In the middle of the day. Lot of light. Lots of witnesses. Not romantic. It should probably be called a meeting instead of a date. For all I know, that's what it is. I wouldn't know either way, we all know I've never been on a date before. I don't even like Thai all that much, so this is already going down as the worst one of my life."

My rambling didn't faze Jess. She just studied me while I spoke and waited for me to finish. "Don't do something just to try to feel. Don't do something just to numb the pain."

I didn't bother telling her there was no way in hell I'd let a stranger touch me. That it had taken time to let the man I loved in. Or that I'd nearly gotten sick over the thought of doing anything with other men I knew and trusted.

I just pulled my hand from hers and stumbled out onto the sidewalk. "Noted. Thanks for the pep talk. See you tomorrow."

Her words echoed in my mind the entire drive back to my apartment, through changing and freshening up my makeup, and the drive to the restaurant.

Nearly everything I'd done the last year was because I was in pain.

Not to numb it, but in an attempt to shield it from those closest to me.

And in the end, I'd ruined us all a little bit more.

Thirty-Seven

Einstein
TWO DAYS AGO

I SAT IN MY CAR, staring at the Thai restaurant as a war waged within me.

I didn't want to be here.

I wanted to go to the oak.

I wanted to find Maverick, to beg him not to leave.

He could hate me—I expected him to. But leave?

No matter what happened between any of us, there was something that bound us all together. That kept us a family.

He couldn't tear himself from that.

He couldn't walk away.

Not because Dare wouldn't allow it but because our bond was thicker than blood. We didn't abandon each other. We didn't leave.

Not even Libby, who had shunned the mafia lifestyle, had left. She had never been able to fully turn her back on it, because to do so would have meant turning her back on us.

And as selfish as it was, I couldn't imagine Maverick not being in this town. Not knowing where he was and that he was safe and *real*.

But if I went . . . if I found him and begged him to stay, that would only put us right back where we'd been.

I couldn't do that to him.

He'd seen my pain, and I knew I wouldn't be able to contain the rest. Everything would tumble free until he knew every excruciating detail, including how much I needed him, how much I'd always needed him.

It had always been that way with Maverick.

He made me want to pour my heart out when every instinct told me that revealing even a hint of what resided within my heart was wrong.

He made me love in a way I'd never thought was real.

In a way some people would never experience.

But I would never forgive myself if Maverick got caught up in this destructive descent I was still spiraling down.

So I would rip out my heart a little while longer to ensure he didn't and hope Dare was able to stop him from leaving.

With a determined breath, I grabbed my bag and stepped out of my car . . . and nearly jumped when I turned and found Alex standing there.

His face fell, and he lifted his hands. "Shit, sorry. Did you not hear me? I said your name."

An uneasy laugh pushed past my lips. "Uh, no. No." I lifted the strap of my bag onto my shoulder and walked to where he was standing at the back of my car. "How long have you been standing there, stalker?"

His face did that pinching thing again.

It really was kind of annoying.

Mostly because it made me think of something—made me sure I knew him from somewhere other than seeing him around town.

"I saw you getting out of your car," he explained and then looked pointedly at the restaurant. "So, lunch?"

I tried to smile. "Uh, yeah. Sure."

I didn't know what else to say.

I wasn't hungry. I didn't want to be here. I regretted agreeing to have lunch with him when I saw him at the coffee shop yesterday.

Because everything about this was wrong.

He paused just as he'd started taking a step away, expression carefully blank. "Don't tell me you own this place too."

We'd loaned the owners money when they were about to go bankrupt a couple of years ago. But he didn't need to know that.

"No. Just the café," I lied.

"Okay, good," he said as he started toward the restaurant.

He kept up the conversation through us being sat in a booth and getting our drinks, but I didn't remember if I responded to him.

Or if I had, what I'd said.

I was replaying the exchange at the oak in my head. Again . . . and again.

I blinked quickly when a drink was slid toward me.

I looked from the little cup to the bottle on the table next to Alex. "I didn't order that."

He gave me an uneasy look. "Yeah," he said slowly,

drawing out the word. "I ordered it a couple of minutes ago. Hey, are you okay?"

I grabbed the tiny cup and asked, "What is this?"

"Sake."

Oh, thank God.

I tipped back the cup like a shot and blew out a steadying breath when I set it back onto the table.

Alex was staring at me wide-eyed. "Well, that's one way to drink it. I guess. Really, are you okay?"

Thankfully, I was saved from answering when the waiter showed up.

After ordering whatever it was Alex ordered, I reached for the bottle of sake, but Alex grabbed it and held it away.

"I feel like I'm missing something here, Einstein. You've only said a few words and you're trying to get drunk off sake. What's going on?"

Tears burned my eyes, and my arms fell heavily to my sides.

Lock it up.

Lock—wait, what's wrong with my arms?

"Hitting you fast, huh?"

"It's sake. It shouldn't." My head dropped forward, and it took all my strength to lift it again. "Nothing should. Not that little. Not that fast."

"Yeah, you're right. It shouldn't." He set the bottle onto the table and leaned closer. "But I wasn't sure if you'd have more than a sip, so yours had a little extra something. A *lot* of extra something. Then you went and took the whole cup like a goddamn shot. Jesus, Sutton."

My blood turned to ice.

My heart started racing.

My chest pitched with my ragged, uneven breaths.

"Wha-what did you just call me?"

Alex blinked quickly, as if he just realized what he'd said, then shook his head. "Einstein."

My fuzzy mind raced, crawled, trying to think.

Oh God.

"I know . . . you're . . ."

I know you. I know you.

I knew him because I'd searched and searched.

Not for him—for *her*.

And only a handful of Larsons in the Tennessee area had come up, none of which were women anywhere near how old Sutton claimed to be.

One of them had been the man in front of me.

"Zachary Larson," I slurred heavily.

He drummed his hands on the table, his smile wide and mischievous. "Surprise?"

It was getting hard to move.

I was struggling to grab my phone.

Struggling to keep it in my grasp.

"Wh're you . . . you . . . do t'me?"

"I needed you to go under fast. Clearly." He winked and then slid from his side of the booth.

"Don'touch," I breathed when he leaned into my side and curled his arm around my waist.

"Oh yeah," he whispered in my ear. "That's working really fast." He raised his voice louder, false concern leaking through when he said, "We need to get you out of here if you aren't feeling well, sweetie."

I'm gonna kill you.

I opened my mouth, but only a whimper came out.

"I can only imagine what's going on inside that genius brain of yours."

He half-walked, half-dragged me from the restaurant, whispering reassuring words to me for anyone who might be watching.

And damn it, no one stopped him because I was fully leaning against him. Head on his chest and arms entangled in his.

I had no control over my body, he was behind every move.

Once we were in the parking lot, he pulled me into his arms and cradled me against his chest like I was a child.

I wanted to scream for help.

I wanted to hit him.

I wanted to ask why he was doing this.

"You should've left it alone. You should've left *her* alone," he said. "Because all of this shit with Sutton taking our daughter from me? It's a game."

Daughter.

Daughter . . . daughter—oh God, Sutton is his wife.

I tried to thrash in his arms.

I tried to claw at his face.

But I could no longer move.

Could no longer speak.

It was getting hard to keep my eyelids open.

"She can try to run and run and run, and I'll let her for a while because I like the slow chase. I like giving her the illusion of safety before letting her know I'm coming for her. And don't be mistaken, this *is* an illusion and I *will* come for her when she least expects me. But if you people help her? Make her disappear? Game over. Because as good as I am at finding people—and clearly, I'm good—you're better at hiding them. And I never said she could leave."

He opened the back door of his car and laid me on the seat before gripping my face in his hands.

It was all I could do to look at him.

To stay awake.

For just a little while longer.

He pressed his cheek to mine and whispered, "You should've left it alone."

Thirty-Eight

Maverick
TODAY

"Avery. *Avery.*" I threw my phone against the dashboard and then drove my hands into my hair, trying to swallow my grief and overwhelming fear. "*Fuck.*"

"Mav—"

I shook off Diggs and seethed, "Go faster."

Dare's voice was low and calm when he said, "Going as fast as I can."

"It isn't fucking fast enough. Did you hear her? She isn't expecting to make it. We need to get there *now*."

He exhaled roughly through his nose and gripped the steering wheel harder. "I heard her. But this is a backcountry road, and we're fucked if we get pulled over considering there is a rifle across your lap."

I gritted my teeth and lowered my voice. "Then don't let us get pulled over."

The car swerved and threatened to lose control when

we hit a massive dip.

"We're fucked if we wreck too," Dare snapped, but he didn't slow when he regained control.

When a call came through the car from Kieran, I leaned forward and smacked at the screen a few times before the call finally connected.

"Learn to handle your car." Kieran's tone was pure taunt.

Dare shook his head. "Hanging up."

"No, no, wait!" Jess shouted. "Seriously, babe?"

"This place," Conor said when Jess and Kieran started whispering to each other. "We were trying to figure out what we are about to walk into. Nothing on the map. Nothing really around there."

The three of us hissed curses.

"Do you think they dumped her stuff?" I asked, unease weaving through my words.

"No," Kieran answered for Conor. "Dare, right around the time you started helping me out, I told you about a bunker Holloway had. Most of our drugs, money—"

Dare hit the steering wheel. "Right. Some of my guys cleared it." Before Kieran could respond, Dare demanded, "Is this it?"

"Yeah."

Cold.

Ominous.

Hinting at unspoken questions.

I gripped my rifle, mostly for something to hold on to. "This is a Holloway?"

"Can't be," Kieran said in that even tone that gave nothing away. "Only five of us knew about it. Four are dead." He cleared his throat. "Guessing Einstein knew?"

Dare breathed a bemused laugh. "Yeah, she knows everything. She was the one to log the hit so she could keep track of it."

"Then they had to have gotten access to her stuff. Because we don't keep record of anything like that. They had to be watching her to know who she works with. It's too coincidental for her to have been taken there."

"Shit, they did." I turned to face Dare, my words all bite and frustration. "I told you the night Libby was taken that someone had gotten into Einstein's system. She was pissed that someone had made it through but didn't know who they were or what they were looking for. I don't know if it happened again. She'd already moved the important stuff." I leaned my head back and tried to calm my breathing. Kieran and Conor were asking what I meant, but I just said, "It was Alex. I told you . . . I fucking told you he was stalking her."

Dare quickly shook his head. "We already talked to him. I asked—"

I shot him a hard look. "Einstein *told me* it was Alex."

It took a second for it to sink in. For confusion and defeat to cross his face. Dare looked sick, as if he'd failed everyone.

His head shook slowly. "Describe—" He cleared his throat. "Describe the bunker, Kieran."

Kieran was talking, but I only caught a few words as my last conversation with Avery replayed in my head over and over again.

"Remember that time we snuck into the theater room?"

". . . marker . . ."

"You're the best thing to ever happen to me."

". . . two rooms . . ."

"You promised to bury me under the oak tree."

". . . go left . . ."

"You promised."

"There, there, there!" Diggs shouted from the backseat a handful of minutes later, leaning forward to point toward the nearly indiscernible metal marker on the left side of the road.

Dare slammed on the brakes, and the car fishtailed to a stop, leaving the passenger side facing the bunker.

I bolted from the car with my rifle in hand.

By the time I saw the lock on the door, Diggs was already shooting it and surging forward to tear it off and open the door.

I felt Dare's presence behind me.

Heard Conor's truck pulling up.

But I couldn't wait.

All of our planning and my training vanished in that moment as I took the stairs two at a time with the butt of my rifle pressed hard against my shoulder.

Because Einstein was somewhere down there. I knew she was.

I could feel her.

And she had been sure we wouldn't make it.

We'd made the fifteen-minute drive in ten, but I had a feeling it still wasn't enough.

If it wasn't—

I faltered when I passed her bag halfway down the stairs.

Either she was there or we were running into the perfect setup.

"Left," Dare whispered behind me when we made it to the bottom of the stairs.

His voice sounded strained.

My chest felt tight.

It felt so damn hard to breathe.

And I was afraid to think of why.

Afraid the reason would be because my soul was already grieving a loss I wouldn't survive.

I shined the mounted light from my rifle onto the door, hesitating when there was nothing more than a deadbolt.

"This can't be right."

Einstein would've gotten out of this.

Why does this feel wrong?

I feel wrong.

But Diggs was already beside the door, and we didn't have time to waste.

He flipped the bolt and tried to push the door open enough for me to slip through, but it wouldn't budge. Not giving any of us time to think, Diggs reared back and kicked the door open, and I barreled though, scanning the room as I—

I stumbled.

Nearly dropped my rifle when I felt the overwhelming pressure on my lungs.

The absence of what was so crucial to breathe.

To *be*.

I staggered forward another few steps, trying to push through the panic rising within me.

As my body begged me to turn.

To find air.

To find Avery in there, because she'd known this was coming.

The alarm . . . her words . . . she'd fucking known.

I jerked when a hand landed on my shoulder and turned

to find Dare trying to force me back to the doorway.

And then I broke.

Shattered.

Soul ripped from my body in grief and denial and crushing agony.

Because there she was . . .

One second, I was shoving my rifle against Dare's chest, and the next, I was across the room and pulling Avery's limp body out of a chair.

I didn't remember moving.

I didn't remember getting her up the stairs and outside or laying her on the ground.

Yelling . . . I remembered that.

Yelling at her to wake up. To breathe.

I pressed against her chest, over and over again, willing her heart to work.

Diggs was there, shoving my hands away and taking over the compressions and telling me when to breathe.

For her.

It never got easier to breathe.

Not when she was a broken reminder of how I failed her.

I twisted my fingers into her hair and pressed my forehead to hers. "You can't leave me. That isn't how this works."

"*Breathe*."

I poured my air, my life, my soul into the girl I loved.

My mouth lingered on hers after the second breath before I dropped my forehead back to hers.

My eyes closed when it became too hard to see.

"I'm supposed to fight for you forever, Avery. Come back. Breathe."

I vaguely heard Diggs counting in the background. "Ten. Eleven. Twelve."

I heard faint crying coming from somewhere.

But all I saw was the girl beneath me throughout the years, swirling through my mind in rapid flashes of the best and worst moments.

"I love you. I didn't get to tell you that enough. I love you, I love you, I love you, Avery."

"Thirty," Diggs called out, louder than the rest. "*Br—*"

Avery lurched off the ground, sucking in a breath that sounded like a cry.

Diggs and I both scrambled to give her room.

And I froze.

I wanted to pull her into my arms.

I wanted to never let her go.

All I could do was stare at her when she fell to her side, coughing and struggling to breathe.

Her eyes were wild when she looked up and easily found me.

Her tears fell unchecked, and she rolled onto her back, her body trembling as sobs ripped through her.

I hurried over and pulled her into my arms, holding her gently as I tried to calm her.

Cradling her face in one of my hands, I brushed my thumb across her wet cheek and searched her face. "It's okay. You're okay."

She nodded weakly, pressing her cheek deeper into my palm.

I dropped my lips to her forehead and inhaled, drinking her in and relishing in the knowledge that I was holding her.

That she was breathing.

"There are less dramatic ways of getting us to stay, you know," Diggs said from beside us.

Avery wheezed out a laugh.

I shot him a glare. "We can talk about that later."

I felt Avery stiffen. Felt the change in the air between us.

She shifted away from me just the smallest of a fraction, but I pulled her back and tucked my face into the crook of her neck.

One of her tears dropped onto my skin, slowly trickling down until it disappeared into the fabric of my shirt. I wanted to hold her in my arms forever, but I knew she needed to be looked at almost as much as I needed someone else to tell me that she was going to be okay.

"We need to get you to the house so Sofia can check you over. You've been gone a long time, and we almost just lost you."

I . . . I almost just lost you.

When I loosened my hold on her, I caught a glimpse of grief before confusion settled in. "Long . . ." She glanced at the darkening sky. "It's been a few hours."

I looked to Diggs and then Dare.

His mouth formed a thin line, and he shook his head, silently letting me know he didn't know how to be the one to tell her.

I brought my attention back to Avery, who was staring at me with an expression that told me she wasn't going to let anything touch her. Leaning forward, I traced my fingers along her jaw, waiting for when she would relax against the touch.

Slowly, she did.

"It's Monday night." Low. My voice was so low that her

gaze dropped to my lips as I spoke. She held stock-still for a beat before blinking quickly as her shoulders and chest moved with rapidly escalating breaths.

And then it all slipped away and was replaced with that nothingness.

Heart of fucking stone.

I pulled her closer, curling my hands around the back of her neck and dropping my forehead to hers. "Don't do that. Not now. Not with me. Not after everything."

Her chin quivered, and her lips pressed into a hard line, but after a few seconds, she nodded.

When she struggled to stand, I helped her and reluctantly let her go. Avery disappeared into a sea of hugs from Jess, Kieran, and Conor as Diggs appeared beside me.

"Thank you," I muttered. "For saving her."

He shrugged as if it was no big deal that he had saved my fucking soul a few minutes ago. "You tell me what to do, Mav. You wanna leave, we leave. You wanna stay, we stay."

My heart twisted as I watched her. "You know what I want."

"Good," he said on a relieved breath. "Because I really didn't wanna leave." He punched my shoulder and started toward the cars. "Give her time to sort through the last two days. Which, you know, for Einstein will take about five seconds. I'm gonna bet she doesn't feel the way she did last week."

I smothered the hope that rose at the thought.

Hoping something like that was dangerous.

After all I'd been through, my heart wouldn't survive it if I let myself believe I could have her, only to be pushed away one last time.

Thirty-Nine

Maverick
TODO: TODAY

WE'D BEEN AT THE MAIN Borello house for . . . God, I didn't know how long.

Lily, Libby, and Maxon had crashed in the living room. Diggs had passed out in the middle of eating.

Dare had told me when he'd come in to check on Einstein.

I hadn't left the room.

I hadn't slept.

I'd just stayed in the chair near the foot of the bed. Watching her. Studying the self-inflicted marks on her cheeks and neck and arms from the times when she'd been deprived of oxygen. Listening to her tell us what she remembered from the date with Alex—or Zachary, I guess—through waking up outside with us.

Dare and Libby's mom, Sofia, was ready for us when we arrived—like always. She'd nursed more of our injuries than I could remember over the years, from fractures to stab and gunshot wounds.

The only time any of us had set foot in a hospital had been when Beckham was born.

I trusted her.

Of course I did.

But I'd looked at the food and water and vitamin drip she already had set up in Einstein's room when we walked in and said, "What the hell is this? She needs—she needs—" I'd raked a hand through my hair and growled in frustration, because I didn't know. But what was in front of us didn't seem like enough.

Sofia had pressed a firm hand to my shoulder and lifted a stern brow. "She needs you to sit and be calm for her."

So I sat.

My jaw ached from the pressure I was putting on it as I was forced to do nothing, even when Einstein panicked and hit Sofia when she realized Sofia was trying to put an IV in.

After Einstein refused water for the fifth time, I finally stood and snatched the bottle from the bedside table and downed a quarter of it, watching her horror-stricken expression as I did.

When I handed her the bottle, she took it hesitantly, studying me as if she was waiting for something to happen.

I'd been back in the chair for nearly a minute when a sob broke from deep inside her.

I'd tensed and rocked forward to go to her, but Sofia held up a hand, silently telling me to stay.

It felt like the first ten years with her all over again.

With her right there, close enough to touch, but not *mine* to touch.

My body was shaking from keeping myself from her as I

watched her cry until her tears dried and then the words came. Tumbling from her mouth in hushed sentences, as if she were confessing her greatest shame.

Her chin had wavered and her heavy-lidded eyes met mine. Just before they shut, she whispered, "And then you were there."

I'd been watching the steady rise and fall of her chest since.

Always. I will always be there.

The words played in my mind on repeat for hours. But the truth was, it didn't matter that I didn't know where we stood. I *wanted* to be there. I *would* be there . . . but when this was all said and done, that might not mean what I wanted it to.

Because the last time we talked, I told her I was done. That I was leaving town.

And she went out with someone else afterward.

"He's gone," Kieran said in way of announcing that he and Jess were in the room.

I slanted my head toward them but didn't take my eyes off Einstein.

"Condo is cleared out. Checked the leasing office, and there's no file on anyone having leased it recently. He covered his tracks."

My hands curled into fists. "He was right in front of us. Right fucking in front of us."

Jess blew out a slow sigh and sat on the end of the bed. "Good way to keep us off his trail for longer. Come back into town to confuse. Once Einstein's location is revealed, he vanishes."

"Hiding in plain sight," Kieran said. "Exactly like Phoenix said that family does."

"Einstein said this Zachary guy targeted her because she was going to help Sutton disappear," Conor said from where he'd been sitting in the corner of the room all night.

I'd been ignoring him.

I didn't want to think about why he was in here too.

"He had balls to come after her, knowing who she was and what she could find out, but he was obviously prepared," he continued. "Maverick said people were getting past Einstein's security a year ago. That means this guy has been studying her and prepping for this for a year."

"That doesn't make sense," Jess said. "Sutton's only been contacting her for a few months."

"But how long had she been looking into us?" Kieran argued. "Einstein searched for her and didn't find a single trace of the woman or the kid."

"You're thinking Sutton has been trying to get the courage to contact us and leave her husband for a year," Jess whispered, her voice heavy with understanding. "And by the time she finally did, Zachary knew and had already made all the records of her disappear so we wouldn't help her."

"Fits what Zachary said to Einstein," I murmured.

"Einstein thinks it had to be more than just Zachary behind it," Conor said. "And what they did to her was mostly psychological . . . playing a game with her before taking everything away. From what Zachary said, it's likely that he'd done something like this to Sutton before, only without a fatal ending. From her emails, she knows that if he finds her, she won't be so lucky."

Kieran was staring at Einstein with that cold frustration. "That's why Sutton won't say anything. She's scared, like Lily said. And if her husband and the others like playing mind games, I think that's the only reason she and her daughter are still alive."

"But for how long?" Jess asked and stood from the bed, turning so she could face Kieran. "We know what we're getting into. We have to get them *now*."

"We're going into cities and towns full of lookouts, Jessica," he murmured. "We've been trying to make sure we wouldn't be walking into a trap, which most of the state is."

"I have to get the folders." When Einstein's groggy voice broke into the conversation, I pushed from the chair and sat on the bed close to her side.

"How do you feel?"

"Like I'm not as smart as I was. Probably the same way Libby does."

A soft laugh pushed from my chest as I took in the color in her cheeks and the brightness of her eyes. I automatically reached for her, to touch her in some way—her hair, her face . . . anything—but withdrew my hand before I made contact. "You look better."

"That's a nice way to tell me I look like I've been through hell. It isn't appreciated."

My head was shaking and my chest was moving with a muted laugh. She sounded like my Einstein. And God, I missed that sound.

She'd forced conversations with the family for nearly a year, but whenever it came to talking to me, it was all bitter resentment and hateful sneers.

That was gone.

I searched her face again . . . because I could, because she was here, and whispered, "You're beautiful."

Her body relaxed with a shaky exhale.

Her eyes bore into mine, asking a dozen questions and telling me hundreds of things.

I'm sorry.

I love you.

What are we going to do?

And then she blinked, breaking the connection, and her body stiffened as she glanced to the side. "Hi."

I shifted my head enough to see the three people huddled closely around us and breathed out a curse.

"See, this is how it is," Conor began.

I tensed, ready to react to whatever he was about to say.

"Your family keeps trying to adopt me, and that's cool." He lifted his hands to include the two next to him. "But you became ours during a bad time. We lost my brother and then this obnoxious, smartass inserted herself into our lives as if she belonged there. And you do. So you don't get to leave us the way you almost did."

Jess jerked her head in Conor's direction. "What he said."

"No dying," Einstein mumbled. "Got it. I'll keep that in mind next time oxygen is switched out for another gas."

"As long as that's settled." Jess leaned forward, pushing me out of the way so she could kiss Einstein's forehead. "We'll be back."

After the guys said their goodbyes and followed Jess out, I released the breath I'd been holding and sat back.

"Don't leave," she begged, grabbing my hand.

My heart lurched and took off in a sprint.

Her chin trembled and eyes watered. "Don't leave. I— Maverick, I'm sorry. I'm so damn sorry, and I know that doesn't—"

"It's okay," I assured her, leaning forward to pull her into my arms.

"No, don't." She pushed herself up until she was sitting. "Don't, I need to say this."

I bit back the words begging to be heard.

I love you.

I love you, I love you.

"I know what I did was . . ." She lifted her shoulders in a helpless shrug. "The worst thing that I could do to you. Unforgivable. I hurt you and us beyond repair, and I will apologize for the rest of my life." A few tears slipped down her cheeks, but she didn't try to stop them. "But all I wanted was for you to have the life you deserve. All I want is for you to find someone who makes you happy. But, God, please don't leave. The thought of never seeing you again wrecks me."

So many things were swirling through my head, nearly slipping free.

I don't want to go.

I don't know how to be happy without you.

But when I opened my mouth, I asked, "Why didn't you tell me?"

Shame and anguish flashed across her face. "Because when I found out, you were so mad about Lily and Dare, and Libby had just found out about the Maxon thing. Everyone was mad about a pregnancy or baby being born, and I panicked."

"Libby didn't know?"

Her eyes flashed to mine before falling to her lap. "Jess, uh . . . she was the one to help me when it happened."

I nodded as Kieran's words replayed in my mind.

"Maybe the last year would've been different if Einstein had felt like she could talk to you."

I'd known when he said it that he and Jess knew something—more than they probably should have—I just hadn't known what.

"I would've been there," I said after a few moments. "I would've been there for you every second. Every thought changed when you told me this weekend . . . every thought would've changed if you'd told me when it was happening."

"Beckham had just been born, and every time I mentioned him, you were so adamant that you never wanted kids."

"Avery, *you* didn't want that before you found out. I understand you found out while half our family had something negative to say about babies, but you know me. You should've known anything that was you and me would've become my entire world."

She nodded, her expression saying what she wasn't.

That she was sorry.

That she'd been beating herself up for letting fears cloud her mind.

"I . . . I've never experienced pain like I did after losing them. I started shutting everyone out who would notice, especially *you*." The last came out as a whisper, as if reliving that time drained the little energy she had left. "I thought I was handling the pain by throwing myself into other things, by not thinking about it. I didn't realize I was suppressing it and making it worse. Spiraling down to this place I didn't know how to crawl out of. And I couldn't let you spiral down with me."

"Avery . . ."

"I can't take back what I did or fix what I ruined." Her eyebrows rose before she lifted her head to look at me. "But I'm sorry, Maverick. You'll never know how sorry I am for not telling you. For all the ways I hurt you. For failing you and them."

"Failing?"

Grief flitted across her face. And I knew in that glimpse that was exactly what she thought she had done.

Failed us.

"Avery, you didn't fail me. You didn't fail anyone." I shifted until only inches separated us and curled my hand around the back of her neck. "I need you to *know* that."

A shuddering breath ripped from her. "I don't."

"Then I'll tell you every day until you do." I dropped my forehead to hers. My voice twisted with my plea. "I want your happiness and your agony. I want your love and your frustration. If you're spiraling down, I want to be the one who pulls you up. Whatever you go through, I want to be there with you, no matter what it is. My heart will never stop beating in time with yours. Don't you get that?"

She curled in on herself, a soft sob falling from her lips before she was tilting her head up and pressing her mouth to mine.

Time stopped. The world faded around us. Chaos of emotions surged through my veins.

And I breathed.

Fully.

Deeply.

For the first time in a year.

Epilogue

Einstein
TWO DAYS LATER

I FORCED MYSELF NOT TO move when Maverick walked into the hotel bathroom and stopped in his tracks.

Forced myself to hold his stare until he broke the connection.

His eyes slowly raked over my body in a way that sent chills skating across my skin and had heat building in my stomach.

Maverick had seen me in nothing but a bra and underwear countless times—hell, he'd seen me in nothing. But it'd been so long, and I'd never stood there on display for him.

My tongue darted out to wet my lips, and I had to clear my throat before I was able to speak. But when I finally did, I didn't recognize my voice. It was low and throaty and raspy. "There's a thing called knocking."

He met my stare through the reflection again, heat and need swirling in his eyes. "We have to, uh . . . we have to go soon."

I bit back the automatic response that bubbled up.

Because Maverick wasn't the kind of guy to get bothered if I made him wait. And we *were* on a schedule. I'd also never taken this long to get ready for anything in my life.

We'd hopped on a plane to Chicago this afternoon with one goal in mind: to get the folders from Phoenix Nicolasi so we could send all the information on Zachary Larson and the operation in Tennessee to Kieran, Jess, and Conor —who were currently driving to get Sutton and her daughter.

Thankfully for us, getting the folders was as easy as going to Phoenix's front door. But unless we wanted to die, he needed to be warned we were coming first. And that warning had a short window of opportunity in the form of an *accidental* meeting at a club.

Pretending to check my makeup and hair, I studied my reflection. "Not every day a girl goes to this kind of club. Need to make sure I'll fit in."

I wouldn't.

We wouldn't.

But Maverick couldn't know that yet.

I sucked in a sharp breath when he slipped his hand around my waist, pulling me away from the vanity and against his chest.

"You're beautiful," he breathed, his eyes still holding mine.

A teasing *I know* was on the tip of my tongue, but I couldn't force it out. I'd never been conceited, but all I could see when I looked in the mirror were the marks where I'd clawed at myself. So much worse than they had been two days ago, and makeup could only cover so much.

Maverick passed the tips of his fingers over the marks on one of my arms, somehow knowing exactly where my thoughts were. "*Beautiful.*"

I rolled my eyes and pushed from him, but my mouth was twitching into a smile.

The honesty and the love were there in his voice, unmistakable as always, filling my soul and melting me.

He grabbed my hand and brought me back so my chest was pressed to his. "If you could see what I see, you would believe me."

"I do." I pushed to my tiptoes to pass my lips across his and then relaxed into him when he deepened the kiss for a moment. "I do, I'm just still trying to wrap my mind around how I deserve this chance with you after everything."

"Don't overthink this in that way only you can do. We belong together. So just be here with me."

"Always," I whispered. After another quick kiss, I pulled from his arms. "But right now, I need to be out *there* getting dressed."

"Funny," he murmured drily and followed me into the sitting area of the hotel room. With a playful smirk, he sat on the couch, directly in view of where my outfit hung on the closet door.

He followed every movement as I grabbed the tiny, slip of a dress and put it on. The heat and need in his eyes magnified until it was palpable as he watched me finish dressing. Until that smirk slipped and his chest moved roughly.

"Tell me you're not wearing that," he nearly begged.

I glanced at the full-length mirror near me—at the faux-leather jacket and knee-high boots—to Maverick. He looked seconds away from storming across the room and tearing it all off me.

Yeah.

I was wearing it.

I simply crossed the floor until I was standing inches from where he sat. "Tell me what's wrong with it," I countered.

"The last time someone tried to touch you, I broke his jaw."

I lifted a shoulder. "Then don't let anyone touch me."

"You're mine." His tone was seduction wrapped in everything that was *us*.

Whispers and pain and longing and a love that was incomparable.

Within a beat of my heart, he'd gripped my wrists and yanked me onto his lap so I was straddling him.

This position was everything . . .

Everything I wanted and needed. And the closest we'd been in so, so long.

I rocked against him instinctively, the move so natural it was like breathing.

A whimper caught in my throat when I felt his erection pressing against his jeans. One brush of the rough material against the lace between my thighs had me wound up so high I could barely breathe.

His hands lightly dropped to my thighs and moved up to my hips, taking the thin material of the dress with it.

Another rock against him and a growl rumbled deep in his chest when I bent to crush my mouth to his. He pulled me closer, pressing me harder against him and swallowing my moans.

I gripped the hem of my dress from where he'd dropped it and slowly lifted it until it was bunched around my hips, raising onto my knees as I did in a silent plea.

A shiver raced down my spine when he trailed his fingers along the outside of my underwear, teasing where I was aching for his touch.

A shuddering breath ripped from me when he slid a finger inside the lace.

A frustrated cry climbed up my throat when our alarms both went off.

I looked from where my phone was sitting on the desk back to Maverick.

Desire and irritation were etched across his face. "Surprised you didn't know that was coming."

Despite my frustration, I laughed. "I did . . . but I got distracted."

"By me."

"By everything about you," I whispered and then pressed a soft kiss to his lips. A shudder rocked through me when he traced his finger across where I was aching for him.

"We have a few minutes."

I wanted to agree. I wanted to let him continue. I wanted to take him to the bed and show him how much I'd missed him. Show him how sorry I was for the last year . . . but I couldn't.

We were here for a reason.

And I had the rest of my life to show Maverick those things.

"We don't," I argued. "We can't miss this window."

"How do we even know he'll be at this club?"

I lifted a brow. "You doubt me?"

An edgy laugh burst from him. "Never. But right now I'd say or do just about anything to keep you here."

A smile slowly formed on my face as I secured my fingers in his hair. "I know . . . trust me. But we have to do this first. Zachary is after Sutton and their daughter. You know how important these folders are."

His eyes searched mine for a few seconds before he said, "All right. Let's go warn some people we're coming."

By the time we made it through traffic and to the club, we were bordering on being late.

Maverick's hand tightened against my hip possessively, and I swayed into his touch as I studied the black metal door to the club.

"Ready for this?"

I wove our fingers together, then tilted my head back so I could look into his eyes. "Don't sound so scared." It was a gentle tease.

There wasn't an ounce of fear in Maverick.

He'd been radiating frustrated energy since we'd gotten on the plane. More so since we'd left the hotel both completely wound up.

The corner of his mouth tilted in that smile that drove me crazy.

Hesitant.

Secretive.

He traced along my jaw with his free hand, his thumb brushing across my bottom lip for a moment before he glanced at the ominous door.

His chest rose and fell with a harsh exhale. "We don't know anything about this guy. We're going in blind. I don't like being at a disadvantage."

"I wouldn't say we don't know *anything*."

"You know details. Specifics. You don't know *him*." The fingers laced with mine tightened. His voice lowered to a threatening tone. "We *know* Phoenix knew what you were up against, what Sutton is up against, and kept the information to himself."

"It wouldn't have prevented what happened."

"What if he has pictures? What if one of the pictures is of Zachary?" The muscles in his jaw flexed. His eyes bored into mine. "Any information would've been better than nothing."

Flashes of hindered thoughts and movements and not being able to breathe ripped through my mind, forcing a sharp inhale.

But I was quick to push them away.

I had folders I needed to get my hands on. Information to go through and send off.

I had to be *here* . . . I could talk it out with Maverick later.

Gripping his shirt in my hand, I walked backward toward the club. "It would've, but you saved me. And what matters now is saving someone else."

He shot forward, weaving his hand into my hair and kissing me fiercely, passionately.

When he pulled away, my legs were weak and I was breathless.

His eyes raked over me, heat and need swirling within them. When they met mine again, he smirked. "To get me through this without breaking anyone's jaw."

A laugh built in my chest and fell from my lips as I led him to the door and knocked three times.

Maverick pulled me closer, as if instinctively.

The door opened, revealing a man in a red suit. Half of his face was covered with a black mask, his matching cape swept along the floor.

He looked like a wannabe Phantom of the Opera.

"Password," the man demanded.

"Club Tempt," I said in nearly flawless Russian.

Maverick tensed, his grip on me tightened.

The bouncer studied him for a few seconds before opening the door wider, granting us access.

I hadn't gotten more than a handful of feet into the hall when I was abruptly turned.

Maverick's voice was so, so low when he hissed, "Was that Russian?" When I only stared, he huffed. "Since when do you speak Russian?"

Since Phoenix held information over my head, and I came up with this plan.

Before I could respond, something behind me caught Maverick's stare. His eyes widened and face covered with a mixture of shock and confusion.

From the information I'd gathered on this place, I could only imagine what he was seeing.

"The fuck kind of place did we walk into?"

I glanced over my shoulder at the dimly-lit hallway.

It looked like we'd gone back centuries to a masquerade party.

If it weren't for the rap music filtering down the hall, I would've wondered if we had stepped through a portal.

Candles lined the walls, illuminating the people lingering there. Everyone was in red or black, their faces covered in masks. The women were in extravagant dresses, while the men were in top hats and cloaks. Everything screamed money. Some were partially naked, their clothes on the floor or hanging from their bodies as they kissed unabashedly.

Also something I'd been expecting, and I knew it only got worse.

I looked to Maverick and whispered, "There will be more of that and probably worse. This club is a cover for a sex ring."

His jaw flexed as he stared at the people in a new light. His chest rose sharply with his rough inhales.

We had dealt with this kind of thing in the past—with people who took part in and ran these operations. Holloway's boss spent years learning the ins and outs of sex trafficking so he could form a ring in Wake Forest. And he tried.

We shut it and him down before it could take off. Hard.

But in being the person behind the computer, I'd seen everything. His plans and his training from owners of other rings—videos and pictures and journals. So, of course, Maverick had either seen or heard about it all too.

Needless to say, we were more affected by these situations than others.

I slid my hand into his and waited until his gaze fell to me. "Phoenix and the families he's connected to are taking care of it. We'd be stepping on the wrong toes if we took action here."

"Then why was it so important for us to run into the guy in this club?"

"I have the blueprints, but I want you to get a feel for

the inside." The corner of my mouth twitched. "You know, in case their families *don't* take care of it."

Excitement and determination flashed in his eyes. "And you didn't tell me before we came . . ." His unspoken questions hung in the space between us.

Why?

Why keep this from me?

"You would've come in intent on killing anyone in your path and this isn't our fight—it *can't* be. Not yet anyway."

After a moment, he nodded and led me down the hall, making sure not to let anyone close enough to touch us.

A few halls later, we stepped into the main room and froze.

The area was filled with people dressed identically to the ones we'd already passed. Many were only partially-dressed, even more were touching and kissing in ways that suggested they didn't care who saw. Then again, judging from their sluggish movements, maybe they no longer had the ability to.

Or maybe they just weren't allowed to.

Whatever the reason, seeing it made what I already knew about the place even more disgusting.

"Look up," Maverick said, his lips pressed to my ear so I could hear him over the music. "The men near the railing aren't wearing masks."

I risked a glance at the section above us and found two men in a heated discussion. "The one in a shirt and jeans is Vic, that's who we're here for. The other is Andrei Petrov, the owner of the club. You're not allowed to kill him," I added quickly when he rocked forward.

Disgust and hatred radiated from Maverick when he said, "Anyone running this shit deserves a bullet."

"Not our fight," I reminded him just as Vic stepped away from Andrei and looked down . . . directly at us.

We stood out in Club Tempt, I knew that. That wasn't what concerned me.

It was the recognition on Vic's face the second he saw me, as if he knew exactly who I was.

Seemed Phoenix had told his friends to expect me.

"Does he know you?" Maverick asked as Vic descended the stairs and approached us, his voice gruff.

"Looks like it."

"Einstein," Vic called out with an easy grin, as if we were old friends. As if this wasn't the first time we'd ever had any contact. "Funny seeing you in our city."

I forced my smile to match his. "You didn't seem surprised to see us here."

That grin of his widened. "I could say the same about you."

"Funny how that works." I glanced at Andrei, who stood at the railing watching the exchange, and then looked back at Vic. "Can I assume you know why we're here?"

His shoulders moved in the barest hint of a shrug. "You could. You would be wrong."

"We need Phoenix."

If he was surprised, he didn't let it show. He simply loosed a slow sigh and said, "Must be bad if you need a Nicolasi who holds all the scary information on every crime family in the world."

Flashes from the bunker assaulted me.

Maverick's hand curled around my waist, comforting and soothing me.

Something in my expression made Vic hiss, "Shit. I'll let him know to expect a visit."

I nodded, swallowing back the sudden tightness in my throat.

"Figured showing up here first to warn Phoenix we were coming would put us on his good side."

Vic snorted and bent close to me, not caring about the way Maverick tensed. "Yeah, keep telling yourself that." After placing a kiss on both my cheeks, he nodded to Maverick and then left the club.

Maverick waited a minute and then pressed his mouth to my ear. "Let's go."

He walked with deliberate, confident steps, keeping me tucked close to his side as he led me out of the club.

I didn't take a full breath until we were outside.

We didn't say anything during the drive back to the hotel, just sat in silence, one of my hands firmly wrapped in his on the console.

Once we were in the elevator, Maverick drew me close. "Now what?"

"Now we give Vic a chance to talk to Phoenix so we can get the folders. Hopefully there's information on Zachary, everyone he works with, and everyone working for him."

"And until then?" he asked when we arrived on our floor.

Heat swept through my cheeks as we stepped off the elevator. My words were nothing more than a breath when I said, "I've kept us apart one way or another for eleven years. I want to make up that time to you."

He pulled me to a stop so he could search my face. "All the shit we've gone through? It brought us here. It's *us*. It's saving each other. It's the tree. It's the pain. I don't want to make up for any of that. I just want a life with you."

Anticipation and need quickly surrounded us as we stood there, watching each other.

"You have me."

"Then nothing else matters," he whispered and bent to capture my mouth.

My heart thundered within my chest the moment his lips met mine.

Wild and free.

Reminding me it was there.

Reminding me I was alive.

The End

Look for more *Rebel* novels from Molly McAdams!
Lyric
Limit

Coming soon from *New York Times* bestselling author, Molly McAdams . . .

The mob's protector and the woman he's sworn to save.
She's frustrating and guarded and the most challenging woman he's ever met.
Gaining her trust is nearly impossible. Protecting her is anything but easy. And when she becomes more than a job, limits are tested.
Now he'll do anything to keep her safe and with him.

Want more Phoenix, Vic, and Andrei?
Check out #1 *New York Times* bestselling author Rachel Van Dyken's *Eagle Elite* series!
http://smarturl.it/RachVDAmazon
Our *Eagle Elite / Rebel* crossover takes place in Rachel Van Dyken's *Envy*!
Amazon: http://smarturl.it/EnvyRVD

Acknowledgments

Cory—As always, thank you for being my constant support. Everything I do is possible because of you. I love you!

Molly and Amy—A massive thank you for the never-ending support and encouragement. Your friendships mean the world to me. I don't know what I would do without the two of you.

Rachel—Thank you for the super fun idea of our mafia crossover and for letting me borrow your characters for a bit! I had so much fun dipping into your world and watching our characters meet!

Regina, Letitia, Malia, & Ashley—Thank you, thank you, thank you for making this book what it is! From the photo and cover, to the illustrations, to the edits. You're all such rock stars!

Made in the USA
Middletown, DE
17 May 2021